Longreave

Daniel Barnett

To my always patient mother, Elizabeth Barnett. It may not be the love story you asked for, but love is the foundation of it.

It just also happens there's a basement.

And it's dark down there . . .

I. The Cowboy

Chapter One
October 2nd

Mark Currier woke inside a child's coffin.

He sat up in the dark, in a bed that was much too small for him. His shirt and slacks were damp. His tie was cinched around his throat. He shuffled to the window in his loafers and opened the curtain, revealing a dresser covered in dust. Inside the top drawer lay a blanket decorated with tiny sombreros. He pushed the drawer shut and left the room, which had been a guestroom for five years now.

Breakfast sat untouched on the table. Mark went to the fridge. Milk. He wanted milk.

"I meant it," said a voice behind him.

His hand quivered. He lowered the carton. Turned.

Alice stood by the counter, perched on one foot. She was stretching her leg calf to hamstring the way runners did after a run. Except Alice didn't run, and she only ever stretched the right leg. Earrings glittered beneath the coppery mess of her hair. There were bruises under her eyes and scratches across her flat stomach where she'd dragged her nails.

"I meant it this time."

He nodded.

"*That's it?*" She rolled her lips in, as if trying to swallow her mouth, then spoke again, softer. "That's it?"

"I'll come after work and get a few things."

She flinched. "Mark. I didn't mean for you. You shouldn't have to."

"I'll talk to David. Ask if I can stay with him awhile." He thought about adding, *you don't have to worry*, but it didn't seem worth the energy. There was a long day ahead. He fixed his tie and left the house. On the porch he paused to look at the old unthreaded wicker chair where his father used to sit and nurse cigars late into the night, for a moment almost smelling the spicy scent of the smoke, and then he walked down the steps into the cool October morning.

•••

Longreave stood on a lonely strip of coast, the only building for half a mile of sand and rock. Built late in the nineteenth century at a time when the country was starving, its architecture reflected the depression. No fluted columns, no balconies, no overhang of roof or trim around the windows, no flourish of any kind. The walls had been red once, before pictures could capture color, but now the four stories of English-bonded brick were salted almost entirely white from sea spray and Longreave, in its old pale age, seemed to be striving for austerity.

Mark parked next to David's Sedan. The sky was a single cloud, low and gray. He took the pebbled stone path up to the hotel's enormous oak door. As he pulled on the handle, a little boy darted out of the lobby.

"Thank you," said the boy's mother, lugging a pair of suitcases. Mark nodded.

"It's that age, you know." She watched her son scramble off with a look that was part reverence, part exhaustion. "Turn my head for one second, and he'd end up in the ocean."

Mark felt something sour rise in the back of his throat. He squeezed past her through the closing doorway.

The lobby was sparsely furnished, the sum of two Chesterfields, a slab of wood masquerading as a cocktail table, and a quilted rug, all shades of brown. A triple-lamped chandelier left bright spots on the hardwood floor.

Nicholas Lorey wiped at the front desk like a saloon keeper polishing his bar. On his left an oil-black staircase projected from the ground. Off to his right stood the elevator, its dull bronze doors crowned by a wrought-iron dial. "Well, Mr. Currier, the hotel has bid farewell to its only guests and we are at last free to run amok. Shall I break out the champagne?"

Mark ignored him and walked into the office tucked underneath the staircase. David was slouched in his chair, his palm pressed to his brow and his eyes lidded. He had on a high school cross country t-shirt underneath his blazer. *Laguna Creek*. The name sounded familiar.

Mark sat down beneath a row of hanging plants. "It's going to rain."

David's eyes twitched open and then settled shut again. "There was a time I could always hear you coming. You would go out of your way to step on every squeaky floorboard. Like Longreave was your own personal piano."

Mark stroked his tie.

"You received my email this morning?" said David.

"I . . ."

"No?"

Mark opened his mouth to tell David about Alice. He saw the words leaving his lips in a comic-strip bubble, printing themselves on the air. He saw the bubble popping and his voice falling apart. "I forgot to check the computer."

"Well, it's just as easy to say it now. I called a staff meeting at ten." David combed his fingers through his fine, silver hair. "I know it's last minute, but it's necessary. For the few of us here."

"What about the Lovers?"

"They'll listen in on the phone." Julie and Matthew were students in Boston. Longreave was their study hall five evenings a week. It was also probably their sex den. There were a lot of spare beds, after all.

"What's it about, this meeting?"

David placed both palms on the desk and rose slowly to his feet. He was wearing sweatpants. "Will you walk with me?"

"I was going to balance the books."

"Already done."

"How long have you been here?"

David glanced over to the wall, where a tiny window framed a ruffled sea. "Long enough."

Mark watched the waves. He could hear the soft chop, chop as they broke against the beach. They sounded like knives in the sand.

Outside the office, David paused to look up at the underside of the steps. "Cracks," he mumbled, "Cracks in all of them."

"I'll get some caulking later," Mark said, but the old man moved on without a word.

Nicholas had his heels propped up on the front desk and was staring across the lobby to the painting of Longreave above the mantelpiece. "Do you think there's another Longreave hanging on the wall inside that one? With another Longreave, even bittier, inside its lobby?"

David set a lump of dollar bills in front of him. "Why don't you run on down the road and get some coffee."

"How thoughtful of you, you old sweetheart. But I'm quite lucid."

"Actually, I was hoping for some myself."

"That diesel fuel you keep in the back not cutting it, eh?" Nicholas dropped his loafers one at a time, heavily, and palmed the money.

Mark's gaze drifted back to the painting. It was a surrealist work, one of Alice's best, the hard edges and colors of the hotel rendered in liquid blurs, so that Longreave looked like a ripple or reflection on the ocean background. A mirage.

"That diesel fuel has run well and dry," Mark heard David say, and then . . .

". . . Mark? Mark?"

Nicholas was staring at him. "Anything for you?"

"No. No thanks." Mark had had been imagining all the Longreaves that might exist inside the painting's oiled world, all the copies of himself that might be standing inside the endless hotel lobbies, each one squeezed smaller and smaller like an image repeated between mirrors.

Nicholas lifted an eyebrow. "Everything all right?"

"Yes. Fine."

"Very well then." Nicholas stepped out from behind the desk and let the partition drop behind him. The keys for Longreave's thirty-three rooms jiggled on their hooks. "Shall I lock the door to keep the hordes at bay?"

"Perhaps you'd better." David's voice sounded oddly sad. He handed Nicholas the hotel key. It was twice the size of the others, with a narrow stem and notched teeth. The original owner, David's father, had made three copies when Longreave was built. The second key had been retired for eighteen years. The third Mark could feel in the pocket of his slacks, its outline rough and somehow comforting against his skin.

Nicholas walked off, his loafers making a slow round of applause on the floorboards.

Soon Mark and David were alone in Longreave.

• • •

Lamps portioned the second floor into bright and dim passages. Walnut doors studded the gray walls. There were eight rooms on each level in the main hotel, odd numbers overlooking the ocean, evens aimed inland, and another nine in the annex that had been built during Harry Truman's second term. Which was where they had to be going. The annex. But for what? The woman and her son hadn't stayed there. Nobody ever stayed there.

A fake lilac bloomed by the elevator. Mark's eyes trailed down to the beads in the flower pot, and a memory snagged him. Alice standing in this hallway, holding up a shining bead over her head, admiring the way it caught the light and winked silver.

"I visited Sarah yesterday," said David.

Mark blinked, and now Alice was standing on one foot by the kitchen counter, beads glittering beneath her hair, scratches across her stomach. "How was—"

He swallowed. He'd almost asked, horribly, how Sarah was.

"How was that?"

"It was cold," David said. "Unseasonably cold. There was frost in her name."

They passed through the arch at the end of the hall. Carpeted steps led them down into a chilly space with high walls and a ceiling that sloped and slanted nonsensically. The foyer. Home to Longreave's second and final elevator shaft, but no actual elevator. In all the excitement of the annex's construction, the builders had forgotten that one little detail. Above the doors was an unfinished dial, its arrow pointing down at nothing. Since Mark was a boy some part of him had wondered if the shaft *ever* stopped, or if it went down and down forever.

He shivered.

The Atlantic sloshed beyond the bay window.

They climbed another staircase, this one reaching up and around the cracked walls of the elevator shaft, and arrived at an open doorway.

Welcome to the annex.

Each floor here was shaped like a square U, twice as long as it was wide, with letters designating the rooms. As they passed 2A and approached the first bend, Mark realized David was talking again, softly. "The ice melted from her headstone, and I saw myself sitting there, an old man with pants he can't hardly keep on his waist anymore and hands aching so bad he can't get them in his pockets to warm them, and I felt . . ."

He cleared his throat.

". . . I felt silly and alone."

Mark braked next to 2C. "Do you hear that?"

There was a hurt look on David's face.

"Are they idiots? Are they daft?" Mark stepped back from the door, stiff. "Who went in here last? One of the ren-o guys? The painters?"

"I—"

"Unbelievable." Mark turned. "Bastards. *Bastards.*"

Down one staircase, up another. Through the second-floor hall, his feet smacking on the floorboards, his blood surging like an ocean inside his body.

"What is it?" said David as Mark returned with the key.

Plastic sheets covered the bed and carpet in 2C. Mark stomped into the bathroom and dropped to his knees by the tub. The faucet was dripping. *Plink . . . plink . . . plink.* He twisted the nozzle. The dripping stopped.

Quiet.

He saw droplets shining on the drain, shining like little beads, and suddenly Alice was a shout inside him. She was in his throat, she was on his lips. He swallowed her down and looked up at David, who was standing in the doorway.

"If you're ready."

"Yeah." Mark adjusted his tie. "Yeah. Where to?"

"Have you visited the cellar lately?"

• • •

There were two entrances to Longreave's underground. The first was tucked in a nook across from the lobby elevator. For decades it had been the favored access point, but then rot had retired the wooden steps on the other side of the door and the door had been padlocked. The other entrance was on the annex's bottom floor, which was reachable only from the floor above, by a staircase so skinny it seemed to have been squeezed into the addled architecture as an afterthought.

Level One of the annex was concrete and little else. It had restrooms, a laundry room, a meager fitness room that no one but the Lovers ever used, and beyond all that, at the very end of the twisting corridor, a tiny door with a sign that read:

DO NOT ENTER.

David twisted the knob. The door groaned open on one final staircase, its steps dipping into darkness. Three long *creeeaaaaks* down, and Mark's feet were gone. Four, and his legs stopped at the knees. His heartbeat jittered, and he choked on the black smell of earth. A lightbulb flicked on overhead. He let out his breath. *It's the annex.* He always felt like a rat caught in a maze when he wandered this deep into the annex.

Which was the reason he never did.

"Be careful," he said. "The steps have a little bend to them."

"I know. That's why I'm glad you're there to pad my fall."

Past the staircase everything was murky. Mark scanned under the low-hanging pipes until he spotted a dangling string. He ventured out and gave it a tug. The space around him brightened. Lit up, alive, the walls were red. Cobwebs twitched against the bricks—proof, if any proof was needed, that they'd come to the most inhabited floor of Longreave. He could feel constant spidery movement everywhere he wasn't looking.

A heavy slosh echoed from the dark.

His insides clenched.

"I have something to show you," said David, headed toward the next string, the next light. They walked on silently, revealing the way as they went, something scurrying always just out of sight ahead. In the hotel above there were walls and railings, corridors and doors, but here in the cellar, Longreave had no annexes. It was one unified enclosure, one grand hall reaching below the woodwork. Halfway through hunkered the boiler, a fat steel tank lying like a larva in a cocoon of pipes, grated stairs twisting up to its hatch. It moaned as they passed, its deep belly gurgling. One lightbulb later, a shadowy bulk to their left became the caved staircase that once connected the cellar to the lobby. Furry bodies whispered underneath the crumbled steps.

Finally Mark pulled the last string. A row of tiny, teeth-like stalactites appeared above his hand.

"There," said David.

And Mark saw. In the cellar's northeast corner, the wall bowed inward. *Bulged* inward. Its bricks were jumbled, stretchers resting at slant, headers poking out from the mold. Along the top of the wall little holes peeked out to the beach. He could hear the waves through them, the come and go, the purr, the hiss.

"Noticed it the other day," said David, "from outside."

"How long has——?"

"How long has it been like *this*? Can't tell you." David rubbed his arms through his blazer. "But as to how long the salt's been wearing away at it . . . that's easy. Always."

"There's not even a cavity. Nothing." Mark turned a discarded chair into a step stool. Standing on it on his tip-toes, he poked his fingers through the holes in the brick and touched the fine sand of the coast. "There should be two walls and a space between for insulation. No wonder it's so damn cold down here."

"Should should should," David sighed.

Mark climbed down and took a step back to survey. "So, we hire guys to replace the bricks right here. One by one, with fresh mortar. And salt-tolerant blocks this time, for God's sake. Twelve feet high and what, twenty feet wide, wouldn't you say? A good team could get it done in a week. Less than that."

"And when more of the wall gives?"

"Then we hire more builders." But even as Mark spoke, he turned. Fully illuminated, the cellar yawned: an ugly, majestic stretch of scarlet, as long as the hotel's history. How many thousands of bricks made up its walls? How many of those bricks were shifting in their foundation . . . inching, grinding their glacial way apart right at this very moment?

"We can buy a treadmill . . ."

. . . *but we can't build a pool.* David's favorite old saw. When big hotels started developing gymnasiums for their guests, David had counted his coins and purchased a shiny Lifestyle TR200 that went up to eight miles per hour. A man did what he could with what he had, and he did no more. Mark ground his teeth. "We take out a loan. I put in the bricks myself. I work down here an hour or two each day. It can't be too difficult, if I just replace a few at a time. It'll be like reorganizing a bookcase. We can hire a neighborhood kid to backpack small loads through the annex."

"Mark."

"Nicholas has a cousin, doesn't he? We pay the boy five bucks an hour and he builds up a little muscle. Everybody wins."

"Mark, I got an offer on the hotel."

Mark stopped. His hand fell. "You've gotten offers before."

"Not like this one." David's voice was quiet. A salt-scented draft rustled his hair. "It's just me now, you know. My daughter, my grandkids, they all live out on the west coast." Laguna Creek. Of course. "I'd like to visit them. Sit on their porch in the sun. I'd like that a lot, I think." David's eyes had closed. He opened them. "The company runs a condo chain. They want to knock down Longreave and put up one of their residences here."

"So that's what the staff meeting is about this morning . . . to discuss the offer?"

"No, Mark. I took it. I sold Longreave last night."

The cellar shrank to a box.

"Oh."

David watched him. "*Oh?*"

Mark heard Alice's voice in his head—*that's it?*—and he understood then, what she meant when she said the world was struggling toward synchronicity. He saw his life assembled like paintings in one of her galleries, each piece of artwork a moment, each moment bonded to the others by some theme in color or structure or style. He walked far down the canvas rows and came to his father, sitting on the porch under a deep blue evening sky, smoking a cigar that smelled of crushed leaves. "When I was twelve," Mark said, "I used to play chess. Do you remember?"

David was still.

Mark sat down in the salty dust beneath the wall. "I carried this scribbled-in copy of The Amateur's Mind by Jeremy Silman around with me wherever I went. I was in love with the game. Had some talent for it, too, for my age. It got me a little positive attention from the teachers at school and a little not-so-positive attention from the students. There were these tournaments in Boston on long weekends, and I would ride back and forth from the city each day. One night I got home, and Dad was outside on his wicker chair." Mark saw gray threads of smoke untwining into the dusk. "It was October. He was in a mood. I used to think it was about Mom when he got like that, but now I think it was about him. Where he was. Where he still was."

David breathed in long and slow.

"I showed him the trophy I won. Small thing. Second place for my age bracket. He told me it was wonderful, that he was proud of me. He meant it." The sky in Mark's memory was dark and smooth and immense, as if the cold Atlantic hung over Manxfield. Frank Currier turned the trophy over in his hands. "After a while, he said, 'I'm going to let you know this now, son, so you don't have to find out yourself. Sooner or later everyone stops caring how young you are you can do something and starts asking how far you'll take it.'" Mark stroked his tie. "Next tournament I entered into the main competition. I lost my first game and got right back on the train, then I spent the rest of my weekend at Longreave with him. With you."

David reached into his blazer. His hand was shaky. "I never considered you an employee. Not you, or your father. Your father was my best friend." He held out a check, slightly wrinkled. Mark took it. Zeroes stared up at him like a row of wide eyes. "I know things haven't been easy for you and Alice since—"

Something cold and wet closed its fingers in Mark's throat.

"—I know things haven't been easy. But I thought this could be good. You and Alice could leave if you wanted, move somewhere else. Somewhere new. You could pack your stuff and fly to Australia. I remember how much Alice and Sarah used to talk about traveling there." David's knotted hands rubbed together. "This could be good. Don't you think?"

In his loose gray sweats, the old man looked as thin as a slip of paper. Mark imagined ripping the check in half. One quick tear, a flick of the fingers, and . . .

. . . *pieces.*

"Yeah, David." He folded the check for two hundred thousand dollars and placed it in his pocket. "Good."

Chapter Two
October 2nd

People collided, Alice knew.

It was a messy affair, nothing clean about it. They came speeding along the blacktop, blind until impact. There was a birth of noise, a steely tangle of anatomy, and like that it was over. People collided and then they held on, the way cars held on after a crash, broken into one. Only the intervention of something larger and more powerful could pull them apart.

And where do they go after that? Where does what's left of them go after that? She spooned her uneaten peanut butter and granola into the garbage disposal and listened to the blades chop and grind. *There. That's where.*

Alice smiled a tight-lipped smile and then set off about the house. She opened blinds and windows. She peeled the linens off the guest bed. She forced in the door of the downstairs bathroom, stepped over the boxes inside, and ran the water in the tub. When she was done, when her breath was a wind in her lungs and the morning breeze was all around, she went into the office where she kept her art supplies.

There was the easel, raised so that she would always be looking up.

There was the canvas, rolled and sealed in plastic wrap.

There was the waxpaper and metal tray, waiting to be made into a palette.

And there were the pigments, vials of light and dark, reflective and transparent colors. Her passion, her poison.

Alice assembled her studio. Easel set, jars in a row. She reached for the pencil, but stopped. No. There would be no outlines today. The structure would come on its own, or not at all. She held up her brush. Could she?

It had been so long.

Alice scratched the tattoo printed down her thigh, 11-25-04, the only ink she'd ever wanted for herself. The living room softened around her. She stared at the white of the canvas and saw something there.

She saw blue.

Chapter Three
October 2ⁿᵈ

A vent rattled: *hick, hick.*

The phone's speaker hushed. Nicholas Lorey's hands were a pasty white ball in his lap. He leaned back in the Chesterfield. "When?"

"Yesterday evening," David said, and shifted on the couch beside Mark, who was sitting with his legs pressed together.

"Not *when* the bloody deal was done. The only *when* that matters is *when* the door and frame marry until death do they part."

David's voice was a helium squeak. "Twenty-four hours—"

"Tomorrow?"

"—from the sale." David rubbed the hotel key between his fingers. "Tonight."

"Lovely." Nicholas planted his loafers on the table and coffee splashed from his paper cup. A muddy stream trickled onto the rug. "For clarification's sake, are we observing damage done to your property or the property of our condominium friends?"

"Our friends."

"Oh dear."

"There'll be an auction," David said after a moment. "Everything except for the beds. Those I suspect are bound for the dump." He turned to Mark. "And Alice's painting, of course. That can go home with you."

Mark glanced at the hotel. Its oiled surface gleamed as though wet. He nodded to hide the lump in his throat as he swallowed.

"Wouldn't want to lose Little Longreave," said Nicholas. "I don't suppose they gave a date for the demolition, did they?"

"No, but I gathered the project won't really get moving until next year."

"That's a long time for Longreave to sit, all lonely."

"It is."

"Mr. Sanders?" came a fuzzy voice on the phone.

"Yes, Julie?"

"It's Matthew, actually. Well, *that* was Matthew. This is Julie speaking now. I'm Julie."

"Yes, Julie?"

"About the shifts we worked last week . . ."

"Your paychecks are in the mail, plus a little extra." David smiled at the phone, and Mark wondered if reassurance by nature came from a place of compassion, or if like so many other things it was just reflex.

The speaker crackled. "Julie and I, we left a few things in one of the rooms. A few personal items."

"Oh. I see."

"No, no, not like that. Gym shorts and a bra—a *sports* bra. For exercise. For when we exercised on our break. When one of us at a time took a break."

David rubbed a wrinkle on his forehead. "Which room?"

"Three-oh-four."

"Your things will make it back to you, don't worry. Take care, both of you."

"But I don't understand." Julie again. "We thought you loved Longreave."

"I do. More than almost anything in the world." There was a limp, gentle quality to the old man's voice that reminded Mark of the ferns hanging in the office. David hung up, placed a check on the coffee table, and walked away across the lobby. The check was for $5,000. Nicholas eyed it for a moment before picking it up and tucking it in his wallet.

"A pretty bonus," he said. "It'd be even prettier if my career here was a financial choice, but sadly, Longreave has never meant as much to my bank account as it has to my sensibilities." He gazed across the table at Mark. "I do wonder, though. If my bonus here is pretty little schoolgirl Sally Somebody, with her braces just out and her breasts just in, what kind of beauty will *you* be kissing tonight?"

Mark's check itched at the skin under his pocket.

"Were you there when Grandpa David peddled off the hotel? Did you help guide him around the details with your strong young hands? Well, not quite young anymore, are they?" Nicholas cocked his head. "Your father would be proud of you, unloading this place off your shoulders with such ease. Both of your fathers would, I reckon. Inheritance is such a *vastly* overrated obligation."

"Go away."

Nicholas flinched. "Excuse me?"

Mark clutched onto his tie and pinched his eyes shut. "Go away," he said, tugging and tugging. "Go away, go away, go away, go away."

The next time he looked, the lobby was empty.

• • •

Mark splashed icy water on his face until he couldn't feel his cheeks. An echoing *drip . . . drip . . . drip* followed him out of the lobby restroom. He walked into the office, where David was knotting a grocery bag filled with the Lovers' soiled workout clothes. "Should I send this box or envelope, do you think?"

"Box," Mark said, staring out the window.

"That needs boarding up. I told them I'd take care of it."

"And the window in the foyer?"

"The bars on it should keep out the vagabonds just fine."

An hour later, Mark walked onto the beach with several lengths of plywood, a hammer, and carpenter nails. Waves groped up the sand. Gulls fell from the clouds like large white raindrops. Inside the office, David was writing apology letters to the hotel's few loyal guests. The room darkened with each panel set in place. Mark broke out in goosebumps as he nailed the last board over the window, and his skin continued to crawl as he headed back to the lobby.

A few scattered reservations dotted the calendar. He called each number back and informed people of the closure.

"But where will I stay?" asked one woman.

Mark stared at Alice's Longreave. "I don't know."

•••

"Are you ready?"

Mark blinked up at the three blurry Davids standing over him. "*Whattimeisit?*"

"Time," David said. His duplicates faded. "Did you rest well?"

Mark sat up on the couch. It hadn't felt like rest, more like being pulled down into someplace dark and held there. "I don't even remember sitting down."

"Forgetfulness is an old man's crutch." David helped him to his feet. "Don't let me catch you borrowing it again without my permission."

Longreave gave a gentle dip and sway, and he must have too, because David frowned.

"Want me to drive you home?"

Mark remembered then. He had no home. He sat back down on the couch. "No, I'll be all right. Just shaking out the cobwebs."

"I wouldn't mind. It's been too long since I've said hello to Alice anyway."

"It's all right. Really. I'm awake now." And he was. Sharply, painfully, awake. Little blades of light poked from each lamp on the chandelier, making it look like some lustrous cactus. "Are you leaving your plants behind?"

"No."

"Why didn't you have the movers move them?"

"They're safer traveling with me." David shrugged. "I'm an overprotective parent."

"Well, let's gather the children."

They crossed the lobby, and Mark was amazed how smooth his strides were, how easily his feet carried him over the floorboards, as if this time were the same as any other time. The staircase slid closer, and he pictured all the versions of himself that had ever walked up it walking up it now, branching left and right through the corridors, opening and shutting doors, folding sheets, replacing soaps, unclogging drains, more Marks than a thousand Longreaves could hold, and yet he could hold onto none of them for longer than a moment. *Slow down*, wailed a voice inside him, and then they were taking down the plants in the office, and then they were walking back through the lobby, and good God, *slow down*.

"Don't forget Alice," said David.

Mark set his pots down before approaching the mantelpiece. Longreave stared down at him, its red body washed against the sea, its windows rounded into glowing blue eyes. He got up on his tiptoes to grip the frame and took in the sweet, musty smell of oil and canvas that used to follow Alice around like perfume.

The sky was heavy and starless.

David reached back into the hotel, shut off the light, then locked the door. Mark felt the click inside his chest.

"I need yours, too," David said quietly. "To give over to the company in the morning."

Mark handed him his key.

The two of them walked down the path. "I'd ask you to help me buckle them in," David said after they'd loaded the plants into his backseat. "but I think perhaps I've asked enough of you today."

The ocean sounded like a moan building inside Longreave.

"Goodnight, kid."

Soon the rumble of the Sedan was lost beneath the waves. Mark climbed into his car with Alice's painting. As he reached for the ignition, his hand stopped and began to shake. He looked up at the hotel. It stood gaunt against the bruised night, like a ship bearing north into a storm. He thought of his father in that theater eighteen years ago. His father, Frank Currier, whose wide solemn face had become his own.

He's sitting near the middle as the lights go down for the second act and the cast retakes the stage. The play is Twelfth Night, and he knows every line by heart. He's whispering them along with the actors when he feels a blossoming of warmth inside his chest. It's quick, if not painless; muted, if not silent. His fingers clench the plush armrest. His mouth locks open. He's dead in an instant, the coronary equivalent of a ruptured tire, and around him everyone laughs, everyone claps. The show goes on.

Mark started his car and drove away.

The show goes on.

Chapter Four
October 2ⁿᵈ

Far off, on land, the sliding glass door opened and footsteps moved across the tile.

An ocean stormed inside the living room. Water slopped and gulped and hissed with a million foaming mouths. The jaws of an enormous wave, so dark it was almost black, closed over Alice. It swallowed her down, spit her up. She broke the surface and someone was on the shore, behind her, calling her name.

"Alice."

Blue filled her lungs.

"Alice."

Blue sprayed from her lips.

"Alice."

A hand touched her shoulder, and her brush stopped mid swathe on the canvas. The floor reappeared beneath her feet, the walls folded up and reattached to the ceiling, and she twisted around with a sputtering scream.

Alex screamed back.

She swooned into him. He had a clean smell—a simple smell, not aftershave or even deodorant, but regular old bar soap. They started laughing at the time. "Jesus, Alex. I almost peed myself."

"I *did* pee myself." He kissed the top of her head and made a little *pphh* sound as he spit out her hair. "Greasy. Are you short on shampoo?"

"Short on a lot of things." Her mind rewound to Mark letting himself out the front door, his shoulders limp in his creased shirt. "It's been a long day."

"I can see that. And a dramatic one, too."

She looked up at his face. It was as familiar as his scent. The blond fuzz on his cheeks. The cheerful blue eyes and sharp, effeminate cheekbones. The red beanie cocked back from his brow.

He was gazing at the painting.

Her day's work hung wetly from the easel, not a speck of white left on the canvas. It had started off an ocean and somewhere along the way become a devourer, a feasting blue anatomy, wave edges pebbled like cracked lips, huge bellies of shadow between the swells. The oil shone, layers drooling over layers. "What a mess," she mumbled.

"Is it finished?"

She felt the pull of it deep inside her, like an undertow. "Not yet."

"How long have you been at it?"

"A few hours." Alice glanced at the dark window. "A few hours longer than that, maybe." Suddenly her legs were quivering, her whole body frail and trembly with hunger. She sank into him and her eyes trailed down his hanging arm to the long-necked bottle in his hand. "What're the bubbles for?"

"It's today."

"What's today?" Then the date struck her. "Shit. Alex. I was supposed to drive to your place, and I completely—did you call?"

"Once or twice." He winced. "Okay, ten times."

Alice hurried into the kitchen, her feet chilly on the floor. She took down two wine glasses, wiped at them with her spotted tank top, and succeeded in fogging them blue.

"A little color never hurt." Alex limped across the tile, favoring his stiff right leg, and set the champagne bottle on the counter. "I've always wanted to try a *bleusé*."

"Not me. I'm iffy enough on the pink stuff." She selected a second pair of glasses.

"You might want to play under the faucet."

Alice looked down at her hands. There was paint on her palms, paint on her knuckles, even a little paint under her nails. She turned the water on hot.

"I talked to Mom yesterday," Alex said.

Steam bowled up from the sink. Her ghost stared back at her from the window, dim and smoking on the glass. "You called?"

"She did."

Alice wrung her hands under the burning tap. "How is she?"

"Same as ever." He stepped beside her and polished the first glass silently. "She wants to know when we're coming."

"And?" Her voice sounded thin around the edges.

"I said late this month or sometime the next."

Alice thought of Vermont in the winter, its canvas of starved trees and snow. "This month."

"I'll let her know."

She attacked her hands with the dishtowel while Alex poured them both a liberal drink. Leaning back against the counter, his shorts riding up his downy legs, he lifted his glass. Tiny wrinkles smiled around his eyes.

"To twelve years sober," he said.

Alice took a sip. Her gaze wandered to the milk sitting on the countertop, and a corkscrew twisted in her belly. They said each cup of milk contained a little pus, often no more than a drop, due to infection in the cows' udders. It amazed her. How you could go on ingesting something knowing it was infected, how you could go on *needing* it even though it made you sick.

Alice emptied the carton in the sink. All of a sudden her breath felt fragile.

"What's wrong?"

She wasn't going to cry. It was silly and pointless, and she was spent on tears. Sick of them, their wet warmth, their salt taste. She shook her head, eyes stinging.

"It's done."

"Oh, *Lis.*" He hugged her, and like a reflex, her fists balled up the back of his shirt. "When?"

"This morning. Last night. I don't know. Does it matter? He's coming back to get his things." She heard the words out loud before she understood them. "He'll be back soon. You shouldn't be here. It'll make it harder."

"Do you want me to leave?"

She opened her mouth to say yes. "Not yet."

"Come." Alex led her to the table, pulled out a chair, and sat her down. The wrinkles around his eyes were still there, but they were different in some subtle way—gentler—all the humor softened out of them. He walked to the refrigerator, his right heel scuffing on the tile. A knot formed in her right thigh. She massaged it.

"Let's get something in you. Something fresh."

"Out of produce."

He closed the refrigerator. "Something warm then."

"Cupboard. Down on your right."

"Directions not needed, dear sister."

At one point in her life she might have wondered how he'd known she was hungry—if he'd heard her stomach growling or simply done the math upon finding her elbow-deep in oil—but she'd long since given up looking for explanations, justifications.

He knew. He *always* knew.

A box of noodles sailed over the stove, then a can of tomato sauce came rolling down the counter. Alex limped alongside it, matching its pace. He selected a pot from one of the hooks, flipped the pot to his other hand, and caught the can behind his back as it fell off the edge.

"You've been practicing."

"Kitchen acrobatics is heading to the summer Olympics," he said. "Didn't you hear?"

"I must have missed that publication of NYN."

He shot her a glare. "You *now* I hate abbreviations."

"I *now* nothing of the sort."

"Well now you now." Alex flicked over a folded square of paper. "Give this a scouring later, will you?"

She smoothed the paper against the table.

Now You Now

Let's tak about the Blak-Caped Chikade, state bird of both Masachusets and Main
and no dout front runer for country bird. A carismatic litle crown wearer, this New
Englander takes its . . .

"Flying over the cuckoo's nest, are we?" she said. Her brother's
bi-monthly column had become a curious success in the local
paper, less for its actual content than its gimmicky avoidance of
silent or otherwise 'unnecessary' letters and the energetically
small-minded personality of Tomas Seudonym Nox. In his
mouth, the English language got its wings clipped. Meanings
shifted and pronunciations changed. No one new or could now
anything, not unless Tomas said so first. Talking (or taking) like
him was a great pastime for Alice and Alex. One they used to
amuse each other . . . and annoy everyone else.

"Always been flying there. Only just now documenting it."
Alex turned on the stove. "Did you know the Chickadee doesn't
migrate? It makes a home and sticks around its whole life. When
things get cold, it gets cold too. Is that loyal or stupid? I don't
know. Christ, it's chilly in here."

Alice traced the scratches on her stomach. She'd given them to
herself in the peak of her fever, after talking had failed, and
shouting, and crying. Her anger, her frustration, like a boiling
bath. And Mark sitting where she was sitting right this moment,
his expression walled off, one hand around his tie. "How was your
swim today?" she asked.

"Tighter than usual."

"I'm sorry."

"Still more pleasant than jogging. Mind if I use the loo?"

"Go ahead," she said, a queer fluttering in her chest, like
Chickadee wings.

Alex limped down the hall. There'd been pictures on its walls
once. There weren't anymore. He stopped halfway to the

bathroom. Turned. "I don't know what's wrong with me. I see an open door and I think, *come in*. It's a problem, really."

"It's fine."

"I'll go upstairs."

"It's fine."

Alex stared at her for a moment, picking at his red hat, then continued to the bathroom. He stepped over the boxes inside, dropped his pants, and lowered himself onto the toilet. As he sat there, his head turned slowly . . . slowly . . . toward the tub.

A creak.

From outside.

From the front porch.

Alice jolted to her feet. Her brother, the open bottle, the bathroom. Oh God, the bathroom. She shut the wine glasses in the cupboard and scrambled for the champagne. Mark was in the doorway. His dark eyes spotted her.

"Hi," she said.

"It smells like oil in here."

"I was going to clean, but I lost track of time."

"It doesn't smell bad." He stood on the welcome mat, his legs hatching up from a nest of shadows. "You've been painting?"

"Yes," she said, and moved herself in front of the champagne bottle. "Though I think I'm out of practice."

"I'm sure it's good."

"You can look if you want."

He touched his tie absently. She could see the veins on his hand. He had such large veins, as if there was too much blood in his body. Or as if . . . Alice thought of water, how it expands when it freezes. "You coming in?"

"I'm just going to grab a few things."

"Okay."

He didn't move.

The eaves played a shrill, singing note. She tried again. "It's sounding pretty ugly out there."

He stepped through doorway, but no further. "The waves were getting rough."

"Were they?"

"Longreave . . ." He motioned her direction, and she almost glanced behind her at the sliding glass door, as if she would find the hotel in her backyard. Something about the idea was unsettling. That a place could follow you. That it could creep up on you, like a person, until you were standing in its shadow.

"I keep thinking it'll rain."

Alice almost said, *Well, I'm glad you made it home before it did.* But that wasn't right, even if it felt natural. "I'm glad it waited until you were off the road." She cringed inside. That wasn't right either. Soon he would be back on the road, and what if started raining then?

"There was a drip in one of the rooms today." The door slammed behind him. He didn't notice. "I was going to talk to the renovation guys about it. I'm not anymore."

Down the hall Alex pulled up his pants. *Don't flush,* she prayed, *please don't flush.*

"No?"

"No." Mark's hand crawled down to his pocket and scratched at something in there. "Longreave. The hotel. It's—"

A swirling gurgle. A glug-glug-glug of pipes.

His eyes widened. He looked lost, a child in a stranger's house, in a man's clothes. He blinked and then started up the staircase without another word.

Her brother emerged from the hallway. "What happened?"

"Nothing," she said, her tension draining into weariness. "But maybe it would be better if you left for now."

"Yeah. Sure. Whatever you want."

She pictured him out in the rain, his beanie swollen. "Take my umbrella."

"I'll run if I have to." Alex slipped out through the sliding door with a wink, and she turned to head upstairs. The painting drew her gaze as she crossed the living room. She was able to see it closer from a distance. There was a shape beneath the waves, or the beginning of one. Perhaps tomorrow the shape would surface.

The bedroom door was open. Good. She had a chance then. Not to bridge the gap between herself and Mark, but a chance at least to watch each other off across the divide.

"It's the second," she said as she entered. "October second. The day Alex got out of the hospital, after his hard spell. His leg was hurting bad tonight. I let him use the other bathroom, so he didn't have to climb the stairs."

Mark dropped an armful of briefs into his suitcase. Walked to the closet. Gathered his button ups—all of them black, all of them long sleeved—by the hooks.

"Please, Mark. Talk to me."

He moved her way, the cuffs of his shirts dragging on the floor. His face was blank. She took a step back, out of the bedroom.

He closed the door.

Locked it.

Alice stood in shock. Then came the anger. Little bubbles of anger, popping as they rose. "We can do better than this," she said, her throat tight as a fist. "I have to believe we can do better than this. Mark. Can you hear me?"

Silence in the bedroom.

Downstairs the water was boiling.

•••

Mark stared at the dresser. He'd forgotten something. Missed a step somewhere. His mother used to say, when packing, start at the feet and work your way up. Socks, briefs—and yes, that was right.

Pants.

He opened the middle drawer and there were his slacks, folded in two neat piles. You had to take care of what was yours. If you didn't take care of it, you didn't deserve it. His father had said that. Outside the bedroom, Alice retreated down the hall. He listened until he could no longer hear her footsteps. It didn't take long. She was a soft walker, Alice. Not like her brother. There'd been an accident when they were kids. She'd been at home when it happened. Cheshire County, New Hampshire. The car went off a bridge near her house and crunched on a dry riverbed. Ugly, tragic affair. Blood soaking into the seats like paint. Both her parents dead. No wonder she never talked about her childhood.

Mark packed his sweats. He'd put them on later tonight, when he—

When he what?

He tried to finish the sentence, but there was a cliff at the end of it. Something scraped inside the drawer. Indented on the next pair of slacks, the last pair remaining, was a rectangular lump. He lifted them.

His blood thickened. His heartbeat slowed.

Mark took the cigar box in his hands. It was smooth and heavy, a gold clasp on the front and two brass hinges on the back. Cracks intertwined on the cherry finish like lines on a weathered palm.

He opened it.

•••

Alice stirred at her noodles as Mark came down the stairs. She lowered her fork. "You never said. If you talked to David."

"We talked."

She needed to swallow. She didn't. "How is he?"

"Better than he has been in a while, I think." Mark set his house key on the ledge by the door. "He says hi."

Wind howled.

"Mark."

He turned. In the soft light leaving the home, he appeared to smile. "You don't have to worry. There's a room for me."

•••

He parked up the coast so his car wouldn't be seen and walked the rest of the way under foggy street lamps.

It was pouring.

Raindrops exploded on the ground. Gutters burbled and choked. Beyond the beach, beyond the world, the ocean heaved like a waking giant. Mark dragged his suitcase up the river of dark beads that had once been a pebbled stone path. He took his father's key out of the cigar box and let himself into Longreave.

Chapter Five
October 3rd

Mark woke in the dark in a room on the fourth floor. He lay in bed underneath a sweaty sheet, listening to the steady drip of water down the window. He drifted off and woke again, sometime later. The rain had stopped, but the dripping had not.

It was in the room with him.

It was in the bathtub.

Chapter Six
October 3rd

Morning painted the window in streaks of orange and swells of gold-tinged purple. Sitting on the floor underneath the sunrise, Mark unpacked his suitcase. His clothes ranged from damp to soaked. He wrung them out one by one in the sink, smoothed the wrinkles against the dresser, and hung them all around the room to dry. When he finished, it looked as though 401 had been wrapped for renovations like the lodgings in the annex, except with cloth instead of plastic.

The smell of his armpits stunned him as he stretched out to make the bed, and he realized it had been over twenty-four hours since he'd bathed. He glanced at the shower. His eyes trailed down the glossy tile to the bathtub and a chill travelled just as slowly down his backside, like rainwater down glass.

Mark rubbed at his bare throat and decided deodorant would do just fine.

Only he didn't have deodorant.

The day was beginning to warm. Whistles sounded from shrubs and branches, and sunlight made mirrors of the puddles on the sidewalk. He passed an old lady walking her Dachshund, but otherwise the coastline road belonged to him and the birds.

There was a supermarket five minutes away, but it was the one he and Alice always used and he was certain that he would run into her there, that they would come around a corner at the same time and bump carts. He had no real reason to believe it would

happen, and yet he felt it bone deep. If he went there, she would
be there. She was everywhere they'd ever been together, and so it
was safest if he didn't go in town at all.

It took him ten miles before he found a place that seemed
suitably distant. He wandered the aisles looking for necessities,
but when he finally reached the checkout line all he had in his
cart was Old Spice, peanut butter, and bread.

He reached into his pocket to pay.

His fingers brushed a damp slip of paper.

A little while later he sitting in a closed cubicle the size of a
handicapped stall. As he waited, he breathed into his palm. His
mouth didn't smell much better than his armpits. The door
opened, and a woman with glasses and brown hair in a ponytail
sat down across from him. "What can we do for you today, Mr.
Currier?"

He handed her the check. "I'd like to deposit this."

"This is a lot of money, Mark," said the woman, who was really
Alice disguised in a business suit. "What are you going to do with
it?"

Mark blinked.

"Mr. Currier?" The woman's eyes had narrowed behind her
lenses. "I asked if you already had an existing account."

"Yes." He shook his head. "I mean, not here. Not with this
bank. I have a joint account somewhere else."

Her polished blue nails clicked on the desk. "Well, let's get
started."

After an hour as long as ten, he tucked his paperwork into the
dashboard and fell back against the seat. His brain felt like
something packaged and numbered, filed away. He stared blankly
at his reflection in the rearview mirror, seeing only the pieces of
his face, not his face. Stiff, short hair. Creased brow. Eyes and
nose and ears, each one a separate digit on a contract awaiting his
name. He licked his dry, split lips and heard David's voice
whisper, *cracks, cracks in all of them.*

Mark put the car in reverse, a new destination in mind.

• • •

It was worst near the top. There, the cracks wove through the woodwork like intricate spider webs. Mark stared up at the underside of the stairs and surveyed the damage, the caulking gun dangling from the tip of his left forefinger. He'd used the money from his new bank account to purchase it along with a bucket of black paint. And not just any black paint. The high-quality stuff. Dark enough to make night look like day.

Mark got to it.

He started crouched on one knee, then worked his way up using the method his father had taught him years ago. *Push, don't pull, on the gun. Squeeze the trigger slowly. Fill fat to narrow.* By the time he reached the middle step, he'd found his rhythm. It wasn't quite beer work—he didn't earn a sweat, only a crick in his neck—but all the same he found himself wishing he'd picked up a cool one from the store. Or a cool six. Better than the measly pickings waiting for him in 401. How had he ended up with peanut butter? He didn't even *like* peanut butter. That was Alice's comfort food, Alice's vice. The thought of eating it now struck him as faintly shameful, obscene even, like stealing a lock of hair to hold onto someone's smell.

At last he finished.

Beneath the floorboards came a small, restless sound—the shadow of a sound—as the boiler stirred from its slumber.

He tapped the almost-empty gun against his thigh and considered his options. The caulk would need an hour or two to dry, and before that, the floorboards beneath the staircase would need to be covered. With what though? Blankets? No. Too absorbent. If only he'd bought plastic sheets from the hardware store—

Plastic sheets. Of course.

Mark almost laughed, the solution was so obvious. He grabbed the key to 2B (2A was exposed to the street, and the thought of

visiting 2C again made all the liquid in his stomach turn over
heavily). As he started for the stairs, he felt a buzz in his pocket.
David. He tossed his phone on the front desk and set off.
Something else struck him when he reached the foyer, and this
time, he did laugh.

He could swipe a sheet of plastic, sure, but he'd have one hell
of a time applying the paint because he hadn't purchased a single
brush. No matter. It just so happened that the renovation guys, as
forgetful as they were with faucets, were more mindful than Mark
when it came to supplies. Most of the rollers and trays had been
purchased on Longreave's dollar, which meant most of the rollers
and trays would be sticking around to collect Longreave's dust.

He strolled into the laundry room down on Level One. Four
industrial-sized washers and driers stood against the wall, but
otherwise the space was bare. Of course it was bare. David had
asked the renovators to move their things because the whole
floor was starting to smell like paint, so they'd taken their station
to the one place where the stench would bother no one. A place
with plenty of room to spare.

The cellar.

All of a sudden he felt like a boy following breadcrumbs deeper
into the woods. *Go back to the hardware store.* But that was silly.
What he needed was right below his feet. He went to the door
marked **DO NOT ENTER.** He pushed it open. As the steps
revealed themselves, slinking down into the cool gloom and out
of sight, a question prickled in the back of his mind.

If he was following breadcrumbs, who was leaving them?

The boiler's husky thrumming shook the dark. Cobwebs hung
over the walls like lacy undergarments. Mark lit the first lightbulb
and revealed the clutter up ahead. There was a flat-nosed shovel
in a wheelbarrow, a couch unstuffed into a bed for rats, a cracked
and empty portrait frame. Behind all that towered the immense
bookcase he, his father, and a more nimble David had hauled
down from the lobby a lifetime ago. The bookcase sat in front of
the annex's elevator shaft, whose doors had never once been
opened in their long existence.

Mark picked over the shelves, which had been stocked by the renovators. Using a paint tray as a basket for his rollers and brushes, he started to turn back.

And paused.

On the lowest shelf, in the dimmest corner, was a hunter's green rollup bag. Mark picked it up by its leather handle. It was lighter than he remembered, but then, he'd been a boy the last time he'd held it. His fingers inched toward the buckles.

No. Not yet.

He gathered his things and rocked to his feet. Looking over the clutter, he wondered how he could have walked right by all of this yesterday and seen none of it.

What *else* might have been standing at the edge of his vision, unnoticed?

Mark made for the exit. He caught the lightbulb's string as he passed. The dark closed around him, and he broke into a run. He was at the top of the stairs, in the doorway to the annex, when the boiler went quiet.

When he heard the drip.

Plop.

His breath stopped. An icy, invisible hand gripped his neck and turned him toward the cellar.

Plop.

He pictured a droplet fattening underneath a pipe, falling, and hitting the concrete. But this was no light peck. This was a lip-to-lip kiss. This was a faucet letting go a drop into a full tub of water.

Mark lifted his foot to back away from the basement.

And took a step down.

He placed the rollup bag and tray by the stairs, and set off with slow, scraping footsteps. The dark was a wall ahead. Every bulb he lit made the wall jump back. Every breath he took clawed his throat. He circled the boiler once, twice, checking the pipes, checking them again, searching for any place on or around the tank where water could collect and spill. Nothing. Nothing. Nothing. And then, far off:

Plop.

Mark thought of breadcrumbs, one laid out after another, encouraging him to take one more step, light one more bulb, go just a little deeper.

Plop.

Blood-drop eyes shone under the collapsed staircase.

Plop.

A warm draft tickled his skin.

Plop.

The cellar narrowed.

Plop . . .

The concrete was no longer cold beneath his feet. The concrete was no longer concrete at all. It was winter, and he was walking down a hallway toward a door cracked open at the end. Heat rattled through the vents. He could hear Alice's brush scrawling away in the office. The door drew closer. From the other side came a deep, sluggish . . .

Plop.

The northeast corner of the cellar brightened, and Mark's chest unclenched. A light breeze was blowing through the holes in the crumbling wall. Beneath them was a large puddle. Some ocean had gotten in during the storm. Some ocean was *still* getting in, soaking through the cracks in the hull. But the waves were calm now. Looking out at the clear sky, Mark felt a similar peace settle over him. He climbed onto the broken chair, reached up, and ran his finger along one of the holes in order to touch the water gathering there before it fell. But there was no water gathering there, or on the next hole, or the next.

The dripping stopped, he realized.

That was when all of the lights in the cellar, all of them at once, went out.

• • •

Mark shouted until his throat was hoarse, his fingers wiggling at the daylight. He shouted for David. He shouted for Alice. He shouted for his father and mother, for God, for anyone dead or alive who would listen.

• • •

He did it on hands and knees, pawing his way along the wall, because walking he felt too exposed. Walking, he couldn't tell if the footsteps he heard were his own. There was a hitching *slur-rrrrr-rrrp* coming from the dark, but it was only the boiler. Even if it sounded like someone breathing through a soggy throat.

Even if it sounded close.

• • •

The cellar had grown. It was up the steps, it was in the annex.

His hand bumped the paint tray at the top of the staircase— *wrong, wrong, that was all wrong*—and sent it scuffling across the concrete. Mark clutched after it. Grabbed it. Held it to his chest, grinning a hard grin. He groped around for the rollup bag and kissed its warm leather, then he looped the strap over his arm and kept crawling, awkwardly now, the tray hopping and scraping as he moved along the wall.

The restrooms crept past on his left.

The sinks in both were dripping.

He pinched his eyes shut, double-wrapping the darkness, and didn't open them until he reached the stairwell. There would be sunlight on the second floor.

Beautiful, *blessed* sunlight.

But the cellar had taken over the second floor, too. Mark clawed at the carpet in despair and remembered Alice dragging nails across her belly. He hadn't even tried to stop her. What kind of a husband, what kind of a *man*, did nothing while his wife opened herself up in front of him? He sobbed. Hard. Then he forced himself across the corridor, reaching ahead for the wall. For a moment he was certain that he wouldn't find it, that he would go on reaching and crawling and never touch anything solid again, and the thought was like touching death.

At last his fingers brushed the baseboard. He pulled himself along and soon the baseboard gave way to something colder, smoother. A door. He felt for the crack at the bottom, and was the dark there a shade lighter? Or did he just want it—*need* it—to be?

Inside 2C a drop struck the drain of the bathtub.

Plink.

He crawled on, biting into his lower lip. His head knocked against another wall. A *new* wall. He'd reached the first turn in the corridor. A fuzzy gray dot hung in the dark ahead. The dot grew into a strip as he dragged himself toward it. He reached out for the strip and saw his fingernail, his knuckle, a curl of hair.

He saw.

Slowly, tentatively, he felt his way up the door to his feet. His legs were unsteady. His breath was thin. He gripped the doorknob and used the key he'd taken from the front desk to unlock the deadbolt. Plastic sheeting clung to his loafers as he crossed the room.

Outside 2B, October's early dusk had fallen.

Inside 2B, Mark Currier stood at the window and let tears roll down his cheeks.

Chapter Seven
October 3rd

Alice watched the sun rise at night.

Crimson waves lapped in from the horizon, where a red sore hung over the Atlantic. She hadn't painted the star. She'd stabbed it into being. The result was more wound than fireball, its body ragged with flames that resembled frays of bloodied cotton.

Disturbing, Alice thought with a smile.

Her first painting was lying on the office floor. She'd worked on the ocean well past noon, undoing yesterday's waves with new ones, but in the end she'd only managed to recreate the same essential turmoil. The shape below the surface—and there *was* a shape, she could feel it—had stayed submerged.

Still the thought of those oiled and stormy waters nagged at her.

Still.

Alice went into the kitchen to wash her hands and was waylaid by a hunger so extreme it made her tremble. Halfway through her bowl of cold spaghetti, she reached for the phone to see what time Mark was coming home.

Then she remembered.

As a little girl, Alice had once found a dog lying behind a bench in the park. She'd been leaning over to pet it—hey there, big fella—when its head lifted and its jaws let out a foamy, whimpering growl that set her back on her heels. *Sick.* The dog was *sick.* She backed away from the phone the same way now.

But it was too late.

She'd been bitten.

Mark was standing by her with a carton of milk. He was at the table, his tie lolling down his shirt like a long blue tongue. He was in the doorway, staring into the house with sad, dark eyes. She ran upstairs, dodged past him, past his suitcase, and shut herself in the bathroom. This was natural, more than natural. This was a part of letting go, just another step in the painful process of being human. You accept the grief, you take it in and build a home for it, or the grief takes you in and becomes your home.

Alice wandered to the mirror.

The ghost of a man drew up behind her, coming into focus, and brushed the hair back from her shoulder. She smiled for a moment. Then the smile fell off her face and she ripped open the drawer. There. Scissors. The blades came alive in her hand. They snapped and twisted and chewed. When she finally set them down, the sink was full of her hair and the hair still on her head was as jagged as a saw blade.

Alice blew a strand from her lips.

Au revoir.

She took off her paint-spotted clothes and climbed in the shower. Soon there was only the heat, the blissful burn. Her eyes closed. A pair of arms reached around her, folding over her breasts. A warm mouth kissed the curve of her neck.

Chapter Eight
October 3rd

David again.

Mark stared down at his phone. Its blue backlight mingled with the glow of the lantern at his feet. He waited until the fourth ring.

"Hello? Mark?"

"It's me."

"I called earlier. To see if you and Alice wanted to have dinner this evening."

"I'm sorry. I was going to get back to you, but I got distracted." An itching heat wormed through Mark's slacks, slow-cooking his shins. He took a step back from the lantern and bumped into the Chesterfield. A second lantern, unlit, wobbled on the armrest.

"Busy day?"

"Eventful."

"What are you up to now?"

"Just recovering from a power outage." A few yards away, the lantern's bright glow softened to a buttery yellow and melted into the dark.

"Huh. There haven't been any problems here."

"It's kind of a local thing."

"Well, how about you two head on over? It's beautiful out, and not so late yet I can't fire up the grill. There's a pair of cold cuts in the freezer for me and you, and some of those veggie patties for the lady. The ones that smell like farts when you cook them."

"Actually, Alice hasn't been feeling so great today. She's about to turn in for the night."

"Oh no. Nothing ugly, I hope."

"Just one of those weather-changing bugs."

There was a pause that stretched as long as the cellar.

"How did she take it?" David asked quietly. "What did she say?"

Mark rubbed at his throat, his collar tight despite the lack of a tie. "You know Alice. She's adaptable."

"And you?"

"To be honest, David, I'm okay. I wasn't sure at first, but I'm okay. I think I needed to get out of that place."

The line went silent. Mark checked to make sure they were still connected.

"I'm okay, too." David's voice was low and a little crackly, like static. "You'll tell me if you're free later in the week?"

"Of course."

"Goodbye then for now."

"Bye."

Mark pocketed his phone and looked up at the mantelpiece, where Alice's painting hung once again. Longreave wavered in the light.

"What am I doing?" he said.

The hotel had no answer for him.

•••

The staircase took two hours to paint. When he finished, he balled up the spotted plastic sheet from 2B and stuffed it in a garbage bag. Sitting in the foyer with his legs crossed Indian-style on the carpet, he ate peanut butter sandwiches and stared out the window to the spot where the ocean stopped and became the sky. It was difficult to find, easy to lose. He couldn't be sure he was actually seeing the horizon, or just looking toward his memory of it.

Mark gathered his leftover crusts to feed to the gulls in the morning then walked up to the second floor and down the dark hall, moving inside a pocket of light. In each hand he carried a black-capped gas lantern, one on, one off. The second in case the first failed. Gas because he no longer trusted electricity. A bodiless, long-armed shape floated at him as he stepped inside 401, and his heart jumped up his throat. Raising the lantern, Mark exposed the pinstripe shirt dangling from the bathroom door. He laughed through clenched jaws and set about collecting his clothes. A few items were still wrinkled, so he got out the ironing board. Then he remembered all the outlets were dead. He sighed.

Before he could change his mind he went into the bathroom to wash the black paint from his hands. As he scrubbed, he glanced at his face in the mirror. When he looked down again, Alice's hands, not his, were stretched out under the flowing water. Long, smooth fingers. Nails each a different color. He wondered if she had worked on her painting today, if she had enjoyed herself. He hoped she had.

He hoped she had been too miserable to crawl out of bed.

Mark turned on the shower and watched water beat against the acrylic until the mirror clouded, then he took off his clothes and climbed inside with the thought of Alice.

After he was done, he shut the door behind him.

His eyes wandered to the rollup bag. Its handles were up, like a dog's perked ears, and for an instant he was six years old, maybe seven, climbing up the porch steps after school. He turned the doorknob and suddenly he was on the ground, massive paws on his chest, fighting off the tongue of a whiskery face. Big eyes, black lips, breath like a garbage disposal. Mooney, his one hundred pound mutt.

God, how long had it been since he'd thought of Mooney?

Mark moved the dead lamp and alarm clock from the nightstand. Sitting on the bed, he laid the rollup bag across his lap and took out his old vinyl chessboard. It smelled like newspapers and maple syrup. The pieces were heavy, tournament grade. He placed them on their squares, naming each one in his head.

Knight, bishop, rook. Last came the royalty, queen to her color. The black king's face was chewed, his crown resting on a scab of tooth marks. Had Mooney done that? No, Mooney had passed when Mark was in first grade, long before his chess days. Some drooling kid must have gotten a hold of it.

After playing around a bit to see if he remembered any openings (he didn't), Mark went to put away the rollup bag and discovered it wasn't quite empty. Folded within a fold was his well-worn copy of The Amateur's Mind. He thumbed through the pages, each one crowded with notes. His father had picked the book up at a yard sale, and it had come home to Mark wearing the handwriting of its previous owner. Neat, compact, slightly feminine. Whomever she'd been, she'd taken the lessons between its covers to heart. Mark had tried himself. He'd read through Jeremy Silman's long list of bad habits and thought processes and done his very best to eradicate them from his own play, but some things were hard to kill and even harder to keep dead.

He shut the book for the evening.

Before turning off the lantern, he reset the board and pushed his king-pawn forward two spaces.

"Your move," he said to the empty corner.

•••

Late in the night, the bathtub's faucet began to drip.

He couldn't sleep.

His mind kept sinking to the cellar. To those holes in the brick. Those growing cracks in the hull.

Chapter Nine
October 4th

They parked by the Charles and walked from there.

The club was a red-bricked basement in a red-bricked alleyway, a perfect match for Alex's hat, which leaned off his head like a beret. He was jaunty this evening, the limp in his right leg masked by a spring in his left. "*M'lady*," he said as he pulled out her chair.

"Stuff it." She looked at the space around them and counted roughly eighty seats. "How many reservations did you say?"

He peered down into his water. "There's a floater in here."

"Alex."

"Sold out." He switched his cup with one of the cups on the other side of the table.

"Won't be room to breathe when it fills up."

"Who needs to breathe anyway?" He flinched and then said, "Did you finish your education of everyone's favorite bird?"

"No silent letters to be found."

When two chickadees bond, they remain together for life.

Alex regarded her. "What's wrong?"

"Nothing. I'm still just shucking off my bygone server skin." She pointed at the menu. "Case in point, eight dollar entrees and six dollar drinks. To our waiter that means we're only worthwhile if we get wasted."

"Well, if it's about our *worth*."

"My thoughts exactly."

A boy in a too-tight v-neck delivered their beers to the table. He smiled at Alex as he left.

"Oh, *look*," said her brother, watching foam bubble over the rim of his cup. "He brought mine with extra head."

"Lucky you."

"Indeed."

"How was work?"

"The cubicle is still shaped like a cube. How was painting? Any more apocalyptic sunsets?"

"It was a sunrise, unless you've forgotten how it works on the east coast."

"Could be I like to think it's the west. What's that thing people always go on about with art?" He hummed. "*Interpretation*?"

"Yeah, and it could be there's no sun in the painting at all. Could be it's something else pretending." She pulled his hat straight.

"Could be." He un-straightened it.

"But no. No apocalypses today." Alice took a gulp of beer. "Today it was the house."

"Your house?"

"What other house is there?" she said, but as she spoke her mind conjured up an eggshell white Victorian crowded in trees with branches like scratches of charcoal. A sunflower-shaped pinwheel spun slowly in the yard.

"Mom said the road's washed out again," Alex said. "So we better be ready for slow-going at the end."

"Ok."

People trickled down the aisles.

"Did you finish?"

"Finish what?"

"Painting the house."

"No. Not yet." She saw home the way her brush had envisioned it. Windows gelled into a slotted mouth. Curved steps rising to a not-quite closed, not-quite solid front door. "Thank you, by the way."

Alex raised an eyebrow. "What for?"

"Last night." After her shower, she'd come downstairs to find Alex waiting in the kitchen with a bad horror movie. Ninety minutes of brain-pulling, head-off-the-shoulders gratuity. Exactly what she'd needed. "And for this."

"Please. I'd scoop out my heart for an hour of jazz."

Alice squeezed his thigh. He gave a tight smile, squeezed her hand back , and lifted it gently off his jeans. Odd, him wearing denim on a mild evening like this. Especially when he'd walked to her house in shorts two nights ago, and under a brewing storm no less. "What happened to showing off your calves?"

"Laundry." Alex fixed his gaze on the stage. "What time is it? Got to be close to curtains now, right?"

From behind them came a light voice, "Five minutes."

A girl sat down at the table. She was with a man, and wearing enough perfume for all the women in the club. Elegant blouse on her, slacks and a collared shirt on him. Upon taking his seat, Boyfriend picked up the water cup with the floater in it and took a long, deep drink.

Alex coughed.

"Hell of a walk up here from downtown," Boyfriend said with a gasp. "But someone *had* to practice in her new heels."

"As if." Girlfriend took his hand. Tight. Her pretty green eyes flicked across the table. "So, how long have you two been together?"

Alice opened her mouth and discovered she'd lost her voice.

Her brother kissed her on the cheek. "Thirty-three years."

"Oh." Girlfriend looked confused. Then she looked embarrassed. "*Oh.*"

The chatter in the club made the silence at their table feel concrete. Alice cleared her throat. "And the two of you?"

"May," Girlfriend answered immediately, gratefully. "It's a funny story, actually. We were down in—"

"Our story is pretty funny, too," Alex said. "There was this whole fiasco with the umbilical cords, you see. We came out strangling each other. And by *came out,* I mean they cut us out.

Our faces were all puffed up and purple when we said goodbye to the belly. Me and my sister . . . we were almost the death of us."

Girlfriend told Boyfriend she had to use the restroom. Boyfriend told Girlfriend he would help her find it. Boyfriend and Girlfriend left the table.

Leaning over, Alice returned the kiss to her brother's cheek.

•••

Lamps made a lovely string of jewelry along the Charles.

Alex and Alice walked down the curving path, their arms touching. Cool air brushed off the water. "Me and my paintbrush, you and your sax . . ."

He winced. "Don't remind me."

"No, you were *good.* You got it to sing."

"Wail, more like."

She sighed. "Was there ever a more bohemian pair in this city than us?"

"Hopefully not," Alex said. "Do you remember that ugly orange headscarf I wore?"

"The Velma turban?" She gasped. "*Yes!*"

"We were living at that shitty place in Allston, and my hair was as long as"—Alex glanced at her, stopped, and burst out laughing—"I'm sorry. It's just, I mean, you look wonderful. Superb."

"What? You don't like it?" She tossed her chewed hair.

"It's . . . it's very 'fuck you.'"

"Well, I picked up the scissors and then I decided they just wouldn't cut it for the aesthetic I had in mind. So I did what any girl would." Alice batted her eyelids. "I bought a chainsaw."

The path led into a tunnel. Shadows occupied its corners, darkness rounding out the geometry of the walls. She thought of her artwork, how none of the buildings she painted ever had a straight edge or right angle. There seemed to be a connection there, some subtext to grasp.

"What are you going to do?" Alex said as they emerged.

"There, ladies and gentlemen, is the million dollar question."

"Forget I asked."

Branches laced into fisher's nets overhead. Stars glittered in the weave. "I'm going to take this step and then the next," she said. "Find what feels good and keep doing it, pick my way from stone to stone, and pray there's another side ahead. Does that make sense? Don't answer please. I'm not finished yet."

Alex slipped as the path turned to dirt. The river peeked blackly over his shoulder.

"I'm going to paint—that feels good. And I think there's something there this time that wasn't there last time, maybe not ever." She saw waves rolling endlessly, a deep blue body of waves waiting to give birth to some secret, submerged life. "It's like, you wake up one morning and you're different. You feel it. It's in you now." She realized she was holding onto her stomach. "I don't know. But I'm not going to stop."

"The griddle cooks when it's feeling hot."

"Something like that." A sigh burst out of her. "And maybe, just maybe, I'll pan off a few along the way. You wouldn't happen to know anybody looking to donate grocery money to a serious *arteest*, would you?"

Alex was quiet. "If it gets too hard, I have an extra room."

"Thanks." She reached to take his hand, but it was inside the pocket of his jeans, moving, scratching. "How's your leg?"

He pulled his hand out. "Holding up."

"Mine are getting devoured." She slapped away a mosquito dabbing at her calf. "We should be getting close to the car."

"Better slow down then." Alex's smile returned, along with that particular luster in his eyes. She could make it out even in the dark. "Why's that?"

"I thought, well, since we were feeling nostalgic . . ."

Out of his coat pocket came a pipe.

"You're kidding." She grabbed it from him. Its mouthpiece was slender and curved. A tiny, ornate lid covered the bowl. As she held the device up, she saw that it was bronze—almost gold. "Nostalgic is right. Did Aladdin sell this to you himself?"

"Of course not." Alex stole it back. "A kitchen guy at the club did."

"You scoundrel."

"Yeah, yeah. Do you want to see if a genie comes out or not?"

•••

It was like swallowing fireflies. Alice
felt
radiant.

•••

For a while, awareness came in frames. They were under the lamps again, laughing and choking, all the world shades of gold. They were on the docks singing *Dirty Water* as their feet splashed in the Charles. They were running down the path with their socks stuffed in their pockets and their shoes dangling from their fingers, and Alex was fine, his leg was fine, the night was beautiful and they were fine.

•••

"You can stay over if you want," said Alex, his back turned to the dark apartment. He'd dozed in the car, curled against the passenger door, and now his hat was bunched up into a frizzy cotton nipple on his head.

"That's okay." She swayed on her feet, her toes holding onto the carpet. *Monkey toes*, Mark used to call them. The thought made her smile.

"I've got a mean stack of blankets in the closet."

"Tempting." She reached up and fixed his hat. "But I should get home. I want to roll out of bed and land in front of the easel."

Alex gave a limp nod. "Yeah, of course."

"You look so tired." She touched his face and felt the delicate curve of his cheekbone beneath the skin. Suddenly her chest was aching, not enough space inside it. She hugged him. "I'd better see you tomorrow."

His fingertips dug into her back. "Tomorrow."

Alice's car started with a purr. She felt an abrupt, uncontainable affection for it—for the crinkly texture of the seat beneath her, for the wheel in her hands, for Lincoln Street, for gravity and the weight it gave to the world. Every moment was a little miracle, every touch a glimpse of a connection to something larger than her and impossible to grasp. The stars were brighter in Manxfield than in the city. They glimmered above, scattered across the night sky like shards of glass across asphalt. Here was proof that not all accidents were ugly, not all crashes left scars. Some made wonders. Some were divine.

If only she could express this to Mark. If only she could show him this sight, crystallize it for him to hold, make him understand. He wasn't alone. She was here. She would always be here, in one form or another, whether they were together or apart. She'd given a piece of herself to him, and he to her, and you couldn't undo that. You could burn it, bury it, drown it, but you couldn't kill it. *God.* If only she had the words.

She let herself into the house, his father's house, the place they'd shared for years. A marriage of wood and plaster and rock. The physical construction of a feeling, of an idea that was called home. This was *theirs,* damn it. This belonged to them and would belong to them, even if everything else was knocked down.

Maybe she did have the words.

If she started small. If she reached out not because she wanted him or needed him but because she cared.

Maybe.

The phone was in her hand, her thumb was darting over the buttons, and now the line was trilling in her ear. The silence between each ring widened into a gulf. Her palm grew sweaty against the plastic.

"Mark?"

Was that static or a breath?

"Mark, are you there?"

"Alice. Hello." His voice came in patches.

"I can barely hear you."

Something thudded on the other end, and either the line went quiet or Mark did.

"The reception's terrible." She bit her lip. That sounded accusatory. *Gentle, be gentle.* "Where are you?"

"Cellar."

His response was so curt it made her bite deeper into her lip. Unless he *hadn't* been curt. Perhaps part of what he'd said had been lost. "Oh. Doing what? Is David down there with you?"

"Just a little home improvement."

"Really?" Had he missed her second question? Or chosen to ignore it? "It seems kind of late to be working. Not that there's anything wrong with working late."

"It's cool."

Alice didn't know if that was slang for, 'it's okay,' or a remark on the temperature in David's basement. She opened her mouth, shut it, opened it again. "How are you?"

Idiot, idiot, you were supposed to keep it light.

Mark took a long time to respond. "Not bad."

"Not bad is good." She grinned, feeling like a terrible actor trapped in a worse comedy. "I was out with Alex." No. She hadn't meant to mention Alex. This wasn't about Alex. She had to get her Alex out of the story. "*I*," she said, "*I* had a nice time tonight." No. No. That wasn't the end of the thought. She had to finish the thought before—

"Glad for you."

She imagined shoving the phone down her throat. "I wanted you to know—"

What?

"—that I—"

That she *what?*

"I called because I—"

A dial tone went off in her brain.

"Because I printed off some papers. I was wondering if I should bring them to David's house, so you can sign them."

"Don't do that," Mark blurted. His voice softened. "You don't have to do that. I'll come by in the morning, okay?"

Alice covered her mouth. Tears welled in her eyes.

"I'll call when I'm headed over."

The line clicked.

A gag caught in her throat. She dropped the phone and stumbled back through the living room, back into the night, not knowing where she was going, only that she was going back, back, back.

The engine's purr, now a yowl.

The steering wheel stiff and croaking in her grip.

The sharp, cold glitter of stars.

Alice fought the dark until she remembered her headlights. The road appeared, and Alex with it. He was limping out ahead of her, leading her, a smile on his face. *You always know.* She settled back against the cushion. Red light. Now Alex was curled on his side in the passenger seat, quiet, asleep. Asleep? No, his breaths were too shallow. Alice swallowed, her tongue dry from the marijuana. Only from the marijuana? Alex had vanished. He was on her left, sitting beside her at the table in the club. She squeezed his thigh to thank him for being there, and he peeled back her hand gently, so gently.

The light turned green.

Her car hopped into the intersection, and outside Alex slipped as the riverside path gave way to sand under his feet. *What are you going to do?* She pressed on the gas pedal. The dotted yellow line began to streak. *If it gets too hard, I have an extra room.* Something in his voice. *If it gets too hard. If it gets too hard.*

Lincoln street. Stairwell. Lock.

"Alex," she called into the dark apartment. "Alex, it's me."

Light dribbled out under the bathroom door, and the carpet gleamed as though wet. She took one step. Two. On the third came a tiny sound—a not-quite human whimper—and then she was running again. Running toward that sick dog sound, floating high up off the floor, part of her here and part of her down by the Charles, running, running . . .

She slammed into the bathroom.

Alex looked up from the toilet, a dripping turkey knife in his fist. The gashes on his thighs bled down his shins and onto his dirty feet. She slapped the knife out of his hand. She slapped him across the cheek. She grabbed him by the throat, falling on her knees in front of him. "Don't you do this to me. Don't you dare. Do you hear me, Alex? Don't you fucking do this to me again." His hat fell off and out spilled silky clumps of hair. "I'll kill you. I'll fucking kill you, you bastard, you selfish fucking bastard, you fuck." She crushed him against her chest. He softened. She brushed his hair, rocking him. "It's okay. I'm here. It's okay. You're coming with me. We're packing you a bag, and we're going, okay? We're going to my house. We're going home."

His breath shuddered out, hot and moist. "He's in me."

"No he isn't." She cupped the back of his head. "Oh, *Lix*. No, he isn't."

Chapter Ten
October 5th

Mark bought bricks on his way to the house.

Alice was sitting in the wicker chair when he arrived. The sight of her there, waiting for him where his father used to wait for him, made his foot hop back to the gas pedal. He would have kept on going, driven around the block a second time or maybe not come back at all, but she'd already seen his car.

He pulled to the curb and a timer started ticking in his head. Five seconds before he got out was excusable. Ten, she would think he was gathering himself. Fifteen, she would know. He stole another glance at her, black baggy sweatpants and a white wife beater. Contrasts on contrasts, a knife cutting his nerves wide open. He got out of the car. His body was a bundle of aches, stiff legs, cramped back, kinked neck, eyes throbbing like joints inside their sockets. There'd been a lot of preparation to do yesterday, heavy loads to carry through the annex and manuals to pore over, and when he'd finally crawled into bed, morning had come in a finger snap.

Mark started up the lawn. In a second Alice would ask him why the back of the Honda was so low, if there was a body in the trunk or something. He got his answer ready.

"Hi," she said.

"I'm working on a project with David."

"Oh. More home improvement?" Steam climbed from the coffee mug on her lap. Underneath the mug was a piece of paper. "Or hotel improvement this time?"

"What's the difference?" He gave a strangled laugh. Her *hair*. What the hell had she done to her *hair*? He tried to turn his attention elsewhere, but all he could focus on was measurements. The reach of her legs from waist to paint-spotted feet, the length of her silence, the distance between them. "The grass is getting long."

"I'll have to cut it."

Mark touched his tie, the last piece of uniform he'd put on that morning. He had to have his tie to see Alice, or she would see through him. He never went to work without a tie. Never since his father passed anyway, and that had been before her time. "You have something for me?"

She nodded. There were little pouches of purple beneath her eyes. He wondered if her 'nice' night had given her a 'nice' hangover to remember it by. As he came up the steps, she rose and held the paper out to him like a waiter presenting a check. She'd been a waiter once, Alice. They'd met in her restaurant while he was visiting the city. She'd served him a hamburger, and he could tell it grossed her out—that *he* grossed her out a little too for eating it—and why was he thinking about that now? Why was he remembering how his hand had shaken as he'd written his phone number on the check? Why *now?*

"It's only the first step," she said. "But it gets the process started."

He stared at the form with glossed eyes. **Joint Petition for Divorce. Joint Petition. Joint.** Control joints are grooves that a builder saws or tools into the wall. They tell the wall to crack here, in these places, and nowhere else. **Joint.** A crease ran down the paper, separating the lines where their names went. Both spaces were empty. "Where's your signature?"

"I'll sign before I mail it in." Alice had her right leg bent behind her and was standing rock-steady in her sweatpants. David had been wearing sweatpants, too, only his had been gray.

Mark felt her watching him the way David had watched him in the cellar, felt the grain of the paper against his fingers, dry and delicate. Moments joined together, like his wrist to his trembling hand. Synchronicity. A second chance to do what he hadn't done then, to tear it in half, tear it, *tear.*

"Do you have something to write with?" he said.

A pen appeared in front of him, magic. He pressed the form to the wall, went to write his name, and started to write his phone number. No ink came out. He dropped his hand.

Alice took a small, sharp breath. "What?"

"The pen's dry."

"Oh." She lowered her right foot, her whole body unwinding with relief. Had she thought for a moment that he wasn't going to sign it? He went to follow her into the house. The door shut. The deadbolt clicked. She emerged a minute later, pulled the door shut behind her, and held out a jar of writing utensils. He reached for a pen. Blue. It had to be blue, the same color David had signed the check.

Alice was staring at something overhead. He followed her gaze to an abandoned birds' nest in the alcove. "Chickadees used to live there."

"Must have left for winter."

"No. Not Chickadees."

He wasn't sure what to say to that, so he didn't say anything.

"Well," she said, a touch of mockery in her voice. "I don't want to keep you."

Mark's hand was steady this time. A few strokes of the pen and it was done, all done. He gave her the signed paper, the pen, and went down into the yard. Leaves twisted from the neighbor's maple. He stopped.

"Alice."

She came to the edge of the porch and stood there in the last inches of shade, her face untouched by the sun. He pulled on his tie. There was something he wanted to tell her. Something that had come to him when all the lights were off, when his whole existence was crawling. A confession? No. An apology. "I'm sorry—"

But he'd left the words in the dark.

"I'm sorry if my call woke you this morning."

"It didn't."

"Okay. That's good. Okay then." Mark walked away across the wet grass, coasting like butter does down a hot pan, leaving a little bit of itself behind as it goes.

•••

Alice closed the door and leaned back against it. Her skin felt tight over her bones. There'd been that one moment as he'd lowered the pen, but that had been a false hope. The rest was all long silences and absent stares, Mark's standard currency for communication. Even his attempt to sign off at the end had seemed empty, out of place.

She shook her head before she could think one more single thought about it, then she padded into the office where she'd printed off the form at five in the morning after clicking blearily through page after page of Massachusetts' divorce code. An ocean gorged on itself in one corner. In another, the same sea boiled under a raw sun. She set the form on the desk and selected a filbert with small, stiff bristles.

The house waited for her in the living room. It was coming into form, yet resisting any real form. The roof curved up into a bowl, its shingles bent into dozens of tiny smiles and frowns. Murky windows suggested nighttime, yet the sky overhead hung crisp and blue. The front door dripped off its hinges, showing an interior that looked as soft as a sponge—and as wet.

The couch sighed behind her.

"What time?" Alex pushed up on one elbow, his eyes half open. "My late?"

"It's okay." She kneeled in front of him and brushed a finger over his feather-soft eyebrows. "I called your work. Told them you were sick."

His cheek settled back onto the cushion. His eyes shut.

Alice looked at his bandaged legs and remembered the peroxide and the gasping, the Neosporin and the pink pile of rags. She sat there awhile before she climbed to her feet and turned to the canvas. Maybe she'd been fooling herself, or just a fool. Maybe time and distance weren't enough, and would never be enough.

Maybe all you could do was cut it off, bleed it out.

She lifted her brush and began painting the lawn Mark had left down, growing the grass out from red roots.

• • •

Mark stood in a ring of lanterns. He had eight now, including the two he kept tied to his backpack for trips through the annex. In the light with him were bags of Portland Concrete and smaller bags of lime, the wheelbarrow and shovel he'd spotted by the bookcase, trowels and chisels of different shapes and sizes, a crowbar, a sledge hammer, and four 15-liter buckets filled with water. The bricks were still in the car. He'd started to unload them, but the road had been too busy for a man pushing a utility dolly to go unnoticed, so back to the trunk they'd gone. That was okay though. He had to tear down the wall before he could rebuild it.

The only question was where to begin.

Mark picked a wedge of salt off the brick. As he crushed it in his hand, the boiler let out a sloshing groan. He glanced outside the lantern ring. The dark flickered where it was touched by the gaslight. He turned his head back to the wall. To solid, *real* concerns. The damage reached about seventeen feet wide, just shy of his original guess of twenty. He'd go the full twenty anyway, for insurance. When a man's foot rots, the surgeon doesn't cut it off at the ankle. He takes part of the leg, too.

Mark stared up at the holes on the wall. They looked like eyes, sky-blue eyes, weeping salt down the face of the brick.

It was time.

Time to put this old, sad thing out of its misery.

He swung. The sledgehammer gouged into a hole and the sky widened in a spray of red chips. He swung again. And again, and again, blow after ringing blow. *This is it! This is me!* He moved down the wall, a swing on each step. Falling rocks bruised his shoulders and head, but the pain was nothing next to the motion of his arms, the heave of his lungs, the zing of the pieces that *he* was creating as they whizzed out of the cellar and over the beach. When he reached the lantern shining at the twenty-foot mark, a strip of daylight underlined the ceiling. The holes were gone. He grabbed a water bucket and drank deeply, gulping and gasping as loud as the boiler.

With buzzing hands Mark worked back the way he'd come, swinging, swinging, the ocean breeze cool against his face. Each impact felt heavier, more substantial, as if he and Longreave were striking closer to some mutual foundation. His bones sang. His teeth jittered. He smashed away brick after brick, and there was the wall behind the wall. And there! And there! And there! Out of breath, he paused to run his fingers over its smooth, salt-white surface. It was dirt, backfilled between Longreave and the fine sand of the beach. A century of moisture and compression had turned it to concrete. *Nature did this with nothing more than time and minerals.* He wondered if a man could do the same with patience and grit. Fortify himself. Cut himself off from hurt.

Mark saw his father sitting out in the wicker chair, alone, all those years alone after the aneurism took his mother. And he swung. He saw Nicholas Lorey in his black suit and bowtie, remarking on inheritance. And he swung. He swung. He swung. He swung. From the wall came a great rumble, like fissures spreading through bedrock, then a slab the size of his torso exploded on the ground and spewed shrapnel. He went on swinging through the smoke, dust in his eyes and mouth, and soon he arrived at the northeast corner of the cellar. It was spoiled too, and had to go. He aimed his hammer straight into the right angle where the walls met. The first blow made cracks. The second tore off chunks. The third forced him to step back as huge blocks crumbled down from overhead and the ceiling gave a terrible groan.

He braced for the fall, for the lobby and everything in it to come crashing down on top of him. The Chesterfields, the coffee table, the mantelpiece. A quick burial. A tomb for him inside Longreave, with Alice's Longreave to keep him company. He waited, tense, lantern light jumping across his sweaty skin.

The ceiling held.

That was that and he was off, no more time to waste. The dead might rest, but there was always more work to be done for the living.

• • •

Mark sat and listened to the boiler, a throb of pain beating between his clasped palms. It was nice to have it there, where he could hold onto it. It felt as if the heart of his pain was in his hands at last.

Rubble littered the ground. His back was propped against rubble; his arms were resting on rubble; there were piles of rubble as large as sofas and smaller crumbs of rubble scattered to the fringes of the gaslight. Dust clouded the lanterns and dimmed their glow. The dirt backfill stood pale and exposed like a colossal bone. Above it stretched a long, navy band of sky. He could hear waves lapping over the beach. The slosh of the ocean mixed with the slosh of the boiler, as if both were one and the same. His eyelids drooped, then he started abruptly to his feet. He couldn't let himself fall asleep. Not while there was a mess to clean.

But as he surveyed his corner of the cellar, the enormity of his mess settled upon him for the first time. There weren't enough

Hefty bags in all of Manxfield to carry this ruin, and provided he *could* get all the pieces out of Longreave, he'd need a semi truck to haul the load. If the folks from the condo company showed up right now, would they sue him for vandalism? Or pat his back for giving the demolition a head start? Hopelessness welled inside him. *A step at a time,* he thought, *take it a step a time.* You don't try to make it through the year or the month or even the week. You try to make it through the day, the minute. You say fuck the pool and you buy a treadmill, and if you keep your head down and your shoulders square, you just might build yourself something of value.

Mark set about plowing debris from the backfill. The going was slow and he had to stop more than once to cool his blistered fingers in the water bucket, but eventually he cleared enough space to begin laying the new wall in the morning. He shut off the lanterns, lit one of the two hanging from his bag, and began the journey back. For a long while his light touched nothing, then the boiler appeared, peeking out of the dark like something playing a child's game. With each swing of the lantern it grew a little fuller, a little more fleshed, until it was right on top of him. A pair of thumps sounded within the tank. *Thddd. Thddd.* Mark walked on in a hurry, his neck prickling. When he reached the stairs, the sloshing stopped for good, draining into a silence that followed him all the way to his room on the fourth floor.

As he peeled off his grimy clothes, it dawned on him that he hadn't thought of the room as Room 401 or simply 401 as he usually did, but *his* room. When did the change happen? And why? He turned on the shower. Was it the presence of his belongings that nurtured a sense of belonging? And if that was so, did all attachment boil down to nothing more than possession? The reflection of ripples moved across the walls and there was Alice, coming up the aisle with a spring breeze playing on her dress and David at her arm. He remembered their words, their kiss, the contract they'd signed first with lips and later with sweat, writing themselves together in the dark of their bedroom. Now her bedroom, her house, everything hers or his, Mark

Currier's or Alice Stokes', the sum of them together weighed and parceled into the sums of them apart. No. Mark swallowed. He didn't believe that. Couldn't. There had to be something else, a factor beyond gain and loss, an explanation for happiness and hurt that wasn't so cold.

Cold.

The water was still cold.

So the gas company had visited today. Good thing the meter was on the other side of the hotel or their representative might have heard some rather interesting sounds coming from the cellar. Lucky Mark. His hand closed into a shaking fist. Lucky? How was he lucky? How could anyone ever be called lucky? Was Alice lucky? She'd been his after all, and nobody knew better than Mark how miserable, how lonely, his silence could be. Was her damaged brother lucky? Were their dead parents lucky?

Was Tommy lucky?

Mark leapt into the shower. Into the jetting cold. He willed his arms open, grabbed the bar soap, and rubbed it over his skin. Grit ran off his body and clogged the drain. Muddy water swallowed his feet. He remembered his trip to the cellar with David, the slow walk down the stairs, the dark claiming another piece of him at every tread. He remembered the sloshing hello from the boiler. Suddenly the cold felt superficial. He turned off the shower, stepped out onto the tile, and picked up his lantern. Behind him came a gurgle—the same sound he'd heard leaving the cellar. The sound of the boiler going quiet.

Except the gas was off in Longreave.

Which meant the boiler should have been quiet all along.

Mark walked out of 401 and down to the second floor. The archway to the foyer stretched like a muscle coming out of contraction. He paused, icy trickles running down his bare skin, unable to escape the feeling that Longreave was opening for him in some way, that it was showing him glimpses of an *other* self, one that dwelled in the play between light and dark—a hidden self that lived and squirmed behind the Longreave he knew. The path closed behind him, folding over itself like black cloth. His feet carried him up around the empty elevator shaft into the annex. 2C was quiet.

So were the restrooms on Level One.

And the cellar when he finally pushed open its door.

Down he went into the chilled air, into the big darkness under the hotel. Soon there would come a slosh, and he would know. He would know. The lantern rattled in his outstretched hand. A hazy moon formed ahead, fattened itself on the light, and became the boiler. He pressed his palm against its side. There had to be something. Because there was no luck, no mercy. Because if God couldn't or wouldn't speak, if all that existed of Him was a pair of waterlogged lungs, there had to be something to balance his absence, some voice to communicate sense into the world. A power worthy of faith. There had to be *something*.

The silence in the tank echoed through him.

Nothing, it said.

Nothing.

Mark stumbled to the staircase wrapping up around the boiler. Shivering, jerking, he climbed the grated steps, got down on his knees, and crawled out to the hatch. His legs braced beneath him, he took hold of the handle. Twisted. The blisters on his fingers opened. The handle groaned. He spun it around, around, then heaved up the lid and shone his lantern down into the tank. His face appeared, floating on smooth darkness. His mouth was wide and black. His eyes were holes, looking down into nothing.

Nothing.

"No."

His other-self nodded up at him. *Yes, yes.*

"No!"

Mark reached down into the phantom's throat—down into the cold, quiet water. He lowered himself, his whole body shaking, as brittle as frost. The tank touched his chest and sent a frigid scream through his nerves. He turned his cheek to the hatch and reached deeper, deeper, his hand stretched down into the vast stillness of the boiler.

"Please," he whispered.

And then he felt a brush of fingers in the cold, drowned darkness. He felt someone reaching *back*.

Chapter Eleven
October 8ᵗʰ

Alice took a sip of rooibus tea, then tucked the hot mug between her thighs. She was re-wearing an already re-worn pair of sweatpants that had seen so much paint they were almost as stiff as denim. Her journal lay in front of her beside a stack of unpaid bills. She had it open on the section titled Art Peeple (A.K.A. Acrylic Junkies), which amounted to three cluttered pages of phone numbers, doodles, and the occasional anecdote or joke. Next to one Harold Knickers was the note: *hates being called Harry but I can't imagine why.* Beneath another name and number, both impossible to make out, she'd scribbled: *Friend and frequent fuck of Levi, somber attitude fixed by a trip to the restroom.* She wondered if Levi's friend had shared some of his mood-booster with her that night, whenever that night had been. It wouldn't have been the first time she said yes to a plant more potent than what grew in a hippie's garden. She'd said yes to a lot of things those days in the city, when it was only her and Alex.

Alice stretched her back as she scanned her professional contacts. Last year she'd thrown away her cell in an attempt to sever all electronic leashes, and now she had to sit at the counter to make calls.

Good for her.

She dialed Gabriel Alvarez, who'd curated her first and only real gallery in Boston. There was a high-pitched shriek. She hung up and then moved down the list to John Books, an art dealer from New York. A robot told her, "The person you are attempting to reach is no longer—"

Strike two. Alice took a scorching gulp of tea as she punched in the number for her old agent.

"Hi?" said a little boy.

"Is this still Melanie's number? Melanie Austen? I'm sorry if this is the wrong—"

"Mom!"

She winced. Her right ear was still ringing when Melanie (and she knew it was Melanie from the first syllable, knew by the unguarded warmth in her voice and the slushy quality of her s's) answered. "Hello, who is this?"

"Hello. Hi. This is Alice."

"Who?"

"Alice Stokes." She'd always been *Stokes* in the art crowd, even after she married Mark and started signing her paintings *Currier*. The silence on the other end stretched a beat too long. She added, "I did the Water Stone series."

"Alice? Oh, Alice! How are you?"

"I'm well," she said, stiffening for no reason she could explain. "How are you?"

"Wonderful. My life's a disaster, complete bedlam. But wonderful. I'm sorry about the toss-around. Nick was playing a game on the phone—what's it called—plants and ghouls. He's four now, Nick, my son. You never got the news about Nick, did you?"

Son. The word sent a shard of ice crawling down her esophagus. *Son.*

"I didn't, no. Good for you. He sounds healthy." And that sounded banal. "You and Richard must be proud."

"It's Gage, and he's no Dick. Shit. *Shoot.* Nick, you didn't hear that! But close enough, and we are. How are you and . . . I really shouldn't guess his name . . . Mark?"

Alice picked a flake off her sweats.

"Did I get it right? Was it Mark?"

"It was."

"And Tommy." She laughed. "I still have the pictures you sent of him as a cowboy. He must be what, almost—"

"I'm painting again," Alice said. "I started painting again."

"Oh. Have you?"

"A few so far. Like the last series I was working on, except . . ."

Her mind wandered to her latest painting. It was of the living room, but at the same time not. The floor was soft and pink, the couch plump and shiny. Red mold carpeted the ceiling. A trail of sunken footprints reached from the entryway to the staircase, but the person they belonged to was nowhere to be found. At the deepest point of perspective, beyond a kitchen whose walls curved and dripped, stood a blackened sliding glass door. She'd marked the canvas there violently, blotting out the backyard with an urgency that was almost desperate.

"Except?"

Alice reeled herself back to reality. "Except, I don't know. More severe. I always twisted things, but with these it's like they want to be twisted. They can't be wrong enough. They're hungry for it." Her stomach growled. She'd forgotten to eat lunch again. Breakfast, too. "Or maybe I'm the one who's hungry. I was never good at describing my stuff. I was hoping—I was hoping maybe I could show you sometime. If you're free to come by."

"Alice . . . I don't do that anymore. I don't even live in New England. I'm in Oregon now."

It was her turn to say, "Oh."

"I'm sorry. I'd love to see your work, of course." Melanie's voice softened. "But it's been six years since you—"

Five. Alice pictured the linens sitting on the floor of the guestroom. *Five years in December.*

"—none of us could get a hold of you. You stopped answering your phone, your emails. I came to your place, you know. Several times. I knocked."

Alice's eyes blurred. She remembered lying in the bed upstairs while someone pounded on the door, lying hidden from a weak winter sun, her arms wrapped around Alex, buried in his clean smell. Every day the same, someone calling at the door, the clock crawling, shadows deepening over the bed until Mark came home from Longreave.

"What happened, Alice? Why didn't you just tell us if you needed a break? Why cut us all off like that?"

"I—I'm sorry I bothered you. Give your kid a kiss for me."

Alice laid the phone in its cradle. What had she expected? For things to have stayed just the way she'd left them? Hit play on the remote and everything slides back into motion? She'd been gone half a decade, a long vacation by any standard, and no world was as cruel as the art world when it came to killing off its inhabitants. She paced to her easel in the living room. Before letting herself even *look* at a brush, she fetched her alarm clock and set it for quarter of five. Sunlight pooled on the windowsill. She stared into the white of the canvas and began to see colors, a spot here and a spot there, leading her like footprints.

A moment later, the sky was dark and the buzzer was going off. A staircase without walls or banisters climbed the page, bending like warm licorice as it rose. Each step was fatter and furrier than the last. The highest had ruptured in a spray of juices.

Alice ran out to her car.

Her brother was waiting outside his office building. As she pulled up next to him, she started in horror. He had no face. On his shoulders sat a red mound, eyeless, mouthless. Then he lifted his head and she realized he'd been looking at his feet. Looking at his feet with his stupid hat turned down where his face *should* have been.

"How long have you been wearing that old thing?" she said after steering onto the road.

He gave a limp shrug. "Forever, give or take."

The hat itched at the corner of her eye. "It's probably filthy. I bet if you put it under a microscope, it'd be crawling. Why don't you get a new one?"

"I don't want a new one."

Alice squeezed the wheel. She stole another look at him, his legs pressed together, one hand cradling the other in his lap, and felt a flash of guilt. He didn't need this right now, especially not from her. "Did you have a good day?"

"It was fine."

"How did you feel?"

"Fine."

"Good. That's good." She licked inside her mouth, searching for something to say. "How were your coworkers?"

"Same as ever."

She thought of the friends she'd lost when she marooned herself in Manxfield. Nobody was ever the same as ever. Time made slow strangers out of everyone. Even yourself. "I'm sure they were glad to see you, after your sick-days."

"Veronica said she'd stab me if I gave her the flu."

"Funny."

"She was holding scissors."

Alice groped for a change of subject. "I was thinking we could go out to dinner tonight. Up in Somerville. How does that sound?"

"That's okay."

"Well, we're out of food at the house, so we'll have to make a stop regardless."

It was crowded at the grocery store, but Alice found a space in the back of the lot. Her brother had reclined his seat and rolled onto his side.

"Are you coming in?"

No answer.

"Do you want anything?"

"Whatever you want."

"All right. Well. I won't set the alarm."

Halfway through the produce, she started to wish she *had* set the alarm. What if he wasn't tired? What if he was faking? She imagined returning to the car and finding it empty. Ridiculous. Her brother had waited for her after work. He wouldn't have done that only to dodge off at the supermarket. She steered into the snack-aisle and pictured him sitting with his hand cradled in his lap. Had he been hiding something in his palm? No, that was stupid. He had pockets, didn't he? She looked into her cart and saw colors. Green and red and orange. "A palette for my palate," she said, laughing nervously.

A woman glanced at her.

"Sorry. Just having pun. Fun."

Headlights swooped past as she exited the store. Their afterimages trailed away across the asphalt, and she remembered footprints leading down a quiet neighborhood street in Dorchester twelve years ago—bloody, broken footprints that had ended by a bench on the boardwalk, where she'd found her brother sitting naked, glassy eyes aimed out over the ocean. Her heart began to pound. The shopping cart slipped away from her. She clutched the trunk of her car and looked in through the rear window.

Alex lay in the passenger seat where she'd left him.

There was a honk.

She spun about to discover a man waving at her from his truck. Then she discovered her middle raised in front of her. She dropped her hand, lowered her head, and walked out into the lane to pull her cart out of his way.

"Bitch," he yelled.

Today, maybe. But who knows who I'll be tomorrow?

•••

After dinner Alex went upstairs to take a shower and Alice sat down to have another go at her journal. Ten minutes later though, all she'd managed to do was prove how few people she actually knew. Or had known. She sat there, listening to the pipes glug in the walls as she went over names that held no meaning to her anymore. At least some of the doodles were entertaining. Like this comic strip. In the first panel a man and woman held hands. In the second, their stick bodies locked together on a bed. The third panel showed the bed frame in pieces on the floor while the top figure continued to plumb the bottom, beads of sweat perched on their white faces. In the fourth and final panel, the splinters of the bed frame had come to life and joined in on the fun. An orgy where lines connected and became angles. A Flatland fanatic's sex fantasy. She must have drawn this up before meeting Mark, back when intercourse had felt like one long search with no end, a rabbit chase for a feeling she could never quite grasp. With him it had been different. Lock and key. With him she'd opened . . .

No.

Not that road again.

As Alice went to close the journal, her gaze caught a phone number squeezed into the left margin. It had no name to go along with it, only a dollar sign. What the hell? Why not? Voicemail picked up as soon as she finished dialing. She almost hung up, but something—curiosity perhaps—made her stay on the line.

"You probably don't remember me—I mean, hello, I'm Alice Stokes. I found your number in an old journal of mine, and I must've been in a hurry or something at the time, because, silly me, I didn't write down your name. So if you do call back, whoever you are, it would be great if you could share that. I'm a painter, by the way. I paint. That would probably be useful information for you to know. Wow, I hope you don't exist. Anyway, I have several new pieces of art for sale. As part of a series. It isn't finished yet. Feel free to call back and laugh at me. Bye. Oh . . ."

Alice rattled off her number and then dropped the phone as if it were dirty. "Well done. Well done indeed."

The pipes were quiet.

The shower had stopped running.

Upstairs, drippy sounds murmured from the bedroom. She pushed on the door and envisioned it sweeping into a soggy pink enclosure, the walls porous and leaking, the mattress curved like a belly on top of a flaccid frame. But there was only Alex standing over his suitcase. Sweatpants clung to his bony hips.

"Wait," she said as he reached for a shirt. "Take them off."

"Why?"

She looked into his eyes, and it was like that day on the boardwalk. She tried but could not find Alex in those eyes. "You know why."

A stream navigated the vale between his breasts. He tugged the string on his waistband and the sweats fell in a heap. The cuts on his thighs had started to scab. She counted them.

"Turn."

He turned. The back of his legs were clean.

"Okay."

Alex pulled his sweats up, still facing the other way. She handed him a shirt. He put it on followed by his hat, then he limped around the bed and crawled under the comforter. She climbed in behind him. He was shivering. She draped an arm over his body and lay there, breathing in the smell of bar soap.

• • •

When she came downstairs to paint the next day, closer to midnight than dawn, the answering machine was blinking. She set a pot of dark roast to brew, leaned over to the phone, and clicked the button.

A man spoke.

"Wonderful to hear from you, Alice." His voice was smooth, refined. "I would love to look at your new series if you can find a time to have me over. Talk soon." He made a small, considering sound. "It appears you and I are equally forgetful regarding my name. That would be Geoffrey Maws. Geoff, if you prefer. Goodbye for now."

Alice tried but couldn't place the guy. She made a note to call him back, then wandered off to make a fresh palette.

By the time she remembered her coffee, it was cold.

Chapter Twelve
October 9ᵗʰ

As Alice set her brush to the canvas, Mark pushed his dolly up the coast. A tall man with nice clothes and nice shoes dusted uniformly gray, he walked under the streetlamps through the crisp, ocean-scented night. He had nothing in his pockets except a pair of keys—one to the hotel, one to the U-Haul. In its trailer was a pallet. The pallet had required a forklift to move from the store. Now the pallet was half its original size and the road to the truck to was just another dark hall inside Longreave.

A very long, dark hall.

He maxed out his dolly under four fifty-pound stacks of bricks and then started back through the neighborhood, all quiet except for a squeak in one of the wheels. Later he'd oil it. But for the time being it would have to make do, just like his bruised body. His ache was marrow deep, no longer a sensation but a definition printed inside his bones, giving meaning to every movement no matter how small. He couldn't remember the last time he'd slept, and he didn't care. It was amazing, really, how little you needed rest when you had purpose.

A door opened up ahead, and he froze as a woman hurried down to the sidewalk, got into a car, and drove off the other direction. If he'd been one house further, just one house, she'd have run right into him. And what then? A casual how-do-you-do? Pleasant weather we're having tonight, isn't it? Why yes, miss, these *are* bricks. I'm building a wall. No, nothing professional—a little personal project is all. Speaking of which, have you read *The Cask of Amontillado*? Mark uprooted himself, part of him wanting to laugh, another part wanting to sob.

He encountered no one else for the rest of the night.

He might as well have been a ghost.

•••

Seven trips and as many miles later, the dark was softening as Mark pushed his last load up the path to Longreave. The windows of the hotel stood black against the salted brick, like rows of undeveloped photographs. He wondered what might be waiting to form in each one, and something—not quite a shiver—tickled under his skin.

It was midnight inside the lobby.

Mark picked up his backpack by the front door, lit one of the lanterns, and locked up behind him. His heart was beating hard. He sat down a moment, but that didn't help, and when he rose, everything around him started rocking and went on rocking as he moved across the floorboards. From the Chesterfield to the front desk lay three thousand pounds of bricks, proof of the work he'd done and a reminder of the work still to come. He left the dolly at the staircase. His body would have to do the hauling on its own now.

Thirty trips.

One hundred pounds a trip.

A stack in his backpack and a stack in his arms.

•••

Orangey light washed down from the beach and touched the beginnings of the new wall laid against the backfill. The wall was almost as high as Mark's knees, and that was where Mark was now. His knees. He struggled out of his backpack's straps and sat there swaying like a man at an altar as he admired his work. First he'd cleaned the edges of the old wall from top to bottom, stripping off the stubborn jags that had survived the demolition and sanding the ancient bricks smooth. Then he'd started to build, binding each layer of young red clay to the old with a fat seam of mortar. It had cost his car its suspension, those first few loads. Hondas weren't made to carry double their weight. That was a man's job.

One pallet a night.

Six pallets to complete the wall.

But first he had to walk back through the annex.

Mark set off, hunched under his empty bag. The boiler came and went, its hatch propped open, its insides quiet.

●●●

He was on trip seventeen when his lantern ran out of gas. The light gave with a sound like someone's last breath, and then the dark had him again. He felt it in his mouth, his throat, his earlobes—every place it could invade. The stack fell from his arms and struck the cellar floor. He reached for the backup lantern and turned the switch. The flame jumped inside the cage, and he started to shiver violently.

At least he wasn't tired anymore.

●●●

401 was a den of cozy colors: warm browns and pastel tans. At first it had been so bright it hurt his eyes, but then he'd pulled the curtain over the window and made it better. In the flickering light, the pieces on the chessboard marched in place. Shame he didn't have an opponent. It would be nice to play with someone other than himself.

Why was he here?

His gaze wandered to the red jug in the closet. *Hello*, he thought, and walked over in three loping steps. He unscrewed the cap off the dead lantern, picked up the jug, and started to pour. Fumes stung his eyes, and now he couldn't see straight, and now kerosene was splashing the carpet and now he needed to pee right now now now now . . .

A minute later, Mark flushed the toilet with a deep sigh. As the bowl drained, the tank gave a dry rattle. Two days ago, like the gas, like the electricity, the water had been shut off inside Longreave.

But this time he'd been ready.

The morning after tearing down the wall in the cellar, he'd gone around to each of hotel's thirty-three rooms and filled the bathtubs. A tedious process it had been, hours of juggling keys and stopping drains and listening to pipes burble in the walls. He'd worked his way down from 401 to 208 and then back up through the annex to 4C, his father's old haunt. More times over the years than Mark could count, he'd found Frank Currier in there with a plastic bag taped over the smoke alarm, taking in the ocean and a late cigar.

Something moved in the tub.

He turned, but it was only light skimming the surface of the water.

As he emerged from the bathroom, his phone started to ring on the portable charger. David, David, David. A little early for calls, wasn't it? Mark blinked at the time. 10:14. How was it already 10:14? No matter. There were bricks to be carried and drips to be listened for. The old man could wait. Mark started to leave.

The old man *couldn't* wait. What if he tried Alice?

Mark sat down on the bed with his phone. The mattress was softer than soft. The mattress was warm tapioca, sucking him down, down. He dropped to the floor and folded one leg under him, heel bone in his butt cheek. Better.

"Hello," said David.

Hi, he thought. Then he remembered to say it. "Hi."

"How are you?"

"Fine. You?"

"Hanging in there." David was quiet for a moment. "I hope I'm not bothering you with my call."

"Not a tit. Bit."

"I'm just now pouring my third cup of coffee—or diesel fuel as our old friend Nicholas would say. Have you talked to Nicholas at all?"

"No. You?"

"Only you. I was just thinking this morning . . . I don't know."

Gummy lines squiggled up and down and across the wall, dividing the paint into rows of rectangles and squares: stretchers and headers. "English Bond."

"What?"

The bricks dissolved. "Sorry, just saying something to Alice."

"Oh, I didn't think she was around. It sounded so quiet on your end. How is she? Feeling better?"

"What do you mean?"

"Her cold."

"Oh yeah, right." He had absolutely no clue what David was talking about. "Much better."

"That's good to hear. These Fall bugs can really dig in deep, you know. Little termite things. Sometimes it feels like you have to burn yourself down and start fresh."

"You have to break it to rebuild it."

"Yeah." David sounded uncertain—or maybe distracted. "It's a week today."

"What's a week today?"

"Since, you know . . . Longreave."

Mark sat in shocked silence. Only a week?

"We should get together, the three of us. Or the two of us, if Alice can't make it. But let's get together."

"Definitely."

The change in David's voice was remarkable, like night to day. "I'll get a little cooking going then. Or would you rather I headed over to your house?"

"No," Mark said sharply. "Not now."

"Of course." David gave a small laugh. "I've been up so long my brain was thinking it's lunch. How about one o'clock? Or dinner? Dinner works for me just as well."

"Not today, I mean. Probably not this week." Panic clutched at Mark as he searched for what to say, and for a moment he was very aware of the space around him, of the darkness under the door and the black hall outside it, of his frail light and the little corner it occupied inside Longreave. "We aren't home. We decided to take a road trip."

"Oh, that's nice. Well, that's nice. Where to?"

Up the coast, he almost said, except Alice didn't like going north and David knew her well enough to know that even if he didn't know why. "Not sure yet. Heading down south a bit. Seeing if we can catch up to summer."

"Just the two of you?"

"Yeah. Why?"

"Just thought with the season that maybe Alex had come along. Two birds, one stone kind of thing."

That was right. Fall was the time Alice and Alex took their annual escape from civilized life. Going walkabout, she called it, because they left technology behind and lived out of the car. A five-day dive off the grid. Mark had a collection of crappy postcards sent to him from states all over the Midwest. "No. No sibling. I'm not even sure if they have a trip planned this year at all." Realizing that, he felt a pang deep beneath his aches. Suddenly he wished he'd packed the postcards. To torch them or to have them, he didn't know. But the option would be nice.

"When will you be back? Do you have any idea?"

"Can't say, really. Might be awhile."

"I was hoping we could talk before I left for California." David's voice was distant, as if he were holding his mouth away from the phone.

"We're talking now, aren't we?"

"Yeah." The old man breathed into the mouthpiece. "Yeah, I guess we are."

Mark's shadow squirmed anxiously on the wall. "If it's okay, I'd better get back to it. Long road ahead."

"Of course. Goodbye."

Mark dropped his phone by the bed and then crawled to his feet. California. What was in California again? The answer hit him as he put on his backpack. Family. For an instant he almost had it, why he'd chosen to stay in this room and not one of the others, why four and zero and one added up to *his* instead of five.

But the connection slipped away.

•••

A tiny fishhook nagged at his brain as he left the room. A feeling that he'd forgotten something, left something behind. He walked back to check the door. It was locked. Of course it was locked. The doors in Longreave were always locked. In the stairwell, he figured out what was *really* bothering him. He'd switched lanterns when the first ran out of gas, and now the light was backwards, his shadow thrown the wrong way everywhere he turned. He lit the lantern on his left side, shut off the lantern on his right, and that helped.

For a while.

He got to thinking about the woman he'd almost run into on the sidewalk, which got him thinking about all the cars that might have passed him by at any moment out on the road, which got him running down the lobby staircase so fast he lost his footing at the bottom and sprawled across the floorboards. There was a sharp cracking sound. Pain soaked into comfort like wine into cotton. His eyes closed, and he was out in the spiced and salted night. Then they opened, and he saw the dolly sitting there in front of him.

"Idiot," he said. "*Idiot.*"

He got up, laughing, and hefted the nearest stack off the floor. He ran it up the stairs, still laughing, and came back down for the next stack. At some point he stopped laughing and started wheezing, and at some point he stopped making noise altogether except for a whistle in his throat, but he himself never stopped.

He had to work.

He had to be *ready*.

•••

Back and forth through the hall, back and forth, bricks on the dolly, bricks off the dolly.

•••

Up and down the foyer-stairs, up and down, up and down, and don't think about the elevator shaft or what it would be like to fall down it, to fall and fall and die falling in darkness before ever hitting the bottom.

•••

All the bricks in the annex, and the dolly too.

Left turn, left turn, dump the stacks in front of 2C.

Right turn, right turn, fetch another load.

Left, left.

Right . . .

•••

Right?

Mark stood in the laundry room on Level One. He'd made a right turn too soon, or a left turn too late, and now he was watching his reflection squirm on the glass lids of the dryers. Trembly all over, he backed into the corridor. The cold passageway transformed the dolly's squeak into a scream. It sounded as if he were running away from something horrible behind him, always behind him, no matter which way he went.

•••

At last, the cellar.

He counted everything: the stacks, the bricks in the stacks, the steps on the stairs, the beats of his heart. He counted pipes, cracks, cobwebs. He counted the boiler, once, twice, a thousand times. He counted and counted, and when he stacked the final pieces of the pallet in place beside the new wall, everything added to zero.

Back to square one.

•••

As Mark lit the ring of lanterns, a junkyard of red came to life around him. He turned the lantern off on his backpack and noticed that its companion had cracked. A fracture ran up the curved glass from base to crown. He flicked the switch to make sure the lantern still worked, and a man-sized scar appeared on the backfill, twisting and jerking as though in pain. He shut off the lantern and shivered, thinking of his reflection on the lids of the dryers. In a moment he was mixing mortar using the water he'd brought down from the bathtub in 201. The cellar began to revolve around him, everything outside the wheelbarrow mixing together like everything inside the wheelbarrow. He went to grab his trowel and walked the wrong way, weaving into the rubble beyond the lanterns. "Don't go wandering off," he told himself.

He laughed.

That was such a father thing to say.

The sunlight warm on his face, he started buttering the wall for the next course—number six. A wave crawled up the shore outside as he knelt to lay the first bricks, and he felt the concrete bulge up beneath him, rounding like a swell of water. Tottering, he planted his hand on the ground.

It was flat.

Of course it was flat.

Next came the corner of the wall. What was the pattern for the corner again? Even rows were headers while odd rows were stretchers, but the corner reversed that rule. More, the corner required *closers*, which were bricks that had been cut in half lengthwise. He'd scored a pile of those two nights ago—or was it three?—to make sure he could focus on the actual bricklaying when the time arrived. Mark retrieved a few and sat down to study the wall again. Its seams wriggled slowly, like long gray worms crawling through red earth. Then Mark realized. The pattern was right there: in the wall itself. He'd laid the foundation. Now all he needed to do was build on it.

Following his own example, Mark finished the corner and started down the main stretch that ran below the beach. He had to get up every few feet to drag the wheelbarrow along after him and fetch a new stack of bricks. Sometimes when he tried to sit back down, a funny thing happened and he found himself *already* sitting down, no memory of getting there. His shadow crouched in front of him on the backfill, trembling like a frightened child. Or an excited one. He remembered what it had been like to be down here in the dark, down here alone or perhaps *not* alone in the dark. He remembered the feel of cold metal against his chest as he reached down into the boiler . . .

Midway through the seventh course, he stopped to mix a new batch of mortar. It was a tricky thing to do on his knees. He had to do it on his knees because every time he stood, waves started rolling underneath the ground again. Mark watched the lumps of concrete break down against the shovel's head and thought of Alice, the way she would mash her granola into her peanut butter when she was worried, stirring and stirring until her breakfast became a paste. When he finally crawled back to the wall, shoving a stack of bricks in front of him, the sun had drifted out of sight somewhere above Longreave.

Somewhere along the eighth course, Mark paused and held up his hands. They were gloved in gray, stiff with crust. He would need to wash them before he went into public. Yes, his shadow agreed on the wall, nodding. But when had he gotten so *many*? He had six hands, connected to six wrists and six arms. Their fingers wagged at him, numerous and twitching, knuckles bending every which way. Mark leaned sideways to take the pressure off his knees and kept leaning all the way to the ground. Suddenly the wall looked very tall. As tall as the cellar, at least. He was going to sit back up in a moment, just as soon as his head stopped expanding. He had to finish this course so he could start the next. There was a lot of bricks left to lay, and the store wouldn't stay open forever. He would use the beach this time, keep off the sidewalk as much as possible. It might be difficult to push the dolly through the sand, but he would be safer beside the Atlantic than the road. Cars couldn't drive in the ocean. That was a well-known fact. The people inside would drown. Their lungs would fill up, and they would drown, drown, drown.

His shadow began to climb the wall, which was strange because he was still on the ground. Only for a moment, though. He rolled onto his back. Above him his shadow poured off the brick into the air, where it spread like a spill of black water, and as the light shrank down, as he sank into darkness, he heard something in the boiler give a timid, waking splash.

•••

The drop fell between his lips and landed on his tongue. It was cold. Any colder and it would have been ice.

Mark's eyelids lifted, then his head, his shoulders, his back. He rose in one long continuous motion and pivoted on his feet. The cellar slipped in and out of focus, surfaces sliding in greasy light.

A night-breeze blew in from the beach and tousled his hair. Rocking, he stared down at the ground.

At the puddles on the ground.

At the puddles in the shape of footprints on the ground.

The toes faced him: two neat little rows of toes lined up side by side, an inch from where his head had rested on the concrete. He felt the place on his tongue where the drop had landed— remembered the exact spot like a desert remembers rain. He tried to swallow, but his throat was too dry. Those puddles. Those small, perfect puddles. He lifted his eyes and saw a lone footprint behind the pair. It was pointed off to the side. One step past it waited another, this one turned away from him and almost touching the lantern by the wall. Two more footprints shimmered beyond the lantern, leading off into the darkness.

Moving on oiled rails, he picked up the lantern and glided after them. They continued straight along the wall, keeping to the path he took every day. The boiler slid by on his right. Beads of moisture sparkled on the steps leading down from the open hatch. *From there. They started there.* At the end of the cellar, he looked back and saw his workstation wavering like a candle flame in the distance. Then he took the old wooden treads up into the annex. And paused. The footprints reached down the hall ahead of him. Straight, clean, full prints. The kind left by slow, unhurried steps. Mark felt the cold bleeding off the walls, that cellar chill stalking him down the corridor, and he knew.

Knew.

What did he know?

Mark turned the corner. The lantern swung in his hand, and the footprints appeared to march across the concrete. They turned right again, then again, climbing to the second floor where they vanished into the rich brown threads of the carpet. He took a step. There was a soft squish. Lowering the lantern, he saw tiny bubbles forming around his loafer. Another step, another squish. He went on, following a trail he couldn't see, walking in the path that had been laid out for him. It was easy, like falling, like coming home. Down around the elevator shaft and its secret darkness, past a bay window walled in black, and through the archway out of the foyer. Footprints gleamed on the floorboards, catching the light like small mirrors. He floated after them into the stairwell, up and up, falling against gravity . . .

To the fourth floor, where he landed.

The trail led down the hall to 401. The door was open. It was dark inside, and quiet. Liquid shadows moved on the walls. As he entered, light puddling in over the carpet, a sound came from the bathroom.

Plop.

Footprints on the tile. Three final footprints leading to the bathtub. It shone in the lantern light like a small, bright coffin.

He walked to its edge.

Looked down.

Tommy lay under the water, pale, perfectly still. Head propped up on the acrylic. Heels resting beside the drain. Black bangs floated up from his brow. His eyes were closed. His mouth was open and dark. Mark sank to his knees. He set the lantern on the corner of the tub by the bar soap. His hands stopped for a moment, shaking, then dipped into the bath. It was the cold of icecaps in the Antarctic, of the deepest trenches in the ocean. His finger slid toward Tommy. . .

. . . and touched him. Not a mirage or a memory, but the boy. *His* boy. Something broke deep inside Mark, came tumbling down like bricks and left a huge windy hole where it had been. He lifted his son out of the tub and clutched him, squeezed him, crushed him to his chest, his voice splintering in his throat. "I'm sorry, Tommy. I'm so sorry."

Lips moved against Mark's neck.

"Daddy?"

He lowered the body in his arms slowly, carefully, not daring to breathe. Tommy's eyes were open and showing nothing but white. The pupils rolled down from inside his skull, bobbled, and widened.

"Daddy."

Mark sobbed and smiled and choked all at the same time. He mopped at his son's dribbling mouth with the cuff of his jacket.

"Daddy, why's it so cold?"

"Shhh, shhh, you're okay."

"It's *c-c-cold.*"

"Here you go, here." Mark pulled the towel down off the rack and bundled Tommy inside it. Tommy gave a larvae-like wriggle, nuzzling against him, and Mark felt a flush of almost unbearable warmth. Warmth enough for the both of them, forever. He climbed to his feet and swayed side to side, rocking with waves that weren't there, taking his son in a slow, quiet dance around the bathroom. "You remember this? You remember dancing like this between me and your mother, don't you? *Ba-dum, ba-dum, ba-dum.* We put you to sleep like this when you were a baby. *Ba-dum, ba-dum . . .*"

A drop of water plinked on the tile.

Mark looked down as a second drop landed in front of his shoes. Wet patches appeared across the towel. "No," he said as water began to trickle from the cloth between his fingers. "No, no, no, no."

Tommy moaned.

Mark rushed out of the bathroom, leaving the lantern behind on the tub, and laid his son on the bed. He unwrapped the towel, unfolding the layers until he came to the bare, shivering body within. It was leaking. From everywhere, leaking, the pores on Tommy's skin drooling like little mouths. Tommy's throat overflowed in a cold gush. Mark stepped back and reached for his tie, but it was on the doorknob. It was on the doorknob where he'd left it after visiting Alice, and what would she do, what would a mother do?

Gulping, spluttering. "*Daddddddyyy.*"

"I know, kiddo, I know, I know." Mark threw the drenched towel into the bathroom, carried Tommy up along the bed, and pulled back the covers.

"Daddy, don't go."

"I'm not going anywhere. I'm right here." He hurried around to the other side, peeling off his dirtied clothes, then climbed in with Tommy and wrapped his arms around him.

"C-c-cold."

"I know."

Tommy's voice came again, low and pleading and lost. "Where am I?"

Mark clutched him tighter and felt pools collecting in his palms, felt the burn in his eyes wash away as the tears finally began to flow. And he knew. Why this room, why 401. He remembered showing Alice up the stairs, a bundle of blankets in her arms. He remembered unlocking the door, pushing it in, and announcing in his most hospitable manner, *Accommodations are on the house, pretty lady, stay as long as you'd like.* He remembered the crib they'd set up in the corner, the dangling yellow stars they'd hung above it, and were the drill-holes still in the ceiling? He remembered the smell of baby wipes, the stink of a used diaper, the mortified laughter as they tried and failed to open the window. He remembered Alice washing Tommy in the tub and later rocking him to sleep, beads swinging from her ears and casting raindrop shadows over his face. He remembered it all, weeks where his family was always right upstairs, weeks where the days glided by like steps in a dance. He remembered climbing to 401 as the winter howled its worst outside Longreave, and lying in bed with Alice, the warm lump of their son cradled between them.

Mark remembered.

"You're home," he said, holding Tommy under the dampening sheets. "We're home."

• • •

The bed was dry when Mark woke, and a finger of daylight pointed toward the closed bathroom door. He sat up, pushing off the covers with arms as heavy as pallets. He'd dreamed—*God,* what a dream. He lowered his hands and was unsurprised to find them trembling. Had he really moved all of those bricks yesterday? And what about the day before, and the day before that, and the nights of hauling and building in between? No wonder sleep, when he'd finally given into it, had taken him to such vivid places.

Mark climbed off the mattress and gritted his teeth as his calves cramped. He shuffled along until his toes bumped something small and hard in the carpet. His phone. With a wince, he bent to pick it up. No missed calls. Then he noticed the date. October 11th. Two days since he'd moved the pallet. Two days since he'd followed the footprints out of the cellar. But that had been a dream, the start of a dream.

Mark heard a small sound.

A splash.

He turned to the bathroom, something like a shiver crawling up his spine. He walked to the door. He opened it.

Tommy sat in the tub, his pale face turned toward Mark. Water spilled from his mouth.

"Turn the hot on, Daddy. It's *cold*."

Chapter Thirteen
October 12th

It was six o'clock in the evening, and Alex was still in bed. He'd taken the privilege of Saturday to heart. Alice walked over to the alarm clock shrilling on the windowsill and smacked the button to silence it, the same thing she'd done once each hour for the last five. But snooze time was over this time. This time, Alex was rolling out of bed. Right side or wrong side.

Before leaving her workspace, Alice turned her painting to the corner. She didn't want to see it until she could work on it more, and she especially didn't want it to be seen. Not until she'd filled in the white hole at the center of the canvas and discovered what was waiting there, and why it made her stomach cramp just thinking about it. She stepped out onto the porch. Wind lashed at her as she glanced up and down the darkening street. No headlights in either direction. She turned back for the house and then noticed the newspaper lying at her feet.

Well.

Well.

Well.

"I think October's a myth in New England," she said as she walked into the master bedroom. Alex was a lump under the blankets. "When the sun's out it's September, but as soon as the moon rears up, hello November."

Nothing from the lump.

"Fall gets its first letter from *fuck*, as in *fuck-yes* during the day and *fuck-no* at night. That's Alice's take on the season. Now you Now." She threw the folded-open newspaper onto the pillow behind him. "Your Chickadee has flown to print."

Standing in front of the closet, she pulled off her wife beater and sweatpants and immediately wondered why she'd stripped *before* deciding on an outfit. There were too many clothes on the rack to choose from, hardly any of them warm, and being naked and shivering didn't help matters. She reached in blind and snagged a glossy blue blouse. Then she decided tonight might be a good night to practice wearing a bra. Not to mention underwear.

Alice walked to the dresser. Her brother's eyes were closed— perhaps a little too tightly.

"If you're embarrassed," she said, sliding a pair of panties up her legs, "you could always leave the room."

"*Hmmm.*"

A sound. Progress.

Alice riffled in the drawer. Where was that faux-fleece bra she had bought for winter? Her nipples were so hard she could sketch an outline with them. Now *that* would be sacrificing herself for her art.

"*Ah-ha!*" She whipped it out and quickly put it on. "Did you know there's a type of bra in Japan made to be warmed in the microwave? No? You didn't? Well, now you n—"

"Shuddup."

Alice smiled in triumph. She chose a pair of tight gray denims that fought her legs all the way to the ass, put on her blouse, and looked down approvingly at herself. One day she might even be presentable for public. One day.

She walked over to her brother and sat down gently next to him. His chest hardly seemed to move beneath the blankets. Feelers of milky-blond hair played out from his hat on static electricity. She hadn't managed to separate the ugly scrap of cotton from his head long enough to feed it through the washer. She hadn't managed much of anything besides getting him to and from work. Which was better than it could have been, than it was the last time. People got bad now and then, the way weather gets bad, and all you could do was wait out the storm.

Would the clouds ever pass over Mark?

She pushed the thought away. "Alex."

"Wha?"

"I'm having company tonight, do you remember?"

"Who?"

"The art guy. The *connoisseur*." She was unable to say *connoisseur* or words of its nature without making herself momentarily French. It was a curse.

"Mmm."

"I was thinking if you're hungry you could go to the café in town. Grab yourself a sandwich, the kind you won't eat in front of me for fear you'd offend my vegan sensibilities."

"Not hungry."

Alice took a deep breath. "I was thinking you could go, even if you're not hungry. You know, stretch your legs. Take in oxygen that hasn't been recycled."

"Have *you* left the house today?"

"No," she said, for an instant transported back in front of the easel, painting cupboards that sagged like wet cardboard. "But I *have* seen what my feet look like."

"Not pretty."

"Not at all. Quite hideous actually." She watched for a smile but didn't see one. "If you hurry, you might even catch the last of the sunlight. Hurry, Alex." She inched the covers down his arm. "Hurry."

He grabbed the covers back and pulled them up to his ear. "You made your point. You don't have to beat me over the head with it."

"Oh, I think I do." She tugged the newspaper out from under him, folded it in half, and smacked him on his hat. "Come on. Maybe your friend Tomas Nox will find some inspiration for his next NYN."

Voice muffled, "What did I tell you about abbreviations?"

"GTFOOB."

"What?"

"Get. The. Fuck. Out. Of. Bed."

His capped-head burrowed under the covers. "In a few minutes."

"Alex. Please."

No response.

She reached for the blankets, about to throw them on the floor, then froze as the phone began to ring downstairs. "That's him." She sprang off the mattress. "He's here." She glanced back at the lump in the bed, her left hand making a brief fist. "This is really important to me. So just—if you're going to stay in bed, just stay in bed."

Alice ran down the hall and vaulted down the staircase. She hit the ground, already turning for the phone ringing in the kitchen, and braked.

There was a man in the doorway.

He had on a shawl sweater worthy of a Fall catalogue. Dark brown corduroys reached down his legs to dark brown loafers. He pocketed his cell phone and smiled a perfect smile, displaying teeth that had been polished, flossed, and polished again. Teeth that were almost too white. "I seem to have startled you."

"A bit," Alice said, more winded than her dash could account for.

"The door was unlatched. It opened when I knocked."

"Oh." She stared at him. Those cheekbones. Christ, they could shave themselves.

"I suppose the polite thing to do would have been to close it and then knock again, but sometimes my judgment falls a bit short." He cocked his head to one side, a gesture almost like a shrug. "You have a lovely home. From the little I've seen so far."

"Thank you. Oh." She suppressed the urge to smack her forehead. "Come in, I'm sorry."

He did, and his hair turned from blonde to gray as he left the half-dark of the porch. He was older than she'd thought, early fifties, with faint wrinkles that accentuated his dimples rather than diminished them and a dusting of pale stubble along his jaw that made her think of the frost found on the ground late in Autumn, at first light.

He locked the door behind him.

"You didn't have to," she said.

"Habit." There was that smile again, brief and bright. "Too many years spent living in New York."

"You lived in New York?"

"I still do." He adjusted the silver-plated watch on his wrist. "Some of the time."

"Would you like something to drink, Mr. Maws?"

"Oh, no. None of that. Geoff, please." He laughed lightly. "But I wouldn't object to a drink, especially if that drink was water."

"You're in luck then. That's all I have."

"Is this your latest?" He nodded at the painting in the corner.

"Yeah. It's in progress."

His gaze lingered on the back of the easel, as if he could see through it. "The others are . . . ?"

"In that room there." She motioned to the office door before hurrying into the kitchen. Geoff followed. He walked quietly in his leather shoes. She wouldn't have known he was behind her at all if she didn't feel his shadow on her back.

Alice filled a highball and Geoff leaned back against the counter while he drank, one ankle crossed over the other. His large, square belt buckle gleamed. "Thank you."

"Of course."

The highball clinked as he set it down, and she thought of Mark, standing with his back turned and his head down over a half-full glass of milk.

Geoff was talking. Or had been.

"What?"

He brushed a thumb along the countertop. "I said you're very clean. It's rare in an artist. Most let everything go around them. Life being superficial next to obsession."

Alice had given the kitchen a bleach treatment yesterday—if two o'clock in the morning counted as yesterday—but he didn't need to know that. "You maybe shouldn't call me an artist until you see my work."

"I've seen your work." His eyes met hers.

"Which work would that be again?" Alice glanced away, at one of the cupboards. She pictured its tiny button handles swelling until they drooped like an old woman's breasts.

"An inversion of the Charles at night, the water radiant with stars, the sky empty."

She remembered that painting, even if she didn't remember when she'd painted it or where it had ended up. "Right."

"You don't sound convinced." He touched his belt buckle, and her eyes flicked there unconsciously. "Believe me, it's yours."

"It's not that." She laughed. "My memory's a little blurry, that's all. A few too many drinks that night perhaps."

"You were intoxicated, no doubt."

Alice felt heat rising to her cheeks. "Well, I apologize."

"I don't mean intoxicated off alcohol. You were a newlywed." He adjusted the watch on his wrist again, his hands restless in a smooth, calm sort of way. "You had a ring on your finger you just couldn't leave alone, and a man on your arm who wouldn't leave you alone. You were like the river in your painting, full of stars. I don't imagine there was anyone around you that night who didn't feel a little drunk."

"The charity auction," she said. Mark had worn a tux and red bowtie to match her dress, and they'd held onto each other the entire event, never not touching. He told her friends he hated large crowds, was terrified of them. She said it was true, he needed her protection. The handsome older man with the pretty young bodyguard. His tux had smelled of woodsy cologne, his sleeve had been warm, and the rest of the night—as in a piece of art—was background. "That must have been, *God*, almost ten years ago. You remember that?"

"It was worth remembering." Geoff walked toward her. She backed up and found herself in the corner by the sink, her butt pressed against the counter's ridge. He took a step closer, and now she could smell *his* cologne, a heady dark aroma, like the first breath off an old bottle of wine. It made her dizzy.

Smiling, Geoff reached for the faucet.

"Thirsty," he said as he refilled his glass. "I hope you don't mind."

"Not at all." Alice looked down at her feet. They were multicolored, spackled in so much paint she appeared to be wearing tie-dye socks.

"Shall we then?"

"Yes. Right. Of course." Alice slipped out of the corner and walked quickly across the kitchen. "I should warn you . . . what I'm working on now is a bit different than the one you saw. It's nothing you would probably call attractive." She glanced up at the bedroom through the railing of the staircase. "It's nothing *anyone* would probably call attractive."

"Aesthetics aren't always about beauty."

"I'm glad you think so." Alice pushed open the office door, hit the light, and stepped back to let Geoff enter. She followed him inside, her heart beating hard and high in her chest. He stopped in the center of the room and scanned the canvases drying on the floorboards.

"What is this?" His voice was low, appalled.

Dismay rose inside Alice on a black tide. She felt her knees go weak. "I told you they weren't pretty."

Geoff waved. "You can't leave your work on the ground like this. The *dust*. Don't you have any other easels?"

"I used to. I don't know where they went." That was a lie. She'd taken her spare easels out into the backyard four years ago and smashed them apart, batted the pieces into splinters. "I was planning on buying more, but I haven't got around to it." Another lie. It hadn't crossed her mind. Storing never seemed as important as *painting*. She let out a shaky laugh. "I guess you spoke too soon."

"About what?"

"When you said I was tidy. That I was rare."

"Oh, you're still rare." Geoff walked to the paintings lined against the wall. "Just in a different sense than I first thought." He looked down at her most recent work. The room was murky. A pink haze swam in the air like coral spawn around a reef. The bed she used to share with Mark bulged, its mattress sweating under a fuzzy red tangle of blankets. A spill resembling pomegranate juice leaked down the footboard to the floor, which had sunken so low it was on the verge of collapse. Beyond the bed the bathroom waited. But there was no way to it. Not across that floor. Feeling herself at a dead end, Alice had returned downstairs for her next painting. There was more of the house to explore.

Geoff moved down the line, silent. Concentration emphasized the already sharp lines of his face. His eyes moved slowly up the staircase, taking it in as if it were a beautiful woman. Or an exceptionally ugly one. His gaze arrived at the top step and lingered on the hazy pink landing. Alice had skipped the upstairs hall. In this house, the staircase fed straight into the miasma of the master bedroom.

Geoff made a small sound, "hmmm," and took one more step.

Alice followed. "I should have arranged these in order for you, the way I painted them. Going *in* instead of *out*. It probably doesn't make any sense." She wasn't sure that made any sense either, or if he'd even heard. She tried not to stare at him, but her eyes continued to betray her. They crept constantly back to his face, little masochist eyes, cutting themselves again and again on his cheekbones. Had he looked her up and down? No . . . unless he'd saved his evaluations for when she was turned the other way. Did she care when or how he looked at her, or that he didn't have a wedding ring on his finger? She had a wedding ring on *her* finger, the gold band pink from paint, and God knew *it* didn't mean much.

Geoff moved on and Alice started after him, only to discover her right ankle had snuck up into her hand. She gave a hop to save herself from falling onto the floor. Geoff didn't notice. His attention was absorbed by the outside of the house, which had to be a good sign, surely. *Surely.*

He stepped to the last in line, the sunrise Alex had called apocalyptic, and studied the red waters. Alice felt a strange pressure growing behind her brow and realized she was holding her breath. She let it out shakily.

"I'm sorry," he said, a dimple in one cheek. "I'm killing you, aren't I?"

"No." She nodded. "Yes. Absolutely."

Geoff laced his fingers behind his head, stretched his elbows back, and sighed. "I don't love them."

"Oh." Her lungs deflated like punctured balloons. "That's okay."

"That doesn't mean I'm not impressed by them."

Alice forced a smile. "No need to get out the ointment and band-aids. I'm not *that* wounded."

"You shouldn't be. I have a habit of speaking my thoughts in the order that they come, not necessarily in the order of importance. Consider it a symptom of living alone for longer than I can remember."

But not without the occasional company, I bet. Not with that face. "I'm sorry."

"No, you're not." He looked at her. She thought of the painting in the actual living room, how he'd stared at the back of the easel as though he could see through it, and all of a sudden her skin felt less like skin and more like a layer of gauzy, revealing cloth. Finally, he said, "We're all who we are, and who else could we be? I'm sure you didn't choose what to paint any more than I chose to be born with a cock. Is that vulgar? I don't mean to be, only honest."

"No." It didn't sound vulgar coming from his mouth. It sounded refined, like *connoisseur.* It sounded French.

"Good." He glanced back along the row of paintings, each one journeying deeper into the house's moist interior. "Earlier I said that aesthetics aren't always about beauty. Well, love isn't always a measurement of appreciation either."

"I forgot what it was like to talk to an art-aficionado. I need to brush up on my abstractions."

"It's been awhile?" he said, not quite smiling, and why did she get the feeling he was referring to something else, something he knew the answer to just by looking at her?

"There was a drought." Except it hadn't been like most droughts. It had been five years of clouds, a long gray engagement with rain that refused to come, while she and Mark dried slowly from the inside out. "This, what I have in this room, is the first stuff I've done in a long time. There was nothing, nothing for forever, and then it was there. All of it at once."

Geoff nodded. "Something opened up."

She saw Mark on the night he packed his bags, walking out into the storm that would soon break over Manxfield. "Yeah."

"Appetite builds." He took a long drink of water. "Have you heard of the Romanian surrealist, Georghe Fikl?"

"No." When she wasn't painting, she hated art. Hated to look at it, be around it, know it existed. Hated it the way a man who can't eat because of stomach cancer hates food.

"He works in oil as well. His paintings center around animals, sometimes butchered, more often than not still alive. Regardless, you look at his paintings and you see meat. A cow stands underneath a red velvet curtain. A bull waits before a grand hallway soaked in scarlet. His settings are all slaughterhouses, even when they aren't. The world he goes to when he picks up the brush is a threatening, provocative place. A carnal place." Geoff turned to her. "And so is yours. Your art—and it is *art*, Alice, there's no doubt about that—is every bit as violent, every bit as visceral, as Fikl's. *More* so. Where he molds the environment around his subject, the doomed beast, you make the environment your subject. It's personification of a more intimate nature. You are inside the beast. You are in its belly. Do you see why I cannot love your work? If I were to hang these on my wall, living alone as I do, I might never sleep."

Alice managed a nod. She was thinking of her walk along the river with Alex, and how darkness had rounded out the right angles in the tunnel beneath the bridge. How a shadow could the architecture of the world.

Geoff lightened his voice. "I should ask how *you* sleep."

"Very well." She rubbed at her arms. They ached from her late-night scrubbing session. "When I do."

He brushed her. "Pardon me."

"It's okay," she said, distracted. The impulse to clean had set on her like a rabid dog. And so she had. Until dawn. It was as though she'd been stripping the kitchen down to the skeleton, the gleaming bone, so she could better capture its essence for the canvas.

"Alice."

"Mmm?" Below her the sunrise and house began to blur, red ocean and red lawn bleeding together.

"Pardon me," Geoff said, a strip of teeth showing between his lips. His cologne smelled as strong as it had in the kitchen. They were standing close.

Because he was in the corner.

Because she'd backed him into the corner.

"I'm sorry." She stepped away. "I didn't even—I guess the tables turned."

"What tables?"

Oh God, she hadn't meant to say that out loud. "Nothing. Just a joke. I joke. As horrifyingly as I paint. Did I tell you that? Now you know. Now you now." She was hot above the neck and cold below, her nipples stabbing at her bra, and when the hell had *that* happened?

"Now I what?"

"There's a column in the paper . . . never mind. Just being Awkward Alice. Chalk it off to out-of-shape social skills. I hope you didn't get the impression I was trying to bully you into taking out your wallet. I know I can be pretty intimidating." She fought the compulsion to flex her bicep and won. Barely.

"Not at all," Geoff said. Which, she realized, was the same thing *she* had said after he trapped her at the sink. He stepped out of the corner and his gaze wandered down the desk. He paused, his eyebrows lifting. "But that just might."

For one hideous moment, Alice thought he meant the divorce form. The divorce form she'd left sitting on the desk, out in the open. But Geoff glided right past it toward the lone painting in the opposite corner of the room.

"This," he said, standing before her ocean, "is beautiful."

"Aesthetically?" She turned over the divorce form on her way to him.

"Yes." His voice was soft, subdued. "Yes, aesthetically beautiful. And also beautiful in the way that your others are beautiful. Because it's frightening, powerful. Because it swallows you."

Alice glanced down at the ocean—at the foaming, feeding mouths—and stepped back as if she'd drawn too close to the edge of a cliff.

"How much would you like for it?" He looked up at her. Hungrily.

"It's not for sale."

His stare sharpened. "Why not?"

"Because it isn't finished yet."

"What do you mean? There was no disappointment in his voice, only excitement. "What else is there to paint?"

She started to tell him about the shape below the surface, but the painting stole her gaze and then her words. It pulled her down. *In.*

"I'll give you two thousand dollars for it."

The number flashed on a neon sign in her brain. Two thousand dollars was enough to keep her going for three months, even longer if she kept up her anorexic diet of granola at sunrise and salad after dark. Two thousand dollars was a Duracell battery for her bank account.

The ocean writhed, waters deep, changing.

"I'll write the check now," Geoff said, talking faster. "Or I'll give you half in cash tonight and the other half tomorrow, after the bank opens. You can use the money to fund a show for the rest of your series. You won't even notice this one isn't there. It's not like them anyway. It's too elemental. It doesn't belong."

Alice's voice exploded out of her. "Because it isn't *finished*."

Geoff quietly closed his wallet. There was an LV symbol on the front. Luis Vuitton. "My apologies. I should know better than to come between an artist and her art."

All of a sudden Alice felt out of breath, bedraggled, like a shipwreck victim that had just crawled onto shore. "No. No, I'm sorry. That's why I invited you here, to see you if you wanted to buy one of my paintings."

"Yes, but when you're purchasing a child and the mother changes her mind, it's impolite to push." He smiled at the look that crossed her face, all his teeth coming out in a full, brilliant exhibition. "Now we are even on horrible jokes."

"You say that," she said, walking away. "But you'd be hard pressed to keep up if we spent more time together."

"Would you?"

She turned in the doorway. "Would I what?"

Geoff walked toward her, his eyes on hers, and she knew once and for all that he hadn't looked her up and down. Not even while her back was turned. He didn't need to. A woman's body was a piece of art with which he was well familiar.

"Would you like to spend more time together?"

Her heart was beating so loudly it seemed to be coming from outside her, from outside the office. *Thump thump thump.* "I . . ."

She backed through the doorway.

Arms tangled around her body, spun her about. She twisted away with a shove.

Alex dropped onto his butt as if he'd shit an anchor. "Owwww, owww, oww. Gravity wins. Gravity always wins."

She stared at him, speechless. His hat was pinched up into a red exclamation point on his head. He was dressed for winter on top and summer on bottom, blue jacket over green shorts. It had been his *thump-thump-thump*s she'd heard, not her heart's. He must have been limping down the stairs, almost running, just as she'd come out of the office.

"Where's your company? I thought you said you were having company. Did he buy one of your paintings?"

"I'm afraid not today," Geoff said from inside the office. He was watching the scene with one silver eyebrow raised.

Alex turned his head. "Oh, hello there. Why not? Didn't you like them?"

"*Alex,*" she hissed.

Geoff fingered his watch. "I like them just fine."

"That's how I feel about them, too. Just fine. They're a bit cheery for my tastes. I mean, if she wanted to do illustrations for a children's book, she should have made them the right size." Alex put his hands on the floor, got one knee under him, and rocked precariously. "I'm okay, Alice, really. Don't help me up."

She could have helped him up right then. By his throat.

Alex pushed to his feet bit by painful bit. Standing in the doorway, he glanced at Alice, glanced at Geoff, glanced back at Alice. Smiled.

"What are you doing?" she whispered.

"I thought I'd take your suggestion and get out of the house for a bit. Breath some fresh air, splash around some."

Alice realized he was wearing swim trunks, not shorts. "But your—"

"My what?"

She'd been about to ask him about his cuts. They'd taken off the bandages, but the scabs were still fresh and the pool was a disgusting place. The pool was nothing more than a disease dressed up in chlorine so people couldn't smell the sickness.

"Your . . . *cold.* You were feeling sick."

He gave a sniff. "I cleared up."

Geoff made a small movement, and as though sensing it, her brother turned. "We never were introduced, were we?" He limped into the office, scuffing his right foot on the floor with each step. "This leg of mine, I swear. I know I shouldn't call attention to it, but it does that pretty well itself. I'm Alex. You'll remember because it's like Alice."

He held out his hand.

Geoff hesitated before taking it. "Geoff."

"*Joff,*" Alex said, double-wrapping his grip. "Fancy name. You've got a silent letter in there. Two, actually. That's pretty special. You can make the O silent instead of the E, and then your whole name changes. Isn't that something?"

"It's something." Geoff extracted his hand.

"Well." Alex turned around with a wince. "It was really nice meeting you, Jeff. Give those paintings a second glance, why don't you? Maybe you'll notice something about them you didn't before. And be kind to my sister. She's a sweet woman, and she works herself to death." Alex looked at her as he limped past. "I just hope I didn't embarrass her *too* badly."

The door opened and shut.

Alice swallowed down a bitter lump. "I'm sorry. He's—"

"It's quite all right. Family is its own beast." Geoff held up the empty highball. "Do you mind if I visit your sink again?"

"Go ahead."

The muscles in his back sketched an elegant, shifting pattern as he walked away. Alice glanced down, her skin prickling with pleasant needles. He returned wearing a moist upper lip, and gave a sigh that sounded only partially refreshed. "It's early."

"Is it?"

"Would you care to have a drink with me, Alice?"

She heard a thumping, and this time there was no mistaking the source. She was alone. They were alone. "I don't think it's good to mix business with private life."

"We haven't done any business."

His eyes held hers. *If only arms could hold like that.* "I'm—I'm still married."

"Still?"

"It's complicated." She twisted her wedding ring through its cake of paint. "My husband, we . . ."

Geoff smiled. "It isn't finished yet."

She saw Mark closing the bedroom door on her. "I don't know. I—maybe I'd better walk you out. I was planning on painting some more."

She hadn't been, but she was now. Most certainly.

"Of course."

Alice stood on the porch, hugging herself, as Geoff strolled down the lawn. He called to her from the curb, where his Mercedes sat like a sleek, black slice of the night. "Thank you for having me over. You'll let me know if you reconsider my offer. Either offer."

With a wave, she turned for the house.

"Oh, and Alice . . ."

Geoff's smile was visible, even in the dark.

"I like your haircut. It's very French."

• • •

Back inside, Alice let the bitter lump come up into her mouth where she could taste it. She went to the phone and pounded in her brother's number. The ringing sounded like laughter.

"Tomas here," came a jovial voice.

Alice skipped through voicemail. "What the hell, Alex? What the hell *was* that? Call me back."

She paced into the living room and pulled her easel out of the corner.

The kitchen was unfurnished except for high, wrinkled cupboards and a counter that dripped like tallow. In the center yawned a white hole where the sliding glass door looked through to the backyard. Alice fixed pear-shaped handles to the cupboards and added a sink made of scabs to the counter. She built a table up from six crooked, furry legs and on top of it placed a fruit bowl overflowing raw meat. She painted pale Rorschach blots on the walls and red growths on the floor and dripping fissures on the ceiling, which sagged from the weight of the bed in the room upstairs. She painted a refrigerator with a plump bottom door and a freezer that hung apart in the middle, like a mouth. She painted detail after detail, weighing down the canvas until it was close to tearing.

The hole stared at her from the center of the kitchen, dry and white.

It stared at her like a blind eye.

Maybe if she could actually *see* what to put there. Alice carried her easel and supplies into the real kitchen one by one and set them down directly in front of the sliding glass door. Chalky moonlight dusted the backyard. The lawn moved delicately, stealthily. She lifted the brush, but her hand froze before the bristles touched the canvas. After a minute of standing like that, she glanced at the clock. Quarter to nine.

Didn't the pool close at eight?

A moment later she was listening to the phone ring. "Tomas here," her brother called out, "Did you now—"

Beep.

"Where are you? I know you're not swimming any more. I swear to God if I find a single scratch on you, that's it. That's it."

She hung up the phone.

Picked it up again.

Waited for voicemail.

"I'm sorry. You don't embarrass me. You know you don't, Lix. Just come home. Okay? Come home."

Alice got up, her legs wobbly. She shuffled through the living room, up the stairs, and fell into bed with the lights still on. She was just going to lay awhile and listen for the phone. She wasn't going to sleep.

But she did.

And dreamed of a bench dripping blood onto an empty boardwalk.

•••

Alice woke in the dark of a strange room. She sat up on one elbow and stared wide-eyed at her surroundings. Slowly she let out her breath. The walls weren't sagging, as they'd looked to be for a moment. She swung a leg over the edge of her mattress and tested the floor with her toes. The carpet was soft but not wet. Of course it wasn't wet.

Light outlined the door.

Alice opened it and blinked at the bright hall. Someone was talking downstairs in a low voice, too low to understand. She weaved to the staircase.

The smell of chlorine hung in the living room like a strong cologne.

Alex was sitting on the couch, one hand over his ear. His head turned to her. "Here she is. Yeah. Sure, I can."

He lowered his hand and covered the mouthpiece of his phone.

"Mom says hi. She made up our old bed for us."

Chapter Fourteen
October 14th

Mark spent the weekend waiting for his dead son to visit. He passed the time by building up the wall in the cellar. Every hour he walked up to 401 and checked the bathtub, and every hour he walked back down with the thought of Tommy clinging onto him instead of Tommy himself.

By Sunday afternoon he was out of bricks. He returned the U-Haul truck, drove his tired car to the store and bought a pair of off-white, six-by-ten tarps and carpenter nails. Back at Longreave in the cold underground, he spent fifteen minutes aging the tarps fifteen years. He rubbed them in brick dust, kicked them through rubble, scuffed and scraped them across the concrete. When the tarps were a blend of red and salted gray, he nailed them to the ceiling so that they hung down over the gap in the wall. The disguise was by no means perfect, but it was better than nothing. If anyone walking down the beach noticed how one corner of Longreave acted peculiarly in the wind—how the bricks at the base of the wall seemed to *flutter*—and decided to give a closer inspection, then so be it. Let people draw their own conclusions. Chances were they would assume that the same person who nailed up the nearby window had also covered up a breach in the wall.

Which would be true.

On Monday morning, after a night of watching the bathroom from his pillow, Mark cleaned himself in 403. He scrubbed his face first, shampooing his beard and hair before dunking his head. Then he stepped into the tub and lowered himself down slowly, shivering, to wash the rest of the body. By the time he finished, he was shaking so badly he could hardly reach for the towel. Still shivering under his clothes, he left the hotel.

The sky was overcast. A ragged wind blew off the Atlantic and tossed his tie as he walked up the shoreline. He'd been too reckless before. He thought of all the trips he'd made up and down the road. All the loads he'd pushed. All the houses and all the windows on those houses and all the people who might have been watching him at any moment. He thought of what he'd risked, *who* he'd risked, and he felt sick. He felt as if he were back inside room 403, lying in a cold tub of water.

As the shoreline curved off behind backyards, Mark climbed up between the rocks and onto the road. His car was parked deep in the neighborhood. A new spot. He wouldn't park it twice on the same block in a week, he'd decided. Most people paid no attention to their neighbors let alone what vehicles they drove, but there was always a weirdo out there with a pair of binoculars, taking notes. Better to stay on the move. Safer.

Mark sat with the engine running and thawed his hands in front of the heater. If only he could hold onto this warmth. Capture it in his skin and save it for his son. His *cold* son. But there were problems a man could fix and there were other problems. There were treadmills and there were pools.

Roasting comfortably, Mark steered his car into town. He drove around for close to an hour, not sure where he was headed. After a while, he realized his tour of Manxfield had begun to tighten. He was following smaller and smaller circles, picking his way along a network of suburban streets, and there was the park he used to haunt in the summer, and there was the dirt lot where he'd tried to dig to China—with a little help from Mooney— before his father caught wind and made him fill in the hole.

Of course, Mark thought, touching his throat.

He'd put on his tie today. There was only one place he could be going.

•••

Grass scrunched under Mark's shoes. From the bottom of the porch he glanced back and saw his footsteps dissolving as the lawn sprang upright again. He climbed the steps, his head down, his hands in his pockets, and stood that way at the door until a spiced puff of wind made him turn to the wicker chair.

It was strange. Funny almost. Of all the memories he had surrounding the chair, he couldn't remember once having sat in it himself. He wondered if it would even hold a man's weight after all these years or if it was sitting here on the edge of falling apart, like so many things.

Mark knocked. A minute passed. He lifted his hand to try again when the door pulled open and he was greeted by not quite the face he'd expected.

Not *quite*.

"Hi there, Mark."

"Alex."

"Today it's Tomas. Tomas S. Nox." Alice's twin tapped at his beanie with a folded newspaper. "I've got my thinking cap on."

"What are you—?"

"Searching for my next Now You Now. Now, I now what you're thinking. *Tomas, you're looking through the newspaper for ideas on a* newspaper *article?* Well, why not? It's not like anyone reads the thing nowadays."

Mark's eyes dropped to the sweatpants Alex was wearing, faded paint stains on each leg. "Are those . . . ?"

"What?" Alex looked down. "Oh, right. I was wearing mine when she did laundry."

Mark pulled on his tie. "Laundry."

"Yeah. Laundry. So, what brings you around?"

"I wanted to talk to Alice." That was the only explanation that made sense anyway. The most truthful one would have been simply, *I'm figuring it out as I go.*

Little wrinkles encircled Alex's eyes. "Then why are you here?"

"Excuse me?"

"You said you want*ed* to see her, not that you *want* to." Alex held up his hands, and his expression deflated into an open, lopsided smile. "I'm sorry. Tomas is a terrible nitpicker. But don't blame him, he can't help it. His whole existence is semantic."

"Is she home or not?"

Alex hop-stepped out of the way, and there was Alice in the kitchen. Her back was turned to Mark, her body outlined in the pinkish red of the painting before her. She was standing very still. Mark had never seen anyone so still, outside of a bathtub.

He moved into the house. A stack of newspapers caught his gaze on the couch, but only for a moment. It was Alice he saw, Alice and nothing else, Alice with her arms hanging limply at her sides and paintbrush dangling from one hand, Alice with her hair poking out like strands of coppery wire and her white tank top showing skin just as white.

"Hey," he said.

Little goosebumps raised on the back of her arms, as if he were a cold breeze blowing her way.

Mark reached for her. He braced for her to jump, to lash at him with the paintbrush. In their early years of living together, he'd startled her in every possible place and manner around the house. In the bathroom while she brushed her teeth. In the middle of a conversation after she'd gotten distracted by the T.V. At the sink, the refrigerator, the kitchen table. She'd been impossible *not* to startle; the moment she looked away, she forgot you were there, you didn't exist anymore, you were dead. It was as if the world were a haunted house, and she was alone in it.

But she didn't jump. She did nothing. He tightened his hand on her shoulder. It was like gripping a doorknob wrapped in a thin towel. Alice had always been skinny . . . but this skinny? He couldn't remember. How long had it been since he'd touched her, not just brushed her or lain by her in bed, but actually *touched* her?

"It's Mark," he said.

Then he saw her painting for the first time.

It wasn't unlike Alice to dabble in the disturbing, but this was different. This was vile, a wet rendition of Hell. Everything soft and pink and on the verge of bleeding, all except for a large blank spot in the center where she'd yet to lay her brush. He looked away from it. At her.

"Alice."

She turned toward him like something coming unwound, a little resistance at first and then less and less. Her eyes widened slowly. "Mark. *Mark*."

He let go. "I'm sorry."

She stared at her shoulder where his hand had rested. "What are you doing here?"

The explanation he'd given to Alex no longer made sense, so he said nothing.

"Why didn't you call first?"

Another question he didn't have the answer to. "I don't know."

"How did you get in?"

He started to tell her the door was unlocked, so *anybody* could have just come in, but that wasn't the right thing to say. Not unless he wanted to start a fight. "Your brother is living here now?" He clamped his jaws. That was even worse.

But she only looked confused. "My—"

Alex limped into the kitchen reading the paper. "Government shutdown one page, healthcare the next. Boring and *boringer*. Where's the news people really want to now?"

Alice glanced at the clock and dismay pulled down on her face. "Oh my God, Alex. Shit. I was supposed to drive you to work."

"No work." Alex bit into an apple and juice ejected from the side of his mouth. "Columbus Day. Hmm. Maybe Tomas should write about *him*. Tell everyone about good old Saint Christopher Columbus, how he braved the oceans and discovered the new world and played patty cake with the Indians at Thanksgiving. Blah. We've already got the elementary schools peddling that lie." He sat down heavily at the table.

Mark took a small step back toward the living room, but Alice didn't move.

"How are things?" she said.

Daddy . . .

"Same as usual. You?"

Alex took another smacking bite out of the apple. He was holding the newspaper up to his face, but Mark had the idea his eyes weren't moving.

"Busy."

"It looks like your painting is coming along."

"*It is*," she said in a clipped, harsh voice that did not sound like Alice at all. She shivered and rubbed one arm.

"You should wear something heavier."

"Whatever I wear I ruin."

"You shouldn't be standing around in that. It's too cold." He saw Tommy in the bathtub, reaching out as water leaked from his nose and ears and mouth. "There has to be something."

She nodded, not quite looking at him. "Are you working today?"

"No holidays at a hotel."

Alex dropped the newspaper abruptly. "Alice, can I use your computer?"

"It's upstairs."

"Thanks." He hurried out of the kitchen, leaving his half-eaten apple on the table.

Mark shifted his feet. Outside, the door to the storage shed hung at slant. Its hinges had gone bad. "The lawn still hasn't been mowed."

"No," Alice said, tracking Alex's footsteps across the floor above them.

"If the grass gets any longer, the community people will start sticking warnings in the mailbox."

She continued to stare at the ceiling.

"It probably only needs one more mowing before winter, anyway. I could show you how. Or I could do it for you, if you'd like."

"I know how to use a stupid lawnmower."

Mark looked away. "The kitchen looks nice."

"So I've been told."

He noticed the stack of mail on the counter. "Anything for me?"

"Only bills. But just in name. I doubt they care much who sends them the check as long as it comes."

Mark wondered if she'd noticed that he hadn't made any deductions from their joint account. She hadn't noticed when he was standing right next to her, so probably not. He reached for the mail. "I can take care of it."

"You don't have to."

"I don't mind."

"I don't want you to."

Mark pulled his hands back and stuck them in his pockets. "Yeah, of course." She didn't want his help; she wanted him *away*. That was the whole point of his last visit here, to start the process of drawing lines, making separations. "Did you have anything else for me?"

"Like what?" Her body was stiff, a straight line from head to toes. *Monkey toes*, he thought.

"To sign? You know . . ."

The tension left her. Her eyes sank, her shoulders dropped, her hand loosened around her paintbrush. "Not yet. I sent the form to the courthouse, but they—they get a lot of mail. It may not come back for a while."

"You'll let me know?"

Alice nodded.

The house was quiet. Mark smoothed his tie. "I've been spending a lot of time at Longreave, and I started thinking about 401 the other day—"

"Why are you here, Mark?"

Because Tommy is cold, Alice. He's so cold, and I don't know what to do. Because I—"I just came by to get some things."

"You know where to find them."

"Upstairs," he answered, but it hadn't been a question.

She turned to her painting. "If you don't mind then . . ."

The brush quivered faintly at her side, like a seismometer needle picking up minute vibrations in the earth.

"Alice, are you okay?"

She attacked the palette with her brush, smashing the bristles.

"Alice?"

"I have to finish."

"All right," he said, but as he left the kitchen he couldn't stop thinking about her unsteady hand or the subtle quaver in her voice, or the way she'd jabbed at the red on her palette, as if she were sticking a knife into an open wound.

He paused outside the bedroom.

Alex was lying on the right side of the bed, Mark's side of the bed, with Alice's computer on his lap. "My sister not in much of a talking mood?"

Mark walked to the closet and stared hard at the clothes, seeing nothing except colors.

"I wouldn't take it personally," Alex said as he pecked at the keys. "She hasn't talked much at all since the other night."

Mark swallowed. He wouldn't ask.

"The other night?" he asked.

"Yeah." Alex yawned. "She had this person over to look at her stuff."

"Who?" Mark pulled something down off the rack without looking.

"I don't know. This art guy. She was really excited about it. He must have left her in a funk though." *Click-click-click.* "Do you like cars?"

"Why?"

"He had a hell of a car. Like sex on wheels." *Click-click-click.* The sound rattled Mark's brain. He realized there was a small pile of clothes at his feet, and knelt slowly to fold them. His body still ached from last week's run of sleepless nights and days, a stretch which was beginning to seem like the course of some strange illness—a scarlet-bricked fever—that had flushed through his system.

Click. Click. Click.

He stacked the last item.

Then sat there.

Wasn't there something else? Something he'd missed before? He stared at the pile. Sweatshirts, turtlenecks, a pea coat and goose-down jacket. He would need all the extra layers he could wear now. Winter was on its way and Longreave was getting cold.

Cold.

That word.

Cold.

Mark saw himself at the bathtub in the morning light, sitting by a lantern that had been dead for hours and a boy who had been dead for years, unable to speak or move. Afraid to touch him. And when he finally did, more afraid to let go.

But he *had* let go eventually, to reach for the towel on the floor. And when he looked back, all that remained of Tommy were the gentle ripples spreading across the water.

Click-click. "How are things with David?"

"They're good."

"You staying in the guestroom?"

Mark didn't respond.

"I remember that room. Cute thing. You could tell he and Sarah liked having guests over, the way they had that room done up. I was their guest one night. It was before you and Alice got married. I got a little sloppy, you remember?"

Mark remembered. He'd gotten a little sloppy himself, and called Alex a gimp. It was a slip of the tongue, a moment of frustration-turned-anger-turned-horror facilitated by too much booze and too many jokes, and it had brought silence down on the house like a judge's gavel. Alice would have walked out with her brother right then had David not walked Mark out first. He took Mark on a long drive, all the way up into New Hampshire. No lectures, just miles. That drive, Mark thought at the time, had saved their relationship. But you couldn't save anything in the long term. You could only preserve it.

"They made me breakfast the next day," Alex went on. "They were so sweet. Sometimes I think about them, their kids. I think if every kid had someone like them, nothing would ever be bad, you know?" The clicking had stopped. "Do you and David carpool to work in the morning? Not *this* morning obviously, since you're here."

"No." A Red Sox logo stared up at Mark from the pile. "Why?"

"Just curious. I thought you might, since you're going to the same place. How's Longreave these days?"

"Fine."

"Huh. I would think it'd be pretty dead."

Mark looked over his shoulder, tense, but the computer screen blocked Alex's face. "Why?"

"Seems like it'd be slow now, with school going and the weather starting to suck."

"Fall and winter are our best seasons," Mark replied, his nerves uncoiling.

"Well, you'd know better than me. October just doesn't strike me as a traveling month, is all." Alex laughed. "But then, it *is* the month me and Alice always go traveling, so what am I saying?"

A computer key clicked inside Mark.

Maybe there *was* a way to warm Tommy, one that had nothing to do with temperature. Mark crawled into the closet, crowded with long-lost things. Alice's burial ground. At last he uncovered it. A shoebox.

Before rising, he tucked it in the middle of his pile.

"Did you find what you were looking for?" said Alex.

"Yes. Thank you."

Alex lifted his head in surprise, and for a moment he looked so much like Alice it was painful. The face that Mark had kissed, woken up to, caressed, stared up at him from under that ugly red hat, and he wondered if he and Alex had ever had a chance from the start, if a man could ever be friends with a man whose face was so familiar.

"Are you—are you on your way out?"

"I just have one more stop."

Downstairs, Alice was standing where Mark had left her. The paintbrush dangled from her hand. Red stained the floor beneath it. She didn't notice when he walked into the kitchen, or when he set the clothes on the table, or when he unzipped the Red Sox sweatshirt and hung it over her shoulders.

"You can ruin this," he whispered.

Mark carried his pile down the hall into Tommy's bedroom, which had been a guestroom for five years now.

•••

"Are you okay?" Mark had asked, and she was. She was okay. The kitchen had a hole in it, a big blank hole right in the middle that grew larger, emptier, *deeper*, the longer she looked at it. A mouth of a hole that begged for her to feed it, that whimpered it was hungry, please, Alice, please. But she couldn't give it what it wanted—grass wouldn't grow in *this* house's backyard, or anything else—and that was okay, too. Art wasn't supposed to be easy. Sometimes art was a razor, and you had to keep shaving and shaving right on down to the bone. And sometimes that meant you skipped a meal or forgot to comb your hair. *Okay*? She was okay. Okay with visits from men she hadn't expected to see, okay with offers from men for works she didn't want to sell, okay with brothers who worried her whenever they left the house, okay with the stack of bills on the counter, okay with sliding glass doors that wouldn't show her a goddamn thing to paint outside them. She was okay.

Until Mark stepped into the hall holding Tommy's blanket in his arms.

The click of the door registered somewhere deep in her brain. Her body turned, and she saw Mark standing outside their son's bedroom with a stack of clothes in his arms. At the top of the stack, folded neatly, was a dark blue blanket decorated in cowboy hats and revolvers.

Bang.

Alice stood stock-still, like someone who has been shot dead but hasn't realized it yet. The brush slipped from her fingers. "What are you doing with that?"

Mark walked toward her.

"I said what are you doing with that?"

He stopped. "I wanted—I *want* something of his."

Alice stared at the folded bills on the cowboy hats, the grooved chambers on the revolvers. Mark walked past her into the living room. She listened as footsteps carried him away, soft and slow. "No." She chased him to the front door. "No, no, no, *no.*"

He turned. He held the stack out to her. His sad, dark eyes looked like reflections of the blanket's cloth.

"Okay," he said.

Alice let her hand fall.

As Mark moved down through the long grass to his car, wind swept the door closed. She swayed away from it.

Her brother was coming down the stairs.

"I found an idea for my article." His face could barely contain his smile. "It'll interest you, I think. Alice."

"I don't care." She walked back to the kitchen inside the kitchen with the Red Sox sweatshirt sagging off her shoulders like a tired cape.

• • •

Tommy wasn't in the bathtub when Mark returned to 401.

He was standing in the doorway, ice water sweating down his thin white body. His ribs showed under his skin with each gurgling inhale. A puddle darkened the floor beneath his feet.

"Daddy."

Mark dropped the stack in his arms. Postcards spilled out of the shoebox and spread images across the carpet: a cardinal roosting in a buckeye tree, two men standing beside a tractor, a light tower off of a lake as vast as an ocean. He fell to his knees and fumbled around, throwing aside clothes in search of the blanket as Tommy moaned at him from a wide wet mouth and stared at him from wide wet eyes.

"Daddy, it's cold."

"I brought you something," he said, clawing left and right. "I brought you something to warm you up."

"Daddy."

"I know, I know." Mark dug his fingers into the carpet and looked straight down. *There.* A collection of hats without heads and guns without hands set against the darkest blue. He held it up to Tommy and smoothed out the fabric, brushed off the dust, shuffling closer on his knees. "Do you remember this? This is the blanket Grandpa David gave you on your third birthday, remember? You remember, don't you?"

Tommy went quiet. He lifted his arm slowly and pointed his index finger at Mark's head, his thumb cocked back. A drop of water grew underneath his fingertip. "Bang."

The drop fell.

Mark nodded, his eyes blurring. "That's right. *Bang.* That's right, partner." He slung the blanket around Tommy and pinched the corners together beneath his chin, making a poncho of it. "There you go. Now you're ready. You just need a hat and you'll be Clint Eastwood."

Teeth chattering, "Kid. East. Hood?"

"Why, he's only the second fastest gun in the West. Not *nearly* as quick as you." Mark tipped an imaginary sombrero. Then he pulled Tommy to him, his voice breaking. "Oh, Tommy. What happened? Did you have a spotty time? It had been so long since you had one, we thought you were through. We didn't think—we didn't know."

Tommy made a *gurrrp* sound.

Mark pushed him back, holding him by the elbows. "Was that it? Did you have one of your spotty times while you were in the bath?"

Tommy's nose began to bleed water. He shut his eyes and shook his head, moaning.

"Did you try to call for Mommy? Could you? Did you know what was happening?"

That *gurrrp* sound again, like a backed-up pipe.

Mark felt the blanket dampening under his fingertips. "Tell me you didn't know what was happening."

Tommy's head shook faster, the skin twisting like cellophane over his windpipe.

"Tell me you weren't scared, Tommy. Tell me you didn't know. Tell me it didn't hurt."

Tommy's tongue lolled out on a sudden flood. His eyelids sprang up, and he had no eyes left. Only holes. *Gushing* holes. Mark tried to scream but no sound escaped his throat. Tommy's head bobbled on a jelly neck. His inch-long penis flapped, streaming. The pores on his abdomen stretched wide, wrinkling his skin into hundreds of twisted lips.

Mark yanked him close, hid him against his chest. Holding his son's face to his faded blue tie, he rocked back and forth, screaming a silent scream as the cold currents came and came, as the body beneath the blanket softened and then gave.

When the scream finally left Mark, it was a sob.

He sat on the carpet in his room on the fourth floor, soaked and shivering and hugging himself, nothing in his arms but a wet piece of cloth.

Chapter Fifteen
October 17th

The milky sky dripped on the woman and boy waiting at the crosswalk. They must have been coming from the auto shop, because there was nothing else nearby except Alex's office building and only car problems would explain them walking around on this spoiled, wind-blown morning. The boy's hood was up and he was pulling on his mother's hand, eager to get across the street, but the mother was waiting for the little person to flash on the sign. She was teaching her son good habits, as any good mother would do. She was wasting her time.

"Alice."

"Hmmm."

Her brother stared at her from the passenger seat, his hat stretched so far down it had eaten his eyebrows. "I asked if you want me to stay home today."

"Why would I want you to stay home?"

"Any reason."

The mother and son walked across the street and up some steps into a diner. "I'll pick you up when you get off."

After a moment of silence, the passenger door opened and shut. Alice pulled out of the parking lot. Three miles from home, she spun the wheel and turned back. The tires lost traction on the wet asphalt, and her car fishtailed across the yellow line. Rain was a bastard, but at least it was honest. Rain revealed the world to be as slippery as it really was.

She parked at the diner.

Inside, the smell of cooking meat sweetened the air. It disgusted her, that smell. It was a mask, like chlorine, to disguise something horrible. It was a plastic smiling face over something that was dead and smiling even wider underneath, rotten lips spread ear to ear, something that wanted to eat you back.

The mother and son were in a booth, beneath a salivating window. His hood was still on, and he was bouncing up and down on the cushion, making it fart, while his mother tried hopelessly to get him to stop. Hopelessly, because she was laughing too.

She needed to know. Someone needed to tell her.

Tell her that you could put a child-lock under the sink. You could crawl across the backyard, combing the grass for nails. You could gate the stairs. You could let him take swim lessons, even though you hated the thought of him at the pool, splashing around in all that chemical-blue water. You could teach him to stay away from strange dogs, to look both ways crossing the road. You could do all those things and more, you could do *everything*, and none of it would do you any good. Because you couldn't get every nail, and you couldn't see every car coming. He wasn't safe. *Home* wasn't safe. You had to run, take his hand and run, hold onto him tight and run, run, run.

"*Mommy?*" said the little girl. She was staring up from her hood, at Alice, who had come within three feet of the table.

The mother set down her fork. "Excuse me? Can I help you?"

"Sorry." Alice backed away, her slippers slurping on the terrazzo. "You look like someone I knew."

• • •

At home Alice crawled into bed and hid herself like a secret between the sheets. The bed was the only warm place in the house, and she was so tired. So tired and so heavy, her whole body one big limp. She pulled the covers over her head and as her breath heated her little pocket of air, she saw the boy (not a boy) from the diner lying broken in the road; saw him rabid and foaming at the mouth; saw him lock-jawed from tetanus; saw him impaled through the neck by scissors, the handle sticking out above his collar like a red bowtie. Over and over and down into sleep she saw him, dead or dying, the perpetual victim of circumstance.

•••

Melanie Austen was at the front door, *knock, knock, knock,* and wouldn't she go away? Didn't she know Alice didn't want to talk to anyone? Alice was with her brother, who smelled so nice and clean and—

Knock, knock.

—just leave her alone! She threw off the covers, and the air slapped her face like a cold hand. Alex wasn't here, only his smell. Melanie wasn't at the door.

But *someone* was.

Alice gathered herself and went downstairs. She peered through the eyehole in time to watch a blurry van pull away.

Tall, oblong boxes crowded the porch. Two by the steps, three by the bell, and five more by the wicker chair. *What in the hell?* She gave the closest box a shove. It was light. Much lighter than it looked. Leaning over, she reached around to pick it up and felt her fingers brush something on the back. Attached to a string was a tiny card:

No strings attached, Geoff.

Alice carried in all ten boxes, laid them across the floor, then fetched a knife. With a flick and slice, she opened the first. Inside, sealed in plastic wrap, was an easel crafted of solid red oak. The surface had been sanded smooth and hand-rubbed with oil, every inch of the tri-mast frame given careful, loving attention—an *artist's* attention. She knew because the very same easel was standing in her kitchen. She'd pined over the brand for years before finally allowing herself to purchase one, just *one*. And now . . .

Alice looked at the boxes spread around the living room. "Fuck you," she whispered. "Fuck. You." It was a joke, a cruel joke. A hearty meal for the girl with no teeth. *Chew, mademoiselle, I know you're hungry.*

She rocketed into the kitchen. Geoff could take back his presents and strangle himself with the strings he hadn't attached to them. Grabbing the phone, she bumped the stack of mail and scattered bills across the counter. Mark, Mark, Mark. Not a single Alice. The only place she ever put her signature was a painting. She didn't exist anywhere but on oil—and if the oil went dry, where was she then? If the brush stopped, where was Alice Currier, who didn't even own her last name, *then*?

Suddenly she wasn't sick with anger, just plain old sick. She ran for the bathroom, still holding onto the phone. The cord yanked tight and the phone flew out of her hand. Alice landed in front of the tub, gagging, no time to turn to the toilet. She saw herself from above: thirty-three and on her knees, living off someone else's money in a house that was not hers, hardly a woman. The gag tugged and tugged. She sucked in a short breath and gagged again, lifting her butt into the air like a stinkbug, getting gravity on her side, but there was nothing inside her to push, nothing inside her at all.

She was dry.

Alice collapsed over the tub. A rope of drool reached down slowly from her lip to the acrylic. Once she'd produced something worthwhile, something that was *hers*, but it had ended the same as her spit. It had swung down on a feeble, thinning thread and died inside the bathtub.

Tommy.

She got to her feet and walked down the hall. In one kitchen and in front of another, she picked up her brush and let it hang at her side, the bristles caked with yesterday's paint. The hole waited. She felt it inside of her, an empty house in her heart. She hadn't meant to leave him alone so long, but there'd been other things on her mind.

The day darkened, and the glass door slid open.

●●●

Alex jumped in from the iced November night. He shut the sliding glass door behind him and turned to Alice, breathing vigorously into his palms. She set down her chef's knife, which she'd been using to lop the heads off broccoli, skin cucumbers, and quarter peppers in a bloodless reenactment of the French Revolution. Also known as dinner.

"Alex."

"Hi," he said, his voice muffled and echoey, "replies the poor parody of Darth Vader, whose face feels frozen into a scary mask right now. *Whoooo . . . Haaah.* What're you making?"

"Roasted veggies over quinoa." She tipped the contents of the cutting board into the stoneware.

"Healthy." He lowered his hands, revealing cheeks that were almost as red as his new hat. He had as many hats as some men had women. A different flavor every week.

"Yes." Any house she lived in would be a meatless house, Alice had told Mark before they married. She knew he stole Tommy off now and then for a pepperoni pizza, but if a little tug-o-warring was the only trauma they were putting their kid through, she guessed they were doing pretty okay. "Mark should be home soon."

Dramatic music played in the living room, followed by loud cheers, an explosion.

"Is that my nephew I hear jumping through the channels?" Alex called out. In response came the skitter of a thrown remote. Alice turned to hide her frown as Tommy pounded into the kitchen, still wearing his raincoat.

"It *is*," Alex said. "Why, I don't believe it."

Tommy gave a shy, "Uncle *Alex*."

"Come here and give me a hug, you. It's as cold as Vanilla Ice out there."

Alice drizzled coconut oil over the vegetables, struggling to get her expression under control. When she turned around, her brother was bent over at the waist, showing Tommy the frost-lines under his eyes where his tears had frozen.

"Tommy," she said, "if you're done with the television, what should you do?"

He looked at her from his deep hood. "Turn it off."

"That's right."

"And don't go tossing the remote," Alex added, with a wink for Alice, as Tommy darted into the living room.

"Don't do that."

Alex pulled his hat to the side, making a beret of it. "Do what?"

Before she could answer, Tommy re-appeared in the kitchen. Sometimes he was more rubber band than boy. "Come here."

"Why?"

"Because I asked you to."

Tommy dragged over to her on feet that were one hundred pounds apiece. He was just under three feet tall, short for his age, and he had Mark's black hair and her pale skin, a contrast that made him look sick when he was healthy and deathly when he was sick. Alice scraped off the crust under his nose.

"Ugh."

"You're telling me." She put together three full place-settings and handed the stack carefully to him. "Get the table ready."

Tommy looked down at the plates and then up at Alex, who was standing with his hands and forearms buried in the pockets of coat, unnaturally quiet. "What about . . . ?"

"Uncle Alex can't stay tonight. He was just coming by to say hello."

Her brother woke at the sound of his name, emerging from himself like a diver returning to the surface of the ocean. A smile bloomed on his face. "*And* to give my favorite pupil his birthday present." He pulled out a narrow box wrapped in blue paper. "I know you got a little freaked out yesterday at the pool, having to go underwater, so I—"

"You can give it to him tomorrow," said Alice. "On his birthday."

The oven climbed to 300 degrees. She could feel the heat growing behind its door.

"It's just a little tiny one. It won't get him wound up or anything."

Tommy turned his head. "*Please*, Mom?"

Alice wondered what sound the stoneware would make if she dropped it. "Go get ready for your bath. I'll be there to turn the water on in a few minutes." She saw his lips purse. "And no *butts*, or things will stink worse."

He slunk over to the table and began to arrange the plates on the table. Extra. Slowly.

"I'll finish that. Go on."

"Goodbye, Uncle Alex," Tommy said, as if he'd never see him again.

Her brother gave a tiny nod, looking someplace past the kitchen, and slipped the box back into his pocket. Tommy went down the hall. His bedroom door closed.

"We've talked about this, Alex. You can't keep showing up this way, unannounced. It's not—"

"I'll call next time, I'm sorry."

She shook her head. "No. That's not what I'm saying. You're not listening."

"I'm listening."

"You're not hearing me then." She walked toward him. His gaze lifted and a pair of glass eyes met hers. Eyes that belonged in a doll's head. "Tomorrow, at the party, you can give Tommy his gift, and I'm sure he'll love it. But tonight was supposed to be for the three of us."

Alex leaned into her, squishing his red hat against her chest. "I just wanted to see you."

"I know. I know you did." He smelled clean, almost blandly so, scrubbed down in bar soap to the last pore. "But maybe—maybe you shouldn't."

"What do you mean?"

Alice felt his fingers moving on her back, searching for a place to sink in, and pictured cold grubs wriggling atop packed ground. She pushed him gently away. "I'm almost thirty. *We're* almost thirty. It isn't right for you to be around all the time. It isn't normal. It's a little . . . *strange*."

Alex stepped back. "*Strange*."

"I don't mean *you*. I just mean . . ." She sighed. "It's not like how it was. You're my brother, and I love you. I love that you're close to Tommy. I really do. But—"

"It's *him*, isn't it?"

"What?"

"It's Mark." He nodded as he spoke. "He never did like me."

"Mark hasn't said a word about you." Ever since losing his temper with Alex during that disastrous party at David's house, Mark had treated the subject of her brother like an extremely delicate vase: stuck it in the corner and stayed the hell away. She paced to the table.

Alex followed her with a limp and a smile. "Sure he hasn't. Sure he hasn't had anything to say about the *gimp*."

"Oh, I'm sure he's had plenty to say."

She shut her mouth. Too late.

Alex went still. His arms fell to his sides, but his smile stayed on his face as if it were painted there.

Alice pushed the last plate quietly into place, then stepped around the table. Her brother didn't move. She reached for the zipper on his collar. "You'd better take off your jacket. If you don't, the walk back will feel like death."

"You told me . . . you told me when we were kids, back at home, that we would always—"

Tommy's bedroom opened. He walked to the bathroom and shut the door behind him.

Alice's hand had closed around her brother's throat. She let go. Her voice was hard and flat. "You don't talk about home in this house. *This* is home."

"Your home."

"Yes."

His face crumpled. He pulled off his hat, balled it up in his hand, and let it fall. It landed on one of the plates, red, like raw meat. He limped to the back door and then out into the night, wind ruffling his feathery hair.

•••

As one Alex closed the door, another Alex dragged it open. He stomped on the floorboards, dislodging mud and damp leaves from his shoes. His hat sat crookedly on his head, and Alice's first reaction was to glance at the kitchen table to see how it could be in two places at once. But the hat wasn't there, and neither was the plate it had fallen on, or the placemat beneath the plate. Only wood, bare.

"Look at that." He held up his hands, as if addressing God. "Alice is in front of her painting. Who'd have thought?"

Alice shut her eyes against the white hole on the canvas and it followed her into the dark, hovering like a moon. "Is that supposed to be sarcasm?"

"No, *no*. Of *course* not."

The tiny hairs on her neck prickled. "It's cold."

"Is it? Is it cold?" Alex walked to the sink, leaving the door wide open. Wind played with the corner of her canvas. She slapped her brush down.

"Is there something wrong with you?"

"Is that supposed to be sarcasm?"

She had a sharp response lined up for that, but as she started toward the sliding door it felt as though she were walking toward the hole on her painting, except this one was black instead of white. She pulled it shut, and her reflection slid into place in front of her. Her face looked hollow. Lost. Why was it dark outside? She couldn't have been standing at the easel for more than an hour.

Dizzy, Alice searched for the clock. 6:30.

6:30?

"*Whooooo*," sighed her brother as he splashed hot water on his cheeks, and all of a sudden reality seemed a little thin, a little frayed, like moth-eaten fabric. There'd been holes in Tommy's cowboy blanket, she remembered. Little gun-barrel holes, peeking from one dark layer of cloth to the next. She blinked, seeing Alex now and Alex then, the past folded inside the present.

"I just have one question," he said. He'd left the sink and was holding a disconnected cable. "Did you tear this out of the jack before I started calling? Or after?"

She started to say she hadn't torn out anything, then she saw herself running for the bathroom while clutching onto the phone. Silly Alice, always holding on when she should be letting go. "It was an accident."

"Well, can't blame you as long as it was an accident."

The date on Alice's leg itched like a scab. "What's that supposed to mean?"

"Nothing." Alex reattached the cable. "Just that accidents happen and sometimes people forget things."

He couldn't have said that. She must have imagined it. Alex wouldn't have said that to her.

"Shit," he said. "I was talking about work, about me walking home from work. I didn't mean—Lis, I'm sorry."

He limped toward her. Alice pushed past him to her painting and picked up the brush. She knew what would go in the hole now. Teeth. The wet ivory teeth of a world that drooled and chewed and swallowed, a world whose every exhale was as cold as November wind. She stabbed the bristles against the canvas, slashed and gouged at the white emptiness.

Alex's hand on her shoulder. His voice soft in her ear. "The brush is dry."

"No, it isn't." But it was, and it was a good thing it was, because teeth didn't belong in the backyard any more than grass did. Alice let her arm fall, limp. "I don't know."

"What don't you know?"

"What it wants from me." Didn't she know, though? Didn't she know, deep down, what belonged there?

"Maybe it doesn't want anything. Maybe it's finished just how it is." Alex, the pacifier. Alex, who always knew what she needed. She felt her breath slowing, her shoulders loosening, then she clenched tight.

Alex didn't know a goddamn thing about anything.

"Let go of me."

His fingers, still warm from the sink, dug grubbily into her skin. "Whatever's going on, you can talk to me about it."

"Nothing's going on." Except for his hand, that was going on *plenty*, and did he really need to touch her to talk to her?

"I know it's almost the time of year that—"

"Nothing."

"If you're missing—"

"Nothing."

Alex quieted for a moment. "By the river, you told me you were going to find what felt good and keep doing it. You said painting felt good. Does it feel good now?"

"It might."

"What?"

"It might if you gave me some fucking space."

Alex's hand dropped from her shoulder. "You're the one who brought me here, you remember."

"Like I could forget."

"If you don't want me in your home," he said, drawing back, "then you should say so."

"I don't want you in my home."

Alex went into the living room. He might have paused before going upstairs, or perhaps she only imagined him stopping to stare at the boxes on the floor. It didn't matter either way. What mattered was he was gone and soon to be leaving for good, and she could finally think in peace. Get her focus back, get rolling again. Obvious now, wasn't it? How could you hope to move forward with a limp slowing you down? Alice stared at the canvas, and already she could feel the change inside her, the hole coming closer, *closer*, like the end of a tunnel . . .

Her brother limped into the kitchen. He had on a new set of clothes, and how was that possible when he'd only just left? Alice glanced at the clock. The minute hand had flipped from straight down to straight up.

"I'll leave in the morning if you still want," he said. "But you can't push away everything. You have responsibilities. We're going home, the home that belongs to both of us, and you need to give me a date. If you don't, I'll set it myself. There's a whole, *real* world out there, and it's time you woke up to it." Alex dropped his phone on the table. "I'll be at the pool. Don't bother calling."

That feeling of *thinness* returned as he limped to the sliding door. Her knees loosened. "Wait."

He stopped on the patio, his back turned.

"The night Tommy—the night before his birthday—what did you bring him? What was in the box?"

Alex stood there a long time.

"A snorkel. So he could breathe underwater."

He adjusted his hat. Then he closed the door.

• • •

With the wind in his hair, her brother limped away across the backyard. Alice leaned her forehead against the cold glass of the sliding door, wishing she could freeze her brain. Or at least numb it.

Later.

Later she could think about her brother. Right now she had a boy and a bath to tend to.

Tommy was standing at the sink when she opened the door. She saw his face in the mirror, wide mouthed and lips slathered in foam, and her heart skipped a beat. He turned to her, scrubbing his teeth.

"What are you brushing for? We haven't eaten yet."

"I had a dirty taste."

Alice thought of the way Alex cleaned and cleaned, spending a quarter bar of soap per shower, a half bar of soap per day. "There's nothing dirty in you. Nothing." She heard how sharp her voice sounded. She softened it. "Come on, rinse that out."

Tommy spit into the sink and then jammed his foamy brush in the holder. "When is Daddy getting home?"

Ten minutes ago. "He should be on his way now. Grandpa David's been keeping him busy at Longreave."

"Is Grandpa David coming to my party tomorrow?"

"You bet. And Grandma Sarah." She got down on her knees to undo his belt. By this time tomorrow the buckle would be wearing a skull in a sombrero. Mark wasn't a fan of the gift— thought it was morbid. But mothers knew best. Cowboys were cool. Dead cowboys were cooler.

"What about Uncle Alex?"

"What about him?"

Her son's dark blue eyes—she saw both herself and Mark in those eyes—trained down on her like gun holes. "He's not coming, is he?"

"Why wouldn't he be?"

"Because you're mad at him."

The splatter of water deepened to a gurgle as the tub filled. "I'm always mad at your uncle. If I wasn't mad at him, it would mean I didn't love him."

Tommy considered this. "Are you mad at me?"

"Infuriated." She patted his butt. "Now climb out of those jeans before my ears start smoking."

He pushed his pants down, underwear too, and Alice found herself with one of those views that only doctors and parents get to appreciate. She picked herself up, lifted Tommy by the armpits, and swung him over the edge of the tub.

He yanked up his feet. "Make sure it isn't too hot."

"It's freezing. Just the way you like it."

Tommy let his toes dip cautiously into the water. He didn't scream, so Alice figured it was safe to let him down. She watched as he laid himself back in the tub, moving every bit as achingly slow as an old person settling into bed. "I'll be back in a sec." She shut off the faucet. "Just have to slide dinner in the oven."

Tommy nodded, water lapping at his chin.

Alice left the bathroom and closed the door halfway behind her, not realizing she'd just seen her son alive for the last time. As she passed the table, Alex's hat tickled the corner of her eye like a drop of blood. She pictured him outside under the ice-crystal stars, head down in winter's first real freeze, and shivered. The oven did nothing to warm her. She started back for the bathroom.

And braked by the phone.

How much time had gone by since her brother left? Five minutes? Long enough for him to walk half a mile, if you didn't factor in the weather and his limp. He'd gotten that limp for her. For Alice, his Alice, who had once upon a dark time whispered promises on nights much colder than this one.

A knot tightened in her right leg.

It wasn't too late to call him, tell him to come back. Mark would be home any moment, and then she could drive Alex to his apartment. He'd gotten the place when she moved to Manxfield, even though coming here meant giving up the regular gigs he booked in the city. As casually as stripping down for a shower, her brother had shipped out of Boston, sold the sax he'd since then nicknamed Soul, and chained himself to a 9 to 5. All because she'd asked him to. Not out loud, no. She hadn't needed words.

He'd *known*.

Alice picked up the phone. In front of her sat the knife she'd used to prepare dinner. She listened to the line ring and in her mind saw what could have been the knife's twin, shining red on a bathroom floor, beginning a trail of footprints that led to a quiet boardwalk.

"Hello," Alex said, and he sounded so all right, so okay, that relieved tears ran down her cheeks.

"I'm sorry, I didn't mean it, you're my brother, Lix, you're my brother and I love you and just come back, okay, come back and I'll give you a ride and we'll talk."

". . . wait for it, wait for it . . ."

Beep.

Alice had been talking over voicemail. She dropped the phone. Blinked at it. Maybe her brother wasn't answering because he didn't recognize the house number. She dug around in her jeans, but her cell phone wasn't there. It was in her jacket. She ran to the front door. The coat hooks were all empty. She stared at them, trying to remember. The car ride home from the daycare. Tommy in the backseat, complaining about one of the other kids. Her in the front, only half-listening, daydreaming about . . .

Alice pushed into the office and shut the door behind her out of habit. Her latest series—and secretly she thought, her best yet—surrounded the room in skyline images of Boston, only there was no sky. Above the city stretched a vast mirror that reflected an alien metropolis of rounded architecture, obsidian ponds, and shadowy green vapors that might have been foliage or clouds. She'd spent the day lost in her *A Tale of Two Towns* and had been in such a rush to lose herself again after picking Tommy up that she'd walked into the house kicking off her shoes and shedding her outer layers as she went.

And there, hanging on the easel next to her newest painting, was her coat.

Alice tore her phone out of the right pocket and dialed Alex. One ring, two, three, waves groping up a thin Dorchester shore, four, five, six, voicemail.

She set the phone down and stared at the colors on her palette until they swirled. He was making a point. He was ignoring her calls to frighten her, and because she knew that, she didn't actually need to be frightened. Nothing bad was going to happen tonight. Nothing bad was about to happen.

Turning with a drunk's easy sway, Alice discovered snowy downtown. Lampposts wore fuzzy caps. Streets sewed together like white thread. Upside-downtown was a different story. There the roads were squiggles and the snow yellow and clumpy as scrambled eggs, the product of a winter that clotted things rather than froze them. Her eyes moved over Faneuil Hall, standing red and proud in the heart of the canvas. Directly above the building, a white hole waited to be filled. *That's no good. No good at all.*

She reached for her brush.

Five minutes later she'd painted Faneuil Hall again, this time hanging down round and moist, like a drop of merlot. She looked at the other little white spots perforating the sky-city. *No good, no good, no good.* She cleaned her brush off on the newspaper and, with the distant sense that she was forgetting something important, opened the jar of Ultramarine to create blue. The bristles made small wet sounds as she dabbed at the oil.

She didn't hear anything else until Mark returned home from Longreave almost an hour later.

Until the scream.

• • •

It tore at the air like a knife at tissue, a gouging, ripping, heart-seeking scream that drained slowly into a liquid gargle. As the last of it died, Alice turned from her painting and floated legless, bodiless toward the office door.

The house stood in bright anti-clarity, everything so clear that Alice saw nothing. She didn't see the floorboards below her. She didn't see the plates on the table, waiting for the vegetables in the oven. She didn't see the hallway or the crowd of Tommys overlooking her from its walls. Tommy as an infant, pink instead of pale. Tommy squeezed between David and Sarah. Tommy in a cowboy costume, pointing a plastic revolver at the camera. Every inch of space taken up in pictures, in her compulsion to block out the white.

Halfway to the bathroom, where Mark sat rocking quietly on the tile, rocking with his jaws stretched wide and the tip of his tie dipping in and out of their son's open mouth, she stopped. Then she turned and walked the other direction through the see-through house. Like a ghost inside another ghost, she walked through the house to the sliding glass door. Home didn't exist. Home was a silent letter inside a word that she'd tried to twist into happiness but always, for now and for ever, spelled despair.

There was only one home, only the first, and it haunted.

Alice walked out into the night. She left the door open behind her, and soon the cold of November moved into the house and took her place at Mark's side. When she arrived at her destination, two shuffling miles later, her feet were frostbitten and her face was craggy with frozen tears.

"I just got your message," said her brother as he answered the door.

Alice fell into his arms.

•••

She walked up the stairs still holding onto her paintbrush. Up the stairs to Alex, who would hold her and lie with her and not say anything, only smell clean and good. She knocked on the door. A minute passed before she remembered.

Alex wasn't there to let her in.

She'd driven him out.

Alice pushed the door open and started for the bed. Then she stopped the way she had five years ago when she found Mark holding Tommy on the bathroom floor. A small, black and white square rested on her pillow. A piece of paper, folded to the size of a hotel mint. On the paper were three words:

Now You Now.

Inside were more. They began with a farewell.

They began, Godby Longreav

Chapter Sixteen
October 17ᵗʰ

For days Mark saw his son only in his dreams. Some had an interpretative quality (Tommy as an ice statue melting in Mark's arms; Tommy as a leaking boy-shaped water balloon), but most, and the worst, were a simple retelling of their last reunion: Tommy, tongue and penis flopping, empty eye sockets flowing and skin pruning around pores that dilated like pupils. All began with Tommy there and ended with Tommy gone, not absent, not in some undefined Elsewhere, but hopelessly, irretrievably *gone*.

To keep from drowning, Mark worked.

On the first day, he traded in his Honda and put its tiny return toward the truck with the biggest bed and meanest suspension. He paid in full, and made sure all mail and extraneous payments would be sent to him online. Then he gave the truck its *true* test run, with one thousand pounds of bricks in the back.

It passed.

His next business was eliminating the long walk through the annex. He used sheers to cut the padlock off the lobby's cellar door and with one lantern on the lip overlooking the crumbled staircase, plus several more spread out below, he put his sledgehammer to use again. It cost him an hour (not to mention a few splinters) to tear the old steps away and shove them aside, but it was worth it once he'd installed the ramp. *Beyond* worth it. Lightweight and sturdy, the ramp unrolled from the size of a suitcase and locked tight into twenty-four aluminum-plated feet.

He shut the cellar door, replaced the padlock, and everything appeared according to the status quo. There was the condo company to keep in mind, after all. More than likely the hotel was just a calendar date to them and wouldn't enter their radar until they were ready to roll out the wrecking ball, but it was better to be safe just in case they decided to send someone to check up on the place.

Just in case.

Dusk hardened into night. Mark coasted his truck to a gap in the rocks halfway down the coastal road, and when he was sure no one was coming from either direction, he drove up over the curb and onto the beach. The sand grabbed at the tires, but they were heavy duty bastards, the best in the business. Approaching Longreave, he thought he saw a light wink inside 4C. It must have been a glimmer of his headlights on the glass because as soon as he shut them off, realizing they were broadcasting his journey down the shore, the room's window went black.

He unloaded his truck behind the hotel. The dolly couldn't push as much weight in the sand, but he didn't have to push the dolly a mile each trip, so the trade off was more than fair. Once the bed was empty, he parked in the neighborhood and walked back along the beach, kicking away his tire tracks as he went. He felt strong and rested as he unlocked the hotel's front door, as if he were starting the day instead of ending it. Perhaps he was, in a way. Night meant the world outside Longreave came into alignment with the world inside, darkness to darkness, an eclipse of more than sun: an eclipse of the *thought* of sun. Mysteries that melted by the light of day became solid.

Night meant possibility.

Night meant Tommy.

But Mark didn't see his son that night. Or the next. It wasn't until dark fell on the third day, as Alice was fighting with her brother over forgotten responsibilities, that Mark found himself not alone in Longreave.

•••

With the cowboy blanket hung over his shoulders and two bricks in each hand, Mark climbed the stepladder. The wall was twenty-one courses now, old enough to go to the bar and get drunk. He laid the bricks carefully, wiped the wet joint smooth with his thumb, wiped his wet thumb clean on his slacks, and climbed down to repeat the process. As his feet touched the ground, the boiler gave a moaning slosh.

Or rather, someone *inside* the boiler gave a moaning slosh.

Mark snatched his backpack and lanterns. Feet pounding, light reeling, he ran across the cellar and up the boiler's grated steps onto the tank.

A moon floated in the black of the hatch.

The moon opened its eyes and mouth and became Tommy's face, spinning slowly around and around, growing smaller and dimmer as it revolved down . . . down . . .

Two small hands broke the surface.

Mark latched onto them. He pushed back with his legs and pulled with everything else and Tommy flopped out onto the tank, facedown, twitching. Mark rolled him over and stared down in horror. The lip of the hatch had scraped a thin layer of flesh off his son's thighs, leaving long bloodless grooves, like tire tracks. A deep *glug-glug-glug* came from his throat. For a moment Mark was paralyzed by the terrible certainty that Tommy had spent the last of whatever juice brought him to Longreave, and arrived only to drain away again.

Then he noticed something missing in Tommy's mouth, the same thing that had been missing that night five years ago in the bathtub. Making a bird beak of his thumb and index finger, Mark reached in between Tommy's teeth and pinched around until he caught what felt like a worm hiding far back below the palate. Slowly, carefully, he pulled Tommy's tongue out of his throat.

The shaking stopped.

Tommy smiled.

"Daddy."

•••

Mark freed the cowboy blanket from between his back and backpack, wrapped it snugly around Tommy, then carried him to the ramp and up into the lobby. *Where were you?* he wanted to ask, *what took you so long?* But he didn't know which questions were safe and which weren't, so all he said was, "Thank you. Thank you."

"Why?"

"Just thank you."

"You're welcome." Tommy planted a dripping kiss on Mark's neck.

The curtain was drawn in 401, the bed unmade. Mark crawled under the covers, shoes and all. Something dug into his hip. He pulled out his phone, set it on the chessboard, and propped himself up against the pillow, holding Tommy in his lap.

After a few minutes, he decided to take a small risk. "Do you remember where we are?"

"Home."

Did Tommy really believe that? Or was he simply parroting what Mark said last week?

Mark pushed a little further. "Why do you say that?"

"Because you're here."

Mark squeezed him and found he couldn't stop. "That's right. And do you remember what 'here' is named?"

"Longreave."

"And do you remember what Longreave is?"

"Home."

"Besides home?"

"A hotel."

"And what's a hotel?"

"The place where people stay on vacation."

That seemed too close to a truth Mark didn't want to consider, so he changed the subject. "What's your favorite movie?"

"Woody."

"What does Woody say?"

"There's a snake in my boot!"

Mark choked on a laugh. He brushed his fingers through Tommy's damp hair. "What's a snake?"

Tommy looked up at him as if he were stupid. "A snake."

"Okay, how about your favorite food?"

"Peanut butter sandwiches."

"What?"

"With the crusts cut off."

"What about pizza? You told me you loved pizza more than anything whenever I took you out to eat."

"I'm sorry."

"Why?"

"For lying."

"You lied for my sake?"

"What's *sake*?"

Mark stared at the ceiling, searching the pattern of stucco for a way to explain. "For a person's sake means to protect them. Like when it's cold, so you give someone your blanket. Because you want to keep them warm more than yourself."

Tommy considered this. He nodded. "That."

God. He is his mother's kid.

"Do you want a sandwich now?" There was half a jar of peanut butter on the dresser along with a few slices of bread that Longreave had kept refrigerated.

"No. *Full.*" Tommy shifted, and his belly sloshed like a miniature boiler.

Mark felt moisture leaking through the blanket into his clothes, and the image of an hourglass appeared in his head, only rather than sand trickling down there was water. Tightening his arms, he said, "Tell me something."

"What?"

"Anything. Movies and animals and games—"

"Like hide and seek?"

"Yes, like hide and seek. How you play, where you play, why you play, who you play with, how you win."

"Don't you know?"

"Tell me like I don't. Tell me like I've forgotten everything about everything."

Tommy told him. You played by finding somewhere secret, somewhere no one would ever look for you, where you could be a secret too. You played in the dark because everything was secret in the dark. You played because it was fun, you played with anyone you wanted, and you won by never being found until you were ready to be found. He told Mark how bugs were the best at hide and seek because they were so small and could fit under rocks. He told Mark about the kinds of bugs there were, about the shape of leaves, about the different sounds shoes made.

"Is that enough?"

"No," Mark said, squeezing harder. "Not even close."

Tommy discussed which trees looked friendly and which looked like they wanted to grab you. He went through all the places sand could get caught. Underwear, Velcro, toenails. His ribs buckled. He looked up. "You okay, Daddy?"

Mark swallowed the rest of his gasp and managed to nod.

The lessons continued. From sand to sun to space, which was the emptiest and darkest thing out there, and then back down to earth and dirt. Dirt, Tommy explained, was like sand except better because it was coarser. Tougher. Cowboys were always covered in dirt. Tommy showed Mark how cowboys looked when they were mad and when they weren't mad. The expressions were identical. Then he showed Mark how to look scary. He made himself a vampire, hanging his fingers down from his upper lip like fangs. *Dripping* fangs. He made himself a clown, using the same fingers to drag the corners of his mouth into a stretched and drooling grin. He pulled the cowboy blanket over his head and *woooo*-ed through the wet cloth.

Mark shuddered.

"See? Told you it was scary."

As the schooling carried on, Mark found the places where his son's ribs had broken and secured his arms there gently. He might have gone on sitting that way through the night, holding onto Tommy like a cast, if nothing had interrupted them.

Around ten o'clock the chessboard lit up and elongated, shadowy fingers reached from the pieces. Mark's phone was buzzing. On the screen was a single word:

Home.

Mark started to turn it off, then saw that Tommy was watching him. "Do you know what this is for?"

"Calling someone."

"And this?" Mark showed Tommy the screen. "Do you know what this says?"

"H-O-M-E. Home."

"Yeah. Home. The other home. Do you remember the other home?"

A flinch, then a whisper. *"Mommy."*

Here, Mark thought, *here is The Question.* And all he had to do to answer it was answer the call. His thumb touched the green arrow and began to slide it. He stopped. What if she couldn't hear Tommy?

What if she *could?*

Mark hung up the phone and tossed it upside down on the chessboard. Tommy groped after it, squirming. *"Mommy, Mommy."*

"No, son. No, I'm sorry. You can't—"

Tommy's head slammed into his chin and rattled his teeth.

"—it's a game, it's hide and seek."

"Mommmmmmy."

"And if you lose, if your mother finds you . . ." Mark felt the heat of tears and pinched his eyes shut. ". . . if she finds you, you'll be taken away from me. You don't want to be taken away from me, do you?"

The thrashing slowed.

"You have to be a secret for now. For both our sakes, you have to be a secret."

His son went limp.

Mark swung his legs off the mattress. Water leaked from the blanket and ran down his forearm as he walked to the dresser. "You want Mommy? I've got something from Mommy. Here, you'll see." He opened the top drawer, pulled out the shoebox of postcards, and carried Tommy back to bed. "You'll see. It's okay. You'll see."

On the chessboard, his phone began to vibrate again.

•••

"He hung up on you," Alice said as voicemail connected for the second time. "And now he's ignoring you." She slammed the phone and then stood there, Alex's latest Now You Now clenched in her hand. *Let's tak about a hotel here in Manxfield,* began the article, and they were going to do just that, she and Mark. No messages, no emails.

They were going to have a nice, long *tak.*

Alice picked the phone back up and dialed David's home number. It was engraved in her memory from years of chatting with Sarah. Grandma Sarah, whom Alice had drifted away from after Tommy drowned. Who had died her own unexpected death. The line trilled cheerfully, and Alice pictured Mark standing over the phone in David's dusty little kitchen while the old man slept. But he wouldn't stay unconscious for long. Not unless Mark answered her goddamn *call.*

She tried a second time.

A third.

A fourth.

By the fifth, she couldn't tell if the phone was ringing or her head. Fragments danced up at her from Alex's article. Reched corporations plum their deep pokets again and restle away another piece of smal-town soul . . . built on the Atlantic . . . raised for sunrises not sunsets . . . wals that have held the likes of Enoc Jonson and Jak Kirby, also nown as CAPTAIN

AMERICA, soon to crumbl . . . recking ball prepares to wave by by . . . Longreave goes to ground and history resins to history . . . wat a nee slaper . . . your friend Tomas can't decide if he should be auditioning for a laugh-trak or reaching for a tisue.

Neither could Alice. She ground the heels of her hands into her eyeballs and then, half-blind, blinking, wandered to the table and slumped into a chair. It took a moment for her to see clearly again. There. The answer was sitting right in front of her.

Alex's cell.

Everyone but her had one.

Alice flipped open the phone and scrolled through the contacts until she found the number for David's mobile. She dialed it. Sweat clammed her palm. She hadn't spoken to David since Sarah's wake, had no right to call him this late, or at all.

"Hello?"

"David. Hi."

"Alice?"

"I hope I didn't wake you. I called the house several times." She realized she hadn't answered his question. "Yes. Alice. It's Alice."

"You didn't wake me. I'm not at the house." He sounded a little winded, as if he'd just come up a flight of stairs. "I'm in California."

"*California?* Mark didn't mention you were going to California. When did you leave?"

"It's been about a week now."

"But why? I mean, what for?"

A pause. "To be with family."

Alice remembered Melanie saying she'd moved to Oregon, and pictured a flock of birds migrating west to escape winter. All of a sudden she felt very conscious of the cold that was coming, creeping down the coast toward Manxfield like someone padding through the hall of a dark and quiet house. A chill touched the nape of her neck. She glanced behind her.

"When did you and Mark get back from your trip?"

Alice straightened. "Excuse me?"

"Your road trip. You guys left town before I did, so it must have been a good one if you just got back. Did the two of you make it pretty far from home?"

She stared at the large white hole where the kitchen used to be. "Alice?"

"Yeah," she heard herself say. "Pretty far from home."

"So, why'd you need to reach me? Everything's okay, isn't it?"

Alice, are you okay?

"I have to finish."

"Finish what?"

Alice looked at her painting. "Inviting people over for a thing tomorrow. Last minute get together. I wanted to see if you could come."

"Oh."

"I'm sorry you won't be around."

"I am too," he said after a moment. "You'll pass on my best to Mark, won't you?"

"Of course. Let's talk again when you get back."

"Sure," David said quietly. "You two take care of yourselves, all right?"

"Yeah."

Alice ended the call. She drifted over to her painting and picked up a clean brush, staring out into the backyard.

Ten minutes later, she grabbed her brother's phone and left the house on bare feet.

On the canvas behind her, outside the sliding glass door of her deformed kitchen, stood a brick wall scabbed in salt.

•••

"Out on the road in some flat, grassy place under clouds that are starting to look a little flat and green themselves. Makes me imagine the sky is a mirror, and that makes me wonder . . . anyway, not sleeping is fun. So is not bathing. Can't wait to get home, hug the both of you, and nurse you back to health after my stink knocks you out cold. Missing my men. Love, Mom." Mark turned to the front of the postcard, where an Olympic torch showered stars over a blue background. "That's the state flag of Indiana. Do you know Indiana?"

Tommy's nose dripped quietly.

"Let's look at the next one." Mark reached into the shoebox and his hand emerged with Lake Michigan at night. The gleam of a light tower lit a bright path across the waters. On the back Alice had written, "I wonder how deep the bottom is," and nothing else. Mark looked at the date.

2009.

The year after.

He set the postcard aside then quickly searched for another. 2010, Kentucky. 2011, West Virginia. 2012, Illinois. The last one she'd sent him. The last one she would ever send him. *I wish you would let me bring you out here one day, just me and you. I think it would be good for us to get away and . . .* He tossed away all three cards. "You wouldn't like these. They're boring. How about we go all the way back? How does that sound, kiddo?"

Tommy's voice was flat. "Okay."

Mark kissed the top of his head and the scalp sank a little, as soft as lips below the hair. He swallowed hard, reached in the box, and came up with a slice of glossy apple pie. "Here. 2003. You weren't even born yet." The writing on the back was barely legible. "Five damn fucking days." He stopped. Cleared his throat. "Well. There are some new words for you."

"Damn fucking?"

Mark flinched. Then he wondered how a few bad words could still shock, even now. He looked at Tommy bundled in the blanket, his little body, his pale face, and guessed it was true what they said about your kid forever being a kid in your eyes. "Your mother had a dirty mouth on her back then. She washed it out for you, I think."

"With what?" Tommy said, water spilling from the gap between his front teeth.

"Nothing. It's an expression. Wash your mouth out with soap."

"Oh. I use toothpaste when my mouth is dirty."

Mark gave in to a grin. "Much wiser of you. But not that kind of dirty. Mommy was different before she became, well, Mommy. So was I, before you. Not bad, just not always so good. A little more exposed maybe. Parents . . . we don't really know what we're doing. We just don't want to do it wrong. So we show the best version of ourselves to our kids. We dress up like at Halloween, pretend we're angels."

"Why?"

"Because we're scared," Mark said. "Because love is a monster. It comes out of a closet we didn't know we had in our hearts, and kills the person we were before."

"That's not nice."

"No, kiddo. It's not nice." Mark pulled Tommy in closer, lacing an arm around him, and felt the stillness beneath his broken ribs. "It's not nice at all."

The phone buzzed once.

Only once.

Mark glanced at the chessboard then back at the postcard. After her colorful opening, Alice had gone on to say, *Take a good look at that pie, Mark. I've got something even sweeter for you when I get home, and you can eat it again and again and again.* "Maybe I'll skip this one, too." He stuck his hand in the shoebox and felt from corner to corner. It was empty. No. That couldn't be. Couldn't be. He flicked through the pile on the bed and counted nine cards total, one for every year from 2003 on except 2004, when Alice had been too pregnant to squeeze herself in the car. Finally, he said, "I think that's it, partner."

A buzz from the chessboard.

"How about we—"

Another buzz. Mark picked up his phone, turned it over, and forgot what he'd been about to say. A stack of texts stared up at him. Texts sent by an unknown number. From first to last, they read:

I'm outside.

I know you're here.

Let me in.

•••

Mark couldn't move.

"Mommy?" his son said hopefully.

"No." It was a wrong number, a friend trying to reach another friend. Maybe a pissed off boyfriend or girlfriend, chasing down an unfaithful lover. Not him. Nobody was looking for him.

A fourth text appeared.

Mark.

Quietly, he said, "I think it's time we play the game. I think it's time you show me how good you can hide."

Tommy shook his head. Slowly at first, then faster.

"Only for a little while. Only while I check something. Then I'll be right back."

"I don't want to hide. I want to stay with *you.*" Tommy squirmed out of Mark's grip and crawled away, shedding the wet blanket across the bed like a snake's skin. He landed with a squelch on the carpet, scrambled up to his feet, and clasped his hands together in front of his naked, dripping chest. "Please."

"Tommy."

"Don't make me, Daddy. Please don't make me."

Mark took a step forward and Tommy took two back, into the bathroom. His feet made slurp-slurp sounds on the tile. "Do you remember what I said, kiddo? About you being a secret?"

Tommy stood motionless, his body running with water and lantern light.

Moving closer. "I need you to do like you said. I need you to make yourself so you won't be found, not by anyone but me." Closer. Blocking the doorway. "And not until I'm ready to find you. I need you to . . ."

Mark's voice turned brittle in his throat.

". . . to take a bath."

Tommy lowered his head and then walked to the tub. He stepped inside—two quiet splashes—and looked over his shoulder. "It's cold."

"I know." Mark swallowed. "I know it's cold."

Tommy sat. He gave one last pleading look before reclining into the water and out of sight. The bathroom darkened as Mark shut the door. He rested his head against the cool wood and waited for the sensation of slipping down, down, down to pass.

The phone lit up in his hand.

Waiting.

Mark took the backpack along with what little light remained in 401. The hall was quiet, and so was the stairwell, all of Longreave still except for him. A black pit waited at the bottom of the lobby staircase. He approached the front door on his tiptoes. Once there, he turned his ear to the oak and listened.

Quiet.

All quiet.

Mark let out his breath. He stuck his key in the lock and felt a buzz in his pocket as he pushed the door open.

Alice stood on the path in a pair of paint-speckled sweatpants and a wife beater. She had a phone in her hand and no shoes on her feet. Lantern light yellowed her bright blue eyes. "Why didn't you tell me? You *motherfucker*, how could you not tell me? All those times you brought up David, brought up Longreave . . ."

The skin on her face went slack.

". . . you tried to tell me."

• • •

Alice stood there, voice gone, phone loose in her hand, staring into the dark of a lobby that looked as large as the night behind her. Mark was dressed to manage a hotel—or a graveyard. Dusted loafers, slacks with gray stripes of crust down the legs, shirt coated in filth and done up to the last button. Two lanterns, one burning, one black, dangled from straps at his sides.

"You aren't here."

"I am."

"You can't be here. You have to go." He glanced at her car, slung across two spaces in the parking lot. "If anyone sees—"

"I'm not going anywhere."

For a moment she expected him to close the door in her face, just as he'd done while packing his bag—preparing, it struck her, to move here. From the home where he'd lived to the hotel where he'd worked since he was a child. The *empty* hotel.

Mark pulled her into Longreave and shut the heavy oak door behind them. He twisted a key in the lock and left it sticking out as he turned to her. "How did you find out?"

Bumps broke out on her arms. His hands, when had they gotten so rough?

He stepped closer, face flickering. "How did you—"

"I looked into my magic crystal ball." She started to laugh. The laugh crumbled. "I talked to David and—what does it matter how I found out? What does it matter why I'm here? I'm here because *you're* here. You should be explaining to *me*."

"Does David know?" Mark asked under his breath.

"What?"

"Does David know I'm here?"

"No. He doesn't know *anything*. You did a pretty good job making sure of that."

Mark's eyes remained fixed on her. "What about Alex?"

She saw the folded piece of paper waiting on her pillow. "Only the basics."

"The basics?" Lantern light made a rippling pool around them, from the old hardwood beneath their feet to the high paneled ceiling above their heads.

"That the hotel shut down. That someone bought the land. It's not exactly a secret, Mark. Did you think you could hide it forever?"

He took a long time answering, long enough for the deep chill of the lobby to settle into her: an icy, ocean-floor stillness. It was Fall outside, but inside Longreave winter was already here. She crossed her arms and hugged herself as the bumps on her arms spread down her body.

"No," Mark said, "I don't think anything is that long."

"What *were* you thinking then?"

"I don't know."

"You don't know what you were thinking? Or you don't know how to explain?"

"Both."

"Try. Help me understand."

Mark looked down at her bare feet. "You can't be standing around like that in here. You'll get sick."

Alice felt the pressure building in her head. "That's what's wrong in this picture. That's what you're worried about. Me. Getting sick."

"Come."

Mark walked off and left her staring at her shadow. It shrank down the door, shriveling from adult to child as the dark closed in around her. Alice turned and chased after the light, frightened to look over her shoulder, frightened at what she might see or not see stalking her across the lobby. She felt something cold and crawly at the base of her neck, a shiver that stayed.

Her shadow.

Her shrinking shadow.

Right when she turned, her shadow had seemed to grow, swelling up to monstrous proportions on Longreave's front door.

She followed Mark up the stairs. "Where are you taking me?"

He didn't answer. It didn't matter. Alice realized she already knew.

As their feet thumped and thumped, she caught herself straining her ears, listening for an extra pair of footsteps. The idea was nonsense, of course. If she heard anything at all, anything that sounded like creaks or thuds on the treads below, it was only echoes.

There was nobody in Longreave but the two of them.

Unless she'd brought someone with her.

Ha. Ha. Ha.

Ha.

They arrived at the fourth floor. Mark's light passed over the clay pot by the stairwell, and for an instant the bed of beads became a bed of pearls. Alice touched the tiny hole in her earlobe and felt a needle-prick of sadness.

"I'll only be a second," he said outside 401. "Wait right here."

Like hell. She could feel the dark behind them, shifting on the walls and ceiling and floor. If she looked back now, she wouldn't be able to see the stairwell. If she looked back now, there'd be no way back.

Mark cracked the door and then squeezed inside. Alice pushed in after him.

He turned his head to her. To the closed bathroom. "I told you—"

"Fuck what you told me. If you think you're leaving me in the dark again, you're out of your mind."

His jaws hardened beneath his black beard. The smell of kerosene thickened around them. He moved to the dresser and took out a pair of socks, which he shoved at her. "Put these on."

"Thanks, *honey.*" She brushed past him to the chair, only for him to walk past her to the closet.

"Wear this." He unhooked his goose-down jacket.

"I'll pass." She started to look away, but her gaze caught on the gap where his jacket had hung. There was no wall behind his clothes, only darkness.

"Suit yourself." Mark swung the closet doors together.

Alice was still holding onto her brother's phone. She had no pockets, so she set it on the dresser before putting on the socks. Her feet were so numb they couldn't tell the difference.

Mark was at the door. "We can talk in the lobby."

"We can talk just fine here."

His jaws hardened again. He set his backpack down, propping the lanterns upright on the carpet. He trudged to the bed. Alice spotted a dark blue tangle of cloth on the covers and looked away quickly, to the nightstand. "I didn't know you like chess."

"Used to."

"You don't anymore?"

"Not sure. Don't have anybody to play against."

Alice stared at the lone white pawn standing in the center of the board. A key twisted slowly in her windpipe, cutting off her breath.

"Mark," she said, "what are you doing here?"

He looked at his lap. "Staying awhile."

"But you're trespassing. Longreave doesn't belong to you. It belongs to those people that bought it, the condo people—"

"They're just some business."

"That doesn't *matter*." Alice clasped her hands tight and spoke again, lower, "This isn't a place to stay. It's dark and cold and I don't know what else. Not safe. What if you have an accident? What if you fall going down those stairs and hurt yourself? Who's going to find you?"

"Somebody would." He pulled on his collar. "Sooner or later."

"And I'm supposed to be fine with that? I'm supposed to be fine just leaving you—"

"You've had an easy enough time until now."

Alice's hands separated, shaking. "You asshole. You stupid, *stupid* asshole."

Mark glanced sharply at the bathroom door.

"*What?*"

"Nothing. Nothing." He looked at her, not quite straight on. "You didn't . . . you didn't hear anything?"

"Hear *what?*"

"The pipes." Mark made a limp motion. "There must be air in them."

Alice rose. It had been months since they were together in the same bed, years since they were together in *this* bed. She sat down next to him, her spotted sweatpants almost touching his crusted slacks. She took his hand. "Mark. Come home."

He turned his head. Up close the black of his beard brought out his eyes, made the dark there into something beautiful and mysterious instead of frightening. "What about Alex?"

"What *about* Alex?"

"He's living with you now."

"It was only for a little while, until he got through a rough patch." She remembered Alex at the sliding glass door, telling her she had responsibilities, telling her to wake up. "We'll talk about my brother later. Just come home. Come home."

Mark turned his head away. "I can't."

Her body clenched. "Why not?"

"I have work to do here."

"What *kind* of work?" She let go of his hand, took his chin, and pulled his face back toward her. "What is there here to work on?"

"I'm building something."

"What?"

"I tore it down, and now I have to put it back up. It's my responsibility."

"Tore *what* down?"

"The wall." Mark stared at the floor as though a window had appeared there, looking down into the ocean darkness of Longreave. "There's no one else to take care of it. Nobody but me. I have to finish."

The key twisted in Alice's throat again, and a wet *click* escaped her mouth. She heard their voices, hers and Mark's, playing back in an overlapping loop. *I have to finish, I have to finish, I have to finish . . .*

"You have to take care of what's yours," said Mark. "Even if it scares you sometimes. Even if you don't know how. If you don't take care of it, you don't deserve it."

"You're not okay." She cupped his cheeks. "Mark, you're not okay."

He shook his head, pulling on her hands. "You wouldn't understand. You don't even mow the lawn."

She choked back a sobbing laugh. "You're not okay. You need to come home, you're not okay."

"Why? So I can be like Alex? So you can play nurse and send me off again when I'm better?"

"*No.*" Her fingers curled in his beard. "No, Mark. No."

He jolted up and away from her. Then he walked to the bathroom, went inside, and shut the door behind him.

Alice looked down at the little twists of hair caught between her fingers, and the cold caught up to her at last, shattering her body into helpless quivers. When she got herself under control again, 401 was quiet. Mostly quiet.

From the bathroom came a low, gentle slosh.

But that wasn't possible, because if the heat was off and the lights were off, then the water was surely off as well.

What could Mark be doing in there?

Alice rocked to her feet, then paused as something higher up the bed caught her eye. A shoebox. Empty. Beside it a dark glossy surface poked out from under the covers. She lifted them and saw a postcard of a lake, saw another postcard beneath it, and another, saw all the postcards she'd ever sent Mark lying strewn across the mattress where they'd slept together for the first time as parents. Slept but never made love because they'd made something *better* and it was tucked soft and safe between them.

Alice covered her mouth. The cowboy blanket, the covers twisted and knotted, the room—*this* room.

Mark. Oh, Mark.

She touched the blanket. Frowned. The cloth was wet. *More* than wet. The cloth was soaked through.

Something rasped softly behind her.

Alice lifted her head, shoulders stiff. The rasping continued like a quiet breath—a slow, easy exhalation. Beneath the kerosene came another smell, wafting on the still air. She turned.

The doors of the closet were inching open.

Inside, the darkness stirred.

•••

Mark thought he heard the splash the first time. The second time, he was sure. He left Alice sitting on the bed and shut himself in the bathroom.

Two anguished syllables floated out of the dark.

"Mommm. Eeeeee."

Mark raised his finger to his lips and crept forward across the tile. By the light dripping under the door, he glimpsed a boy's profile sitting erect in the tub. He knelt.

"Dad—"

"*Shhhh.*" Mark covered Tommy's mouth. He put his other hand around the nape of Tommy's neck and gently laid him back down into the tub. Tommy tensed as his head went under. Mark felt lips moving against his palm, water filling the space between his skin and his son's, and he smiled what he hoped was a reassuring smile—a smoothing smile. A small, cold hand reached up and touched Mark on the forehead, the cheeks, the mouth, as though learning his face, and then a tremor sent waves lapping inside the tub. "*Shhh,*" Mark said, "*shhh,*" and held on until the hand dipped back below the surface, until the neck relaxed in his grip.

Shaking, he stood.

The light under the door disappeared. There was a rustle, a bang of wood. *Alice.* He ripped out of the bathroom in time to see the bedroom door swinging shut. He leapt to catch it. Too late. The dark closed around him completely, and something else with it, a smell he couldn't quite place.

You can buy a treadmill, he thought in sudden terror, *but you can't build a pool, you can't build a pool, you can't build a pool.*

He didn't hear someone padding toward him across the carpet . . .

He didn't feel something cold tickle the back of his neck . . .

The doorknob turned in his hand, and he stumbled out into the darkening hall. A fading glow bled from the stairwell. The steps lost shape and seemed to melt beneath his feet as he ran down them. "*Alice!*"

He crashed against a wall and pushed on, calling her name again, his voice echoing through the hotel. As he reached the second floor, a sock-clad foot darted out of sight ahead. Shadows raced him to the lobby staircase. Its oil-black steps were slippery with running light. He leapt down them in two strides and hit the floorboards at a sprint. Alice was at the front door with his backpack, the lanterns dancing wildly on their straps. There was a *thunk* as she twisted the hotel key in its lock. He spun her around by the shoulders. Her face shone. Eyes wet, nose snotted, teeth slick and gleaming.

"What is it? What happened?"

She answered by flinging his backpack. One of the lanterns— the one that was on—smashed against the floor. Its light flared for one brilliant moment, like the farewell pop of brightness from an exploding sun. The lobby blackened and she was running down the path. As he started after her, he heard a low steady hiss. Gas. A vision came to him of Longreave in flames:

Salt fell off the walls in charred clumps.

Rooms filled with smoke.

Water boiled inside bathtubs.

Mark tore off his right loafer, wedged it under the door, and followed the hiss of gas to his backpack. He felt around for the broken lantern and turned it off before flying down the path to the parking lot, holding the hotel key in one hand and his shoe in the other. "Wait," he said, yanking open her door as she tried to shut it. "You can't go until we finish—"

"There's nothing to finish here or anywhere. It's all already *done*."

The engine snarled and the handle ripped from his fingers, then the car was out of the lot and onto the road, roaring up the coast away from Longreave.

Mark put on his shoe. He started running.

• • •

The lights were on in the house, and the porch was lit up like a stage. Mark jumped out of the truck. His calf clenched, and he went down gracelessly, too winded to shout, too weak to catch himself. Only then, sprawled on the curb, did he notice.

There was no car in the driveway.

Maybe Alice parked down the road. Mark picked up his aching body, then limped to the front door. He lifted his hand to knock, lowered it, and took the doorknob instead.

It turned.

"Alice? Alex?"

The painting gave a tired flutter in the kitchen. Mark stared for a moment at the boxes spread across the living room. "Hello?" Still limping, he went up the staircase. *There are two gimps in the house tonight,* he thought. Except he didn't think so, not really. He didn't think there was anyone in the house but him.

The bedroom was empty.

He stood awhile, looking in at the tangled sheets on the mattress, the clothes dangling from the dresser, the suitcase missing in the closet, then he turned off the light and shut the door. He turned off the light in the hall as well, and the one above the staircase, and the one in the living room, slowly tracing his way from switch to switch, reenacting the ritual he'd performed every night for years. Alice could never be alone in a house knowing any corner of it was dark. She avoided shadows like most people avoided germs.

When he arrived at the entryway, one light remained.

Mark entered the office. He gave no more than a passing glance to the artwork on the floor, and what he saw was red. Raw. Wounded. He reached for the lamp. Paused. A piece of paper rested facedown on the desk. A piece of paper creased down the middle. He picked it up. Turning it over, he thought of the final message Alice had sent him from outside Longreave, as they stood feet apart through the door, the message he hadn't discovered until she was gone.

I hear you.

Standing there in the last little light of the dark house, Mark felt a strange whisper inside his chest, like a closet beginning to open.

• • •

Mark slipped and sank his way down the beach, unable to tell his thoughts from the sand, his sand from the thoughts. Waves whispered static against the shore. He could not say what caused him to look up as he neared Longreave—maybe the brief scent of spice that carried past him on the wind, maybe nothing—but when he did, he saw the light again inside Room 4C. It was tiny, a pinprick of yellow hovering behind the window. It drifted through the dark on a lazy horizontal, stopped, and brightened before floating down and out of sight like a slow, luminescent raindrop.

Mark glided the rest of the way.

He found his backpack in the lobby and felt for the backup lantern—the one that had cracked on the night of Tommy's return. It had more cracks now. They made flowing veins of shadow on the floor and wall. He took the key to 4C and then he took the staircase, hardly hearing his footsteps, hardly feeling his legs or the cold, moving through the hotel as though he'd left his body behind at the door.

The annex smelled of streets in early October, of dry leaves crushed into red and orange spices on the sidewalk. A ribbon of smoke trailed down the stairwell between the third and fourth floor. Mark ran a finger through it as he climbed. He was met by many more when he emerged, some as low as his knees, others so high they caressed the ceiling. They filled the air, ethereal and gray, wisps of autumn incense.

He followed them to the end of the hall, where 4C waited behind shifting clouds.

He unlocked the door.

Frank Currier sat in his chair by the window. He was naked except for the towel draped over his big lap, his chest and stomach as brown as the cigar in his left hand. Smoke breathed from his mouth. "Hey there, kiddo. What took you so long?"

•••

Mark stood in the doorway, watching smoke twine from his father's navel.

"What are you waiting for, an invitation?" Frank puffed on his cigar. "Has all this walking around in the dark made you a vampire?"

Mark stepped in and heard the door shut distantly behind him. "You're here, too."

"I never could get out of this place." He paused. "Looks like I passed the gene on to you. Sorry about that."

"Dad." Mark felt his brain working on an impossible math problem, trying to divide eighteen years by the distance in feet between them. "*Dad.*"

Frank gave a lung-depleting sigh. "I had hoped, with you and my grandkid having spent some quality time together, that the two of us could skip the phase of our meeting where you're stunned stupid."

"Tommy. You know about Tommy?"

"Word drips around."

"You've seen him?"

"No."

"How come, if you know he's here?"

Frank smiled, and smoke drew the shape of his lips in front of his face, a ghost smile that blew apart with his answer. "It's a big hotel."

"Who else?" Mark wobbled. "Is Mom, is she—?"

"I wouldn't know."

"What do you mean?"

"I'm not sure how accurate your memory is of your mother and I—you always did have a knack for shutting out things—but we were not a picturesque pair. I was passive aggressive, she was plain old aggressive. A bit of a shrew, by my estimation. Though, to be fair, I could on occasion be write down an ass." Frank sniffed escaping smoke back into his nose. "We stuck it out together as long as we had to. You know how the line goes."

"Until death do us part." Mark saw Alice dressed half in white and half in black, holding out a divorce form missing her signature. All at once the night caught up to him. He sat down hard against the door.

"Thank God. I was worried you'd want a hug."

Mark traced one of the feelers leaving his father up to the smoke alarm.

"Don't worry. The battery's out of commission, like your dad." Frank shrugged. "Not that it would matter much."

"So, the smoke isn't real."

"Real enough in some ways. Not real enough in others."

"And you're the same. Tommy's the same."

Frank looked out the window. "I always liked the view from here. It beat the parking lot, to be sure."

Mark recalled the annoying little lesson Alex had given him on precision in word choice. "You say it in past tense, like the view's not there anymore."

"You ever draw a line in the sand?" Frank's eyes stayed on the glass. "You scribble it up away from the waves and the line stays straight. But if you scribble it *down*, close to the water, the line blurs and blurs. After awhile there's no line at all."

"That's what Longreave is, you're telling me. A line drawn close to water." Mark envisioned the dead floating in a dark ocean, searching for a shore to crawl onto, a place worn down by the tide where they could stop and rest awhile.

A hotel.

Frank turned from the window. His beard appeared blacker than before, as if some of the night had reached in and held onto him. "Longreave is a bunch of walls put up a long time ago, by people who had no idea how to build anything. It's nothing with no one in it."

"Is that supposed to be an answer?"

Frank stroked his cigar. "You know, kiddo, I often wondered how you managed to win a single games of chess."

Mark flinched. "Why?"

"You never could make any sense of the board around you."

"And you always were an encouraging bastard."

"I'm afraid the rules *clearly* state that you aren't allowed to speak ill of me."

"Sorry. My dad didn't teach me much in the way of manners."

Frank let out a laugh. His face clenched and he palmed his left breast. After a moment, he let go and tapped ash off onto the towel.

"Does it . . . does it hurt?"

"Not so much, not anymore." Frank blinked away the smoke filling his eyes. "Just a little ache now and then."

Mark glanced into the bathroom, toward the still tub of water, and his breath caught as if his throat had filled with hooks. "I held him down."

Frank only stared.

"When Alice was here, I held him under the water so he would be quiet." Mark touched his lap, still damp from Tommy. "So she wouldn't hear him. It was like, like I—"

"You didn't. You can't."

"But what if it hurt?" Mark looked up, seeing Tommy with his eyeless eyes gushing, with his pores bunching his skin. "What if I keep on hurting him even though I don't mean to? He doesn't *know*. He doesn't know he's dead, so what if one day I do actually kill him, the part of him that thinks he's alive? What if I hurt him or scare him so bad he doesn't come back?"

"Kids are forgiving when it comes to their parents. They'll take most any wound you give them and wear it without complaint." Frank was quiet. Thickening strands of smoke joined around his body, like threads sewing into a blanket. "I'm sorry what I said to you that night, after you came home with your trophy. I wanted to tell you happiness isn't about talent, it's about courage, *conviction*, but I couldn't speak the right words. I was too much of a coward."

Mark answered softly to keep his voice from breaking. "It's okay. I'd probably have gotten tired of the game anyway."

"Thanks for that, even if you don't mean it." A gray cloudbank hid the ceiling. "You'd better get going. It's late. You know how us old people get when we stay up too long."

Mark scrambled upright. "You can't go yet. You only just got here."

"Kid, if you think I ever left, you're even dumber than I thought."

"What about Longreave? You never answered. What is it about Longreave that makes it"—Mark could only come up with a phrase that made the question circular—"what it is?"

"Remember Mooney," Frank said, his face coming and going behind shifting curtains.

"My *dog*? What about him?"

"Everything."

Mooney. Big white eyes, black-brown hair, breath as foul as garbage left out in the sun. The lumps in his neck had gotten fatter and fatter until he'd died under the porch one wilting day when Mark was in the first grade. "I remember him. I do."

"Then you'll be all right."

Mark started forward and stopped as the smoke thinned around his father, showing patches of crinkling flesh. "*Dad.*"

"It isn't always until death, you know, the way it was for me and your mom." Frank's hand appeared, palm facing up, as if to hold onto the smoke. His fingers were the crispy brown of tobacco leaves. "Sometimes it's longer than that. Sometimes it's forever."

The smoke shifted again, and Frank Currier had no mouth to speak from, or face to support one. Then the curtains blew apart for good. There was nothing behind them, nothing but a chair and a bath towel with a few cinnamon dashes of soot.

• • •

Mark made his way through the many stairwells and hallways of Longreave, and when he arrived at 401, he felt as though he'd stepped out of his father's room straight into the room he shared with his son. But Tommy wasn't in the bathtub, no matter how long Mark looked down into the water, and he looked down into the water for a long time.

He might have stayed there all night, watching, waiting, if his phone hadn't started to buzz on the dresser.

Alice.

Mark ran into the room and then realized. His phone was still in his pocket. *This* phone—Alex's?—was a flip model. On its display glowed an 802 number. He answered the call.

"Hello?"

Breathing. "Who is this?"

"This is Mark. Alice's husband. She left her brother's phone with me by accident. And you are?"

The voice, an old woman's voice, rose a notch. "Alice's husband?"

"Yes, ma'am. You know her?"

"Alice *Stokes*?"

"Currier. Our last name is Currier. Who am I speaking with please?"

The line dropped. He pressed re-dial and got a busy tone. He tried again and got a high-pitched screech. Holding the phone, he walked to the window and gazed out over the ocean, that view his father implied had ceased to exist except in memory. As waves kneaded the curved line of the shore, the display went dark in his hand.

802. Like the number of a room. *802.*

He ran an area-code search on his own phone. The results loaded slowly. They sunk in even slower.

The call had come from Vermont.

Mark sat down on the floor with his postcards. He arranged them into chronological order and read the writing on each one, not just Alice's messages but the print as well. It was a small detail, in the margins, but viewing the collection as a whole it became hard to miss. Surely she hadn't expected him to hold onto every card she sent from the road.

Not him.

Not her unsentimental Mark.

He returned the cards, none of which had come from the same state and yet *all* of which had been manufactured by the same company, to the shoebox. He crawled into bed without shutting off the lantern.

Its flame had grown sputtery, wild. Its cracks threw epileptic shadows on the walls.

One shadow in the circus was plumper than the rest. It had limbs and a head and a watermelon belly, and kept completely still while the others twisted and squirmed.

Mark didn't notice.

He didn't notice that black had made a move on the chessboard either.

Under cold covers, he drifted off to the thought that maybe he wasn't the only person with secrets after all.

•••

A little after three in the morning on Interstate 93, a brother and sister whose names were as similar as their faces crossed the New Hampshire state-line into the deepening Vermont woods, headed home.

II. The Pool Salesman

Chapter Seventeen
October 18th

Alice Currier woke in warmth and wetness.

She sucked in a breath like someone emerging from deep underwater and sat up, clutching the covers to her breasts. Her heart hammered at her tonsils. Moisture slickened her back. She was sitting in a puddle of sweat—a *pool* of sweat. Too much sweat to be sweat, and too-strong smelling, too much like chlorine.

She reached between her legs slowly, almost sensuously, and touched the crotch of her pants.

The soaked crotch of her pants.

It took all Alice had to hold off the sobs building in her gut. She curled her fingers around her vagina and squeezed, hard enough to hurt, hard enough to penetrate, pushing the piss-saturated cloth inside herself on one nail.

A gasp escaped her. She bit down on her lower lip and forced her finger in to the first knuckle. Her spine twisted, throwing her head to the side. Across the king-sized bed, on the far end of the windowless room, her eyes found the closet.

Its doors were cracked open.

Alice rolled over and tightened into a trembling ball. There was nothing in the closet, in *any* closet. If she turned over again right now, the dark under the hangers would be completely still—and the doors definitely wouldn't be open any wider. She would see. All she had to do was look over her shoulder.

Take a peek.

She started to and then decided looking was even more stupid than not looking. Looking meant she needed to *prove* nothing was there, when she already knew that. She knew that. Alice pushed off the mattress. She hit the light switch and the bedroom lit up as loud as a scream: white walls and white ceiling and pale blue carpet *bright, bright, bright*. It was the shape of a house, the room—the kind of house a kid would draw in crayon and have stuck to the refrigerator. To her back was the floor, to her sides were the walls, and ahead of her, tapering toward the closet, was the pitched roof. No light made it into the closet, she observed with a shiver.

Alice peeled off her wet clothes, not thinking of Tommy's blanket and how it had been wet too, and especially not thinking about what had happened after she touched it. She tossed her garments on the covers and stripped the bed. Where she'd slept there was a damp yellow patch the shape of a flower. A garden of stains surrounded it. The stains were old now, like her. They'd dried and turned brown.

Feet whispered down the hall outside, dragging shadows underneath the door.

The big brass knob started to turn.

"*Wait.* I'm not—I'm not—w*ait.*" The door pushed in slowly, breathing against the carpet. The sound was horrible, the very worst sound there was.

"Pancakes are getting cold." Alex shut the door behind him. He blinked at her. "Why're you—Alice, what is it? What's wrong?"

She shook her head. "*Don't.*"

"Don't what?"

He looked over at the mattress. "Oh."

"Mom will hear. Mom hears *everything.*"

"Oh, Lis. It's okay." Alex opened his arms to gesture, and that was all the invitation Alice needed. She leaned into him, her face finding the crook of his neck.

"Not since Boston. Not since we moved to Boston."

He stroked her back. "It doesn't matter. We'll turn the mattress over later."

She thought of the bedsprings stuffed inside, stiff and old, poised to squeak. "But Mom—"

"We'll be quiet about it."

"But the smell."

"There's spray in the bathroom."

"But—"

"I'll take a shower, and when I come back to get dressed, I'll give the mattress a spritz. You can tell Mom I decided to clean myself up, if she asks. You don't even have to lie."

"But . . ."

But she had nothing after the but.

"Go on. Have yourself some empty calories and a side of empty conversation with Mother Dearest. She doesn't eat anymore, only thing fills her up now is talking. She's on the vernacular diet, strict like."

"Alex . . ." She remembered telling him she didn't want him in her home and later begging him to leave that home with her. Love and guilt swelled inside her like competing balloons. "Thank you."

"You want to thank me, you can start by remembering where you lost my phone."

She swallowed. "I told you."

"You're positive you didn't leave it at David's house?"

"I had it when I left. I know because I forgot it was yours and tried to call you on it. After that . . . I'm sorry."

"Whatever, I'll use it as an excuse to buy myself a fancy new one when we get back. I should be thanking you, really."

"You're welcome then." The balloons grew a bit bigger. Together they felt about as big as a hotel room. Was Mark in 401 now? she wondered. Was he sitting around alone in the giant dark closet of Longreave?

Alex brushed her hair. "You've got almost as many knots as Mom."

"She'd be thrilled to know I take after her."

"Do you really think that?"

"That I take after her?"

"That she'd be happy if you did."

"I don't know." She pulled her head back. "Do you?"

He regarded her. "I think—what I think is you'd better go keep her company before she comes looking for it."

Dressed and cradling her dirty laundry, she let herself out of the room. The hall was long. It stopped to the left at a tiny bathroom, but stretched on and on to the right, past the den and kitchen, past the garage door, all the way to the master bedroom. As a kid she'd felt the hall *was* the house, and that the rooms attached to it were nothing more than closets.

Alice took a deep breath and inched out into the kitchen.

Beverly Stokes sat low at the table, dark sunglasses taking up most of her face. The skin of her cheeks was soft and loose, pulled down into pouches that looked as if they would come right off the bone with a pinch. A large mole marked her neck. Her hair was gray and knotted, like her hands, which rested on either side of her empty plate.

Alice kept walking, quietly, and was almost clear of the kitchen when:

"How did you sleep, dear?"

She hugged the covers. Turned. "Fine. Just have a little laundry to do. Clothes I brought."

"Of course. The detergent's on the top shelf, but you know that. Nothing ever changes around here, just gets older."

Beverly's sunglasses remained on Alice as she backed away.

The laundry room was a segue to the garage. Tufts of insulation showed behind the walls. A dead lightbulb hung from the ceiling. Alice loaded the washer and wondered if her mother could hear the difference between a big load and small load. Last night she'd heard Alice and her brother coming up the road. They'd found her waiting on the porch, in the dark, her nightgown wind-stuck to her withered frame.

Beverly was in her chair, so still she might have been asleep. Or pretending to be. "Are you going to join me or just stand there?"

Alice jumped. "Sorry. I—I was looking out the window." Squeezed between the sink and refrigerator was a view of the backyard. Needlepoint branches itched at the pale sky.

"Find everything okay?"

"Yeah." Alice took a seat.

Down the hall the shower started. Her mother's head cocked at the sound.

"Are these all right for me?" Alice motioned and immediately felt stupid. "The pancakes, I mean."

"Would I offer them if they weren't?"

Biting her tongue, Alice forked one onto her plate. "They look wonderful."

"Do they?"

"They do." She took a nibble. "They taste even better."

"That's nice. I was worried they'd have no taste, with how much I had to take out of the recipe. I don't know how you do it."

"Do what?"

"Live without so many ingredients."

Were they still talking about food? "I get by."

"How are things in the city these days?" Her mother's ring finger tapped on the table. "Are you seeing anyone?"

Syrup stuck to Alice's throat as she swallowed. "I've been so busy with work. You know me."

"I should."

Alice set down her fork. "Did I say something wrong?"

Beverly Stokes gave a raspy haw-haw, more like a cough than a laugh.

"What's so funny?"

"I just remembered the joke where the mute writes to his upset friend . . . *was it something I said?*"

"Haven't heard that one."

"No?" Beverly moved her jaw side to side, loosening its joints. "That's a shame. And I just spoiled the punch line, too."

Is this empty enough, Alex? "Where'd you hear it?"

"Made it up."

"I didn't know you made up jokes."

"They come to me once in a while. Poof, and they're there. Nothing really worth sharing, though. Nothing you'd be sad if you didn't hear."

Alice impaled her last piece of pancake.

"Have another." The pouch under her mother's chin quivered slightly—eagerly?

"One is fine for me." Still chewing, she carried her plate to the sink. "You made enough for a whole week."

"You're staying a whole week?"

"That's not what I said."

"Well."

Alice wet the sponge. "Maybe a week."

The countertop was dusty, like everything in the house. Her eyes trailed down it, and paused on the telephone. Its cable dangled free.

"I thought you got our message we were coming last night."

"I did."

Alice plugged the cable back into the jack. "Your line was disconnected."

"Was it?"

"Must've gotten snagged."

"Must've."

The shower was still going. *Really selling it aren't you, brother?* Alice thought as she finished washing off her plate.

A sound came from the table. "*Mm.*"

"What?"

"I forgot to mention I ran out of vegetable oil."

"Do you need me to get some?"

"Andy is bringing groceries by tomorrow." Beverly's voice was soft, pleasant. "But I ran out before I cooked your pancakes, so I used lard on the pan. Is that important? Is that something I should have let you know?"

Alice turned, her insides cramped and hot. The back of her mother's head was so tangled it could have hid a second face.

"Dear?"

Alice walked to the front door and put on the slippers and robe waiting there. Her stomach rolled like an overloaded dryer. "I think I'm going to step outside awhile."

"You aren't upset, are you, Alice?" her mother called after her. "You aren't angry with me for forgetting to tell you one *little* thing?"

Wilting daffodils leaned over the path.

She cut across the crescent drive and onto the rutted dirt road. The day was cold and clear, the sun bright and useless. At one point she thought she heard Antique Andy, her mother's neighbor, rumbling up in his vintage Ford, but it must have been some other vehicle on some other lonely country lane because the sound faded. Woods pressed in close. Wind rustled like snakes in the trees that still had leaves.

Alice emerged onto the bridge.

She slowed.

The guardrail was torn wide open on the side that faced downstream, back when there'd been a stream to face. Splinters jutted from the chewed metal. Bolts clung to twisted posts. The county should have filled the gap long ago, just like they should have filled in all those ruts. But there were more urgent matters than fixing up forgotten roads and bridges.

Alice sat down and dangled her legs over the edge. Thirty feet below her mother's slippers waited the riverbed. If she looked hard enough, if she tried, she could almost see broken glass glittering in the sand.

Chapter Eighteen
October 18ᵗʰ

Mark stood on a bridge in New Hampshire, his hands in his pockets. It was the only bridge within three miles of Midland, which was the only town in Cheshire County as small as the one Alice had described from her childhood.

The riverbed wasn't dry like she'd described, but he figured that didn't mean much. A lot could change in twenty years, especially surrounding a bridge. This one wasn't quite level anymore, and the planks had come loose here and there, which was why he'd parked before walking onto it. With an extra thousand pounds in the back, his truck would have snapped those planks and sent him falling. Not very far though. Certainly not far enough to kill him. A lot could change in twenty years, but he didn't think a drop off this bridge had ever killed *anybody*.

He kicked a pebble. It made a tiny splash in the stream, two feet later.

Hands still in his pockets, he walked back to his truck.

•••

The Amateur's Mind had a lot to teach about bad thinking in chess, but little to say on the actual basics, so Mark bought a book of openings on the way back to Longreave. He hadn't been surprised that morning to find one of black's pawns had moved.

He didn't feel there was much left to surprise him. If anything struck him as interesting, it was the particular move black had made. c5 was a grab for the center, and also the beginning of the Sicilian Defense—hardly the choice of someone who knew nothing of the game. It certainly wasn't the kind of move Tommy would have made, assuming Tommy could manage a correct move at all, and based on the few games Mark had played against his father, Frank Currier knew as much about chess as a nun did about sex. Still, anyone could make *one* good move with a little luck, so Mark had shrugged it off and developed his king-side knight before leaving the hotel.

But now, standing over the board, he felt a tingle down his neck.

Black had responded again. Another pawn move. The *right* pawn move. He checked his book and there it was, d6, the second play of the Sicilian. New players never went two for two. It would be like shooting a gun downrange, blindfolded, and hitting the target both times. His heart beating quicker, Mark pushed his d-pawn forward. For a moment he sat there and watched the board, half expecting black's c-pawn to slide on its own and knock over his piece. Then he made himself get up and leave the room. He had a wall to build.

He got as far as the stairwell.

Surely it was too soon. *Surely.*

He jogged back to 401 and with a trembling hand, unlocked the door. Light washed in over the chessboard.

It had changed.

Black's c-pawn now rested on the square Mark's pawn had occupied just a minute ago. The captured piece was gone. He checked for it on the carpet, under the bed, in the closet—even in the bathroom—but it was nowhere to be found. It had vanished into thin air.

Like a ghost.

Laughing under his breath, Mark completed the exchange with his knight. He set the black pawn beside the board. "See? You take the pieces, but you don't *take* them. You leave them for the next game."

Silence. Wriggling shadows.

Mark twisted around . . .

. . . and let out his breath. He'd had the momentary impression someone was standing right behind him, standing very still. But that was ridiculous. Almost as ridiculous as playing chess with someone who wasn't there. "Okay then," he said, needing to hear a voice, any voice. "Okay, friend, you're up." He started for the door, went back, and shoved the book of openings in his bag. "We don't want you cheating."

Mark poured over the book outside 401. Brick dust on its cover mixed with the sweat on his palms and became a paste, which he wiped off on his slacks. He let himself back in casually. It was his turn. He made his move, casually, and strolled out into the hall. Right before the door shut, he yanked it open.

The room was empty.

"Sorry. Just kidding."

Mark closed the door, staring inside the whole time. He counted to ten. Once more, black had answered.

"Looks like we're going by the book, eh?"

But soon the book had been tossed out the window. Black castled king-side. Mark castled opposite and stormed the enemy stronghold. He didn't notice the deadly countermeasure arranged against him until it was too late. After giving up a few pieces (all of which evaporated between turns), he tipped his king in resignation. "All right. One-zero, you, whoever you are. It's been fun. Too bad you're a thief."

He went down to the basement thinking of empty rooms, of secrets kept behind closed doors.

•••

Last night's mortar had hardened in the wheelbarrow, and his shovel was stuck inside like Excalibur in its stone. He broke it free with the sledgehammer and used a chisel to chip off the residue, then he got to work on the wall.

Sunlight winked along the tarp. Darkness lapped around the lantern ring to the sound of waves. Twice he paused and stared off, thinking he'd heard a splash, but he'd imagined it both times. He was down to the final stacks of bricks when a rock skittered behind him. He spun.

"Hello?"

The dark returned his voice, softer.

". . . hello?"

There were probably a hundred rats down here, crowded among the cobwebs, watching him with blood-drop eyes. He'd spooked one, was all. He'd spook one again to prove it. Mark tossed a chunk of brick.

He heard it break.

He heard the pieces scatter.

He heard nothing after that.

A chill tickled his arms. He made a fist. He wasn't down here to skip stones, damn it. He was down here to *work*.

Mark flew through the remaining bricks. He gave his tools a hasty clean, untied the lantern Alice had broken from his backpack, and replaced it with one from the lantern ring. He could have replaced the cracked lantern, too, but he didn't. It seemed wrong to put down something that had survived so much.

Shadows followed him across the cellar, sliding across every surface like living seams. He was grateful when he reached the ramp to the lobby, and even more so once he'd bolted the door behind him. That didn't stop him from pausing occasionally to listen as the hotel talked to itself in whispers and moans. He started up the staircase.

Something tapped quietly under the front desk.

Tapped twice and went silent.

He turned. "Hello?"

This time his voice didn't echo. It was swallowed. He approached the desk on feet that felt like lumps of ice inside his loafers. The keys trembled on their hooks as he lifted the partition. The space under the desk was deep and dark.

And empty.

Tap. Tap.

Mark looked up, past the other side of the desk. Past the lantern light. "Is someone there?"

Tap.

A long, dragging pause.

Tap.

The knot of his Adam's Apple dropped into his stomach. He stepped out from behind the desk, moving slowly. The elevator emerged, its bronze doors set in shadows. Its wrought-iron dial pointed to L, for lobby.

Tap. Tap. Tap.

Brittle. Like an old fingernail.

"Who's in there?"

Silence.

Mark leaned an ear against the cold elevator doors. The lantern was hot against his leg. He counted to ten the way he had during the chess game, between moves, then he let out his breath and took a step back. Nothing. Just one of the cables or gears settling down from disuse. Just tired, creaky Longreave.

Tap.

Low inside the elevator.

An image arose of Tommy, black mouth wide on his white face, hands reaching up as he sank into the boiler. What if he'd swum up out of the wrong shaft? What if he'd surfaced in Longreave only to find himself trapped inside a dark box, gagging on his tongue, finger twitching . . .

Tap. Tap. Tap.

"I'm coming, kiddo, hold on." Mark wedged his nails into the crack between the doors. As he pulled, a deep groan reverberated through his arms. The doors separated an inch, two, dividing the elevator in darkness. Panting, he let go and dropped to his knees. "Tommy? Son?"

From the crack came a small, raspy breath.

LONGREAVE

Mark jolted upright. He forced the doors wider, then he angled the lantern light down into the elevator and revealed a slice of dusty checkered floor. There was another rasp. Another. Another. Another. He could almost see Tommy huddled in the back, body shaking, chest jerking.

Mark grabbed the doors one last time, to shove them all the way open.

That was when he realized.

The breathing wasn't coming from down low. The breathing was coming from straight ahead. From the dark in front of his face. He let go. Stepped back. The breathing grew louder, hoarser. It shook the air.

Mark ran for the staircase, and didn't stop until he was in 401 with his back pressed against the door.

His heartbeat slowed.

Not for long.

The chessboard had been reset on the nightstand. All the pieces were in place, ready for a new game.

•••

At midnight, Mark ran of excuses to stay in his room.

He scraped the last of his cold beef soup from the can, put on his backpack, and stepped out into the hall. His breath showed on the air. A light sweat clung to his forehead. He was gripping his truck key so that its point stuck out of his fist, a self-defense trick he'd learned from his father and later shared with Alice, causing her to roll her eyes.

Alice. Thinking of her and not knowing where she was made him feel alone—truly alone—for the first time since he'd found Tommy in the bathtub. It made Longreave bigger and darker than it already was.

Mark crept down to the second floor. He could hear the quiet in the lobby below, actually *hear* it, a not-sound so loud it muted the creak of floorboards under his feet, the click of the lantern at his side, the rapid beating of his heart. When he blinked, he saw the elevator imprinted in his eyelids. And when he looked down the lobby staircase, he saw bronze doors hiding at the bottom, cracked open just wide enough for an arm to reach in.

Or *out*.

Mark swallowed his breath. The elevator wasn't really there, he knew that. Just like he knew he'd been wrong thinking there was nothing left to surprise him. There was always something to surprise you, as long as you were alive. Maybe even if you weren't. He knew that if he walked down the staircase, his lantern would reveal nothing at the bottom but floorboards, which would lead him to the front door, which would take him outside to stars and streetlights and his load of bricks.

He knew that.

But his legs didn't.

There's a line in everyone, like a shore, where fear ends and terror begins. A line that to cross is to drown. Mark's line was drawn at the top of the lobby staircase, and not a single step further. He turned back with a jerk.

Shut in his room, he began to pace. Tomorrow he'd buy an army of lanterns—one for every step across the lobby and a dozen extra to brighten his way through the cellar. He'd buy every lantern in every store in Massachusetts. Tomorrow.

Dressed in his pajamas (all four sets of them), Mark crawled into bed. He switched off the lantern. In the dark, his breath sounded strange. Dislocated. He couldn't tell if he was breathing—or someone else was.

He jolted up like a Jack-in-the-Box.

A Mark-in-the-Box.

A moment later he was crouched by the toilet, splashing cold bathwater on his face as the shadows from his lantern played on the walls around him. He needed to get his thoughts off boxes and things inside boxes. He needed to . . .

His brain tiptoed downstairs to the lobby.

To a pair of gleaming doors.

Mark launched out of the bathroom and then stopped, beard dripping, body trembling, by the foot of the bed. Had he ever been so scared in his life? Perhaps in the cellar when the lights had shut off, but that had been pure reaction, a blind groping panic. This fear was different. It had eyes.

It *breathed*.

What had changed?

Mark looked at the chessboard. It had no answer for him, but maybe, just maybe, it could provide a distraction. He sat down at the nightstand. His opponent could have made the first move after resetting the pieces—it was the winner's right—but had chosen instead to stay black. Fine by him. He'd play carefully this time. Give away nothing.

Mark started the game and left the room.

Ten. Nine. Eight. The hall flickered in the corner of his eye. *Seven. Six.* The dark was moving because the light was moving, not because there was something moving inside it. *Fivefourthreetwoone.* He unlocked the door. "Let's see how your Sicilian works now that I'm warmed up."

But his opponent hadn't played The Sicilian. At first it seemed his opponent hadn't moved at all, then he got closer and saw the tiny bump in black's first rank. e6. A quiet answer to e4, one space forward for Mark's two, no doubt meant to appear passive. Well, it wouldn't fool him. He grinned, his teeth chattering ever so slightly, and set his d-pawn next to his e-pawn. The center was his.

Until the next move when black contested it. "No *thank* you," Mark said, turning down the exchange by pushing his e-pawn up one more square. He was given one more chance to open up the game, but he chose not to. The last game had been open. He'd lost the last game. So once again he pushed his threatened man forward, and from then on things were locked tight, the board divided by a diagonal blockade of pawns.

For a while, Mark felt safe.

For a while.

Bit by bit, like bricks, the opposing pieces built walls around him. His queen got stuck behind a knight, which got stuck protecting her as black pawns advanced to the sixth rank, the seventh, lengthening the blockade and shrinking Mark's side of the board. He started lingering outside 401 between turns, unable to take his eyes off the dark. The restless dark. The dark that waited eagerly for him to show his back so it could slip forward and steal another inch of light from him.

After forty trips from the room and as many plays, when most games would be down to its final pieces or already finished, Mark had lost without losing a single point. He sat on the bed and searched for a move, *any* move, his hands clenched in his lap. All he could see was black. Everywhere, black. Black soldiers and black squares, darkening the board. He blinked and the blockade became a staircase. A *black* staircase, like the one to the lobby. At the end of it waited the black king, his scabbed face peeking from a box of pawns.

Mark heard a rasping breath in his head. Heard it *struggle*, as if pushing from a clogged mouth and throat. "I don't want to play anymore."

He tipped his king. Then the black king, so he couldn't see its face. Then the rest of the pieces, knocking them down with both hands. Fumbling, panting, Mark stuffed the pouches and rolled up the board and carried the bag to the dresser, where he shoved it in beside Alex's phone and the shoebox of postcards.

Longreave was still. Quiet.

No.

Not quite still.

Not quite quiet.

Something moved in the hall. Moved with a brittle *tap, tap, tap*. It clicked closer. Paused. Scuffled and sniffed outside the room. His nails cut into his palms. His stomach pressed down painfully on his bowels.

The hall went silent.

He moved to the door. The knob felt like a naked bone in his hand. He twisted it slowly . . . slowly . . . and leapt from the room, jabbing the lantern out ahead of him. Shadows squirmed away down the hall.

The empty hall.

Mark stood there, his knuckles white on the lantern, until his knees wobbled and he tipped against the door. It had closed behind him. He unlocked it. The door pushed open from the inside and an inhuman face leaned out of the dark. Tongue lolling. Fangs dripping. Claws sank into his chest. He fell back onto the floorboards, a scream caught in his throat. Then the tongue was slobbering across his cheeks, licking after his mouth as he twisted his head back and forth, laughing.

"Stop, oh Christ, stop, Mooney, stop, your breath smells like *death*."

Chapter Nineteen
October 19th

Chips of ice floated in a black pond overhead. Alice stood barefooted on the cement, her hands inside her sweatpants. The backyard was enclosed in brick. Weeds underlined the wall and sharp branches crowned it, stabbing up with tips that resembled wrought iron in the dark.

It had happened again.

Hands had dragged her out of a dream she could no longer remember, except that there'd been hands on her there too—and a vague face above, swimming in the blue glow of a bedside light—then her brother had melted into focus overhead, shouting out of a mouth that seemed disproportionately large, half the size of his skull and hollow and wet, and Alice had felt the scream she couldn't scream gushing out between her legs, hot as blood.

The picket gate whined.

"Not right now," Alice said, staring at the concrete. "I don't want to hear it's okay, I don't want you to tell me to come back to bed, I just want to be left alone."

"I left you alone all year. Isn't that enough?"

Alice looked up and saw her mother across the pool. Light from the kitchen window painted a quiet portrait of her, an old woman in a worn nightgown standing at the water's edge.

"I thought you were Alex."

"I know what you thought." Beverly had removed her sunglasses. Shadows had taken their place. "I know what you're thinking now."

"If you did, you wouldn't be talking to me."

"You're thinking you can't wait to leave back to Boston, that you wish you'd never come. Like you do every time. You're thinking you'd be happy if you never had to come again. But you don't *have* to come see me, I know that and you know that, too."

"Hmm."

"*Alice.*" Beverly's voice dropped. "Why didn't you tell me you have a husband?"

The woods gave a *shhhhhhhh*. Weeds stirred in the plant bed. Between Alice and her mother, the pool was still, not a single ripple on its surface. Green clouds of fungus hung in the ice-sealed water.

"What did you say?"

"I get you don't want me involved, but why couldn't you tell me? Why couldn't you tell me you found someone, so I knew you were happy? What would be the harm in that?"

"You know about Mark?"

Beverly nodded. Her head lost its groove and started turning side to side. "I know about him, *about* him, but I don't know anything."

"How?" Speaking felt like childbirth.

"I called Alex. After I got your message saying you were on your way, I was confused because it was so late, so sudden, so I called Alex. And Mark answered."

"What did you tell him?"

"About what?"

"About *you*, you old bitch. What did you tell him?"

"Nothing! *Nothing.*"

"Did you tell him your name? Your last name? Did you tell him about here? Did you tell him about *home*?"

"No! I didn't tell him anything. I knew you'd never come back if I did. I didn't say anything. I said—"

"*What*? What did you say?"

"I said I had the wrong number and hung up."

"That's it?"

"Then I unplugged the phone because I was scared and I didn't know what to do. That's it. I swear, that's it."

"If he calls back, you—"

"He won't. Not after this long."

"If he *does*—"

"I won't answer. I'll let it ring." Beverly lifted her arms, seemed unsure of what to do with them, and let them fall back to her sides. "But Alice, who is he? Is he nice? He sounded nice, but sometimes they sound nice and they aren't, sometimes underneath they're rotten. Is he, Alice? Is he nice?"

"Yes," Alice said quietly.

"Good, *good*." Her mother clasped her hands. "What else is he? Is he tall? Is he handsome? You were always so pretty, I knew if you ever just let yourself out there, you'd be snatched up, I *knew* it. How did he ask you? Are you going to, *oh Alice*, are you going to have kids?"

Alice looked down. Her reflection floated in the pool, trapped under ice.

"I'm sorry," Beverly said, shaking her head, almost flailing it. "I asked too much. You don't have to say any more than you want. Only what you want."

Alice licked her lips and felt her spit turn cold. "It's okay. I'll tell you."

Her mother stilled. "You will?"

"Yeah, sure. I'll tell you everything." She started slowly around the pool's curved edge. "He is tall. And very handsome. Dark eyes, dark beard. It's going a bit white now, just a bit . . . a dash of salt, you might say. But it makes him even handsomer, I think." Alice came to the halfway point. Beverly followed her path, mouth open, a smile trembling on her lips. "He asked me to marry him on the beach by his work, with a pair of beads he had fashioned into earrings. He didn't have the money for a ring, and I didn't care, and we did have a kid. Tommy."

Her mother made a small strange sound, a fluttery gasp. Tears ran from the shadows above her cheeks. *"Tommy."*

"Tommy died. He had a seizure in the bathtub and drowned. He would have been four the next day."

Beverly choked back a sob.

"And now Mark is gone," Alice said, still moving just as slow. "He's gone and probably out of his mind as well, and it's just me and Alex the way it was before, and you know what else, mother?" Alice drew up to her side. Whispered into her ear. "You know what else?"

Beverly covered her eyes.

"You were wrong. I wasn't thinking that I can't wait to go back. I was thinking that I never left, I only thought I did. I was thinking how much I am like you after all."

Alice kissed her mother softly on the cheek, then walked away from the pool.

Chapter Twenty
October 24th

When Mark got back to Longreave from his morning errands, he was ready. He whistled his way up the ice-crusted path, set down his grocery bag, and stopped at the door. Some large weight was pressing against it from the other side. As he turned the key, he tugged on the handle and jumped into the hotel, catching his dog's mammoth front paws in the air.

"Why, yes. Of *course* I'll take this dance."

Mooney, his jaws hanging in an all too human expression of shock, wobbled on his hind legs as Mark led him in a two-step shuffle along the receding edge of sunlight and back to the front door, stopping it an instant before it shut. He let Mooney down. The dog looked up with round, almost glowing eyes—eyes like full moons—before lowering his head and slumping off into the dark.

"No one likes a pouter." Mark gathered his things and headed across the lobby. The elevator appeared for one flickering moment, a dark spine running down between the doors. He paused at the staircase. "I guess I'll have to taste-test these biscuits myself."

From the couches came a lazy smack of lips.

"Fine. Have it your way."

Mark listened for the sound of paws all the way up to 401. He was still listening when he unlocked the door and Mooney landed against his chest. "Okay, okay," he gasped through lashing tongue and slobber. "You win. You win."

Apparently content, Mooney curled up on the bed as Mark unloaded the groceries. The two of them had been keeping a regular schedule around the hotel, building in the daytime and moving in fresh stock at night.

The wall was halfway done.

"She wasn't there again this morning," he said softly, turning over a jar of peanut butter in his hand. He hadn't meant to purchase it, but it had snuck home with him all the same. "Tomorrow it'll be a week. For both of them."

He glanced at the bathtub.

The last items in the bag were a stick lighter and package of incense, cinnamon scented. There'd been a strange smell in the room lately. Not always. Not now. It liked to seep in while he was in bed, between the thin hours of two and six in the morning. Sometimes the smell was so strong that upon waking he had the wild, sleepy notion he was floating inside a swimming pool.

• • •

Tommy might have had no room in his stomach, but the same wasn't true for Mooney. The mutt ate as if he had no stomach at all, only a hole. A hole that *actually* went all the way to China, unlike the one he and Mark had dug in the dirt lot when they were pups. He scarfed his biscuits straight from the bag.

Then he ate the bag.

His mere presence woke up the appetite in Mark, who put away three overloaded sandwiches, gorging himself so thoroughly he had to get out of bed before he gave in to a nap. Leaving the room, Mooney loped ahead and snacked on the beads inside the clay pot. They sucked noisily down his throat, like ball bearings into an empty vacuum cleaner. Mark got down beside him.

"Not those, okay? Anything but those."

Mooney gave a clinking cough.

In the cellar he became a four-legged blur, flitting in and out of the lantern's glow. It was as if the dark didn't exist for him anymore, as if the word had lost its meaning. Mark wondered if brightness hurt his eyes now, the way it did for some nocturnal creatures, or if death had undone any distinction between light and dark.

The water had frozen over in the buckets. Mark broke the ice and began mixing mortar, his breaths white on the air, his hands gloved to keep from cracking in the cold. Occasionally he paused to throw a rock. It didn't matter if the rock was fist sized or dime sized, or if he winged it so hard the echoes of it skipping sounded miles away. Mooney found it. Mooney always found it (and frequently ate it, too). After the wheelbarrow went dry, they took a trip to 303's bathroom. By the time Mark finished refilling the buckets, his knees were throbbing from kneeling on the tile. The empty tub stared up at him. His father said kids forgave their parents for almost anything, but what if he'd been wrong? His father had been wrong plenty in life, so why not *now*?

A warm snout nuzzled his cheek.

"You're right. There's nothing I can do." He put a hand on Mooney's neck. He could feel lumps there, fatty little eggs nesting under the hide, waiting to hatch. "Nothing I can do."

As work on the wall dragged, Mooney began to trot off for long periods of time. Perhaps he was finding more to eat, or perhaps he was booby-trapping the cellar with steamy ghost-dog shits. If shitting was something he even did. Eventually he returned for good and flopped onto a pile of rubble, dusting his entire right flank.

"You need a bath, boy." Mark caught a whiff of himself through his many layers, and grimaced. "You're not alone." On the way back, Mooney hung close, his shaggy ears pressed flat to his head and his ink-dipped tail pointed straight at the ground. "Don't worry," Mark said lightly, "I'm not going to make you take a bath. Don't have enough water as is." But he was thinking of the lumps clustered around Mooney's throat, like a collar made of cancer. Thinking of the nook below the porch and the hot, heavy air on the day he'd crawled down there and found him, swollen and covered in stickers, death's first lesson.

Mark laid his hand on Mooney's thick head, wondering if it was possible to experience a good thing—any good thing—and not also think about its end.

•••

There was a soft pile waiting on the ramp, but it had not come from inside Mooney. Jaws locked open in a scream, red eyes bulging from its skull, the rat lay curled with its tail between stubby hind legs.

Except for that face, those *eyes*, it might have been sleeping.

"Was this you?" Mark looked down at the head glued to his thigh. Mooney stared up at him mournfully. "Don't play innocent with me, pal. I remember the way you used to chase squirrels, and it wasn't to make friends. So, what was it? The rocks didn't run fast enough for you? You decide to find some real sport?"

Mooney's sagging black jowls seemed to frown.

Kneeling, Mark combed his fingers through the rat's stiff fur. The body was still warm. It had no teeth holes, no wounds of any kind. He pulled his hand back shakily, half expecting the corpse to twist its neck and sink fangs into him. As he rose, something moist glimmered between the ramp's aluminum plates.

A splinter from the old staircase.

A *thick* splinter.

It was six inches long and soaked red from base to point. Mark looked at the rat, at the pink tail tucked between its hind legs, and an icicle slid into his guts. Crouching once more, he pinched the tail and pulled it back. Blood dribbled from the rat's anus. Mark jerked to his feet and reached for Mooney, needing to touch him, feel him.

Mooney wasn't there.

Mooney was at the bottom of the ramp, his head raised, his body stiff. Beyond him the lantern light melted.

"Do you see something?" said Mark. "Is someone there?"

A draft stirred deep in the cellar. The dark let out a cold, dying breath against his face. He backed toward the lobby. "Come on."

•••

Mark's sleep was short and infected by bad dreams. Dreams where dead things bled in the dark. Dreams where the bricks he reached for turned soft and warm and twitching in his hand and bit him with needle teeth. The last dream ended as Tommy rose from the bathtub in a dripping cowboy outfit and pulled the trigger on a revolver, shooting Mark in the chest.

He sat up in bed, sweat slimed and close to panic.

He was dirty.

Dirty.

By the tub in 307, he began to strip. His reflection floated on the mirror: beard in grubby shags, forehead spotted with mortar, neck shining as though rubbed in massage oil. Behind him Mooney panted like a failing heater, if that heater had been loaded with old eggs. The air pruned Mark's penis as he removed his boxers, and he felt a nip of confusion at where he was and what he was doing. Then he saw his toiletries on the sink and his tie on the doorknob. Alice. He was making himself clean for Alice, because she was coming home. He got down on his knees and, without pausing, dunked his head into the water. But there was no water.

That was a lie.

A mirage.

The tub was filled with fire. Liquid fire. His nerves lit up like Christmas lights before blinking off all together, leaving him thoughtless and numb, an observer rather than a participant. From a window deep in his mind, Mark watched himself shampoo his scalp, rinse it off, and crawl into the tub. Bliss met him there. Warm waves smoothing out beneath clear skies, the whole world stretching blue and unwrinkled toward a far off horizon . . .

Something furry hung over him. A massive, rotten worm felt around the inside of his mouth.

He gagged.

Mooney pulled his head back, tongue dangling, and stared down at him inquisitively. *Where . . . what?* Mark became aware of the lantern's heat against his face, of the clothes lying around and under him on the tile. Finger by finger, his hands woke up. He walked them along the floor, collecting his clothes and dragging them over his naked body. He began to shiver. The shivering got worse until his teeth were chattering and his legs were kicking in place, the way a dog's legs do when it dreams of running.

When the tremors subsided, he could sit.

But not stand.

Not yet.

Mark tugged his clean outfit off the toilet and got dressed, moving one piece of himself at a time. A foot. A knee. The left cheek of his butt. By the time he finished, his joints felt like joints again, not rusted ball bearings. He peered into the tub. A skin of grime coated the water. *How long was I in there? One minute? Five? Ten? How close did I come to—*

He pictured Alice finding him inside the tub, finding him like he found their son. He laughed. Then his laughter broke apart, and he sobbed for her. For what he'd almost done to her.

Would I have come back, like the chess pieces? Back to Longreave?

Mooney began to slop at the bathwater, the sound of which brought to mind a certain passionate kiss. That was all the motivation Mark needed. He got to his feet, grabbed his toothbrush, and attacked his mouth. Next he set about grooming, whereupon he made a discovery—one he tried to ignore, and then reason around, and was forced finally to admit. There *was* gray in his beard, and no, the gray was *not* dust or mortar. He snipped away the bad hairs, watching Mooney's head bob in the mirror.

Slurp, pant, slurp, slurp, pant, slurp . . .

Trimming around his ears, he thought of Alice's crude new look and his horrified first reaction to it. How must she have felt when Longreave's door opened and he appeared in the dark lobby, like some caveman? Stunned? *Horrified?*

Perhaps they were both a little crude at their roots.

And perhaps, if they cut down low enough, they'd find their roots were tangled.

His hair combed, Mark put on his tie. The sound of drinking deepened to a full-gulleted *glug-glug-glug* behind him.

"Okay, boy. Time to cut you off."

Mooney's head had disappeared below the lip of the tub. His tail whipped like a shaggy, sporadic fan.

"Hey. Talking to you."

There was no panting, only those glugs. Those deep glugs. Mark moved closer. He saw neck and more neck and finally dark, thrumming bathwater.

Mooney's head was completely submerged.

A pair of matted ears surfaced. Mark began to tingle all over, inside and out. It felt like a chill except it wasn't cold, it was the opposite, a hot shiver through his body.

Clenched onto the ears were two tiny hands.

Mooney lifted his head and Tommy rose with him, face besieged by licks, mouth gushing water and laughter.

Mark smiled. Then he reached up to his throat and touched his tie, and his smile faded a little.

But only a little.

It wasn't as if Alice were coming home today, anyway.

•••

Alice sat in the shower until the water was cold, then dressed back into her dirty clothes and walked downstairs to open Geoff's gifts. She carried the easels into the office and attached her paintings to them, working counterclockwise around the room to the ocean. That one she lingered in front of for some time. Drying had darkened the oil. The lips of the waves were cracked, as if parched.

Alex was hunched over the phone in the kitchen. "I *told* you. My cell broke. That's why I called you from the house before we left. That's why I'm calling you from the house now."

Her brush was crusty. She took it to the sink and held it under the tap.

"I had no idea you emailed me until this morning. We didn't have internet—"

Water ran pink down the drain.

"—no, I don't know what kind of place doesn't have internet these days. All I know is there's none at our aunt's. Yes, there was a service, why?" A pause. A laugh. "Of course I didn't save the pamphlet. It wasn't a fucking play. It was a funeral."

Alice walked to her painting, dripping brush in hand. The bristles weren't all the way clean, but that was okay. Neither was she.

Her brother's voice lowered. "I'm sorry. It's been a stressful week. I know, I know it's asking a lot." He let out a breath. "Okay. Yeah. Okay. I'll be by later."

The phone clicked.

"They let me go."

Alice dried the brush, looking through the sliding glass door to the backyard. Dead leaves littered the lawn.

"Aren't you going to say anything?"

She laid down fresh waxpaper, opened a jar of linseed oil and a jar of pigment, and mixed the two on the palette.

"Alice."

"It doesn't matter."

"What do you mean it doesn't matter?"

"I mean it doesn't matter."

"I have bills. An *apartment*."

"You can stay here. You already are, anyway."

"And what about you?"

She frowned at the consistency of the paint. "I'll figure something out."

Alex swatted the counter and then left the kitchen. Outside the *other* kitchen, Longreave's salt-scabbed wall blocked the backyard, but it wasn't what really belonged there.

It was only a placeholder.

Half an hour later the wall was gone. In its place shimmered a pool, a hint of drowned brick swimming in the depths. She walked to the counter and picked up the phone. It rang twice.

"Alice. I hope my mail found you well."

"I've been thinking."

"Have you?"

"I'd like to take you up on your offer." She heard herself telling Mark there was nothing to finish, it was already done. "Both of them."

• • •

It was noon when the smell of chlorine seeped into the room, but with the drapes pulled it might have been midnight. Mark lay asleep in bed, a boy on his right arm and a dog between his legs. The fumes breathed in under the door, up from the drain in the bathtub, down from the faucet in the sink. The cracks in the walls—and there were many cracks in Longreave's walls—hissed oh so softly, like a nest of dozing snakes.

Mooney lifted his head. He did not smell the gas. He could not smell. It was a feeling around him, a thickening in the air. It made the lumps in his neck itch.

The doorknob twisted.

Mooney's growl started low and grew until it shook the bed. In the dark dreamless place that was not quite sleep where Tommy drifted, the growl spread like a ripple across black water.

The knob twisted back.

Chapter Twenty-One
October 26th

"That's it," Mark said as Tommy hoisted the brick up over his head with tight-lipped concentration. "That's it . . ."

Tommy's eyes took on a panicky sheen. He swayed back toward the edge of the stepstool.

Mark looped an arm around him. "Got you, kiddo."

His son laughed—a sound like someone gargling mouthwash. "That was close."

"Sure was." Beyond the lanterns, Mooney appeared for an instant. He'd been acting strange all evening, circling their position, swimming in and out of the dark. "Try again?"

"Don't let go."

Mark told the lie every father does at least once. "I won't."

"Promise?"

"Promise."

Tommy swallowed. From his shoulders hung the sodden cowboy blanket, its corners tied at his neck with a bit of thread. He'd been leaking into the fabric for two days straight and growing lighter all the while, losing a little of the curve in his belly, gaining an extra degree of definition in his ribs. But still he persisted. Two draining days, and still he was *here*. He lifted the brick, wobbled, and planted it neatly on the wall.

Mortar dribbled.

His mouth dribbled.

"I did it." He turned. "Did I do it?"

"Yes. And by yourself."

Tommy looked down at his waist. He looked long and hard, as if expecting Mark's arms to materialize around him. Then he exploded into jumps and shouts, his feet making landed-fish sounds on the stool, which was suddenly and enthusiastically shaking.

"Easy, kiddo, *easy*," Mark said, planting a steadying foot on the ground.

Tommy's voice died down. "Did it . . . did it . . ."

"You did." Mark took the back of his son's neck. "You did, and that's great. That's wonderful. Because if you don't put down one, you'll never put down two. No one ever finishes what they don't start. But it's finishing that matters. It's what you've built in the end that matters. You understand?"

"I think so, maybe."

"Then what do you say?"

Tommy lifted his head, stressing the line of his jaw. He looked every bit the cowboy that moment, there on the stool with his shoulders square and his face oiled tan in the lantern light. "Give me another brick."

•••

Tommy didn't tire like a four-year old, but he did get bored like one. After half an hour of hard work, Mark decided to show mercy. "All right, kiddo. You can play now." He swung him down to the ground.

Tommy held up his arms. "Again."

"No way. You're too heavy." Except that wasn't true. He was too light . . . and something else, something worse. His bones had felt wrong. *Spongy* wasn't quite the right word to describe them, but Mark had a feeling that soon it would be.

"But—"

"I've got a better idea." Mark set a piece of rubble in Tommy's hand. "Throw this."

"Why?"

"Just throw it."

"Where?"

"Anywhere."

Mooney had stopped acting like a shark and was watching them. Watching the rock. There was a look in his eyes, eager and somehow regretful. It was the look of a recovering alcoholic staring down into a beer. *I shouldn't,* it said, *I really, really shouldn't.*

Tommy let the rock fly.

It hardly landed before Mooney came trotting back with it, but Tommy was delighted all the same. Death changed some things, but not all of them. No, not all. He ran to meet Mooney, sliding on his knees and leaving a skid mark of flesh on the concrete. A moment later the rock was off again, and the game was on.

It was a good game, too.

While it lasted.

•••

"Mooney's missing."

"Why do you say that?"

"Because he's missing."

"Give him a minute." Mark scraped at the mortar, and sniffed. The wheelbarrow had a funny smell, almost like a fuel pump. It made him uneasy and he couldn't say why. "He'll come back."

But Mooney didn't. Not after a minute, or five minutes, or ten.

Mark turned away from the wall, now forty courses high. His palms were clammy inside his gloves. He kept thinking over his son's last toss. It had been a great one, a real zinger way out into the cellar, and so what if the rock only bounced twice? So what if he'd heard the rock skip and skip, still moving fast, and then . . .

Nothing.

Nothing at all.

"*Moooooooneeeeeeeeeyyyyy,*" Tommy called from the furthes lantern, the tail of his cowboy blanket glowing like a lampshad his silhouette thrown back long and bat-shaped behind him. *"Mooooooooneeeeyyyyyy."*

"Okay," Mark whispered to himself. "Okay."

He lit his cracked lantern, then picked up his crowbar. It felt like a large, crude key in his grip. Holding it unlocked a black box inside his heart, and for one trembling moment his fear was so solid he could feel its shadow over him. He walked to Tommy, who spoke without looking away from the dark. "Mooney wouldn't run away."

"No. He wouldn't."

"What if he's lost?"

"Then we'll find him." Mark hooked the crowbar on his belt. "Or he'll find us first."

"What if he doesn't?"

"He will."

There was pain in Tommy's eyes. "How do you know?"

"It's his nature. Dogs know their way home."

Boys, too.

Mark took his son's hand, and together they went out into the nightscape of the cellar.

• • •

For a long, cold time they wandered and shouted Mooney's name, listening to shrunken voices call back to them from the dark. Finally, Mark thought to ask, "Tommy, what can you see?"

"Huh?"

"What's the closest thing to you?"

"You."

"esides me."

" were somewhere. That Mark knew, but not much more.

ht corner where he worked, his north star, had vanished.

of its glow remained. Which meant they'd either passed

ithout noticing and it was standing between them and

the light, or—a possibility he did not want to consider—every lantern in the ring had shut off.

Every single one.

"I see . . ." Tommy heaved a sigh. "I don't get it. What's this got to do with finding Mooney?"

"Think of it like a game. One we can play while we search."

"Like I Spy?"

"Yeah. I Spy. You start."

Shadows twisted from Mark's lantern like threads in a living cobweb. He watched his son look side to side and tried not to think of spiders, or things like spiders, creeping toward them through the dark.

"I spy . . . with my little eye . . . something *big*."

"The boiler?"

"What's the boiler?"

Mark almost said, *Where I found you last time.* "Well, it's big and metal and it's got pipes all around it. You know pipes, don't you? They're what water goes through. And it has a staircase, and a hatch—a hole on top."

"No, not that. It's bigger. A lot bigger."

Mark felt a little chill. There was nothing in the cellar bigger than the boiler. Nothing, at least, that had been there in the light. He swallowed. "Hint?"

"It's red."

He heard red and saw blood, saw something huge and covered in blood, and his throat closed tight as a fist. Then it loosened and he gave a shaky laugh. "The wall."

Tommy frowned. "That was too easy. Your turn."

"Okay," Mark said, pretending to search. There were no walls in his world, only smooth darkness all around, so he'd proved his theory. Tommy could see. Better than him, if not completely. And he'd learned something else, perhaps just as important. Tommy thought Mark could see too, and why shouldn't he? What little boy had ever assumed himself capable of something his father was not? It was one of the sacred illusions of childhood, faith in the parent, and the hardest to kill. But it could be killed, oh yes, and once it was dead, it never came back.

"You're taking too long."

"Give me a second." He started to move, steering in the direction that Tommy had 'spied' the wall. For ten steps there was nothing and then, like a trumpet blast to his eyes, there were bricks. Bright, scarlet bricks. But still the ring of lanterns was nowhere to be seen.

"Daddy?"

What stood past this wall? Land? Or ocean? He hoped—prayed—it was the former. Because if they were facing the Atlantic right now, then they were standing in line with his workstation, and it really had gone black. Mark couldn't believe that. Not when he'd just re-fueled the lanterns the other night.

That smell in the mortar. That funny, petroleum smell . . .

"Daddy."

"Okay, okay. I've got it." *Let this work. Please.* "I spy, with my little eye, something shiny."

Tommy gave the dark a quick scan. "The thing you said. The Boil Her."

Well, the boiler *was* shiny. But the boiler would be in view no matter what side of the cellar they were on, so it was useless as a landmark. "Try again, kiddo. I'll give you a hint. It's long."

Tommy scanned again, slower.

"It's shiny and long and sloped," Mark said gently, screaming inside.

"What's 'sloped?'"

"Sloped is like a hill." He spread his arms at an angle. "You can walk on it."

"The ramp?"

"*Yes!*" Mark swallowed, dizzy with relief. "Yes. That's it. You did it, kiddo. You're on fire today." They were by the entrance to the lobby, which meant the lanterns were out of sight but still burning, and that was a beautiful thing, a *wondrous* thing.

Tommy was staring at him strangely. "But the ramp isn't there."

"What do you mean it isn't there?"

"It was there when *I* spied, but then we walked over here, and now you can't see it anymore because it's behind the Boil Her. You can't spy what's already gone, Daddy. That's against the rules, and I don't get why we're playing this stupid game anyway when Mooney is still missing. " Tommy cupped his mouth and walked into the dark. Soon there was nothing to chase but a voice howling, "*Mooooooooooneeeeeeey. Mooooooooooneeeeeeey.*"

Mark chased him down, breathless. He glanced back in search of the wall, but it was lost. Like the ramp, like Mooney. Like them.

"I forgot how to play, I'm sorry. One more?"

"No."

"One more, and we'll go on looking for the big guy."

Silence. Pursed lips.

"I spy with my little eye the closest way out of the cellar."

Tommy pointed. "The stairs."

Mark took his son's hand again, tight this time, and hurried that direction. In his mind he saw the last rock Mooney had run off to chase. Saw, instead of heard. It skipped once, twice, and then something in the dark reached out and grabbed it.

• • •

Faster and faster, dragging Tommy along behind him, and there it was at last, ten feet ahead:

The annex staircase.

"*Stop!*"

Tommy's knees locked and he was yanked off the ground by one arm. Mark heard a sound, both little and very loud, a pellet-gun *pop* that rang in his ears like an explosion from Dirty Harry's magnum. He wheeled around to see his son crash face-first on the concrete, the cowboy blanket caped out behind him.

"*OhGod.* I'm sorry, I'm sorry."

"You were about to run right into it!"

"Into—into what?"Mark hardly himself speak. He was staring at the funny way Tommy's left arm dangled.

"The puddle!"

Mark turned his head toward the staircase. The ground beneath it was dry. "What puddle?"

"The *puddle*." Tommy's arm flopped as he rose, dragging the knuckles of his hand across the concrete. His shoulder was sunken, the skin there loose and pouchy. A hysterical note entered his voice. "It's right there. Don't you see it?"

Mark nodded quickly. "Of course, yes, of course. The puddle. What about the puddle?"

"We were about to run into it." One front tooth wobbled as he spoke. "It's deep, Daddy, it's so deep I can't see the bottom, and you were about to drag me into it. Why would you drag me into it?"

Mark watched his son's mouth move and remembered how it had felt moving against his palm, underwater. "I didn't mean—"

"*Why?*"

"I didn't mean to scare you. Or hurt you. I—"

The dark trembled behind Tommy and Mark caught himself wondering what might be moving inside it, creeping closer in a shuffle or crawl.

"—I'll carry you." Mark picked him up by the armpits and felt nothing where the left shoulder should have been, only boneless skin, stretching around the blade of his hand like a wet, deflated balloon.

"No! We'll sink!" Tommy squirmed up Mark's body.

"No we won't. Dad's too big to sink." He started for the staircase, his loafers quiet on the dusted concrete, his son tensed against him.

"Is it cold?" Tommy whispered.

"Very."

Mark glanced back from the top step, half expecting to see footprints shining on the ground where he'd walked. But there were none.

"Daddy."

"What?"

"Look."

Down the corridor of the annex's first floor, as far as the light touched, lay a different kind of trail. His heart plunged like an elevator down an empty shaft. The trail was made of hairs. Brown and black hairs.

Mooney hairs.

•••

"I can walk now."

"Are you sure?" Mark said, uncertain. There was a movie playing in his head. In it Mooney was being dragged down the hall by his tail, his eyes closed into white slits, his tongue trailing from his mouth.

"The puddles aren't as deep here."

Puddles. Plural. How many puddles are there in Tommy's Longreave? Mark set him down. "Let me know if one looks too big for you, okay?"

"Okay." Tommy picked up a hair, gave it a shake as if to dry it off, then took a step and picked up another. "He must have been running *really* fast."

Mark un-holstered his crowbar. As they reached the first turn, he tightened his grip and jumped around the corner. The lantern swung, and for an instant it was all too familiar: the cold walls (now colder) seeming to come alive, the trail (now fur instead of footprints) leading down the squirming passageway.

Like reliving a dream and discovering it had become a nightmare.

More hairs waited on the steps in the stairwell. A new film reel began to whir on the projector: Mooney, black snout and dripping mouth, skull thumping and thumping up to the second floor . . .

Where Mark stopped.

Down the hall the dark breathed in and out, in and out. He glanced behind him, and the dark was there too, blocking off the bottom of the stairwell. It almost made him miss the wide-open of the cellar.

Almost.

Tommy started down the hall, gathering up the hairs camouflaged in the carpet with his one working hand. He stopped at 2C. "Mooney's in there."

"How do you know?"

Tommy smiled. "I can hear him."

Mark remembered standing outside this same room with David, listening to the soft drip of water through the door. He shook his head. "I can't—"

And then he heard it.

Panting.

Low, *raspy* panting.

• • •

The panting stopped.

But *first* it drew away from the door, deeper into the room, like a cuckoo bird sliding back into its hole.

"Silly dog. What's he doing hiding in there?"

I don't think that's Mooney, Mark was about to say when Tommy dropped his collection of hairs and reached for the knob. Panic froze him. Relief thawed him out again. "We can't get in, kiddo. It's locked."

"No, it isn't."

The door clicked open, and as the dark inside reared back from the lantern light, something came at them across the carpet. Came at them in a low, rustling crawl. Mark lifted the crowbar and cracked it against the frame, bringing a ghostly dusting of plaster down on their heads.

The plastic sheeting settled on the floor.

"Nothing is locked in Longreave," Tommy said lightly, before walking into the room. "Mooney! Mooney!"

Mark shouldered in after him. The vague fluttering over the window became a curtain, and the crouched thing by the closet turned into a chair. He stared at the bed. Like the floor, it had been wrapped for renovation.

It wasn't anymore.

The plastic on the covers was torn and twisted, as though a struggle had taken place there. Tommy kneeled. "Mooney?" A hand covered his face and dragged him under the bed, screaming a muffled scream. Mark blinked the vision away and Tommy was already back on his feet, walking to the closet, reaching for the button-shaped doorknobs. "Maybe he's in here."

Mark choked on his heart. "Don't!"

Tommy froze.

"Come to me."

"Why?"

"*Now.*"

Tommy slunk over and Mark grabbed his good arm, pulled him close. "He's not here. Mooney's not here."

"How do you know?"

"I just know."

"But—"

"We're going back to our room and that's the end of it. That's it."

But when Mark tried to turn, he couldn't. He stared at the closet, at the crack running down between the doors like a thread of fine black silk. There was nothing in there. Nothing grinning at him from the dark.

Then prove it.

"Wait here."

Scraps of plastic stuck to his loafers as he inched toward the closet. He wasn't afraid anymore. His fear was too big for him, a whale swimming inside a pool. He hooked the crowbar between the doors, then eased them open.

The closet was empty.

Except . . .

"Daddy?"

That smell. It hung faintly in the boxed air, an extra ingredient in the blend of dust and mildew. Mark thought of the mortar. There'd been an extra ingredient in it too, hadn't there? Kerosene. Drained from the lanterns and poured into the water buckets. A little in each. Just enough so he wouldn't notice. *This* wasn't kerosene, though its aroma was similar, though the two words almost rhymed.

Breathing in the smell of chlorine, Mark let his gaze slide down to the closet floor.

"Daddy?"

I spy, with my little . . .

"Daddy, what's in there?"

The eyeball stared up at him, so bright it almost glowed. A long, pink root clung to it like a tail.

"Nothing." Mark shut the doors. "Just like I said."

But as he looked at Tommy, he saw the rat from the ramp. The rat that had died slowly and torturously on the inside, skewered by a stick that had started at its hindquarters and must have come close to reaching its mouth.

• • •

They walked in silence until they rounded the abandoned elevator shaft, at which point Tommy made a sound like someone sucking liquid through a punctured straw. The foyer was underwater. At least to him it was. To Mark it was the same as always, except now he wondered if there was a different Longreave for Mooney as well, and for his father, and for the *other* guest wandering the halls with them. And, if Longreave in the afterlife became a reflection of who you were or how you died, what might the hotel be like for someone whose way of hello was a bloody gift in the dark?

Mark carried his son across the pool that wasn't there. He didn't let go of him at the other side. He didn't want to ever let go of him again.

But he did, at the fourth floor.

He was thinking of chess pieces, of *black* chess pieces that moved in the shadows and laid hidden traps, when he turned down the hall to 401.When he heard something crawling up the steps behind them.

Only *crawling* was too pretty a word.

The thing in the stairwell was dragging itself, limb by limb, toward the light and panting as it came, choking, struggling for every terrible breath.

"Go to the room." Mark set Tommy down. "*Run.*"

The breaths grew and grew and then broke apart into what sounded like sobs—or laughter. An arm pawed onto the landing below. An arm with no flesh, no hand. It was bone wrapped in yellow guitar strings of tendon and richer, heart-red ropes of muscle, and it was dripping. Blood steamed on the floorboards. Vapors hissed through the air, twisting and pink and reeking of chlorine.

Mark heard himself scream. He covered his mouth, but the scream continued higher. Just as he realized it wasn't coming from him, it was coming from down the hall, the stump pulled back out of sight.

Outside 401, Tommy lay pinned on the floor.

Mooney sat on top of him, endeavoring to lick the skin off his face.

• • •

Tommy's bad arm swung like a stuffed sock as he rose. He was smiling. "I'm a cowboy, and Mooney's a pirate."

"A pirate?"

Tommy covered his right eye. "Argh."

Inside 401, on the bed, the outline of a dog bobbed its head slowly, almost lovingly, over the covers. As Mark approached, he thought of the oil machines always there in the background of old westerns, those big metal giants whose parts rose and fell endlessly as their tongues licked deep into the earth."Hey, boy. What you got there?"

Mooney lifted one pale eye.

One was all he had.

Between his paws lay a skeletal hand, its fingers curled into claws.

It stretched longer than the hallway at home in Vermont, longer than any hallway she'd ever known. Its walls and floor and ceiling, all pink and shining and spotted in red mold, started at the corners of the canvas and closed together as the perspective shrunk, twisting ever so slightly clockwise until they reached the center of the page, where an upside-down door opened into a rightside-up bathroom. The bathroom was as tiny as a thumbprint, and a ruddy steam congealed the air inside, so she couldn't be sure. But, leaning in, she thought she could spot someone standing there, either dressed in the steam or made of it, someone who had a head but no face. She drew closer. Closer.

"I wonder if I can say hello without startling you."

She spun on her heels.

A white set of teeth smiled in the entryway. "I suppose not."

Alice lowered her brush and smeared red across her thigh. "Shit. *Shit.*"

Geoff filled in around his smile, like the cat in Wonderland. The front door was closed behind him. Locked too, by the look of the deadbolt.

"How long were you—"

"Watching you?" He moved into the living room, his shoes as quiet as slippers. "Only a moment, from inside. *Out*side, however

. . . you have a beautiful window, Alice. I couldn't resist the chance to observe an artist in her natural habitat."

"The psych wards should have open houses more often." She crossed her arms over her tank top, which had torn to show an extra inch of cleavage. Not that she had much cleavage to worry about.

Again, that smile. Geoff produced a neatly folded cloth from his back pocket.

"Of course you would own a handkerchief. What is it? Prada?"

"Payless." He gave it a wag. "Call me unsophisticated, but I don't believe in spending money on anything used to wipe your nose."

Alice mopped off her thigh, taking the chance to breathe. "You must think I'm a total mess. I mean, a real fucking specimen."

"A little filth adds flavor," he said as she handed back the dirtied handkerchief.

"I was planning on cleaning up, you know. I got an outfit ready upstairs this morning so I wouldn't be scrambling to find something right before you got here. So you wouldn't see me like, well, *this*." She waved at her barefooted, denim-shorted, wife-beaten self.

"I'll take you as you are."

She licked her lips. They were suddenly dry. "And where is that you're planning on taking me?"

"I know a little place."

A man like him probably had a collection of bars to match his women. "Would this place be close to your place?"

Geoff stroked his jaw, and its silver dusting of stubble whispered under his hand. "Very."

• • •

He paid for the painting in cash, twenty green bills that burned in her pocket until she thought her leg would catch fire. When he stepped out, she stuffed the money into the desk.

She tried not to look at the ocean on the floor.

She tried.

Geoff returned a minute later, but Alice didn't hear. She was too busy watching the wordless blue language of the waves. They had a message for her, written like Braille in the bumps on their lips, a message waiting for her to deliver it from the depths.

Her hands tightened. "It's *finished*."

"Pardon me?"

She saw Geoff standing behind her. "Sorry. Nothing."

He lifted a frame carved of some fine wood. "I hope this is the right size. I had only my memory as reference."

That was modesty talking. Geoff had an eye for art. Artists, too.

The ocean lost something once framed. It seemed quieter, tamer, a lion in a cage. Alice looked the other way as Geoff carried it from the house. She put on her coat to follow him.

There was a laugh.

Her brother sat in the hall upstairs. He looked a bit like something that had been put in a cage himself, his legs dangling through the railing, his face squeezed between the posts. "Go earn that paycheck, sis."

Alice showed him her middle finger.

She left.

•••

Her painting went in the back and she went in the front, onto a seat as dark as the smell of Geoff's cologne. The leather announced every move she made with a sigh. She shifted her butt, *ahhhh*. She crossed her legs, *ooohh*. Finally she sat still, fingers laced in her lap, the seat sweating underneath her.

They talked about nothing she could remember as soon as the subject changed. She watched him, watched his lips. Wondered what it would be like to draw those lips with charcoal and oil, to draw those lips down her body, between her breasts and across her naval. There was a lump in her stomach. It kicked like a baby when he looked at her, and sometimes when he didn't. Sometimes it rolled over and she felt so swollen, so sick, she had to fight not to open the window and shove her face into the cold wind.

As the conversation waned, Geoff's hand strayed to her knee. To her thigh. Alice pinched her legs and trapped it there, whether to keep it from leaving or prevent it from venturing further, she didn't know.

She saw Longreave in the shadows that the clouds dragged over the road.

She closed her eyes.

The sound of the motor was a wave under the hood, a wave that crashed and crashed but never broke and carried her away on its swell.

•••

Dusk bled roses over Boston.

Alice hugged herself at the bay window of Geoff's fourth-story apartment while he disappeared somewhere with her painting. He reemerged empty handed and glided into the tiled kitchen. "Are you cold?"

"A little." The space beneath the high ceiling swallowed her voice.

"There's a vent to your side, by the couch." He opened a cupboard. "Slide over there."

She took a step left and felt hot air thrum her shins. The statue of a man statue stared down at her with smooth blank eyes. Its face had not been given a mouth.

"Better?"

"Yes," she lied, looking away from the statue with a shiver. "I used to love the South End when I lived in the city. We would come here for shows, me and my brother."

Ice clinked. "You lived in the city?"

"Down on Ashford Street. Trashford, to the college kids. My first night I saw a girl frenching a dog on the sidewalk. Where's this place you're taking me?" She turned and jumped. Geoff was standing right behind her.

"I startled you again." A slice of white showed between his lips.

"No. I mean, a bit. I was distracted." She saw the lowballs in his hands, one large ice cube apiece.

"One to keep us warm."

"Okay." She swirled the drink. The ice cube rattled inside the glass, and she thought of the ocean in the other room. The ocean she'd sold, and the wooden frame that contained its storm. "Scotch?"

"Brandy." He sat.

"How many brandies have you served here, I wonder?"

"I haven't had any Brandys over, I'm afraid." His smirk warmed into the real thing, and he gestured next to him. "Please, Alice, sit."

The couch might have been cut from the same cow as the seats in his car. Its cushions sighed deeply as she sank into them, and she had the brief, almost funny idea that if she looked down between her legs, instead of leather she would see the pink of the corridor she'd painted—the pink of a large, moist tongue. The idea was so almost funny she thought she'd never laugh again. She took a big swallow of brandy. "How long have you stayed here?"

"A few years." Geoff placed his drink on the fogged coffee table beside him. An identical table sat beside her. A twin. She wondered what Alex was doing, if he was already tucked in down in the guestroom. He'd slept there the last couple nights. The bed upstairs was no longer safe. No bed was, if she was in it.

"Do you like this place?"

"As well as any. And you?"

"Me?" Alice scanned the apartment and was greeted everywhere by shining surfaces, sleek surfaces, surfaces polished well enough to hold a reflection. She remembered his response to her art. "I don't love it."

He gave a soft, dignified clap. "Ah, I see. Well, I suppose I must allow you your moment of revenge after I criticized your interior design so harshly."

"I *suppose* so."

"I'm curious, though." He swept his arm. "What particular aesthetic doesn't agree with you? Is the ceiling too stable? Are the walls too dry?"

"Ha ha." She rolled her eyes. "It feels, I don't know, a bit sterile."

"Are you calling my place an old maid?"

"Of course not." She took a quick drink. "It's more of an empty cock than a barren womb."

"So *vulgar*." Geoff laid a hand on his breast. "Why do I get the feeling you're trying to hurt me?"

"Perhaps you're too sensitive."

He stared at her, the hand that he'd set over his heart now resting lightly on his belt buckle. Alice tipped the glass to her mouth, and the ice cube gave her a cold kiss. She'd finished her drink. Somehow.

"May I pour you another?"

"Why not?"

She turned her head to the window as he went into the kitchen. A lazy sprinkle of lights glimmered over the park across the street. Looking at them, she felt a spike of heat under her sternum as her love for Boston leapt up inside her like a lantern flame. Things had not necessarily been good here, but she'd been young, and still capable of finding pleasure in running for the sake of running. Here marked the brief moment in time before Mark, before Tommy, before *good*, where the brush was in her hand, hers alone. Days of oil and nights of jazz and footprints leading everywhere on frosted sidewalks. Everywhere and nowhere.

Geoff returned with brandy for her and a tall glass of water for himself. He paused when he saw her smile. "What?"

"Nothing. Thank you."

"There's more if you'd like."

"I didn't mean for the drink."

"Oh." He rubbed his thick chest, slipping two fingers between the buttons of his shirt. "What for, then?"

"The view."

"So you *are* fond of my apartment."

"No." She took a sip, her eyes lifted to him over the glass. "Only where it looks."

"I should go down to the street in that case."

"I'd rather you stay here."

"Is that so?" He spread his legs and his corduroys sighed with the couch.

"Yes." She gave another quick sip. "We wouldn't want to spoil the sight."

Geoff drowned his wince in water. "So, Miss Currier—"

"You're wrong on both accounts there."

"How so?"

"I'm no *Miss*, and as far as last names go, *Currier* is worth less these days than the handkerchief in your pocket."

"Your husband—"

"Has decided he prefers the dark and cold to my company." She drank to hide her expression. The brandy burned like sweet kerosene.

"Foolish man."

She nodded, and there was a curious little bounce to everything, as if the apartment were nodding with her. "You don't know the half of it."

"Then tell me."

Alice stared at him, at his hand resting upturned on his leg, like an invitation. She shook her head. "You wouldn't want to hear the story. It's too long, too strange. Besides"—she lowered her voice and glanced around furtively—"it's a secret."

"I like long, and I love strange."

"You said something similar about art and beauty, I recall. Before you saw *my* kind of strange."

Geoff sat there quietly.

"I shouldn't." Alice glanced down into her glass. She hadn't gotten buzzed since Cambridge with Alex, but she was getting there, by God, the bees were coming in a swarm. The night came back to her with sudden clarity: the river, Aladdin's bowl, the run through the lamp-studded dark, both of them like the stars, so very high . . . and then the low, the dreadful plunge beginning with her phone call to Mark, all her best intentions turned to bad results. "What the hell?" she said, looking out at the sleepy Boston skyline. "Worlds apart, as they say."

Geoff waited while she finished her drink.

"He's at Longreave."

He raised an eyebrow. "Longreave?"

"It's his hotel. Only it's never been his, and it's *really* not his now that it got signed over." The divorce form swam up in her mind and floated just as quickly away. "But the man never did know how to move on."

"I'm afraid I don't follow."

"He's living there, my husband. He's living in that locked up black hole of a hotel, just waiting for the wrecking ball to come and knock it all down. With him still inside it, maybe."

Geoff leaned toward her slightly. "No one else knows?"

"Only he and I. The happy couple." Alice tried to laugh, but only exhaled.

"And your husband, he's chosen not to leave this derelict place due to what, some misguided sense of loyalty?"

She shrugged. "Sure, let's call it that."

"What would you call it?"

"A *mystery.*" She swept her hand, the way she would laying a background stroke across a canvas. "I doubt he even knows himself. He tried to explain, but it was all nonsense. Like an art-school grad going on about how some particular piece is demonstrative of this or that, or captures the essence of blah-blah-blah."

"The more spoken, the less said."

"Exactly." She set her glass down before it ended up shattered on the enameled floor. "He went on about walls and building things, but the only wall he's building is around himself. Not as if he needs any help there."

Geoff considered this. "There is no greater hiding place than the one we make of ourselves."

Alice blinked and 401's closet was waiting for her in the microsecond of darkness, its doors cracked open. "Well."

"Well, what?"

"I guess the story wasn't so long, after all."

"Things often feel bigger than they are when they're trapped inside."

"Comforting words from Mr. Maws. Do you moonlight as a therapist when you aren't playing art connoisseur?"

"No. I moonlight as an art connoisseur when I'm not playing therapist."

"You're serious?" Alice sat up straight. "You're a shrink. *That's* what you do."

"Yes."

She ran her fingers down the leather armrest. "And here I am on your couch."

"Here you are." He looked at her in that calm, un-searching way of his. As if everything about her was painted on her skin, plain for him to see. Her heart quickened, blending beats. She glanced to her right and there, hanging in front of her face, was the stone phallus of the statue.

"Am I supposed to feel better now that we've had our little session?"

"Do you?" His belt buckle gleamed like the floor like the kitchen like his moist, steady eyes.

"No."

"Maybe we should go a little deeper."

"Oh yeah?" she said, more breath than voice. "Where should we start?"

"How about here?" He brushed the tattoo on her thigh.

She shuddered. "There?"

"*Eleven, twenty-five, oh four.*" He traced each number, his finger moving slowly, warmly, up her leg. "Who died for you to get this?"

Swallowing, "Why did someone have to die?"

"Only tombstones carry dates on them."

"Tombstones don't carry dates." She tried to shake her head, but it stuck in place. His fingers slid along the line of her shorts, climbing her thigh on cool nails. "They don't *move*, and they definitely don't move on."

"Do you, Alice?" He came closer. Their breaths mixed hot and sweet on the air between them. "Do *you* move on so well?"

She shut her eyes, scrambled to think. "Grief is a house."

"Is it?" Their mouths brushed. "Or is it perhaps a hotel?"

"You have to build a home for it, or it builds—"

His lips spread into a slight, soft smile against hers. "You have to build a home for your house?"

"Why do you want to know all of this?" she said, her voice breaking. "Why do you want to know where it hurts? So you can lick my wounds?"

Geoff pulled back. She opened her eyes one at a time.

"I'll lick whatever you want, Alice."

A word lit up her mind. One single word, so large it left no room for anything else. *Happening,* she thought, *happening happening happening.* Geoff moved his hand down the inside of her thigh and cupped her crotch.

Happening

The zipper on her jean shorts purred.

Happening happening

Her panties red. Her breaths short and fast.

Happening happening happening

His long middle finger slid in between the denim and her underwear. "What do you want me to lick?"

She squirmed. "I want you to—"

"Yes?" Geoff gave a little press, drawing a gasp out of her.

"—I want you to stop."

"It doesn't feel like you want me to stop." He sank his finger through her panties, and Alice opened to him wetly, like flesh under a knife. "I'd say, in my professional opinion, you feel a bit peckish."

Her lungs were between her legs, far away. Her breath traveled forever to reach her mouth. "*Please.*"

"Please what?"

Alice twisted up from the hips, her body winding until her cheek touched the leather cushion. "I want—"

"I know what you want, and I can help." Geoff climbed down from the couch, then lifted her off her butt. She felt her shorts sliding down her thighs, her panties trailing like a silky kiss along her skin. "The thing about appetite . . ."

The empty water glass on the coffee table. His brandy sitting beside it, untouched.

"Have I lost you, Alice?"

"*Please.*" Tears ran down her cheeks.

"The thing about appetite," he said, lowering his face between her raised legs, "is that it builds without you ever knowing it's there." A tongue flicked out, unseen, and a rope cinched inside her stomach. Geoff rose, his lips moist. "It builds." Down again. A deeper lick, a tighter rope, a pair of eyes watching her from a crevasse of skin. "And builds." Those eyes. Those still, staring eyes. Had she seen them blink? Had she seen them blink even *once*? The rope became a noose around her middle, dragging her down. She clawed at the couch. "And builds." He lowered one last time, his mouth cut off by her pelvis, his eyes like the eyes on the statue, and as the rope dragged Alice down into herself, her body stretched out away from her, as long as a corridor. At the end of it, far off, she saw Geoff's head but not his face. Geoff had no face left, only a pit of sunken steaming skin.

Alice craned her neck back and screamed.

The rope let go.

Geoff surfaced. His grin was wide and wet, a shark's grin. "Until you're starving."

•••

Alice got up on tingling legs. "Where are they? Where are my panties?"

Geoff held up a red wad. "Here you go. Fitting color for you, I might add."

"I'm leaving."

He nodded. "Okay."

The tile felt as if it were made of cold needles. Alice looked back, the panties dangling from her hand. "I'm going now."

"Okay."

As she turned her head, the walls ran together and formed a smooth round enclosure, a shining circus tent. She walked to the front door. A bathtub and toilet greeted her on the other side. She took a backwards, swaying step. "Where's out?"

Geoff pointed to another door.

Alice stumbled toward it. She would go down to the street, and find a phone to call Alex, and Alex would come to take her home. Her eyes welled at the thought. For a moment her brother felt so close she could smell his soaped, clean skin. She stepped into the stairwell, but there were no stairs. An enormous bed sprawled before her. Above it hung two paintings. The first was her ocean. The second was her river, the one she'd auctioned off all those years ago as a newlywed. A grave of drowned stars glowed in the water.

"It was you," she said, turning. "You bought it."

Geoff stood in the doorway. His shirt was unbuttoned, and his corduroys were folded neatly over one arm.

"Of course I did." He walked toward her, his penis as hard as marble. "I have good taste."

Chapter Twenty-Three
October 29th

They spent the day half at work and half at play. In the morning, Mark woke starving and smelly and out of the supplies to satisfy either one of these conditions. He filled two Hefty bags of clothes, sat Tommy on the bed, and got down on one knee in front of him. But he couldn't bring himself to say goodbye, so all he said was, "I'll be back. Wait here for me." To Mooney he whispered, "You watch him. You *watch*." He left Longreave with a cloud over his heart and made his run through town like the proverbial bat out of Hell, eager to return to its roost. First the dry cleaners, then the department store for bricks, then the grocery store, then back to the dry cleaners to collect his load, and then, last but not least, home. His *other* home, where Alice's car sat parked in the driveway, dust on the license plate and doors. Mark returned to the hotel thinking of dirt roads, of bridges, of Vermont. He rode in quiet, but not *in* quiet.

In the back of his mind was a room full of clocks. There was a clock for Mooney and a clock for his son and a clock for Longreave.

The clocks were ticking.

Ticking.

When he unlocked the front door, the duo was there: transplanted from 401 to the lobby. Tommy sat criss-cross on the floorboards. One hand—very small now, very soft—rested atop Mooney's head. He jumped to his feet, also small, also soft, and an empty sleeve of skin swung from his shoulder. Mark dropped to catch his son in the early-morning sunshine spilling into the hotel, and he felt the cloud over his heart lift.

The cloud stayed away for the afternoon. Mostly. There was a brief spell near dusk when a hint of chlorine wafted in under the door, but Mark lit a stick of incense and was soon able to forget that he'd smelled anything.

He brought the bricks around in record time, flying up the coast on his feet and back down in his truck. Tommy rode the dolly during their trips across the cellar while Mooney drifted along the fringes, vanishing on one side only to reappear on the other, his footfalls soft and steady. If they weren't alone in Longreave, at least they were being left alone.

The thought was far from comforting.

Mark double-checked the fuel in the lanterns and got to work. He and Tommy laid two stacks together before boredom, that magnet always looming over children, pulled the boy off to play with Mooney. There were rounds of tag (Mooney dominated), matches of hide and seek amidst the rubble (Tommy dominated), and strange staring contests (winner undetermined) in which the pair would sit facing each other for minutes at a time, mesmerized, Tommy's two eyes locked to Mooney's one, the whole cellar still except for the water running down Tommy's skin and the occasional plop of mud from the pit in Mooney's skull.

They did not play fetch.

That game had been put to rest.

Sometime after eleven the duo ventured off to climb the highest mountain of bricks. They were almost to the summit, a good six feet from where they'd started, when Tommy slipped. His boneless arm tangled python-like around Mooney's neck, and together they rolled down the slope. Upon landing the dog leapt to his feet and took off in a roaring bound while Tommy, harnessed to him, bounced on his back and screamed in glee. Around and around they tore, dodging in and out of the rubble with the blanket (by some miracle still clinging to Tommy's shoulders) flapping along behind them.

And that's how the cowboy found his horse, Mark thought with a smile.

By twelve the smile had stretched into something hard and painful. Mark had to urinate. Badly. He dance-hopped from place to place, grinning through clenched teeth, mercifully unaware that miles away in Boston Alice was waking up soaked in an another man's bed. When Mooney began to slurp mortar from the wheelbarrow as if it were a trough, the sound made Mark do a partnerless dosey-do.

Just a few more bricks. Just a few more—

Mark dropped the trowel, a realization dawning on him, divine. He was pissing right now. Inside his pants or out. He ripped open his belt, pushed down his slacks and spun around, a human sprinkler. Staggering away from the wall, he directed his stream out over the rubble. His gasp sank into a sigh of relief. He closed his eyes.

In the dark, there came little creeping footsteps.

Then a heavy hiss, as of a fire hose.

Tommy stood beside him, his one remaining hand wrapped around his tiny penis. The stream issuing from it was beyond disproportionate. It was monumental. Tommy's urine arched like a clear, flowing rainbow out over the ring of lanterns, disappearing into the dark right as it reached its peak.

Mark gaped.

"I think you've got me beat, kiddo." He started to laugh and Tommy did too, and they went on pissing and laughing, laughing for the senseless joy of it, laughing like only boys can in their crazy outpost on the shoreline of the world.

It happened suddenly, perhaps the only way it is ever meant to happen. It happened, Mark would think later, with the swift severity of a teacher reminding his pupil of a lesson he'd been too quick to forget.

The structure dissolved from Tommy's face. His jaw flapped in a grotesque parody of laughter before coming unhinged. The crown of his skull dropped as though into a sinkhole. His brow folded back into his forehead, followed by his eyes, nose, mouth, and chin. Tommy continued to stand, a decapitated thing urinating an impossible current, and then, as the sinkhole grew wider, hungrier, he diminished with increasing speed, draining into himself from the top down until there was nothing left to drain.

His cowboy blanket landed in a drenched heap. The arch of his stream collapsed with a delayed, trivial patter.

Ten seconds.

From there to gone.

Ten seconds.

Mark sat down in the puddle spreading on the ground, his pants around his thighs. With a whine Mooney joined him, and together they listened to the steady lifeless pulse of the Atlantic outside Longreave.

Chapter Twenty-Four
October 29ᵗʰ

At ten in the morning, in a clean set of clothes, Mark descended to the lobby with Mooney at his leg. They walked in slow, synchronized steps, like pallbearers at a funeral. The hotel lay hushed around them.

When they reached the immense oak door, Mark stopped and stood there in silence. He hadn't spoken since Tommy, in the famous words of Nicholas Lorey, bid farewell. He wasn't sure where to begin. He only knew he had to begin if he was going to finish.

"I'm stepping out for a while, boy. I need to take a walk and clear my head, but that's not why I'm telling you this. I'm telling you this, I guess, because I'm scared."

He ran a hand down his coat, impressing the tie beneath into his sternum.f

"All vacations end sooner or later, and I have to think about after. That's a pretty defining word, isn't it? *After.* A real wrecking ball of a word." He took a deep breath and let it out as slow as possible, stretching the moment until he realized, with a pang of regret, the moment had already passed. "I'm going to see about a girl. The only girl. I'll be back as soon as I can."

He rubbed Mooney's neck. The lumps, each one as large as a golf ball, squirmed under his touch.

"You take care of yourself while I'm gone. You *stay.*"

Mark went out into the daylight, but part of him stayed behind in Longreave. His thoughts kept returning to the hand Mooney had fetched from the darkness, the hand that had become a pile of chlorine-scented dust by the next morning, and he couldn't help but wonder.

How long before Mooney wandered into the darkness and a hand fetched *him*?

• • •

Seagulls scratched across the cloud-bumped sky like fingernails on a rash. Alice watched them from the passenger window of the Mercedes, her forehead pasted to the glass. She was wearing the shorts and jacket she'd left the house in yesterday. But no shirt. That was bundled inside the plastic shopping bag between her legs. She'd tied the bag to trap the smell inside, but the smell was on her skin too, so the bag was useless really. A band aid over an itch. And she itched, all right.

She *itched*.

"I find his work to be quite stark as a whole," Geoff said. "Not as in barren, but devoid, yes. Devoid of pretense, utterly exposed and utterly ashamed. Each painting you see strips another layer, shows a little more, until you discover yourself observing a body of work that's just as beautiful as it is hateful, disgusted by its own existence. A body of work that has its arms and legs spread and is begging you to devour it, digest it, save it from the cruel fate of *being*."

She shut her eyes and Geoff's voice whispered to her from another place, a dark place, where his face was secret and his hand was a second, softer whisper moving up her thigh. *You really are filthy, aren't you, Alice?* Moving on top. *Aren't you?* Something damp and soft and growing on her abdomen. *Aren't you? Aren't you?* Then the soft thing not so soft inside her, and *yes,* she moaned, the soaked sheet wrapped around her body winding tighter.

When Alice looked out the window again, the seagulls had shrunken and donned black caps. "Chickadees."

"What?" said Geoff.

Her gaze drifted down and landed on a familiar slideshow of houses. "Let me out. I want to walk."

The Mercedes stopped. Geoff took her arm as she reached for the handle. He too was dressed the same as yesterday. Same dark corduroys, same button-up shirt, same bright smile. "I'll pick you up tomorrow night."

Alice nodded.

She walked in the gutter, the shopping bag dangling from one forefinger, until a parked van forced her onto the curb. The breeze was gentle but sharp, a razor tickling her legs. She watched her feet move and imagined she was on the edge of a long and tall bridge, a bridge whose guardrail had been torn off. Without realizing, she reached under her jacket and slowly, steadily, dragged her nails across her belly. Soon she could no longer see the gutter at all, only a distant paleness, like sand. She turned when she needed to turn, crossed roads when roads came her way, and the bridge went on beneath her, pointing her home.

Where it ended.

"Alice."

She looked up, her feet resting on open air.

Mark stood in front of her, his shirt tucked in, his slacks pressed. Sunlight dappled his loafers. Blue silk spilled from the fist at his collar. "Can we talk?"

Everything was still.

Then wind ruffled the plastic bag, and she was falling, stomach up her throat, falling, bile in her mouth, tears in her eyes, falling, falling.

Mark.

Geoff.

Mark.

•••

Mark procrastinated his way to the house. A new pair of shoes at the shopping center, a stroll through the community park, a pack of mint gum chewed and spit into the cup holder. He racked up fifteen minutes and three flushes on a public toilet, turning back to the stall each time he tried to leave. And still his clothes looked drab, and his legs felt tight, and his breath smelled stale. And still he had to shit.

He sat across the street, choking the steering wheel, then killed the engine and climbed out of the truck. Using its door to block the wind, he removed his extra layers. A gust stole leaves off the neighbor's maple, and he was pierced by a moment of unexpected and stinging empathy for the tree, whose long life was defined by letting go. Growing itself out every year, only for Fall to tear it all down.

If he noticed someone approaching down the sidewalk, it was in one of the back rooms of his mind, behind closed doors and branching corridors. He smoothed his tie, smoothed it again, and started for the house. As he stepped onto the curb, something came to him on the wind. A snatch of rhyme, sung soft and tonelessly in a child's voice.

> "London Bridge is falling down,
> falling down, falling down,
> London bridge is falling down,
> My fair Lady."

He turned and there was Alice walking toward him in a jacket and paint-stained shorts, Alice with a shopping bag swinging in one hand and her eyes on the ground. Terror washed over him. He felt as though he were back in Longreave, facing the stairwell as the dead thing climbed—laughing and sobbing—into the light.

"Build it up with wood and clay,
Wood and clay, wood and clay,
Build it up with wood and clay,
My fair Lady."

Fifteen yards off. Fourteen. He couldn't move, couldn't breathe. She was coming, and he was in her path, and she was coming. Cheeks where he'd moved his fingers, breasts where he'd laid his head, kneecaps he'd pretended were doorknobs—*I'm afraid these locks are busted, m'dear*—and used to gently spread her legs. Coming. Every line on her face, every curve of her body and cell in her skin, *all* of her, coming right for him.

"Wood and clay will wash away,
Wash away, wash away,
Wood and clay will wash away,
My fair Lady."

Six, counting down, five, four, and this was seeing after your eyes forgot light. This was standing after a long, black crawl. This. Right here. This was the cellar door.

"Build it up with bricks—"

"Alice."
She stopped. Lifted her head. Stared.
Mark squeezed his tie. "Can we talk?"
They stood in place, like mirrors reflecting an equal and opposite stillness. An invisible hand brushed the hair back from her right ear, where the bead he'd given her used to hang, and she began to sway.
"Please. I know it's a lot to ask. After everything."
Alice stepped back, the plastic bag clutched to her chest.
"Just give me ten minutes to explain. To try. Please."

"I don't have any room for your insanity," she said, before walking up the lawn and into the house and slamming the door behind her.

Mark's arm fell.

This, he thought, *this wasn't how it was supposed to happen.*

•••

In the quiet house, the crash of the door was harsh, startling. Alice twisted around to peer through the spy-hole. A surrealist painting wavered outside, the lawn drawn in broad green ripples, leaves spilled across its surface like giant drops of lemonade. A brown smudge hovered over the sidewalk. She blinked out her tears and the smudge became Mark, moving away across the street, climbing into a truck.

Truck?

Since when did he drive a truck?

Since when did he have the money for a *truck*?

There was a creak upstairs. "Alice?"

She jumped, tightening her arms around the bag and forcing out a gush of urine-stench. Alex. He would see her. He would see her, and he would *know*.

"I take it the date went well," he called.

"It did. It was nice. Really nice." She walked into the kitchen.

His voice floated after her. "You going to tell me about it?"

A fist punched inside her stomach. She covered her mouth as she turned down the hall. Her footsteps were calm, controlled. She shut the bathroom door behind her and dropped in front of the toilet, but the lid was down and it was *happening, happening, happening*.

With her bag of dirty laundry cradled against her chest, Alice vomited into the tub.

•••

Back at the hotel, Mark patted Mooney on the head and walked into the cellar without speaking a word.

He worked down in the cold, in the chilled salt-breath of the Atlantic and yellow heat of the lanterns. He worked his new shoes dusty. He worked his brown slacks gray. He worked the day away in silence, and as night tucked Longreave under a star-studded blanket, he began to sing softly, slowly, under his breath.

"Build it up with bricks and mortar,
Bricks and mortar, bricks and mortar,
Build it up with bricks and mortar,
My fair Lady."

The lumps in Mooney's neck grew fatter, fatter.

"Bricks and mortar will not stay,
Will not stay, will not stay,
Bricks and mortar will not stay,
My fair Lady."

Chapter Twenty-Five
October 30th

"Alice, Alice." Mark took a deep breath. Lowered his voice. "*Alice.*"

On the bed, Mooney blinked his one eye.

"Can we talk? No. Let's talk. We need to talk. You and I, we're talking. We're having a conversation. I'm not leaving until we talk. Yeah, I'm not leaving until we talk. I have something to say, and you're going to hear me out."

Your insanity—

"We should sit down. Sure, the couch is fine."

Your insanity—

"I know things are crazy between us."

Insanity—

A bubble swelled and popped in Mooney's open eye socket. Mark wiped brown goop off his cheek. "You're right, buddy. It's no good. I'm no good."

Reddish-orange light was bleeding through the curtain, and the incense was smoking its last on the dresser. He'd lit it before going to bed. Not because any strange scents had been present in the room, but as a precaution. It was a secondary nightlight, a night*smell*, his ward against creeping odors and the things that creeped with them. He knew it was pitiful to put faith in such a childish concept, that you couldn't kill a smell any more than you could kill a ghost.

And yet . . .

And yet, as he'd lain there breathing in the spiced smoke, an idea had come to him and guided him down the narrow hazy corridor between waking and sleep. He'd believed his father was in the chair by the closet, watching him over a slowly dwindling cigar. There was no image to accompany the feeling, only the dreamlike conviction of it, the warmth. Perhaps he'd only wanted his father there, *needed* him there like the child needs the nightlight, and so his mind had done the rest.

Your insanity.

Mark pushed himself off the floor and stopped, rocking, his head surprised to find itself up so high. He looked at Mooney, at his fat and pulsing neck. It throbbed all over, as though a crop of hearts were growing under his skin.

"How you doing, big guy?"

Mooney didn't move.

After a lingering stare, Mark turned for the bathroom. What had he expected, anyway? A response?

Your—

"Insanity?" Mark said to the mirror, the door shut behind him. "You want to ask me about insanity? About Longreave? Well, why don't I ask you about Vermont?" His reflection stared back at him, tight jawed. "Look whose tongue the cat stole now. That's right, Alice, the cliché is out of the bag. I put a few things together of my own while you were gone. Did you think you could hide it forever, your little vacation spot? I've got a hotel, you've got a whole state, and you don't have room for *my* insanity? Why, yes, as a matter of fact I don't have any idea where the hell I'm going with this. No clue at all. I'm just pointing fingers because fingers are like secrets, which are like assholes, everyone has them and who gives a shit, and can I please fucking kiss you now?"

Mark sat down heavily on the toilet. If he launched at Alice about Vermont, he'd only succeed in getting her hackles up. At best. At worst? Well, that was just it. He didn't know. Whatever she'd buried there, she'd buried deep. Below ten years of marriage, below five years in Boston, below everything he knew or thought he knew about her. And things left underground for a long time . . . they don't always react well to open air and sunlight. They get used to the dark. They *rot*.

Your insanity—

What was in Vermont?

Your—

His. Exclusively his. The property of Mark Currier and no other. Sign on the dotted line and mail it to the courthouse. He dug at his temples, driving bolts of pain into his head. For a brief, blissful moment he was gone, Alice was gone, everything was gone except for the pain, the blinding, blackening, *purifying* pain. But as he let off the pressure, her voice returned, whispering the same two words over and over again.

He swayed out of the bathroom. "Mooney, buddy, I don't know what to do."

Except for a splotch of mud on the cover, the bed was bare.

"Mooney?"

His heart began to pound. It filled his neck: a sick, swollen beat of Morse code that said, *Your insanity, your insanity, your insanity.*

"*Mooney?*" he shouted.

• • •

Thirty-three.

Longreave had thirty-three rooms, and Alice had thirty-three years, and so, as Mark pulled the keys off their hooks in the lobby and stuffed them into a plastic shopping bag, a loose association formed in his mind between the hotel and his wife. A bridge running the impossible distance between Manxfield and Vermont, connecting the home of his secrets to the home of hers. At the end of the bridge there was darkness.

The same darkness waiting for him behind the doors above his head.

He looked up at the paneled ceiling, the handles of the shopping bag twisted around his knuckles. Mooney hadn't been under the bed, or in the closet. He hadn't been in the cellar either, not for all the minutes Mark spent shouting his throat raw down there, replaying last week's hunt alone. Nor was there sign of him on the annex's ground floor. No hairs, nothing. Only empty restrooms and a lone treadmill and laundry machines with windows like portholes, each painted deep ocean black. Only the creaky quiet and uncertain stillness of Longreave.

Mark stared at the panels above, panels like the squares on a chessboard, and was unable to shake the feeling he was playing into a game he wanted no part of, one he had no chance to win.

He saw Mooney, half blind and choked by a collar of lumps.

He saw fingers curled into claws.

He saw the rat.

Holding the crowbar in one hand and the keys to Longreave's many doors in the other, Mark made his first move up the stairs.

• • •

He worked the hotel top down, the same way he'd worked Alice in their distant days of lovemaking, leaving no spot untouched, no niche unexplored. The fourth-floor rooms were untenanted except for shadows. On the third floor he began to understand Longreave for what it truly was: a collection of hiding places. Nooks within nooks within nooks. In the rooms were bathrooms. In the bathrooms were bathtubs, veiled by drapes. And behind those drapes, standing with skinless arms and fingers spread wide, awaiting the moment when the curtain sweeps back and light falls upon the stage . . . there was nothing. Again and again, nothing.

The closets were boxes holding . . . nothing.

The beds were lids on top of . . . nothing.

The nothing grew inside him, like a pit. It grew until he felt hollow. He walked with stomping steps just to hear his feet on the floorboards, to prove he was there. But he wasn't convinced. He'd kept company with ghosts, and they'd seemed real enough, too. He started the second floor yelling for Mooney and he ended whispering, "Mooney, where did you go?"

Lantern light caressed the archway to the annex.

The annex.

For a moment Mark could hear the hotel's mystery guest dragging its dismembered, delighted self up the stairs. Suddenly the crowbar didn't cut it. He walked down to the lobby and from there, into the cellar. His footsteps were heavier coming out than they were going in, because *he* was heavier. He marched up the ramp to a sound like drumbeats, his grip tight on the sledgehammer. "I'm coming, Mooney. I'm coming."

● ● ●

Mark gazed at the strips of plastic scattered on 2C's bed, like confetti left over from a party. An exclusive, *secret* party, where Mooney had lost an eye and acquired a hand. He tried to envision the struggle that had taken place here but could not. His mind refused to go down that road. That road, it said, was a dead end.

Dead end. There was a lie for you.

The dead did not end.

Mark picked his way into the room, his soles sticking to the carpet's fake skin. The shopping bag dangled from his left shoulder, and with every step it jingled faintly, as if filled with jewelry. Earrings, perhaps. He turned for the bathroom door, the first stop of three in a routine that was becoming ritual. Bathroom, bed, closet. Bathroom, bed, closet. A slow, clockwise search. As the bed became a sliver in the corner of his eye, he stopped and twisted back to face the mangled covers, a hammer slamming down inside his chest, heartblows instead of heartbeats. He had no reason for the spike of fear, except . . .

Except he didn't want to put his back to the bed. Didn't want to let that nook below the mattress slide out of sight. Because it might not be empty. Because this time it might not be nothing.

He realized he hadn't called out to Mooney once since arriving at the annex. Which was why he'd come here in the first place. To find Mooney.

Wasn't it?

"Hey boy? You under there?"

He took a step. Fingers of light tickled at the dark under the bed.

"I know you can't answer, but the thing is—well, the thing is I don't know what the thing is. Having a tough time with words myself. A tough time in general, to be honest." He blinked, and his eyes were wet. "If you had to leave, you could have let me know. You could have given me a sign, so I knew to say goodbye."

Your—

"Mooney?"

Insanity—

Mark wrung the sledgehammer, lowering himself bit by bit. An instant before his knees touched the carpet, before he saw beneath the bed, a voice inside screamed, *Behind you!* He spun at the bathroom door. It was cracked open. Had it been cracked open a second ago?

He didn't think so.

Mark took a step toward the door and saw a hand, extending just as cautiously as his foot, reach out from under the bed behind him. He turned. The hand slid back into the dark, gone without a glimpse.

He stood there, tight, trembling. Something was here with him, in 2C. *It* was here. He'd heard the drip in here that day with David, and he'd found the eye in here that night with Tommy, and now it was morning—the clock goes round and round—now it was morning, and 2C had a new secret for him to uncover. It was licking missing lips under the bed, it was peering through the crack of the bathroom door, it was in front of him, behind him, oh God, which was it?

"Stop fucking with me!"

With an underhand swipe Mark caught the mattress and flung it up, box frame and all. Dust bunnies scattered out of hiding—but nothing else. Already turning, he kicked through the bathroom door. Tiles flashed like teeth in a snapping mouth. The bathroom was empty. The shower curtains were pulled aside, and the tub was empty too. Unless . . .

Unless *it* was lying *down* in the tub.

Lying submerged like Tommy, chlorinating the water with its blood.

Mark's skin was hot and sticky under his clothes. The tub sat innocently across the room, four feet of bleach-white acrylic. Too short for anyone but a child to fit inside without contorting. But that was the fun of games, wasn't it? To hide in unexpected places, make unpredictable moves. To catch your opponent by surprise.

He moved closer, no sound but his strained breath, his small footsteps. He could see it waiting for him in the bath, limbs jumbled, twisted. It would rise when he looked down upon it, and as the rosy water ran off its body, whatever face it had would come unmasked. And then . . .

Then.

Then.

Mark leaned over the tub, opening his mouth to scream, and felt a tiny draft of air pass his lips. The bath was empty, just like every other bath before. He lowered his hammer and walked back into the room, where he stopped.

The closet.

Of course. There was a grotesque synchronicity to it. On his last visit to 2C he'd found Mooney's eye in the closet. Now he'd find the rest of him there, or maybe, just maybe, whatever had left that eye. He licked chapped lips. Not the bed or bathroom after all, but the closet. Door number three. Three and three makes thirty-three.

Insanity—

Was it? The dead didn't end, they came back. Sooner or later, *everything* came back. Life was a criminal returning to the scene of the crime, and it kept bringing Mark here. To 2C. Hotels had hiding places, true, but they also had history. If he searched the annals of Longreave, might he discover 2C had a story? Something ugly buried long ago that now, with the rooms as dark and cold as crypts, had dug itself out of the grave? A psychopath whose last victim and breath were taken between these very walls—a psychopath with a penchant, perhaps, for chess? You heard about it all the time in the news, freaks staining the lives they touched. Well, how about the *places* they touched?

You never could make any sense of the board around you.

Mark pushed away his father's voice, reached for the right door of the closet, and pulled lightly at its knob.

Nothing.

Nothing, that was, on *one* half of the closet.

He switched the hammer to his other hand. *This is it. This right here, this is it.* Part of him was on the sidewalk, watching Alice walk toward him all over again. Sucking in a deep breath, he ripped open the closet's left door and exposed . . .

"Nothing." Where Mooney's eyeball had been, there was now a brown spot on the carpet, like a coffee stain. He said it again, louder, "Nothing," then he wheeled out into the hall. "Nothing!" Up the stairs, a shout on each step. "Nothing! Nothing! Nothing!" Through the rooms on the third floor, nothing! in the bathtubs, nothing! under the beds, nothing! in the closets, and up again, announcing himself to the unlit annex, "Nothing, nothing, *nothing!*"

Mark only slowed when he arrived at 4C, Longreave's final unexplored room. He paused in the doorway, filled with a horrible certainty. The closet was open, empty. So was the bathroom. At least, as far as he could tell from the door. He crept to the tub on tiptoes and peered over its lip. "Nothing," he said weakly, "nothing."

The bed.

Age had bowed the mattress and box frame, lending the dark beneath a gentle curve, like a smile.

Mark nodded.

It had planned this. *It* had known he'd come looking for Mooney, and *it* had known he'd save the annex for last, and *it* had known what looking would do to him. How each room, each peek, would strip away at his nerves. How his arms would tire, and his resolve would wear until he became reckless. *It* had guided Mark here, or rather let Mark guide himself here, his own nature leading him along as smoothly as contrails of smoke. And now here he stood, in 4C, by the chair where Frank Currier used to smoke his cigars. Wasn't that just Shakespearean? The son cometh home to the father's chamber and finds waiting for him a new ruler. A black king.

Mark inched closer. Thirty-three rooms, three hiding places apiece, down to one room and one hiding place. The closet and bathtub left open, exposed, to ensure he checked under the bed last. Every move he made predicted. Controlled.

Well, not this one.

He untied the backup lantern from his bag. Bending over slowly, his eyes never leaving the smiling darkness under the bed, he set the lantern on the ground and turned the switch. The flame sprang awake.

It thought he had to get nice and close to reveal *it*.

But *it* didn't think of everything.

He tipped the lantern on its side, straightened himself, and gave it a kick. The lantern rolled under the bed, bouncing gently. Around it the shadows burned away like old wrapping paper.

Mark blinked.

There was nothing down there.

Nothing.

He let out a soundless cry, a nothing-cry, and brought the full weight of the sledgehammer down on his father's chair. Its seat snapped in two, its legs splintered, and in the crash he heard a front door slamming shut.

Your insanity.

The hammer slipped from Mark's fingers. He sat down in the rubble, alone in Longreave.

Chapter Twenty-Six
October 31ˢᵗ

When Alice finished washing the bite marks on her thighs, she put on a pair of Alex's sweats and went back downstairs.

The house was dim, quiet.

She opened the curtains, brightening the living room. One shadow remained in the corner. "Happy Halloween," it said.

"What are you—what the hell are you doing there?"

The shadow lifted its black-hooded head, un-hunched its black-clothed body, and stretched its black-sleeved arms.

"Waiting for her highness to return." Alex yawned. "Had an idea if I sat somewhere uncomfortable, it might keep me from dozing off. But no dice."

"You didn't need to stay up for me."

"Who *needs* to do anything?" His eyes dropped to her sweatpants. "Thought I got all my clothes from your room."

"I didn't think you'd mind." The sweats she'd worn to Boston were stuffed in a garbage bag upstairs. They smelled.

He gave a limp shrug, dragging his shoulders against the wall. "How was your night?"

"It was nice." Her thighs were raw and hot, walking in ants. She fought the urge to scratch them. "We had a nice relaxing night."

"That's a lie if I've ever heard one."

She swallowed. "What makes you say that?"

"The purses under your eyes are practically Prada. You don't earn a set of that pedigree from a *relaxing* night."

Alice let out her breath. "You caught me. We had a nice, *exhausting* night."

"I'd ask for the details, but I'm sure I don't want to know." Alex watched her. He had bags of his own under his eyes. Not quite designer quality, but leather, at least.

"I'm sure you don't." She smiled. A muscle twitched in her cheek.

"Well." His gaze remained glued on her. "As long as it was nice."

"It was." Alice moved over to her newest painting, blank except for a shriveled pink door placed at the center of the canvas like meat on a white plate. She remembered the slice of veal Geoff had chewed through as a precursor to the main course, dabbing his lips between each delicate bite. "Very nice. He's a nice man. And we have so much in common when you think about it. With our interest in art."

"I'm happy for you," Alex said, struggling to his feet.

She spun on him cheerfully. "It's just so nice meeting someone who can express himself, you know. Who isn't afraid of *wanting.* Or saying what's on his mind. You know what he told me this morning on the way home?"

"What?"

"The sun was starting to show—it was dark when we left—and the sky was glowing this violent shade of red. He motioned out the window and said, *every day begins in murder.*"

Alex sniffed.

"Then he looked to me and said, *dawn sets the night on fire.*"

"Pretty. He should write a column for the newspaper."

"It reminded me of my painting. The sunrise you so lovingly labeled apocalyptic. It made me feel closer to understanding it. All of them." She waved her hand. "I don't know why I even bothered telling you."

Or what about Geoff's words caused her skin to crawl.

Alex shuffled for the kitchen, his hood coming off to show his red beanie. "You must have imagined I'd care."

"Wouldn't be the first time I was mistaken." She turned to study the canvas. The door was small, which meant it was set deep in the perspective, far away, though not quite as far as the bathroom in her last painting.

Alex hadn't left the room yet.

"What?" she said.

He fished his tongue around his mouth. "While you were over at Geoff's, you didn't have any . . . problems, did you?"

"What kind of problems?"

"You know."

Alice felt blood rising in her cheeks like red sunlight. She laughed. "If I did, do you think he'd be picking me up for a third date tomorrow?"

"No. Guess not." Alex started to go and stopped again. "You should take a nap. You really do look exhausted."

"Thanks, but I'll pass."

The bed *had* called to her while she was upstairs, but she was scared to lie down on it. Scared of what might happen to those white, unstained sheets. At least with Geoff she didn't need to worry about such things.

He made her sleep on the floor.

•••

Alice shook the jar of red pigment and when nothing came out, she set down her brush. It was useless without the right color.

Still, she had a hard time moving.

She'd painted the corridor again, except in this installment the bathroom at the end was closed—and closer. The obvious impression should have been that she, the viewer, was moving down the hall. But the opposite was true. The hall was moving *her*. It scrunched like an accordion, bundling into pink and sweaty folds, dragging her toward the closed door and whatever waited on the other side.

Alex was carving a pumpkin at the kitchen table, a joint stuck in his mouth. "Behold as the queen emerges."

"You can't smoke in here."

He scraped out the pumpkin's seedy brains, dumped them in a salad bowl, and offered her the joint between slimy fingers. "Thought you'd never quit."

She took a hit, then tossed the joint in with the seeds. "I didn't. I'm going to the store for more paint."

"Too bad. We could've finished the face together." He turned the pumpkin and a pair of empty overlarge eyes landed on her.

"Too bad." Alice stared down uneasily at the outlined and soon-to-be yawning mouth. "Can I get you anything while I'm out?"

"A job would be nice."

"Okay then." She started for the door.

"Candy."

"What?"

"Candy." Alex plunged his knife in and out of the pumpkin's face, slicing the mouth wide, making it scream. "Kids'll be coming around looking for candy tonight. We wouldn't want to let them down."

•••

Of all the doors Mark opened during the week, the last he expected to find a monster behind was the door to his house. He'd been too distracted on the drive over ("Alice, I'm here to talk . . . Alice, let's talk, Alice, *Alice*.") to notice the wand-wielders and superheroes populating the streets, so when the pale-faced, long-fanged ghoul answered his knock, cackling, he almost stumbled back off the porch.

The ghoul narrowed its black eyes at him. "Aren't you a little old for trick or treating?"

Mark tried to collect himself. He was still missing several pieces when he replied, "I'm not here for that."

"That's a relief," Alex said, running his tongue along his protruding teeth. "Because we're low on treats."

Mark stole a glance into the house. "I need to talk to—"

"She's out, I'm afraid." Alex covered his mouth with a red-nailed hand. "Oh no, there I go breaking character. A creature of the night, *afraid*. That's preposterous."

"She isn't here?"

"No, she's out. Didn't I just say that? Perhaps it's the fangs," he said, slurring. "They're no good for pronunciation."

Mark wondered how good Alex's pronunciation would be with the fangs shoved down his throat. "I know she doesn't want to talk to me. But I'm not going anywhere, so just tell her, tell her to please come out."

Alex's painted face sagged. "No one *ever* believes the monster."

"She really isn't here."

"Cross my still heart." Alex drew an X over his cloaked breast.

"Well—"

"—well, *indeed.*"

Mark clenched his jaws. "Are you going to tell me when she'll be back?"

"If only I could."

"How about where I can find her then?"

"That I might do. Under one condition."

"What's that?" Mark said through a tight throat. His patience was stretched thin, and so was the rest of him. He'd lain awake all night listening to the wordless voice of the hotel, the creaks and moans, the whispers. Hearing everything and hearing nothing, despair opening inside him like a hungry black mouth.

Alex batted mascara-lined eyelids. "You don't go talk to her."

"What kind of deal is that?"

"It's like you said, she doesn't want to talk to you. So I'd be one dead undead if she discovers I sent you her way."

"Fine. Deal."

Mark saw his smile mirrored back at him, ghoulish.

"Now *I* don't believe *you*."

"Then I guess I'll come inside and hang out with you until she gets back."

"I'm pretty busy, to be honest. Decoration preparation and all." Alex started to close the door, but Mark leaned in and caught it.

"I'll help."

"That's all right."

Mark felt the pressure of the door build against his hand, but held it steady. "You know the great thing about owning a house? I'll give you a hint. It's the same thing that separates me from a creature of the night, such as yourself."

"What?"

"I don't need an invitation."

Alex let go and sighed. "She's at the art store."

"Which one?"

"It's Manxfield. How many art stores do you think there are?"

"Take care, Alex." Mark trotted down the steps, light on his feet. The day—or night, as it was soon to become—was looking up for the first time.

"Oh," Alex called, "I almost forgot."

Mark turned.

"Do you remember the guy I told you about? The art guy? She's been spending a lot of time with him lately. And *late*, too. So late she doesn't come back until early." A red nail wagged at Mark. "You're looking pale all of a sudden. Maybe you should check your neck for bites."

Flashing its fangs, the ghoul shut the door.

As Mark stood on the sidewalk, stricken, a young boy with a white tablecloth over his head *woooooooo'ed* past him.

•••

Mark almost didn't make it there, kept catching himself steering onto roads that would take him back to the hotel. But then he was parking his truck next to Alice's car, and then he was inside the store wandering the aisles, each so long it could have moonlighted as a hallway inside Longreave.

He stumbled onto her in the back, a basket brimming with red vials hooked over her arm. She was standing completely still, staring down the acrylics aisle as if there were something at the other end of it, something she couldn't quite make out. Suddenly it was too much—the size of the store, the chemical tang in the air, the brightness—all too much. He stopped and rubbed at his temples, longing for the soft glow of his lantern, the dark.

"Help you find anything, sir?" said a boy stocking one of the nearby shelves.

Alice returned to herself with a twitch, and met Mark's eyes.

"No," he said. "I've already found it."

She blinked at him, turned her head the other way, and started down the aisle.

He went after her. "Alice, *wait.*"

"What do you want?"

"To talk to you. What do you think?"

"I think I need to have a chat with my brother about discretion." A vial wobbled out of her basket.

He caught it as it fell. "Here."

"Keep it. I took too many anyway."

"Cleaned them out, did you?"

Instead of responding she licked her lips, and for the next few seconds her lips were all Mark could see. Their texture, their curve, their color—red, like the vials—imprinted on his brain like a bruise. He saw himself leaning to kiss her, saw her leaning to kiss someone else, and jealousy crashed over him in a tidal wave.

The bastard. The fucker. He'd kill him, whoever he was.

Mark released his fist and forced his eyes down off her face. Her arm was trembling. How long had she been standing at the end of the aisle, holding that thing? "Let me help you." He reached for the basket.

She switched it to her other side.

Mark bit down. "Alice. If I could just have one moment."

"You've had several, by my count."

"I've been thinking."

"Always a relief to hear."

"I've been thinking about us."

Alice stopped and turned to face him. He opened his mouth. Shut it. She started off again. At the checkout stand, he caught back up to her. She was unloading her basket one vial at a time and stamping them onto the conveyer belt.

"This is hard for me, you know." He set the vial he was carrying down with the others. "Talking about my feelings."

"Feelings are hard for everyone, Mark."

"It's especially hard for me." He grimaced at how whimpering that sounded. "I know what you think about me living at Long"—He glanced at the people around them and then lowered his voice—"I know what you think, but it's only temporary."

"You've just figured that out?"

"I mean, what I wanted to say, what I *want* to say." Mark swallowed. Finding his way through the annex without a lantern was easier than this. "Being there has put things into perspective for me. I know what I want now."

"You want to talk. We've covered that."

"No. I mean, yes. But no. I want—"

One of Alice's hands crept down between her legs and began to pinch and pull at her sweats.

"I want—"

The conveyer belt had stopped. The checkout girl was staring at them. "Cash or debit?"

Mark dug out his wallet. "Debit."

Alice held up a hundred dollar bill. "Cash."

The girl, hardly out of high school, smiled a cramped smile that said she would very much like to melt under the register. Finally, she reached up and took Mark's card.

From the corner of his eye, he saw Alice's jaw knot.

"Would you like a receipt?"

"No. Thank you." Mark wrapped his arm around the paper bag before Alice could grab it. He headed for the exit, his thoughts coming in a manic, unbroken flow. *I want I want I want I want want want* . . . out through the automatic door and into the last hours of the last day of October . . . *I want I want I want I want* . . .

Alice pushed past him, her shoes smacking the tarmac.

"You're mad."

She shook her head.

"You're *not* mad."

She gave a short hard breath, almost a laugh.

"Are you going to talk to me?"

"You're too much," she said. "Really."

Halfway to their vehicles. Mark felt the steps ticking off like seconds on the timer of a bomb. There wasn't enough time. There was never enough time. *I want I want I want I want I want I want I want—*

"You."

"What about me?" she said.

Their vehicles leapt closer and out of his mouth came, "I know you're seeing someone."

Alice slowed as though she'd hit a speed bump. She sped back up, her face blank.

"I don't care," Mark said, and immediately regretted his choice of words. "I mean—what I mean is, it's okay. It's okay. I'm not upset."

At her car, countdown over, *bang*.

The trunk slammed. Mark realized Alice had already taken the bag off him. She slapped a wad of green into his still-raised hands.

"What's this for?"

"What do you think?"

He thumbed through the bills. "Eighty—you're kidding me. Your stuff there cost *eighty* dollars?"

"No. Seventy-six. But you can keep the change."

"Take it back." He shoved the money at her. "Please."

"I don't want it." She turned for the door. He caught her and spun her around, her back to the bumper.

"I want you to have it."

Her eyes were big, beautiful, and dry. "You don't listen to anything I say, do you?"

"I have more. I have more than I need." His tie felt heavy on his chest. "I should have told you. I was going to tell you."

She pulled her head back and regarded him almost cautiously. "Tell me what?"

"David, when he sold Longreave, he wrote me a check."

"A check for how much?"

"A lot."

"A check for how *much*?"

"Two hundred." He let out his breath. "Thousand."

A strange smile crept across Alice's face, and she broke into high, hysterical laughter. Mark waited for her to stop, but she didn't, just kept laughing and laughing until the sound of it was hoarse, painful.

"It's yours, too," he said quietly. "Half of it. More. As much as you want. I'll go to the bank right now and transfer—"

She shoved him.

"I don't want your fucking money."

They stood under the darkening sky, both of them silent.

All of her, all at once, went limp. "It was never about money."

Mark flexed his hands helplessly at his sides. "There has to be something here. There can't—there can't be nothing."

"Goodbye, Mark." She walked over to the driver's door, opened it, and climbed onto the seat.

He leaned in after her. "Alice."

"Please don't see me again," she said, her eyes aimed out the windshield. "Please just leave me alone."

His hand slipped. The door shut.

Mark stood in the empty space left by Alice's car and watched its taillights drain, like the day, into dusk.

•••

Alice watched Mark shrinking in her rearview mirror and knew what Geoff said had only been half true, that dawn may set the night on fire but night always had its revenge, that murder wasn't a beginning or an end but a cycle in which the dead came back to kill and be killed again.

When she walked into the house, Alex regarded her warily from a mask of white and black paint. "Are you mad?"

She pulled out a big bag of candy and gave a bright smile. "Why would I be mad?"

Chapter Twenty-Seven
November 6ᵗʰ

For five full days Mark said nothing to no one, not even himself. He hardly left Longreave, or had a thought outside Longreave. He moved around the hotel like a man on rails, following the same path between the cellar, lobby, and 401. During this time the wall stopped growing and creeping fingers of frost began to inch down the backfill from the beach, which had taken on a paleness that rivaled snow. The skin on his hands stiffened and cracked like old leather. More white hairs appeared in his beard.

He'd been a fool, so focused on building something new that he'd neglected the mess he'd made with the old. He'd pushed the rubble aside the way a boy shoves candy wrappers and soda cans beneath his bed, to be disposed of later. But later was a lie that parents fed their children to comfort them. To instill belief in a benign world, a world that would wait, when the truth was the world was a clock turning and turning. His father, honest asshole that he was, would have told him. His father would have told him that the world would turn away from you if you let it. That its heart was fashioned in cruel gears, and it wanted to leave you behind.

And so, because it was there and it was his, Mark tended to the trash. In the day he worked quietly, methodically, loading pieces of bricks into bags and moving the bags to the lobby. At night he filled the bed of his truck, and in the morning he visited the dump outside town. He didn't worry about the in-between time, when anyone from the condominium company could open the front door and discover the garbage piled in Longreave's lobby. He didn't have it in him to worry. On occasion as he worked in the cellar, he would catch a whiff of chlorine, there and then gone, as if carried past him on a phantom wind. He didn't concern himself with these occurrences either, merely noted them and moved on. A day might come when the smell would solidify into something real, something that walked and breathed if not lived, but that day hadn't arrived yet.

Pound for pound the rubble equaled the fresh brick he brought in from the department store, but the moving went much faster. He worked past exhaustion into a meditative state that was not quite waking and not quite sleep, where Mark Currier ceased to exist except as a pair of working arms and legs. He ate little and slept less, and when he *did* sleep, bags populated his dreams. Truckloads of bags. Landscapes. Sometime the bags started to twitch, pulsing like the lumps in Mooney's neck, and he would wake with the feeling that he wasn't alone, that a visitor was in his room, sharing the dark with him. But whenever he reached for the nightstand and turned on the lantern, 401 was empty.

By the fifth day all rubble had been cleared. He found a broom in the junk pile by the bookcase and swept the remaining red crumbs and dust into a hill, which he then bagged and carried over his shoulder, wearing an expression of simple contentment on his face. The job was done. His house was clean.

He paused, looking over at the demolished staircase by the lobby's entrance.

Well.

Almost clean.

As he chipped away at the heap, light began to spill through the web of broken boards and drip, thick as honey, into the shadows below the ramp. The shadows grew fewer for every stick he threw on the dolly, until the nook was lit except for its deepest corner. On his hands and knees, he crawled under to collect the final stray splinters, and there, in that corner, lay a patch of darkness the lantern couldn't wash away. A patch of darkness spread evenly across the concrete. He picked some up and let the clumps fall from his fingers. It was soil. Rich, fertile, soil. The kind found beneath a porch on a hot summer day.

Mooney.

That night Mark slept well.

The next morning he stepped out of Longreave for the first time in almost a week.

•••

One row of stretchers, double layered, followed by a row of headers. The same number of bricks per row, with even lines of mortar sealing the bricks together. Joints, these lines were called. They made the individual pieces into something strong, something that would last a lifetime.

Or longer.

Mark folded the tarp up the backfill to make more room, pinned the tarp in place, then climbed down to begin the next layer. As he bent over the wheelbarrow, he stopped and straightened, his neck twisting toward the shifting dark beyond the lanterns. After a moment, he shook his head and went back to work. He was rising to his feet, wet trowel in hand, when he heard it again.

A *click-click-click*, far off in the cellar. His mind turned strangely to Alex lying in bed, punching at the keyboard of Alice's computer.

Click-click-click.

Vaguely metallic.

Now when Mark tried to imagine Alex, he couldn't. All he could see was a finger, its skin peeled down to the shiny bone. The finger was tapping against the boiler, teasing, soft.

Click-click-click.

Mark knelt slowly, set the trowel in the wheelbarrow, and reached for the sledgehammer leaned against the wall.

The clicks turned to thumps.

The thumps grew faster.

It came loping at him from dark, low to the ground and dripping wet, like something that had crawled out of the ocean. Two faces, the top bobbing and the bottom drooling, both wearing a grin. As the thing emerged fully into the light, Mark lost all strength in his arms. The sledgehammer clattered to his feet.

Tommy rode into the lantern ring, a furry scruff of neck clenched like a harness in his hands. Both of his arms were intact, and he sat tall astride his mount, whose eyes were as round and bright as the moon.

The cowboy and his horse slowed in front of Mark.

You have to break it to rebuild it, he thought.

And he thought that if this was insanity, then insanity was sweet, and he wished he'd tasted it sooner.

• • •

After dark, with Tommy wrapped in the blanket on his lap and Mooney lying warm at his feet, Mark opened the package of postcards he'd bought from the store. There were fifty in the pack, one for every state in the country. Vacation postcards.

He laid the first on the nightstand. The front displayed a hunk of cheddar speared by a starry flag. With a small smile, he recalled the look of distaste Alice had flashed him as he bit into his cheeseburger on the day they met. He turned the card over and stared at the blank square on the back, not sure where to start.

Then he wondered, why not there?

Why not start at the beginning and work from there? Build off that first memory in the restaurant and see what grew?

"Hey, kiddo." He picked up the pen. "What did I tell you about laying bricks?"

"If you don't put down one, you'll never put down two."

Mark nodded. "That's right."

A moment later, he wrote, *Dear Alice* . . .

Chapter Twenty-Eight
November 9th

The dog was sick. She could see it behind the bench, lying in a bed of empty chip bags and soda cans. Its hide rose and fell in jagged hitches.

Alice walked toward it down the path. Wind carved hissing swaths through the grass on either side. It was too tall, that grass. She couldn't remember it being so tall the last time she was here, or so red. She squinted up at the scarlet sun through the haze of heat hanging over the park, and blinked sweat out of her eyes. When she looked down, the dog was closer—much closer, as if the path had shrunken. Now she could smell its sick smell, hear its whimpers. They sounded thin and pitiful, almost human.

Panic clutched at her throat. She turned to run the other way and found herself standing over the dog. A puddle of spit foamed around its head. It was sick, *sick*. She didn't want to see it, didn't want to touch it, but her eyes were stuck open and her hand was reaching out, fingers trembling, toward the back of its matted skull.

With a moan, the dog lifted its head and twisted a smooth, *hairless* face up to greet her. Its features were bunched together, crammed on a canvas that was too small to fit them. Blue eyes, brown eyebrows, bubbling mouth. A gush of warmth emptied down Alice's legs, and she watched in muted horror as the thing at her feet stretched open its jaws and cried out to her in *her* voice.

•••

Alice climbed out of bed and walked straight to the shower, where she stayed until her skin was almost as red as that nightmare sun, then she returned to the room and gathered up the blanket of puppy pads spread on the mattress. She'd bought the pads from the housebreaking section in the pet store, too scared to be seen shopping in the human store for something equivalent. Once they were stuffed into the growing trash bag under the bathroom sink and the bed was remade with linens, she jogged lightly down the stairs. Alex lay sprawled on the couch in his swim trunks, one bare foot poking over the armrest and tapping at the air. Outside, the sky was beginning to dim.

"What would you rather now as a proud member of the ignorant masses?" he said without glancing up from the computer. "How a salt marsh becomes a salt marsh? Or why Manxfield's salt marshes are the best marshes in the country?"

"That's a tough one." Alice tweaked his big toe. "I always had a thing for the unsalted variety, personally."

"How little you now," he said dryly.

She plopped down beside his head. "Why don't you explain pool etiquette? You can compare slow and fast lanes, expert and beginner strokes."

Alex raised an eyebrow—or lowered an eyebrow by her point of view. "Tomas Nox *does* do a masterful dolphin."

"You can even mention the importance of changing after a swim, so you don't stink up the whole house."

"I only have 250 words. Not sure I'd have space to cover that." Alice pulled his hat down over his eyes.

He let it stay there. "You have a good rest?"

"Yes." She'd taken to naps lately. These days, night didn't provide much time for sleep. "A very restful rest." Her gaze drifted to her latest painting. Another corridor. All she'd been able to paint were corridors, each more compact than the last. In this one, the third, the viewer stood mere feet from the end. The walls and floor and ceiling had bunched into tight folds, which surrounded the bathroom door like a rounded pink picture frame.

The door eased open, breathing out on oily hinges . . .

"How about dinner and a movie?" Alex asked.

The door squished shut.

"Can't, sorry. Geoff is picking me up." She glanced outside reflexively.

"Again?"

"He just can't get enough of me." A shiver ran up her back, and she crossed her arms. "Chilly in here."

Alex was quiet. She had the uncomfortable feeling he was watching her through the weave of his hat. "When?" he said.

"Not for an hour or so." She clapped her hands, launching to her feet. "Long enough to satisfy the first half of your proposal, if you so desire."

"All right then."

"Then all right." She strolled into the kitchen and her eyes chanced on the stack of envelopes on the counter. "Any fun mail for me?"

No response came from the living room.

"Alex?"

"I didn't check."

She thumbed through the pile—bills, bills, a notice to mow the lawn, more bills—and sighed. It seemed, strange as it was, that paying bills late didn't stop the next round from coming on time. "What shall it be?" she called, opening the refrigerator and looking in at the woefully bare shelves. "Lettuce with vinegar? Lettuce with broccoli *and* vinegar?"

"I don't think dinner will work after all."

"What? Not hungry anymore?" Alice walked back into the living room and stopped when she saw the sleek, black car parked at the curb outside. "Oh. Well." Her legs loose, she glided to the door.

"You forgot something."

She turned, smiling, and lifted her coat off the hanger. "What would I do without you?"

"That's a frightening idea." He pushed off the couch toward her. His muscles must have tightened up badly after his swim, because his limp was more pronounced than usual. "Why don't you invite your paramour in for a while?"

"I would." The skin under her sweats itched maddeningly. "But I think he has something planned for me tonight."

"Too bad." Alex glanced out the window. "And here I was thinking he and Tomas Nox would get along rather well, sophisticated gentlemen that they are."

"Tomorrow." She leaned in and hugged him. Tight. "Tomorrow we'll do dinner, okay?"

"Yeah." Soft in her ear, almost a breath.

Alice stepped out with her hands in her coat. Deep in the right pocket, her car keys scratched at her finger and like that she was in the house again. "Don't need these." She dropped the keys on the ledge. "It's not like I'll be driving tonight, anyway."

Geoff was a shadow behind the tinted window.

"How's my artist?" he said as she shut the door behind her. "Hungry, I hope?"

She nodded weakly before looking back at the house. Alex stood on the porch in his swim trunks. She raised a hand to wave, then realized he couldn't see her. By now she'd be a shadow to him, too.

•••

Geoff's plate was a palette arranged in shades of red, steak cooked rare, mashed potatoes stained pink by chopped beets. He ate with relish. Between bites, he paused to point his fork at her. "Why don't you take that off?"

"I'm okay."

He smiled. His teeth were colored. "Go on, make yourself comfortable."

She pulled off her shirt, crumpled it into a ball under the table, then suppressed a gasp as her back touched the cold steel chair. Geoff watched, chewing.

"The painting, is it going well?"

Alice glanced down at her bare plate. "Yes."

"You hesitated."

"It's . . ." Alice felt her nipples hardening and reached up instinctively to cover them. Making fists, she forced her hands back into her lap. ". . . a little slow."

"Picking at the details, are you?"

"No."

"Do you want to talk about it?"

Are you going to talk to me?

Alice choked on her breath. There was a lockbox in her mind, a safe where her most painful and precious memories were stored. It opened briefly and showed her Mark standing in the parking lot, his profile bowed, a defeated man floating away on a sea of asphalt. Over a week had passed since she told him to stay away from her, and he had. Perhaps she'd been wrong. Perhaps he did listen to her after all.

"You're rather aloof today, Alice." Geoff scooped up some potatoes with his spoon, careful to leave no beet *jus* behind.

"I'm sorry. It is my work. I guess you could say it isn't going smoothly." A hallway flickered behind her eyes, wrinkling as the walls contracted, as the door at the end was drawn closer. That door, that door, there was something waiting behind that door. Waiting for her brush to bring it to the surface, like the shape below the waves. She pictured her ocean hanging in Geoff's room and wondered what exactly she'd sold, and if it was lost to her now the way Longreave was lost to Mark, if she was just going on in denial with each new painting, trying to open a door that had already been shut for good.

"Maybe what you need is a change of scenery."

"What?"

Geoff licked his teeth behind his lips. "Maybe you would find your process, how should I say, *silky,* once again, if you surrounded yourself in a new habitat."

An invisible dish rag dripped ice water between Alice's breasts. "What are you saying?"

"That room behind you is my office."

She looked over her shoulder at a plain white door. It had always been closed during her visits, but now it stood ajar.

"*Was* my office. I cleared it out this afternoon."

She turned her head back to him, the muscles tight in her neck. "Why did you do that?"

"It will make a wonderful studio, I imagine." Geoff laid his knife and fork diagonally across his plate, dabbed his mouth with his napkin, and got up from his seat. "I figure we can move things into it slowly, begin with an easel or two." Loosening his tie with one finger, he started for the bedroom. "Have a peek, why don't you, before joining me."

Alice waited until he was gone and then pushed out of her chair. Her heart fluttered like a trapped bird. She went to the coat rack, fumbled her jacket off the hook, and reached for the doorknob. For one horrible moment it wouldn't turn and why wouldn't it turn, *why*? Then she undid the deadbolts—both industrial grade—and opened the door.

A dozen carpeted feet stood between the apartment and the stairs. As she stared out, half naked, one dozen became two dozen, three, the walls and floor and ceiling stretching into a sepia corridor.

She shut the door.

She re-hung her coat.

Geoff was sitting on the edge of his bed. Part of him—the part between his legs—rose for her when she entered. "What did you think?"

"I liked it," she said as he unbuttoned her jeans, making her sway on the balls of her feet.

"No panties this evening?" There was a touch of disappointment in his voice.

"No." Panties only meant more to throw away at the end of the night.

"It's okay." He brushed her cheek. His hand formed a fist in her hair and pulled her face down to his lap. "I know how you can make it up to me."

He told her to look at him.

She looked at him.

And discovered she could see her ocean framed above his head.

•••

The pillow in her mouth kept Alice from moaning while Geoff chewed her legs from the knees up, his eyes swimming closer in the half gloom, shining as though through murky water. But when he tired of foreplay and turned her onto her stomach, the pillow fell off the bed out of reach, and there was nothing to muffle her dog-like whimpers, nothing to do but clench the covers and pretend they were waves, pulling her down into a deep dark place where the world was still, silent, dead. Which was why she didn't notice when Geoff's hips stopped rolling. Not until he screamed and flopped next to her onto his belly, jerking like a landed fish. Between his legs was a hand, clamped around his smooth testicles.

How'd that get there? The hand connected to a wrist, which joined to a long downy arm, which led to . . .

"Sorry it took me so long," said Alex, standing at the foot of the bed. "I was right there with you the whole drive—man, that Mercedes sure does stick out—but I had to wait for someone to let me in downstairs, since I couldn't buzz. Fortunately, names and room numbers are listed on the mailboxes, and of course I could never forget *your* name, Jeff. By the way, did you know you left your door unlocked?"

"I'll kill—"

Alex twisted his fingers, wringing a yelp out of Geoff's throat.

"No? Well now you now." Her brother glanced at her as she rolled over, and his eyes paused on the bite marks lining her legs.

Paused for a long while.

When he spoke again, his voice had grown strangely hoarse.

"Get your clothes on, Lis, and go downstairs. I'll meet you in a moment." He turned his head. "Joff and I are going to have ourselves a nice little tak."

•••

Such raw essential pain, Geoff had never known. He had become acquainted with it in this very bed, glimpsed it in a desperate gaze, tasted it in an escaping moan. But *known* it? Truly feasted on it?

Not in his life.

He drooled on the mattress, one bleary eye on Alice as she quietly pulled up her pants, put on her shirt, and walked out of the room. The front door opened and shut. The grip on his balls loosened. A little.

"Up and over so we can see each other," Alex said, "And be easy about it. We wouldn't want anything precious to tear."

Hissing through clenched teeth, Geoff rolled onto his back.

Alex glanced at the penis pointed up at him, still hard and wet. "That's some poker you got there, but you won't be needing it anymore, so go ahead and put it away."

Geoff managed a thin smile. "Can't."

"I wonder about that, I do." Alex gave a small, considering tickle before locking his grip tight.

Four fingers. Four divine points of pressure. Geoff felt as if he'd finally found God. When he was allowed to breathe again, his prick had sunken to half mast. Panting, he said, "You'd better hold on forever. Because the moment you let go, I'm going to break off that hand."

Alex nodded absently, his gaze wandering around the room. "What a place you've got here. I always wanted to live in a place like this when I was a kid. Clean, bright, everything so slick not even a shadow could stick. I'd leave the lights on always, of course. For Alice. She gets jumpy in the dark. You'd understand if you knew."

"Knew what?" Sweat trickled between Geoff's pecs.

"How much does a place like this run, anyway?"

Geoff pushed up onto his elbows. "More than you could afford."

"I'm aware of *that,* Jeff. No need to rub it in." Alex pumped his hand, and Geoff collapsed back onto the mattress, his chin craned skyward.

"What do you want?" he gasped.

"Mind if I join you?" Alex sat down with a wince. "This leg has been killing me today. I try not to let it show in front of Alice, because she's guilty about it. She thinks she should've been in the car too, but if she *had* been in the car, there's no way I'd have done it. Wouldn't have had the balls." He looked sideways at Geoff. "That was a joke, my friend, if you couldn't tell."

"Fuck you."

"You'd like that, wouldn't you?" The humor dropped out of Alex's voice, and left something black and cold in its place. "I know all about guys like you. Explored a lot of damp holes in your life, haven't you? Doesn't matter if it's got two legs or four, or how old it is, or if it's family, so long as it can get wet, right?

"Your sister gets plenty wet."

A muscle twitched under Alex's eye.

"What's the matter?" Geoff said. His palate wasn't the only part of him well trained; so was his nose, and he caught a whiff of something interesting now—what the sommelier side of him might call a colorful bouquet. "Is it hard to hear that your sister gets wet for me? That she comes to me practically *drooling?*"

"Be quiet."

"Or perhaps I'm giving myself too much credit." He laced his fingers across his stomach the way he did during a session. "Perhaps I don't factor into this little story of yours at all."

Alex's gaze was blank. A dead man's stare.

Yes, here. It was here. If oil was Alice's medium, then flaws were Geoff's. He painted people, took portraits of the secret, ugly faces they hid from public. From themselves. This was *his* art, and under the skin of this boy's feminine mug, he was beginning to sense a masterpiece. "How *does* this story play out in your head? Does it end with your sweet sister—and sweet she is, believe me—untying that tight knot on your swim trunks? With her calling your name as you—"

Alex's hand twisted viciously. *"Be quiet."*

Geoff laughed. He beat his palm against the mattress as tears burned into his eyes. *"What a pair!* What a pair she's got between the two of you. You limping after her, and him running off to hide in his hotel—it's too good, I can't, I *can't.* No wonder she's ruined."

"What did you say?"

Alex was looking at him, one of his soft and peculiarly pale eyebrows raised like a feathered wing.

"About what?" Geoff said. "Alice? She's not exactly what one would call a *healthy* girl."

Alex turned his head, showcasing his delicate jaw line. He began to nod. "I always did find it strange she couldn't remember where she lost my phone." Geoff felt the tickle of a nail below his ball sac, and shivered. "And Mark, well, he made it clear enough after Tommy where he'd rather spend his time. Not at home, no. Not with his wife who needed him. Never." A slow smile spread across Alex's face, and as it widened, one of his fingers began to move back and forth along the sensitive stretch of skin between Geoff's groin and asshole. Looking off into space, Alex said, "Here's what's going to happen now. I'm going to leave." Back and forth, back and forth. Long, lazy strokes. "And this will be the end of it. Your last scene in the story, in your terms. Alice will never hear from you again. I will never hear from you again."

The caressing finger became a massaging finger. Geoff let out a shuddering breath.

"You stop existing the moment I step out of this apartment. Remember that, if you remember anything. Take it to heart.

Because if you forget . . ." The finger pressed harder, deeper, kneading into the tender meat between Geoff's legs. He could feel the threat of pain, close now, as close as a lover. The sheets dampened beneath him. With almost clinical fascination, he observed that his penis wasn't so limp anymore. Was, in fact, quite firm. ". . . if Alice happens to run into you at the supermarket or at an art show, a week from now, a year, it doesn't matter when, if you forget and you become *real* again, even for a second . . ."

Alex looked down at him.

". . . I'll fuck you myself."

Geoff's eyes flicked to Alex's swim trunks and then back to his face, so similar to his sister's. That didn't sound so bad, he decided.

Alex caught the glance and shook his head. "Not that way. I'm afraid we'd have to find something a *bit* less conventional."

Geoff blinked, confused.

"My poor man, I've led you all wrong. Here, let me help you understand." Alex took Geoff's hand. He pressed it against the crotch of his swim trunks and then rubbed Geoff's fingers slowly, firmly, back and forth—the way he had moved his own finger moments ago. And for the second time that night, Geoff felt something he had never felt before in his life. Horror. True horror, like a worm in his insides, pushing up into him with a blind, mushroom head. He tried to scream, but could not.

There was nothing beneath the trunks. Only a fold of skin, like a vagina, except no vagina Geoff had ever encountered ran side to side.

"*This* way." Alex reached behind himself. "With *this*."

His hand emerged holding a steak knife, pink shreds of meat caught in the serration, and Geoff—unable to scream— discovered he could still urinate.

•••

Alice stood on the sidewalk below a frosted streetlamp, hugging herself, certain that the door at the top of the steps would never open.

When it did, she burst into silent tears.

Alex limped down into the hazy gold light. He was carrying two framed paintings, one in each hand.

She threw her arms around his neck. "You know. You *always* know."

Chapter Twenty-Nine
November 15ᵗʰ

On an evening when many families were stoking fires, Mark sat over a postcard on his bed, nuzzled up against a damp lump under the covers. A stick of incense smoked on the dresser, and two lanterns burned on the nightstand. The first was for light and the second was for extra warmth, but only his feet were truly comfortable. After some training, Mooney had learned to lie across them instead of by them, and that was where the dog had been draped for the last half hour, asleep or putting on a very good act.

Curled across the front of the card was a golden comma of sand (a snapshot from sunny California), which Mark glanced at periodically for inspiration. Now and then as he wrote a smile touched his face. Of the eleven letters he'd delivered so far, this was his favorite. He felt unlike himself writing it. He felt young. For once he wasn't straight-lipped, serious Mark Currier, but lighthearted Mark Currier, full of wit and brevity and a sense of— strangest of all—*fun. Somewhere in the World it doesn't Suck,* he titled the message, after an old joke of theirs. He followed with a list of the marvels that winter in New England provided: used condoms and cigarette butts and sandwich wrappers preserved in ice like prehistoric fossils, black snow piles on curbs, sidewalks turned into skating rinks. He could picture Alice smiling as she read it, putting her fingers to her lips occasionally, caught off guard by a laugh. She would like this one. She would be unable not to like it, whether or not she liked him right now.

Mark set the pen down, rubbed his hands in front of the lanterns, and let out a long visible breath before picking the pen up again.

He hadn't caught a glimpse of her or her brother since Halloween, and for the last week the curtains had been drawn over the windows of the house, giving it a hibernating look. The only sign anyone lived there at all, besides the car in the driveway, was that every morning when he stole up to the porch to deliver his postcard, the mailbox was empty. For now though it was enough to know she was reading what he sent her. There'd be time for them to talk face to face in the future, but until then he had plenty more postcards.

A low, swishy sound came from the bed. Mark threw back the covers.

Tommy's eyes were open. "Are you all done, Daddy?"

"One brick at a time, partner. Ready to get a move on?"

"Yes, sir."

"Then saddle up."

● ● ●

It began to snow lightly as Mark drove down the coast. By the time he pulled behind Longreave, flakes the size of cotton swabs were falling out of the blackness. Some stuck to the beach, but most drifted into the ocean and became lost in the tossing water. He watched awhile from the shoreline, wishing Alice were here with him to share the spectacle, then he dropped the tailgate to unload his bricks. His hands were tingling under his gloves, and not from the cold. This would be the last time he was out here, like this, working under the night sky.

The wall was almost finished.

Inside the lobby Tommy and Mooney faced one another, joined by three feet of rope. Their shadows danced on the mantelpiece, but their bodies were still.

It was no longer midnight in Longreave.

It was high noon.

Tommy drew the revolver from his holster and shouted, "*Bangbangbang*," jamming on the plastic trigger. Mooney swayed on his paws before keeling onto the floorboards with a heavy thump.

"Maybe I'd better buy him a gun, too," said Mark, "so he stands a chance."

"Horses don't have guns." Tommy holstered his shooter emphatically.

"They don't, do they?" Mark lifted a stack off the dolly. "And do they typically partake in dust-offs?"

"What?"

"Do horses often have shootouts with their compadres, compadre?"

"Only Mooney. Because he's not really a horse."

"Oh. That makes sense."

Tommy grabbed the rope and tugged to no effect whatsoever on Mooney, who was still playing dead. Mark had lassoed them together last evening, tying a noose around his son's waist and a second noose around Mooney's neck. "So your horse can't run off again," he'd explained to Tommy while tightening the knots.

But that wasn't the real reason.

The real reason was that smell. Two weeks ago, after his son came riding out of the dark atop Mooney, the smell of chlorine had begun to grow stronger. More frequent. They'd be walking up the stairwell or working on the wall when it would steal in around them, an invisible fog, a sickness crawling on the air. Then Tommy had soaked into the bed one night and the smell had retreated to whatever hole it called home . . . until yesterday when Tommy returned and it crept back out of hiding like a snake drawn by the pitter-patter of a rat.

No, the rope was not to keep *Mooney* close.

•••

Mark woke with the postcard in his hand, and a good feeling. He changed into a clean set of clothes, hopping to keep warm. His blood rushed like electricity in his veins. Today he would see Alice. He didn't know how he knew, but he knew. Today, when he arrived at the house, he would find her waiting for him.

He kissed his boys on the head (*smack, smack*), checked the knots on their rope, and then slip-staggered up the beach through two inches of fresh snow, the postcard tucked in his inner breast pocket to protect it against ocean spray, as sharp and fine as crystal dust this clear morning. All the way to the house he told himself not to get his hopes up, not to be let down if the curtains were drawn and the porch was empty, this was only one day, one postcard, one chance of many to come. But when the house slid into sight, his breath stopped.

Alice sat in his father's wicker chair, her head down, her face half hidden inside the hood of a sweatshirt. Swallowing his heart, Mark stepped out of the truck. He shut the door with a little extra force. She didn't look up. The side of her jaw and one delicately arching cheekbone caught the sunlight as he approached. "Alice," he said, then he glimpsed her legs through the railing of the porch. They were bare from the knees down, and silky with pale hairs.

Alex lifted his head. "Sorry. The other half."

Mark stared.

"Missed you yesterday, what with my horrible habit of sleeping in. But last night I set my alarm clock, and wouldn't you know, the early bird really *does* catch the worm." Alex tilted his chin inquisitively. "You have something in your jacket there? I can take it off you if you'd like."

Mark removed his hand from his breast pocket. "What did you do with them?"

"*Them*? It isn't wise to speak in pronouns, Mark. Didn't we already talk about this sort of thing? About the importance of care in choosing words? If you just say '*them*,' I might think you're talking about the sugar packets I dumped into my coffee this morning, in which case the answer would be I threw them in the trash."

"What did you do with my postcards?"

"I threw them in the trash."

"*Bastard*." Mark took a hard step forward.

Alex held up his palm. "I wouldn't come any closer if I were you."

"And why the hell not?" Mark continued up the lawn.

"Well, the closer you come, the better the chances are there'll be a ruckus. And a ruckus means Alice will wake up."

"Good. I can tell her the shit you've been up to."

"All I'm saying is Alice, like myself, isn't much of a morning person. These days, anyway. And that means she'll be grumpy if she has to come out here and break us up from rolling in the grass. Do you really want that to be the way your reunion goes? I mean, after all the *time* you put into those letters . . ."

Mark stopped, one hand on the porch railing, splinters digging into his palm.

"*Woooooh*," Alex exhaled in relief. "I was never good at fighting. Always ended up using teeth, and I just broke my fangs biting into a caramel apple on Halloween. I make a poor monster, I guess."

Mark wasn't sure about that last part, but he bit back the urge to say so and instead asked, "*Why?*"

Alex regarded him for a moment. "I want her to be happy."

"And I can't do that."

"No," he said. "No, Mark, I don't think you can. I believe you want to, I believe you would try. I read your postcards."

"Before you threw them out."

Alex blinked once. "Before that. And they felt sincere. They did. But you're a runner, Mark. When things go wrong, you run and you hide. After Tommy, you disappeared into that hotel of yours, and I took care of her. I watched her sleep walk around the house, looking in cupboards, under beds. Searching for him. For you." Alex pulled off his hood and hat and ran his fingers through his scattered milk-white hair. "I've been taking care of Alice my whole life, Mark. And you may have been the best, I'll admit. But no man has ever been good for her."

"Except you."

Alex shrugged. "I'm her brother."

Mark's legs shook a little as the anger drained out of him. "It's different now. *I'm* different."

"I think you think that, Mark. But people don't change. We try, but we're like planets." Alex drew a circle with his finger. "We keep coming back to where we started."

Mark spoke without thinking. "And you and Alice, where did you start?"

A twitch.

"I know where you two really go on your trips. I know about Vermont."

There was a long pause. "If that's all you know, Mark, you don't know a thing. You have no idea where we come from. *What* we come from."

"So tell me."

Alex's voice became quiet. "That, *that*, is a road you don't want to go down, my friend. You won't like what you find at the end of it."

"I don't care. Whatever it is, I don't care. I've heard worse. *Seen* worse." In his mind the stump of an arm reached up, ribboned and dripping, from the dark.

Alex gave a small and not completely steady laugh.

"That's it then," said Mark. "You're telling me how it is. You're making the decisions."

"That's it."

"This is bullshit." Mark walked up the last two steps. "I'm going inside to see my wife."

"The door's unlocked. One piece of advice, though. If you do decide to talk to Alice, never ask about Vermont."

"There's no *if*. I'm going."

Alex didn't say another word until Mark reached for the doorknob.

"How are things at Longreave?"

Mark froze.

"Are you enjoying your stay? I would think it must be rather lonely, but then, you always seemed fond of its company."

"She told you."

"Of course she did. Alice doesn't keep secrets from me." Alex cocked his head. "You didn't answer my question. Are you enjoying your stay?"

Mark swallowed.

"Would you be sad if it ended?"

"You wouldn't."

Alex lifted his forefinger and traced a slow circle in the air.

"No. You won't."

Mark gripped the doorknob. From the corner of his eye he saw Alex's finger moving around, around, around. His jaws clenched. His eyes blurred. He turned and walked down the steps, and as he crossed the lawn he pulled the postcard out of his pocket and crumpled it in his fist. He kept waiting for one last comment from the porch, a goodbye, maybe just a chuckle, but the silence said enough.

• • •

Mark remembered none of the journey back to the hotel. He climbed into his truck and Longreave's giant oak door slammed behind him. Before the echoes faded, he was striding through the dark.

"Daddy," Tommy's voice trailed after him. "Daddy, *wait*."

Mark switched on the lantern tied to his backpack and its flame coughed up a chunk of lobby. Into the light came Mooney, pulling Tommy along by a taut length of rope. Mark started up the stairs, his jaws bolted shut. Up and up he went, seeing Alex's finger twirl with every turn. Up and up, around and around, climbing in circles. His breath burned in his throat; his eyes burned in their sockets. He emerged onto the fourth floor, his son moaning close behind.

"Daddy, stop it," Tommy called. "Stop running."

"I'm not—"

Mark kicked out at the nearest object.

"—running!"

With a groan, the clay pot tipped over and shattered. Beads spilled out of its mouth and burst out of its broken sides and flooded the hallway in a sparkling, musical wave. They blazed in the light like pale pearls of fire, and as they rolled off into the dark, they were extinguished.

Slowly, the tinkling died.

One bead returned from the shadows by 401, clicking across the cracks between the floorboards, and stopped against his shoe. Mark picked it up. Held it in his palm. He was watching the way its curved surface flickered, thinking vaguely of starlight on water, when a pair of realizations crept up on him. The first was that it was quiet. So quiet the walls seemed to breathe.

The second was that he could smell chlorine.

Closing his hand around the bead, he turned. Tommy and Mooney stood by the stairwell, as still as gunslingers in a face off. Except they weren't facing one another. They were facing the other end of the hall.

Mark walked to them. He heard a low rough sound, menacingly soft. Mooney was growling.

"What is it, son?"

"There's a man."

A cobweb of fear settled over Mark's heart. "How close?"

"Close."

"Who is he?"

"I don't know." Tommy clutched onto Mooney. Water leaked out of his grip and soaked into the dog's thick hide. Beyond them, dark filled the frame of the corridor like a black photograph waiting to develop.

"The man." Mark swallowed. "What does he look like?"

Tommy's voice was hushed. "He's big. Bigger than you. And he's naked. I can see his bones in places, he's so naked. You know when you get dressed fast, and you forget something? He looks like that. Like he forgot to put on all of his skin. And his *face* . . ." Tommy turned to Mark, his eyes big and wet. "I don't like him, Daddy, and I don't like the way he's holding out his hand to me, and I don't want to look at him anymore."

"Okay." Mark wrapped an arm around his son. "Okay, let's go."

They picked their way to 401 through the scattered beads, forced to stop every few steps as Mooney jerked to stare back down the hall. Each time the darkness was as close as it was the last time, and each time Mark thought he saw movement inside it, until finally they reached the safety of their room.

"He can't get in." Mark backed away from the door. "It's locked."

"No it's not," Tommy said. "Nothing is locked in Longreave."

There was something in his voice now that the panic had left it, something in his voice and the way he stared at Mark. It made Mark think of the way *his* father had looked to him, after the coroner drove off with his mother's body. Frank Currier, sitting in the wicker chair with an untouched cigar smoking on his thigh. Frail. Tired. And, for the first time, human.

Mark walked to the bed, sat down, and put his head in his hands.

Only when the bead slipped out between his fingers, only then, did he realize he'd held onto it. It glimmered up at him faintly from the carpet, like a lost earring.

Chapter Thirty
November 16ᵗʰ

It was after dark, and a low breeze was yawning into the cellar. Mark had taken down the tarp to finish the wall. It lay rolled on the swept floor behind him like an enormous white grub, at home underground. In the flickering lantern light it appeared to wiggle suggestively, and as Mark worked, he felt a similar squirming deep down in his gut.

He was close now.

And so was the smell of chlorine. Close, and just a little salty from the breeze. Mark listened to the waves and imagined a vast pool tossing against the shoreline outside—an ocean with chemical blue waters, its tide creeping closer and closer to Longreave. He paused every few bricks to stare out past the lanterns, the fingers of one hand stroking the bead inside his breast pocket. Soon enough he finished the first layer.

Two left, he thought.

It was a big thought, too big for him to hold onto yet. He let his attention wander from the wall to his son. Tommy paced back and forth, the concrete wet under his feet. The noose had slipped down his stomach and was hanging unevenly off his waist, similar to the way some cowboys wore their gun belts.

Mark got down on one knee and caught him by the arm. "Hey there, partner. You on watch? Somebody set to hang tomorrow?"

Tommy stared blankly. Gray streaks of frost lined his hair.

Mark picked the cowlick away from his son's forehead and felt it crunch between his fingers. "What's going on, partner?"

Tommy's eyelids twitched but didn't move.

They'd frozen open.

Mark tightened the noose, unable not to notice the little flecks of skin clinging to the rope, and released him. Tommy turned and continued his slow march past Mooney, who lay unmoving except for the lumps in his neck. *Those* moved plenty.

There was a footrace going on in Longreave. It had taken place before, and it would take place again . . . and again . . . and again. On the last two occasions Tommy had crossed the finish line first. But this time, Mark had a feeling the runner with four legs would come out the winner.

He did the only thing he could do.

He put his gloves on and got back to work.

The second layer took him almost twice as long. Not because he had to stop to make more mortar, or because he heard any sounds in the cellar that gave him pause. It was his hands. It was as if his hands could tell the end was drawing near and didn't want to be done. He kept seeing Alex twirl a finger from his father's wicker chair, seeming to say, *get a move on, buddy, hurry it up.* Kept finding himself on the stepladder without any bricks to set, just standing there with his head tilted back, listening to the wind.

But most of all, he kept picturing the beads explode out of their pot in a dazzling flood, filling the fourth floor with sudden brightness.

It was exactly this image that was on Mark's mind when he climbed up for the third and final layer, to fill the gap and conclude the job he'd begun over a month ago. Standing on the top step, the ladder creaking dangerously below his feet, he rose onto his tiptoes and looked out barely—just barely—over the lip of the wall.

In the glow spilling from the cellar, dark waves speckled by starlight lapped at the snow-covered beach.

He watched.

He watched for a long time.

A few hours later as he carried a new load out to his truck, the glow was still there, a stage light over the wintry sand.

•••

By morning, the mascots of twenty-seven states were lying crumpled or in pieces around 401. A thread of dying smoke curled over The Rockies on the dresser. Mooney drooled on the Grand Canyon at the foot of the bed. A decapitated eagle lay in the bathroom, where its short and pitiful flight had ended.

Mark woke fully charged on an hour's sleep. The worming feeling in his gut yesterday had been caterpillars and the lot of them had hatched into butterflies overnight. He threw off the covers, exposing an open-eyed Tommy and creating a draft that whirled some Midwestern cornfield off the nightstand. "Wrangle up your ride, kiddo," he said as he paced in search of his tie. It wasn't on the front door where he usually hung it, so it had to be in the bathroom.

But his tie wasn't there either. He stood behind the closed door for several seconds, bewildered, before realizing his tie was already on his throat. He hadn't taken it off since leaving Alice's house yesterday morning.

Alice. Had there ever been a name with a sweeter slide to it? *Alice. Alice. Alice.*

He reached for the knob, then paused as he heard a sound in the room.

Click.

Click.

Mark pulled the door back slowly.

Tommy was out of bed. He stood by the sledgehammer propped against the dresser, the cowboy blanket loose on his sagging shoulders. His revolver was out and he was pointing it, *click,* at his own trembling silhouette, *click,* on the wall.

Mark walked to him. He closed his hand over the gun and guided it down. "Hey there, hey."

Tommy's fingers held the handle in a death grip. In his wide and staring eyes Mark saw a reflection of himself on the cellar floor, the day the lights went out.

"Are you thinking about that man in the hall?"

Tommy shook his head.

"What is it then? What's got you so scared?"

"Cowboys don't get scared."

"I don't know about that," Mark answered slowly."I think even the bravest cowboys know fear. *Especially* them. I think, if they were never afraid, if they never wanted to get down on their knees and crawl, they wouldn't know what it meant to stand."

Mooney let out a long, rattling breath.

"You're leaving," Tommy said.

Mark stared back, at a loss. "Only for a little while. Only a couple hours, to find a jeweler."

But after a couple hours all he'd found was himself laughed at repeatedly upon speaking his request, and by then his search had taken him to the narrow downtown streets of Boston. He wandered, directionless, seeing Mooney huddled and still in every shadow, hearing the click of a revolver with every step.

A meaty smell wafted out of an open door. Mark stopped, his stomach growling, and looked in along a familiar row of booths. He'd eaten here before, once. He'd given the waitress his phone number.

His waitress wasn't as pretty this time, but the burger tasted just as good as he remembered. He wiped the grease off his fingers, then removed the postcard from his pocket. On the front was a picture of Faneuil Hall.

"Get your check?"

"What?" He looked up. "Oh, yeah. Yes please." When the girl returned, he asked, "What's the street number for this restaurant?"

Frowning, "Why?"

He turned over his receipt to write on it. "I need a return address."

She told him, still frowning. He asked for directions. She gave him those, too.

They led to a four-story building, drab on the outside but inside a crow's paradise. There were shops for trinkets, shops for jewelry, shops for trinkets that doubled as jewelry. On the top floor, he approached a spectacled man gluing fake diamonds onto earrings. A woman sat reading in the back of the room, her feet propped on a desk. The man listened to Mark speak and, unlike the others, didn't wave him out the door. "You show me."

"I'll have to take you to my truck. It's a bit to carry."

"Is it far, your truck?"

Mark shrugged. "Pretty close."

Five blocks later, the man was complaining, "I say something is close, I think next door. Maybe next, *next* door. Not—"

Mark threw back the tarp on the truck bed, opened one of the Hefty bags, and the man swallowed the rest of his words.

"How much?"

"Five hundred pounds," said Mark. "Maybe six."

"No. How *much?*"

"Get it to me by Friday, and the price is yours to set."

The man smiled, displaying more than one gold filling. "We drive back and you park in parking garage. Right under building. *Very* close."

Their transaction concluded in a sweaty handshake at a quarter to two, the floor of the shop all but hidden beneath trash bags. This didn't seem to concern the woman one bit. She continued to read without so much as a glance at her surroundings, and when Mark stepped back through the door immediately after leaving, she gave no indication she noticed.

"It is not quite Friday yet, my friend," said the man.

"Actually, I was wondering if I might borrow your wife's hand."

The woman lowered her book with a laugh. "My brother's wife is still an idea in his head, fortunately for her. As for my hand, I'm afraid I have no knife to remove it."

"No knife needed." Mark reached into his breast pocket. "Only a pen."

•••

Strolling down the sidewalk, Mark watched sparks drip like golden rain from the girders of an naked building and remembered how it had stormed on the day he moved into Longreave, how the hotel had resembled a ship cast out into deep and violent waters.

He stopped at a postal box, pulled the flap, and lifted a sealed envelope to its mouth.

You're leaving.

His fingers tightened.

"I'm not."

Mark let go, and as the letter rustled into the mailbox out of reach, he gave a small prayer that it would find its way home.

The drive coasted by smoothly. He listened to music, even sang along with a few oldies. His body was warm, his stomach was full, and there was room in his heart for a comfortable future. Humming, he let himself into the hotel.

"Hey, you two," he called as he crossed the lobby. "I'm back."

A click of nails came from the staircase.

And, softer, a slithering *bump, bump, bump.*

He raised the lantern. Its trembling flame revealed Mooney, head bowed and heavy pawed, walking down the steps from the second floor. Mud dangled off his jowls. An empty noose trailed after him.

Chapter Thirty-One
November 22nd

There was nothing special about the day, nothing that made it any different from the day before, or the days before that. It was a Friday, there were more clouds than sky above Manxfield, and the thermometer on the sliding glass door read just below freezing, as it had the whole week. But on this day, instead of returning to bed after changing her sheets and taking a shower, Alice went downstairs. Her legs were trembly by the time she reached the living room, and the house seemed larger than she remembered. Colder, too. Yet when she processed these sensations and analyzed how each one made her feel in turn, she found she had no particular desire to climb back under the covers, and so she continued into the kitchen.

"Alex?"

A sore bulged on the refrigerator. She let out her breath. It was only a ladybug magnet. Pinned under it was a slip of paper.

Goooooooood morning, Lis!

If you're reading this then I'm already dead—whoops, wrong note. Take two: if you're reading this then you're up and about and maybe wondering where I've run (as if I could) off to. The bed in the guestroom is getting a touch cold at night, so I'm fetching some extra blankets from my apartment. Speaking of cold, you'll find breakfast in the refrigerator. Top shelf, figuratively. Bottom shelf, literally. Serve yourself, or be served when I return. The choice, m'dear, is yours.

Love, your rambling brother, Lix.

Alice crumpled the note with a smile. She wandered over to the fridge, more curious than anything, but the instant she popped the Tupperware and released the smell trapped within, she was starving.

Ten minutes later, her stomach full and her taste-buds fried from superheated tofu scramble, she dropped her empty bowl in the sink. As she walked by the counter, her eyes landed on the mail. The mere sight of it brought her close to panic. She hurried on, and when she emerged safely into the living room, she felt as though she'd run through a thicket of sharp branches and barely managed to escape, her good mood clinging to her like a shredded shirt.

"Baby steps," she breathed. "Baby steps."

Before long, her baby steps had taken her into the office. An incomplete clock of artwork surrounded her, one painting at every hour except six, eight, nine and twelve. On this clock-face the day opened with a gruesome sunrise and developed into a clear morning, cloudless skies overlooking a malformed house. At three o'clock the perspective moved to the house's entryway, at four it climbed the staircase, and at five it arrived at the spoiled master bedroom. Next came a jump downstairs to seven o'clock and a red kitchen whose back door gazed out to a pool that glowed bright blue despite the dusk. And then, as the day progressed into night, one last corridor stretched from painting to painting. There was no guestroom in this house, or if there was, it had been entombed by the supple walls. All that remained was the doorway at the end of the hall and the indistinct figure of someone in the steam, someone more horrifying perhaps than the house itself, because at this point the perspective halted, as if the person behind the camera had stopped to turn and run, only to discover it was too late, the corridor had a will of its own. The door, wide open at ten o'clock, slammed shut at eleven. The room dragged closer . . .

At midnight stood a bare easel.

Alice stepped around the easel to her desk, where a pair of paintings lay side by side. Sliding her gaze left to right, she followed the glowing Charles downstream to the Atlantic. Its dark blue waves tossed and tossed. Beneath them—deep beneath—something else tossed, too. She thought of all the times she'd woken the last two weeks, urine-soaked blankets tangled around her body as though she'd been rolling in her sleep, struggling to surface from some nightmare.

Alice turned the wooden frame over, unclasped the back, and slid the canvas out carefully before clipping it to the midnight easel, hanging the ocean at the end—and also the beginning—of the clock. Stepping back to view the painting, she felt a familiar tug in her belly, a fishhook right behind her naval. The sensation was not painless, nor was it entirely uncomfortable. Now when she scanned the raging waters, she saw lips as well as waves, spittle as well as ocean spray.

It hit her, the same way it had in the kitchen.

Hunger.

With a length of canvas fluttering from her hand, Alice strode into the living room. The final, squashed leg of the corridor still hung on the easel there, and the closed door at the end rattled impatiently in its frame. She took the corridor down and laid it on the floor, where she could see it while she worked.

Easy, she told herself as she clipped up the fresh canvas and prepared the palette, *baby steps, baby steps*.

She stretched her right leg.

The door had settled. Alice looked up at the easel, and it was there too: a pink shadow on the paper. She swallowed.

"If it doesn't, it's all right. You can try again tomorrow."

But it did.

Slowly, smoothly, the door at the end of the corridor eased open.

•••

The sink was too small for its mirror, the steamy air tinted everything red, and there was a slight strain to the architecture—pulling the walls in and pressing the ceiling down—but after the rest of the house, the bathroom looked almost ordinary. A carpeted lid covered the toilet bowl. A glossy sheen brightened the rounded floor tiles. A bunched curtain dangled from the shower rod, which curved down slightly at both ends so that it frowned over the bathtub.

The tub sat in the center of the canvas, a plain thing, its lip moistened by the steam. Except for its yawning faucet, there was nothing to separate it from the tub waiting down the hall in the real house. Alice was lifting her brush dreamily to the mouth of the faucet when a thought snuck into her head.

Alex isn't home.

Or was he? It wouldn't be the first time someone had slipped in without her noticing. She walked to the window, pulled back the curtain, and squinted out over the sunlit snow.

No car.

Alex wouldn't have gone for a swim without coming back to check on her first, not after two weeks of delivering punctual meals to her bed and keeping a cycle of sheets running through the washer. Licking the inside of her lip, Alice went into the kitchen to check the clock. Noon. Had he gotten pulled over perhaps? He didn't have a license. He got too nervous driving with strangers to ever pass the test. She saw how the story would play out: the cop asks Alex for his identification, Alex declares that Tomas Nox requires no identification, the cop relocates Alex to a holding cell and gives him one phone call. Alice glanced at the answering machine.

There were no messages.

She sat down at the counter. Could he have gotten into an accident? Sure, he *could* have. He could be dead somewhere, crushed in a crumpled tin can that had once been her car, but even as she considered this possibility, she didn't feel worried. It was impossible to feel worried after such a fine paint. She propped her elbows on the counter, went to place her chin in her hands, and realized an instant before she smeared her face that she was still holding her brush.

Alice stared at the wet bristles.

Blue.

What had she been going to paint that was blue?

She tried to stand, but her legs were happy hanging off the stool. Just as well. She'd only end up back at the canvas if she got up now, and then she'd never hear if Alex called. Hardly aware of what she was doing, she began to sort the mail. Junk went straight into the trash, and so did the notice to mow the lawn. When a plain white envelope appeared in her hands, she set it automatically with the bills. Then she paused. Picked the envelope up again.

Alice Stokes.

Not Currier.

Stokes.

The penmanship was clean and effeminate: tiny circles over the i's, a gentle lean to all the letters. She glanced up at the top left corner. The fading bite marks on her legs began to itch. Boston. The envelope was from Boston, and unsigned. But the address wasn't Geoff's. The address was . . .

. . . the address was familiar somehow.

From where, though?

Using her nail, Alice opened the flap. A blank, creased piece of paper peeked up at her. Something thin and rectangular was tucked inside it. She unfolded the paper and saw red. Blocks of red. Bricks.

Longreave.

No, she realized, Faneuil Hall. Massachusetts was written in gold across the building's iconic façade. She was holding a postcard. She turned it over, and her first thought was that the handwriting on the back was not the same as the handwriting on the envelope. She didn't have a second thought. She was reading.

Dear Alice,

I'm sitting in a cold room as I write this, with only memories to keep me company. That's okay, though. They are good memories, for the most part, and I am warm.

I know I've been gone long, far longer than forgivable, and that the chances of this finding you willing to receive it are . . . well, the image of a castaway bottling a letter and floating it out to sea comes to mind. I've spent a lot of time thinking since the last time we spoke. About what you said, about what I wanted to say but couldn't. The truth, Alice, is you terrify me. You always have. It's why my hand was trembling the day I met you when I wrote my number on the receipt, and it's why my hand is trembling now. The thought of you won't stay dead in me. I kill it, but it comes back. I run, but it follows me down every hall, wherever I go. Is it a romantic thing to say you haunt me? I don't know. What I do know is I never want you to stop.

You asked me once, through a closed door, if I could hear you.

I hear you.

Now let me show you. Meet me Saturday night at eleven, where the water meets the sand, and let me show you that we can do better than this.

From the other side,
Mark Currier

Alice was squeezing her mouth—almost crushing it. *The day I met you, the day I met you.* She flipped the envelope and took in a breath so sharp it pulled at the skin of her palm. The return address, she knew why the return address was familiar. Oh God, how she'd hated working in that restaurant. Hated the food, hated the smell, hated the burgers for not being brushes, the customers for not being canvases. Hated all of it, including herself for how much she hated it. Until him.

Until Mark.

He'd wandered in from the cold, looking lost at first and then only looking at her. His scarf had been tied clumsily, and he'd been wearing this silky blue tie that went about as well with his plaid shirt as crocs go with a nightgown. But there'd been something about him, something she hadn't been able to put into words until she touched his sleeping face in the dark. Running her fingers over his cheekbones, his jaw line, his lips, she'd thought, *If I painted him, he would look exactly the same. He would look exactly like Mark Currier.* And she'd fallen asleep then, comfortable with the lights off for the first time she could remember.

Saturday.

Tomorrow.

Alice lowered her hand, hardly breathing, and started to read again—slower, from the beginning. She got as far as *memories* when the front door burst open.

"*Lis*!" Alex's voice carried up and away, his feet pounding the staircase. "The editor of the paper—Dennis Hicks—he called me out to breakfast. He wants Now You Now to go daily. He wants Nox on full time. Full time! The pool etiquette article, he loved it, *they* loved it. He showed me the fan mail, and . . ." The bedroom door swung open up above. ". . . *Lis*?"

Her brother's footsteps returned downstairs, softer. He limped into the kitchen, where she was sitting with the postcard and its envelope tucked inside her sweatpants. A smile bloomed across his face. "There you are. Did you hear what I said? Of course you did. The whole neighborhood probably—"

His mouth shut. He blinked.

"You're up. That's . . . that's wonderful, Lis. And look at the color in your cheeks. Where did *that* come from?"

Her skin burning, she said, "Must be your tofu scramble."

Chapter Thirty-Two
November 22ⁿᵈ

Mark spent a long week watching Mooney decline. The dog's fur fell out in patches. His breath grew hotter and stickier and fouler until Mark started burning incense even though the smell of chlorine was nowhere to be found. Mud dripped constantly from his black nose and crusted his pale eyes, which had grown dim, and the once bottomless pit in his stomach had been filled in like the hole they'd dug as youngsters. Sometimes he stopped breathing. He'd lay in place for hours, still but for his throbbing neck, and then his chest would shudder into motion with a grinding, crunching sound like food in a garbage disposal.

On Thursday night he tried to jump into bed with Mark and fell backwards onto the floor and then Mark had to pick him up because after that he kept falling when he stood. It was a full moon out, large and luminous, but in Mark's dreams the moon was black. In one of them he was holding Alice, except she was so feverously hot that his happiness at having her with him was poisoned by his worry for her. When he came to, he was hugging Mooney and it was morning. *The* morning. Time to go to Boston to collect what his money had paid for and begin the preparations for tomorrow night. But right then all Mark wanted to do was make time move slower. He lay in bed scratching the wrinkle of Mooney's brow until it was late afternoon and the trip couldn't be put off another minute. On his way out he started to say goodbye, but his voice stopped in his throat and he left without speaking a word.

The jeweler met him in the parking garage. "My friend, come and see!" His eyes were bloodshot, and his mouth smelled like a coffeepot. "All week it took, eating in the office every day and last night sleeping there too—but now a vacation is coming. A long vacation by myself—ha! If *she* thinks she is invited, she will have a surprise! A postcard is what she will get. My hands, you see my hands?" The jeweler held up fingers that were curled into pincers and apparently stuck that way judging by the difficulty he had opening the stairwell door. He urged Mark on as they climbed—"*come, come*"—despite the fact that Mark was right beside him. The shop looked exactly the same as before, down to the Hefty bags on the floor and the disinterested sister with her feet propped on the desk. Except this time when Mark opened one of the bags, *he* was the one who stared.

"Well?" the man said, leaning from foot to foot. "What do you think?"

"I think—I think you deserve that vacation."

The man crossed his arms proudly. "I already have my hotel."

"So do I," Mark said softly, closing the bag.

The man clapped his hands. "A vacation for both of us then! How is yours? Is it nice? Does it have pool?"

Mark thought before he answered. "Sometimes."

His sister glanced up at this, but the man seemed to find Mark's answer perfectly normal. "Good, this is good. How deep?"

"Very."

The journey back was slow. There'd been an accident on the freeway. A bad one. Broken glass strewn a hundred yards. Police officers treading in heavy boots. An ambulance in no hurry to reach the hospital. He glimpsed a pair of black bags—bags that were much longer and skinnier than the ones in the bed of his truck—and all of a sudden he didn't want to go back to Longreave. He wanted to go on driving the way he had with

David after the house party soured, just go on driving late into the night.

Instead he parked on the beach where he always parked when bringing in a load and carried around the first of the Hefties. He paused with his hand on the front door. He could feel some large weight pressing against it from the other side.

Shadows greeted him in the lobby.

Mark set down his bag.

When he finished unloading, he parked his truck up the coast and returned down the shoreline on foot, walking with his head low and his fingers in the lint at the bottom of his pockets. He felt nothing as he opened the front door, and he heard nothing but his footsteps as he climbed to 401. He wasn't surprised to find the room empty. He wasn't surprised at all. Turning around, he let the door shut behind him.

No draft stirred in the cellar. No water dripped. Mark walked down into the familiar cold and darkness, neither hurrying nor holding back, moving very much like a man on his way to work.

The air below the ramp was warmer, slightly humid.

Mooney lay curled in the corner. He didn't lift his head. He had no neck to lift it. The lumps had burst open and what remained of his throat resembled a popped balloon, muddy skin ripped into flaps. Mark sat down next to him. He leaned back against the wall. After a moment, he said, "I was a lonely kid. Preferred inside to outside, liked winter better than summer because the cold gave me an excuse to stay shut in with my latest obsession. Before chess, it was comics. Anything superhero, and all the better if it could fly. Tommy had his cowboy hat, but I had my cape. I would jump off the bed in my room—same bed and same room my son slept in—and try to stick in the air. Not sure when I grew tired of always landing. Probably after I watched Mom hit the kitchen floor."

Mark rubbed Mooney's ears.

"I remember when she brought you home from the pound. I was in the living room doing I-don't-know-what, and I saw her from the window. So did Dad. She came staggering up with you in her arms like some oversized suitcase, *you*, this puppy twice the size I was, and like hell if I didn't go running to the door to tackle the both of you, the way you always did to me. Dad was so pissed he almost gave himself his heart attack early. But he was more jealous than he was mad, I think. Jealous my mother got to be the one to make me that happy. Grownups . . . we aren't any better than we were when we were kids. We still want all our toys, even the broken ones. We're still selfish."

Mark's throat filled with mud.

"You don't have to do this. You don't have to do this anymore. You were my first friend, my best friend, but I don't need you anymore. Are you listening, you big dope? I don't need you *here* anymore. So don't you keep—don't you keep coming back for me."

Without moving, Mooney licked Mark's hand. His pink tongue crumbled. Then the rest of him fell apart, adding another layer to the soil below the ramp.

It took a while for Mark to crawl his way out, but he did, and by the time he left the cellar he was standing tall. He walked up through the familiar cold and darkness, neither hurrying nor holding back, moving very much like a man on his way home from work. *Tomorrow*, he thought, *Alice, tomorrow, Alice, tomorrow.*

Tomorrow he would see Alice.

But for now he was alone, and that was all right by him.

In 401 he untied the lantern from his backpack, set it on the nightstand beside the stick lighter and package of incense, and shut off the light. His eyes were closed before his head touched the pillow, and he was drifting off, almost asleep, when the voice floated out of the dark.

"I finished my bath," it said.

• • •

The temperature dropped twenty degrees in the next two hours as a cold wind—the first real bite of winter, weather reporters were labeling it—arrived in Manxfield after a long trip down from the north. It blew through town, turning garbage bins into flap-jawed monsters and pushing swings in empty playgrounds. It rattled windowpanes and whined through attics and made at least one wicker chair creak on a porch. At the beach, where the ocean was beginning to churn blades of ice onto the sand, the wind sharpened itself into a keen whistle along the eaves of an old pale building, one that had been standing by the water for over a century.

Above Longreave the full moon was a little less full, and its light fell gray and ghostly over the hotel.

Inside 401 Mark and his dead son were sleeping.

For now.

• • •

"Daddy."

At first Mark thought he'd dreamed Tommy's voice, it was so soft. But then,

"*Daddy.*"

Mark opened his eyes in the dark. His son lay pressed against him, wet lips brushing his ear. "What, kiddo?"

"It's cold."

"Where's your blanket?" Mark said, feeling around groggily below the covers.

"It's moving up and down my neck, and it's cold." Tommy sucked in a shivering breath. "His finger is so, so cold."

Mark smelled it then. Thick in the room, almost a physical presence.

Chlorine.

He fumbled blindly at the nightstand. An icy, numbing panic settled over him. The lantern wasn't there. His hand bumped the package of incense and then closed around the stick lighter.

"Make him stop, Daddy. Make him stop touching my neck."

Slowly, his arm shaking as if it weighed a hundred pounds, Mark lifted the stick lighter above Tommy and pulled the trigger.

The flame lit a face in the dark.

It was missing things. Skin for its skull, which was the smooth, stark gray of the boiler. Eyelids for its eyes, bright and blue and unmistakably merry. Below that, the pieces that were there were broken. The bottom jaw hung unhinged, joints exposed and splintered, supported only by a few scarce strips of flesh and tendon. The mouth was a yawning wound cluttered in the back with bits of teeth and mashed gums, and it was bleeding. Wherever there was tissue, there was blood—slick and red and steamy.

Mark dropped the lighter as he rolled away.

The room plunged back into darkness.

He landed on the floor. Tommy began to scream, then a huge bang shook the room and sliced the scream's volume in half. Mark scrambled out of the covers on hands and knees. His head slammed into the dresser.

"Dadddd—"

"*Tommy!*" he shouted, lunging after his son's voice. His hand brushed something lying in the carpet and an instant later he hit the closed bathroom door. "I'm here, I'm here." The knob refused to turn. He backed up and threw himself against the door. Once. Twice. He might have been tackling a wall. The wood didn't so much as creak.

A string of low, raspy breaths bled through the doorframe.

Breaths from a blocked-up throat.

Breaths both pained and laughing.

Helpless, Mark reached for his collar and—what was that? He repeated the motion and there it was again, a ripple in the black, a disturbance. His hand. He could see it move, even though he couldn't see *it*. He turned. To his right the darkness was not quite complete. The faintest glow outlined a limp, rectangular shadow.

Mark darted over and ripped open the curtain.

Moonlight spilled in, monochrome. He spotted Tommy's cowboy blanket lying by the bed, and past that, near the front door . . . the lantern? No. Better than that. As he crossed 401, he remembered shoving away from the dresser and brushing something on the carpet, something with a long and thick handle.

He turned back to the bathroom, a familiar weight in his hands.

Nothing was locked in Longreave.

Not if you had the right key.

Mark brought the sledgehammer down, smashing off the doorknob in one clean strike. The door stayed put. Seeing mortar, seeing bricks, he delivered a second blow straight into the door's center. Woodchips peppered his face. He swung again. The hammer crunched through and got stuck. He twisted and yanked, tearing open a jagged hole, like a mouth. Like the mouth of the thing in there with his son.

"Daaaaaaaaaaaaaaaaaadddddddddddddyyyyyyyy."

"I'm coming." Mark swung. "I'm com—"

A hand wearing its skin like a shredded glove reached out of the bathroom, closed bony fingers around the hammer, and pulled. Mark slammed into the door as his own hands were dragged through the hole. His knuckles ripped. Splinters dug into his flesh, drawing blood. The hammer left his grip and with a loud, bonking splash landed in the tub.

Then it was quiet.

Then, horribly, it wasn't.

A soft sound came from the bathroom. A *sighing* sound, rough and smooth at the same time, like someone running his palm along sandpaper. A sound that made him think of stubble and sweat, of his beard moving against Alice's cheek as they made love under the covers.

"Tommy," he whispered. "Can you hear me?"

A small, pale finger poked out from the crack under the door. He got down on his knees and held onto that tiny piece of his son.

"I need you to listen, Tommy," he said, trying not to hear how the sounds in the bathroom were changing, growing steadier, almost rhythmic. "I need you to listen carefully, to every word I say. Can you do that? Can you do that for me?" Tommy's finger curled tight around his. Mark closed his eyes and for an instant he was under the ramp beside warm mud, Mooney's mud. "You're dead."

Moaning, muffled, *moist*.

"You died five years ago. You had a seizure in the bathtub, a spotty time, and you swallowed your tongue, and you sank, and you drowned. You're dead." His son's finger twitched and pulled back into the bathroom. The crack under the door let out a gush of cold water. Mark went on, almost shouting now, his eyes pinched shut. "You're dead, Tommy. You're dead, you're not three, you're dead. You're *dead*."

There was a creak.

Mark stopped. The door had opened an inch. He lifted his hand, hesitated, then gave the door a push. It swung with a whine into the empty bathroom, skimming across the shallow, chlorinated pool on the tile.

•••

Mark found his lanterns sitting in the hall. He lit both. Back in the room, he opened the dresser and removed the rollup bag. With his copy of The Amateur's Mind off to the side, he set up the chessboard wearily. Behind a dark row of pawns stood the black king, his scabbed face flickering underneath his crown.

"New game," said Mark.

Chapter Thirty-Three
November 23ʳᵈ

Mark stood on the beach behind Longreave, his back to the water and his hands in his pockets, looking up at the stars. The wind had undone the part in his hair, which had grown down to his ears, and the waves reaching up the dark sand now and then touched the heels of his loafers. It was a bitterly cold night, the kind of night that could freeze a man's blood, but not Mark Currier's. He was used to the cold, no more aware of it than he was the names of the constellations or what they forecasted.

A low, musical note moaned from the eaves of the hotel. His gaze flicked down to 401, but didn't linger there for long.

Alice was coming.

He checked his phone. Eight after eleven.

Alice had to be coming.

•••

Alice wasn't going.

That was why she did errands all morning and mowed both lawns in the afternoon and spent the evening cleaning up the bedroom. To tire herself out. And the long, hot shower she took, washing the paint from under her nails and scrubbing the knots out of her hair, *that* was to make her whole body loose and relaxed, so she could melt right into sleep . . . just as soon as she said goodnight to Alex. Downstairs was extra chilly though, so she put on jeans instead of sweats.

The clock caught her eye as she walked through the kitchen. Quarter after eleven. Too late to make it anyway, even if she wanted to see what Mark was waiting to show her, which she didn't. She'd wasted enough time on that man, enough for a few lifetimes, and damn him if he thought she would run into his arms after one little letter.

A frenzied *clickclickclick* was coming from her brother's room.

He'd been working nonstop since Tomas Nox's promotion, churning up new ideas and getting ahead on articles, and it sounded as though his engines were really steaming tonight. What if interrupting him made him lose his groove? A terrible, terrible feeling it was to be yanked out of your world. Sometimes you couldn't get back in, no matter how hard you tried.

Quietly, she returned to the kitchen.

A thought struck her. She'd parked down the block just in case the temptation arose to go for a drive, but it occurred to her now that tomorrow was Sunday and the street sweeper came on Sunday—or maybe Tuesday. She wasn't sure. Better to be safe at any rate, and re-park in the driveway. She put on her shoes by the sliding door, where she'd left them after mowing the lawns, then took a page from her brother's book and slipped out the back. Hugging herself to keep warm, she jogged to her car and was grateful to discover she'd forgotten her coat on the passenger seat. The dashboard clock blinked awake.

11:19.

Alice drove home.

She didn't stop there though.

• • •

As the half-hour mark came and went, Mark struggled to keep his eyes off the hotel. He kept glimpsing movement inside the rooms and glancing at the windows, only to find the reflection of waves sliding blackly on glass.

He pulled on his tie, one hand up beneath his coat.

Alice wasn't coming.

•••

"Evening," said the police officer, leaning his bald head into the car.

"Hello. Hi."

The cop's eyes, just visible through his tinted glasses, scanned the backseat before returning to Alice. "You know what red means, don't you?"

In her mind a faucet poured crimson. "I'm familiar with the color."

"License and registration. If you'd be so kind."

The faucet continued to bleed into the tub. But she hadn't painted the bathwater yet, and her bristles had been blue when she stopped yesterday. Blue. Not red. *Blue.*

"Ma'am."

"Sorry. Here." She reached to her right and then saw her purse sitting at home on the kitchen counter. "*Not* here. I forgot it."

"In a hurry this evening, are you?"

"Please, officer." 11:31. "I'm already late—"

"Big Saturday night?"

Alice bit her lip. Nodded.

"Well then," he said, his breath steaming as it left his mouth. "How about a little walk to warm up for the dance floor?"

"*What?*"

He opened the door and held out his arm, like a chauffeur. "After you."

"I haven't been, I'm not—I swear."

"I believe you," he said sadly. "In my heart, I believe you. I really, really do. But this brain of mine is agnostic, and it'll need proof."

•••

Mark turned his head, held his breath. Something. He'd heard something for a second . . . *there*. There it was again.

Far up the coast, soft but growing, the sound of an engine.

A wave crashed behind him and spilled around his shoes. As the foam settled, the night became quiet once more.

Mark let go of his tie.

He'd tried. No one could say otherwise. But life wasn't like it was in Longreave. In life, when you let something die, it usually stayed dead.

•••

The hotel emerged from the dark, a spot of white forming on a black canvas, and a chill slid between Alice's ribs like an ice-pick. Her foot moved to the brake without her telling it to and stopped the car. She wasn't going inside, only to the beach. Whatever Mark said or showed her—if he was even there anymore—she wasn't going inside Longreave.

Bundling herself in her coat and leaving her car up the coast where no prowling eyes could connect it to the hotel, Alice set off under a golden chain of lamps toward the bleak silhouette overlooking the ocean.

•••

Mark picked up his things and started through the lobby, feeling the bang of the door behind him in his bones. He took the sledgehammer everywhere with him now, like his lanterns. Its steel head scraped on the floorboards as he walked.

A long trudge brought him to his workstation. The ring of lanterns threw light up against the tarp, which was held up not by nails anymore but pieces of duct tape, to ensure that a single hard yank would pull the whole getup free. He leaned his hammer against the bricks, then looked up at the wall. Now was as good a time as any to finish it, he supposed. No sense in waiting when the world didn't. He climbed the stepladder. As he reached the top, he heard a quiet voice outside Longreave.

"Mark?"

A smile appeared slowly on his face. He reached for the tarp.

•••

Alice picked her way along the rocky path, her right hand on Longreave to guide her. After the streetlamps, the dark seemed sudden. Dense. Soon there was only a residual glow to see by, and then nothing but starlight. The slop-slurp of the ocean deepened. It sounded huge, a monster of unimaginable appetite and size whose mouth was endlessly salivating. Apprehension pricked her. "Mark?"

No answer.

The dark ahead began to move down low, and the night sky divided from the rolling Atlantic. Salt sharpened the air. She couldn't make out her shoes, or anything beneath her shoes, and she lost her footing as she stepped onto the beach. It was blanketed in pebbles, slippery with them. There'd always been rocks here, but *this* many? A retreating wave slid back down the sand, and the sound of the water on the shore was strangely light, almost musical.

"Mark?"

She looked around, biting her lip.

"Mark? Are you—"

Something rustled behind her and then there was brightness, blinding brightness, as if all the stars above had fallen onto the beach. The ocean sparkled, black waves pinpricked with dancing white pearls. The sand blazed, not sand at all.

"Hello, Alice."

She turned on the sand that wasn't sand.

The very bottom of Longreave's wall had vanished, impossibly, and been replaced by a long glowing strip. In the middle of the strip floated Mark's face. His expression was one of simple gratitude. "You don't have to keep them, don't worry. I just wanted you to see. To know."

Bending, Alice picked up one of the grains at her feet. Fitted to it was a tiny piece of metal, which came off when she pinched it to reveal a tinier hook. "How did you . . . ?"

"Wait there," he said. "I'll be right out."

●●●

Alice had her back to Longreave as Mark walked onto the beach. He stopped and took her in, there against the silver-studded backdrop of the Atlantic. She was radiant, and not just because the ground she stood on glowed. It was the details of her, printed on her posture and in her clothes, details he'd forgotten but now returned easily to him, like lines from an old and favorite book. The way her hips leaned to the left, offsetting the tilt in her right shoulder. The slip of neck beneath her chopped hair, copper turned to gold in the light from the jeweled shoreline. He watched her waiting for him by the water, and he knew this was one of those few moments a person is granted in a lifetime, knew he would remember this moment until the very end.

Perhaps, he thought, *perhaps longer than that.*

"I had a pull-cord ready."

She turned.

"I was going to give it a tug." Mark picked up a string laid across the beads. There were thousands of them, every one made into an earring. "Drop the curtain for a nice dramatic effect when you arrived."

"I'd say you still managed to accomplish that," she said, sounding a bit winded.

"I hope it's not too much. I forgot you weren't a fan of cheese."

"Oh, I think I can make an exception." Her gaze wandered their bright corner of the beach. "Just this once."

Mark tossed the string into the cellar. "I should probably keep the speech I prepared to myself. I don't know if your stomach could handle it."

"Speech?"

"Well, it's more like a poem. Nothing elaborate. Just a brief fifteen or so stanzas written in iambic pentameter. I didn't have any ink to dip my quill in, though, so I had to use my own blood. Red, I must say, really enriches the passage where I talk about our hearts beating together."

Alice was looking at him curiously.

"What?"

"If I didn't know better," she said, "I'd think you and my brother have been hanging out. His talent for self-deprecation seems to have rubbed off on you."

Mark picked at the inside his pockets. "Did you tell him you were coming?"

"No."

"It's all right if you did." He tried to sound light despite the large stone resting on his chest. "I know you two don't keep secrets from each other."

"I'm pretty sure I kept it a secret from myself, honestly. That I was coming."

The stone lifted, and he let out a shaky laugh. "As long as we're being honest, you had me worried there. For a second."

"You said you wanted me to scare you in your letter. Besides, I owed you one."

"For what?"

"Keeping me waiting."

"I'm not—"

He swallowed.

"What aren't you?" she said, her face guarded.

"I'm not done." He could feel the rows of black windows looking down on him like eyes. "There are things I need to take care of in Longreave, things I can't abandon now. I don't expect you to understand, and I can't explain. Someday, maybe, I'll know how to tell you. But tonight what's inside there is inside there, and I'm out here." He pointed at the ground between them. "I'm out here with you."

Waves came and went, stealing jewelry from the shore. Wind played a series of rising notes along the hotel's eaves.

"*So?*" she said, with a touch of impatience.

Mark walked to her. He put an arm around her waist and ran his hand up her cheek, brushing back her hair. A bead glittered on her ear, bright as a pearl.

"You wore them."

Alice stared up at him. Her eyes were very blue. "Of course I did."

• • •

They kissed.

They kissed standing below the stars, and on top of them.

They kissed until Alice couldn't breathe, there at the place where the water met the sand in the shadow of Longreave.

"Take me home," she said when their lips finally came apart.

Mark pulled back. "Alice—"

"Take me home *now*."

Chapter Thirty-Four
November 24th

They snuck into the house like two drunk kids. Gestures instead of words. Tiptoeing steps. Regular, lengthy pauses to kiss. Once with Mark against the sliding glass door, a second time with Alice against the table, a third in the living room against only each other, their mouths like magnets.

He followed her up the staircase dizzily and the next instant they were in the bedroom, as if they'd skipped the upstairs hall entirely—as if the upstairs hall didn't exist. Door shut, lights on, clothes coming off. There was a sledgehammer in his pants, beating dully at his senses and making it impossible to think. His ears rang; his blood ached. He kissed her lips, her neck, her collarbone, kissed until he ran out of skin and then he made more, yanking the strap off her shoulder and freeing one breast. Her nipple hardened against his tongue, and God, Mary, Jesus, Joseph, all the names in the Bible weren't exclamation enough.

They fell, and the bed was there.

"Help," she gasped, fumbling at his pants as he fumbled at hers. *Slow it down,* a voice whispered, *slow it down so you remember.*

He got up with an effort and made for the light switch.

"*No.* Leave them on."

The bedspread was balled in Alice's fist, and the blue popped fiercely from her eyes. He dropped his underwear as he shuffled back to her, and her expression changed. But then she pulled him down and kissed him and he forgot all about the fear that had touched her face. Together they tugged at her pants, and as her thighs began to show, she stopped tugging and grabbed his wrist.

"Turn off the lights."

"I thought you said—"

"Please."

Getting up was hard. He heard Alice undressing under the covers. He hit the light switch, and the room went black.

Familiarly black.

"Where are you?"

"Here," he said, not quite sure where here was. He followed her shallow, uneven breathing through the dark, one arm out in front of him. Any moment he'd feel a door . . . and then a mouth of wooden splinters, and then a half-peeled hand . . .

He bumped into the bed.

"*Mark?*" Alice whispered uncertainly, as though he might be someone else.

"Yes." Warm, trembling skin waited under the covers. Alice made a little sound as his penis brushed her stomach. The contact was smooth, silk on silk, maddening. She wrapped her fingers around his shaft, and for one naked second it seemed possible, likely even, that he would die. He rolled on top of her, and now she was kissing him again, and not only with the lips on her mouth. Her hand moved up and down, stroking and pulling, pulling him in, in, in—

"Stop," she moaned. "Please stop."

He froze, his body one long throat with a lump of meat caught inside it. His arms began to shake. He tipped onto his side.

"I'm sorry, Mark. I'm sorry, I can't."

Five years, five fucking years, you brought me back here, why would you bring me back here and—

"Mark?"

The lump went down slowly, painfully, and Mark started to feel like himself again. "It's okay."

"Will you lay with me? Just lay here with me?"

"Of course."

She wiggled up against him and pulled his arm over her, pressing his palm to her breast. She was quivering. He remembered how he'd hated her for one selfish moment, and that hate sliced back at him like a knife.

"I'm sorry," he said.

"You didn't do anything. It was me. I—I get nervous sometimes."

"In the dark?"

She stilled. "I didn't think I told you that."

"You didn't."

"I guess you probably figured it out easy enough." She gave a brittle laugh that broke into an uneasy silence. "You . . . what else do you know?"

Never ask about Vermont. Mark let his lips rest on her neck a long time before answering. "Know about what?"

"Never mind." She squeezed his hand against her breast. "Mark?"

"What?"

"I do understand. About Longreave. And you don't have to tell me, you don't have to tell me *ever*, if you don't want."

Mark heard her. He heard her very well.

"Okay. All right."

Alice kissed his fingers, her lips soft on his split knuckles. "The beads were lovely. Like something out of a painting, or a dream." She drew a tensing breath. "Don't let me fall asleep, all right? Promise me you won't let me fall asleep."

"I promise."

She relaxed. "Talk to me. Tell me a story."

"I don't know any stories."

"It doesn't have to be a *good* story, just a story."

Mark thought. "There once was a boy who played hide and seek in his father's hotel."

"How old was he?"

"Old enough to play the game. Not so old he understood why he was playing."

"Why was he playing?"

"Because his father told him to."

"Why?"

"Because the boy wasn't supposed to be at the hotel. The boy was supposed to be away with his grandparents on a long vacation, and if his mother found him there, his father would lose him for good. So he told the boy to hide."

"Where?"

"Somewhere nobody would ever look. Somewhere his mother would never find him."

"Did she? Find him?"

"No. She didn't. And when she left, his father couldn't find him either."

"Where did he go?" Alice nuzzled closer, making herself small.

"The boy doesn't remember. It was a big hotel, and easy to get lost in, especially for a boy his age."

Her breath drew in deep and slow, then went out deeper and slower. "Was he scared?"

"I don't think so. I think he might have been sleeping, or something like that." The shadows in the room had softened enough for Mark to make out the bathroom door. Inside, a faucet was dripping. "His father was worried about him. So worried he didn't stop to think about the hotel's new guest."

"He shouldn't have done that to you."

Mark lifted his head in surprise. "Who?"

"Your dad." She smacked her lips. "That was bad. Making you hide. Dads can be so rotten."

"Alice?"

A light snore floated from her pillow. In her drowsiness, she had taken the boy in the story for Mark himself and assumed the worst of his father. Of *all* fathers. Mark let his head back down and whispered, "It never crossed my mind that the day Longreave's new guest checked in, the day I first smelled chlorine in my room, was the same day my wife had visited the hotel."

Hours passed.

Mark lay awake. He thought of bridges and area codes. He thought of Alex on the porch. *You have no idea where we come from,* what *we come from*. But mostly, he thought of eyes. Bright blue eyes. Eyes like small swimming pools.

Make him stop, Daddy.

Mark turned to Alice in the dark. With one fingertip—one *cold* fingertip—he touched the back of her neck and traced her spine, just as last night's visitor had done to his son. She shivered violently in her sleep. There came a low, leaking sound. A Tommy sound. Mark held her under the moistening sheets, his heart broken by horror and understanding.

"Oh God," he breathed. "Oh God, Alice, I'm so sorry."

•••

Alice woke knowing what had happened, feeling it on her, cool and sticky. She threw Mark's arm off her body and dragged herself, retching silently, out of bed.

"Alice."

"I told you," she said, lurching into the bathroom, "I told you not to let me fall asleep."

She slapped on the light and then banged through the shower's glass door. Cold water bucketed her head. The breath shriveled in her throat. She pinched her eyes shut in the icy rain, her hands balled against her thighs, her toes clenched on the floor tiles.

A pair of arms reached around her, folding over her breasts. A warm mouth kissed the curve of her neck.

•••

"I remember being here like this with you," Mark said, "when Tommy was a baby."

They stood with their heads together, their bodies gently swaying. Alice watched the steam thicken through the hot beads of water gathered in her half-lidded eyes. "You'll have to be more specific."

"We were splitting time between the house and Longreave. We'd just gotten back from a few nights at the hotel, and we were terrified—"

"Terrified?"

"Tommy was only a month or two and, new parents that we were, we were terrified to leave him alone. Like he'd combust if we stepped out of the room. But, once again, being new parents, we had acquired a very noticeable smell. An almost, how-do-you-say, *aura*."

"Oh, conundrums."

"Well, after much weighing and deliberating, stink edged out paranoia. We left the door open and snuck—"

"You're forgetting one thing."

"What?"

"How horny we were."

"*That*." Mark tightened his arms around her, and she felt a soft little movement against the cheek of her butt. "*Might* have played a role in tipping the scales."

Alice looked down the streams pouring over her body. The bite marks on her legs were gone. Heat had blushed her skin and washed them away. She ran a finger across the bolded date—11-25-04—dripping on her left thigh. "It's tomorrow."

"Yeah," Mark said softly.

"He would have been nine."

"Yes. He would have."

"What do you think he'd be like? Do you think he'd still love cowboys?"

"Probably not." Mark's lips moved against her neck, feeling out words. "At least, not in the same way."

"Do you think, if he showed up at the door in an hour like nothing ever happened, do you think we'd recognize him?"

"I know we would."

"Just think, though. His hair might be long, or brown instead of black—kid's hair, sometimes it gets lighter as they grow older. He might have put on a hundred pounds."

"Your son, fat?" Mark laughed. "Are you kidding?"

"I'm serious. He could be a whole new person."

"He could be six feet tall and bearded, the only third grader alive capable of buying beer, and we'd still know it was him in an instant."

"How can you be sure?"

"Because he'd know us. He'd look at us, and it would be impossible not to recognize him. It would be in his eyes, like a reflection in a mirror. It would be in his eyes, who we were to him, who he was to us." Mark paused. "We change, people change, but we see each other the same. We stay ourselves in each other, even when that self of us is dead. We stay family."

He's in me, Alice thought, and saw her brother bleeding on the toilet. Then she saw Tommy in a different bathroom, holding a toothbrush instead of a knife. *I had a dirty taste,* he'd said, and it had probably been nothing more than post-nasal drip, but . . .

Her throat pinched. "I scolded him."

"What?"

"I was scared for him, of him, I don't know. I was so scared of doing wrong by him, of fucking him up—he got a cold that winter, and I kept thinking, every time his nose dripped, I kept thinking how *pale* he was, how sickly. I was too hard on him. I should have been more, I should have told him more that I, what if he didn't, *Mark*, what if he didn't—"

"He knows." Mark moved his hand down from her breast, to her belly. "He knows."

Over the next few minutes, the water cooled.

"We should get out," Mark whispered behind her.

She gripped his penis. "Not yet."

"Alice . . ."

"I'm asking you to." She began to stroke, and soon she felt an answer.

He slipped inside, hard, but also soft. For a second it seemed he would never end, that he would go on reaching into her until he touched her heart. Then he was sliding the other way, the friction going out just as gentle as it was going in, just as unbearable. She closed her eyes and thought, *this, how could I ever have been scared of this?*

It didn't last long. Next to a year, or two, or five, it hardly happened at all. Alice was still climbing when Mark climaxed, and yet, as she listened to the water running off them down the drain, their breaths slowing together, she felt as if she had come, in a way. She felt as if she had come home.

Chapter Thirty-Five
November 24th

"I have to go."

"Already?"

"If any early riser heads out before church to take a walk by the water . . ."

They were lying on the stripped bed, Alice in a pair of sweatpants and nothing else, Mark in less than that. Her hand rested between his legs on a little pillow of pubic hair.

"Point well taken." Alice smiled. "Set aside a handful for me, will you?"

"Is that all you want?" Mark said, smiling back. "A handful?"

Alice curled her long fingers around his testicles and leaned in close. "It's a start," she breathed as their lips touched.

"I really have to go," Mark said, several minutes later.

"I know."

He kissed her again, quick and firm, then got up to collect his clothes from the floor. As he put on his tie, Alice said, "Will you be back tonight?"

Mark's hand paused mid loop. He looked into the closet and saw a muted scene playing out in the shadows there. Saw Tommy standing in the laundry basket as though it were a bathtub, calling for Mark, mouthing *Daddy* to the darkness around him. But Daddy was not there to answer.

At least, not *Tommy's* daddy.

"If I can."

Alice was quiet.

Mark turned around, and his eyes went first to her eyes, staring into the bathroom, and then to her hand, picking at the left leg of her sweatpants, scratching at the date tattooed beneath the cloth. "Of course," he said. "Of course I'll be back tonight."

As quick as a twitch, she was smiling again. "Good. That'll be nice. So, you're off to clean beaches, and then what? Got a lot of other things on your plate today?"

"Nothing big."

"Well." Alice gave her thighs an enthusiastic double-pat. "Good luck. And while we're on the subject of *good*, perhaps I should also say, *bye*."

"Not yet." Mark walked back to the bed.

"No?" She looked up at him, a puzzled tilt to her head. "Does your tie need a little straightening first?"

Mark leaned over her. "Just a little."

•••

Mark carried the taste of Alice downstairs on his lips. He knew what he had to do, and he dreaded it. But his dread was still a shadow—like the future, waiting to be formed. The present was solid. The present was *sweet*.

He slipped through the kitchen. All the lights were on, same as they'd been when he and Alice snuck into the house. He passed the hall, paused, and took a few steps back. The bathroom was dark. Alex had been up at some point in the night to use it, but was asleep now, judging by the crack beneath his door.

Mark kept walking.

He stopped on the threshold of the backyard, wind sucking away the warmth around him. Then he turned around for the second time. There was one more thing for him to do.

He knocked once.

Alex responded instantly, without a trace of sleepiness. "Come in."

As Mark opened the door, light extended a finger into the room and touched the thin figure in Tommy's old bed. Alex was propped against the headboard, his pale hair wandering about like one of the cobwebs in Longreave's cellar, his winter hat resting in his lap. He was picking at it the same way his sister had picked at her sweatpants.

"Did you get lost on your way out? Or are you here to implore me not to make a certain phone call?"

"Neither." Mark switched on the light before closing the door behind him and walking across the room. He wanted to distance his voice from the hall as much as possible. "I'm here to apologize to you."

Alex watched him. "What for?"

"For treating you like a gimp when I should have treated you like a brother."

Alex opened his mouth and left it open.

Mark ran his thumb idly along the dresser, its surface wiped clean of dust. "And to say—"

The top drawer was pulled out a few inches. Inside, where Tommy's cowboy blanket had lain for years, a pile of white briefs partially covered a manila envelope and a fancy kitchen knife with brown flecks stuck to the blade.

Mark shut the drawer. Whatever was in there didn't concern him.

"—And to say that if you need anything, let me know. I'll be around." He walked past Alex, who had stopped dismantling his hat, and gave one last look around the room from the door. "It's nice to have family living in here again."

•••

Night was lifting as Mark shoveled jewelry on the beach. The ocean began to burn where it met the sky in the distance, and the waves rolling toward Longreave caught fire. Finished, he covered the bed of his truck. A few earrings remained lost in the sand, pieces of buried treasure which people would uncover and take home over the years and eventually forget, not realizing what rare and precious evidence they'd found.

In his room, Mark dialed the number he'd copied from Alex's phone and then sat down by the chessboard.

The pieces were in play.

"Hello?" said a soft and hoarse and very old voice.

"Hello, ma'am. This is Mark Currier. I need to speak with you about Alice's father."

A pause. "I think you have the wrong—"

"His eyes were blue. And he built pools, or maybe he cleaned them, because he always came home smelling like chlorine."

Another pause. Longer. "She wouldn't tell you that."

"You're right. She wouldn't."

"Then how—?"

Mark marched his king forward one square, into black territory, and the endgame began.

"You live in Vermont. Where?"

Chapter Thirty-Six
November 24th

Alice lay sprawled across the mattress, drifting on calm currents. She wasn't asleep. Far from it. She thought she would never sleep again in her life, she felt so awake, but that didn't stop her from dreaming.

She stood on the beach, face to face with Mark under Longreave. The glow from the cellar outlined his tall, square-shouldered profile and silvered the gray in his beard, giving him a regal, almost kinglike, appearance. He walked closer . . . and now he had her pressed against the kitchen table, and now he held her beneath the covers, and now in the shower, their bodies sealed like a love letter inside an envelope of steam.

Alice smiled on the bed, then the currents carried her on to other destinations, not all of them as bright as the beach. She visited the boardwalk and found Alex waiting at the end of a bloody trail of footprints. She lowered Tommy into the bathtub. She watched a belt buckle, its skull grinning under a cowboy hat, sink into the mossy waters of a pool. But these memories were different somehow. They had less *traction*, like a shore whose sand has been replaced by beads. She stopped to look at them, but didn't linger.

Mark was coming back.

Mark was coming back *tonight*.

The ceiling lifted and gave way to the starry expanse over the beach, where she stood once again, illuminated by the light shining out of Longreave. "I had a pull-cord ready," Mark said behind her, and as she turned to face him—

There was a faint knock on the door.

"Come in."

Alex entered. Fuzzy red strands poked from his hat, which was frayed so badly it resembled a mad-scientist's hairdo. "Wasn't sure you were awake."

"I am. I didn't think you'd be, though."

"Yeah, well." Alex looked off to the side and swallowed, his Adam's Apple tugging at his throat. "How was your night?"

"Fine," Alice said quickly. "Yours?"

He nodded, still not looking at her, and she felt a twist of guilt inside her gut. Why hadn't she told him about Mark? Out of everyone in her life, her brother had put the largest stake in her happiness. He would want to know. He had the right to know. *But what if he isn't happy for you?* said a quiet voice, curiously similar to her mother's. *What if he doesn't understand?* Somehow the idea that Alex might not grasp what last night meant to her—that this pearl cupped in her hands might look only like an ordinary bead to him—was even worse than the thought of his disapproval. She pictured herself trying to explain and her mouth went dry. She might as well perform self surgery and bare her heart.

"So," she said, "you about to start writing?"

Alex gave another nod. "Soon."

"So much people need to now, so little time."

A crooked smile came and went on Alex's face. His right hand shifted against his leg. He was holding onto a manila envelope. "I—"

"What?"

He tossed the envelope onto the bed. "I'm sorry for the things I do. For the way I am sometimes."

"Alex," she said, but he'd already left the room. As his footsteps moved down the hall, she reached for the envelope. It was packed thick. She stuck her fingers inside and felt something glossy, like a photograph.

Or . . .

Alice flipped the envelope and out they spilled. Postcards for monuments and food dishes and vacation spots around the country. Postcards from far away places.

Postcards from Longreave.

She turned over the faces of Mt. Rushmore and read, in Mark's handwriting, Imagine how many people and how long it must have taken to build something so large, so lasting . . . incredible what we can accomplish when we come together, isn't it?

Downstairs her brother's door clicked shut.

Yes, she thought.

Incredible.

An hour later, with the postcards scattered on the bed but still very much on her mind, Alice went down to the office. She unframed the painting of the Charles that Alex had reclaimed from Geoff, then carried it out to the easel and unclipped the canvas that was currently hanging there. Soon she would finish the bathtub. Very soon.

But first she had a little more dreaming to do.

Alice hung up the river, its waters aglow with stars. Not so far away, by Longreave, the rising sun crowned the ocean in red.

•••

Mark slowed to a stop halfway across the bridge. Through the hole in the guardrail, he could make out the dry, snaking path of the riverbed below. He sat there for several minutes, then he drove on under the hidden noon sun.

The house was white gone gray and long, very long, skinned in panels that looked as if they'd been stretched. Dusty windows looked into dollhouse-sized rooms along the lip of the rooftop, suggesting a squashed second floor. Above the front door the paint wore a shadow of numbers where the street address once hung. He didn't need to read them to know he'd found the right place. Nowhere had ever reminded him so much of Alice's artwork.

The closed quiet of his truck made the silence outside feel empty and strange. Wind stole through the frosted-white woods. Water dripped soundlessly from branches weighed down by icicles. In the yard, a sunflower pinwheel missing one petal spun in a bed of drooping plants. He watched the flower go around and around and saw Alex moving his finger in a slow circle.

Where we started.

The front door opened, and a hunched woman appeared in the doorway. She had a face set in big, frowning wrinkles and a frame like an apple chewed to the core. On her nose sat a pair of horn-rimmed sunglasses.

"You're her," he said in a small voice.

In one even smaller, she replied, "You're him."

Mark held out his hand and then let it fall as she turned and walked into the house. He glanced down at the upside-down welcome mat beneath his feet before following her. The living room was dim. Shadows swam the blue carpet. Bare shelves crowded the walls. The smell of dust hung heavily in the air, laced with something sweet and generic that stirred up an association of store-brand ketchup and corn-syrup sodas. No chlorine. Of course not.

Of course not.

"Do you live with anyone?" Mark said, crossing a long hallway into the kitchen. She let out a soft laugh and touched the back of a chair. "Here."

"Thank you." The seat creaked under him.

"You're probably thirsty, driving all the way up here from Boston." Her slippers sounded vaguely like Mooney's paws as she moved to the sink. She gave the counter the same light touch she'd given his chair, and Mark realized with a stab of pity that she was blind.

"A bit further than Boston, actually."

Her hand twitched. She took a plastic cup from the drying rack. "Whereabouts?"

"Manxfield."

"Manxfield," she echoed.

"It's south. Near the ocean."

She filled the cup, her face turned to the one light source in the kitchen, a small window by the sink. Outside, branches scratched the bellies of clouds. She shut off the water. "How long have you two lived there?"

"Eleven years."

"Oh," she said, as though Mark had just told her it was going to drizzle on Tuesday. She came to him, set the cup down, then took a seat across the table. "And you and Alice, are you still . . ."

It dawned on Mark that this meeting was as much for her as it was for him.

"Ma'am?"

"Beverly."

"Ma'am, perhaps it would be easier if you told me what you do know."

Her sunglasses centered on his eyes. "I know if my daughter finds out I let you come here I won't ever be in the same room as her again."

"She won't."

"I hope you're as certain about that as you sound."

"The reason I'm here"—Mark pulled on his tie—"I'm here to make sure Alice never has to talk about here."

"You're protecting her."

"I suppose I am." He added, "Or trying to respect her, at least."

A pause. "How did I die?"

"Huh?"

"If you didn't know I was alive, she must have told you I was dead." Beverly licked her lips. "So how did I die?"

His mind turned to the bridge, to the hole in the guardrail. "There was a car accident."

A small hiccup escaped Beverly's mouth. She adjusted her sunglasses with shaking fingers and said, softly, "I know about Tommy."

Mark shifted in his chair.

"And I know you're supposed to be—well, you don't seem like you are, but I never was too good when it came to telling about men . . ."

"What am I supposed to be?"

Beverly performed a gesture reminiscent of her son. She drew a circle in the air next to her temple.

"Alice said I was crazy?"

"She mentioned the possibility."

"This was when she visited you in October?"

Beverly nodded.

Mark took a slow drink. "She had reason to think so."

"Are you?"

"No, ma'am. No, I don't believe I am."

He could feel the subject behind his visit inching closer, creeping up on them like fumes. Then Beverly's face brightened. "What did the hen say when the farmer dropped her egg?"

He flinched. "What?"

"Fowl!" She smiled, displaying several gaps between her teeth.

He wasn't sure how to respond, so he didn't.

"I don't get up to a lot these days, so I make up little jokes. I thought of that one yesterday. You"—her smile shrank, and he had the distinct impression she was watching him hopefully behind her glasses—"you wouldn't happen to have any jokes would you?"

"No, ma'am."

"Alex always brings a joke when he comes. He's a writer, my boy, he writes funny articles for The Boston Globe." Beverly sat up straight. "What am I telling you this for? You've read them yourself, haven't you?"

Mark swallowed. "A few. They're very good."

"He shares them with me over the phone, and I just think they're wonderful." She settled back into her chair, her body seeming to melt in size. "You and Alice. You're with Alice now?"

"Yes, ma'am."

"And you'll be staying—I mean, that won't be changing?"

Mark saw Tommy pulling the trigger on his own trembling shadow. "Not if I have any say in it."

"Good." She gave a tiny, almost unnoticeable, nod. "So, tell me, how is my daughter?"

"She's . . . okay."

Beverly ran a hand over her wrinkled shirt, all expression wiped off her face. "My children, Mark, are many things, but *okay* has never been one of them."

Silence hung in the air, with the dust.

"Who was he?"

"Who he was and what he was are different things entirely. I doubt anyone could ever answer the first question, not his parents, whoever they were, not even him perhaps, but as for *what* he was, as for the man my husband was, I think I can speak with some authority." Beverly made fists of her knotted hands, her knuckle bones gleaming through papery skin. "You were wrong, so you know. He didn't build pools, or clean them."

"Was he a swimmer?" Mark said, thinking of Alex.

Her eyebrows rose above her sunglasses. "A swimmer? No, he was a floater. He'd lay out with nothing under his back but the water, his belly up in the air, until the whole front of his body got so red it looked like it wanted to steam. He loved pools. Loved the geometry of them, loved the way the walls sloped down and became the floor, everything curved and molded together, one part. Loved the smell. Loved it all. It might have been the most curious, useless obsession in the world—certainly it was the most innocent, when it came to *his* obsessions—but he found a way to turn it into a career."

"How?"

"By selling them. He started out of his truck, pawning off those plastic kiddy tubs, those big blue saucers you always see lying in the weeds of somebody's yard. On hot summer days, he'd come driving by like the ice cream man, handing out his stock for five bucks a pop. Ten, if it was *really* hot. He didn't have a jingle though, so he just went nice and slow and whistled out the windows instead. He had some whistle, he did."

Mark pictured the face that had appeared over him in 401. The gaping mouth, the throat clogged with broken gums and teeth.

Not anymore, he doesn't.

"The Pool Salesman," Beverly said. "That was how I knew him before I knew him. When we met, *formally* met, my folks had died and I was living alone in their house. This was down in Addison. Now, I was never pretty like my Alice, and the boys who ignored me in high school went right on ignoring me until I was thirty. Guess I would've been sold pretty much anything by the time he knocked on my door, so long as it came with a nice smile.

"That summer turned out a real parcher. He upgraded his catalogue to include beach balls, water noodles, what have you. By Fall he'd saved up enough he didn't have to head south for winter like usual. He tucked in with me, got to drawing designs for the real thing, and when summer rolled around again, he wasn't selling out of his truck anymore. He was selling to hotels all down the east coast, straight from home. If you've ever been on vacation this side of the country, chances are you took a dip in one of my husband's pools."

A rash of bumps broke out over Mark's body.

"He had this house put up for us. We moved into it, Alex and Alice were born, and things were good for a while."

Mrs. Stokes went quiet, her face limp below her sunglasses.

"What happened?"

"What happened is the sweet man I said *I do* to down in Addison became an even sweeter father who liked to spend time with his children. What happened is I stopped asking questions I didn't want to know the answers to. Like why someone would build a bedroom for his kids but not have any windows put in it. Or why it was always his turn, not mine, to go settle the twins down when they started crying in the night. Or why, when they got older, I never seemed to hear them crying until *after* he'd gone to put them back to sleep. What happened is I learned that some men are sweet because they're sweet, and some men are sweet because they're rotten and they have to hide the flavor."

Mark felt a curious tightening sensation in his throat, as if a tiny crank had begun to turn inside his windpipe.

"They were three and a half the night I finally got out of bed because of the sounds. It was miserably hot. My sweat stuck on me like a second layer of skin. I walked down the hall. I walked very slow. The light was on in the pool, and a soft blue glow came in through the kitchen window. I kept walking. A part of me expected to turn back, *knew* I would turn back. I think it was that part of me that led me a little further, a little further, until I was outside their bedroom. That part of me, it spoke with the same reassuring voice you sometimes hear in a nightmare. It told me everything was okay. It told me soon I would be back in bed. Soon I would wake up.

"I pushed on the door. It opened quietly, and for a few moments it was like I wasn't there. The bed was lit by the nightlight on the dresser, lit blue, like the pool in the backyard. Alice's diapers were dangling off the covers. She was naked. So was her brother. So was their father, beneath them. They looked like a pair of ventriloquist dolls in his lap, their faces identical and blank, their mouths hanging open. I don't think they even knew they were moaning."

Mark wanted to leave. He wanted to have never come here at all.

"I won't say what he was doing to them, what he was making them do to him. To each other. At last, my husband turned his head. He did not seem surprised or upset to see me standing there. He got up, tucked Alex and Alice in, and turned off the nightlight. Then he took me by the arm and walked me back down the hall, through the kitchen, to the garage. He didn't say a word the whole way." Beverly Stokes pinched the loose skin on her throat and stretched it thin, taut. "Do you know much about chlorine, Mark?"

"Only its smell." As he spoke, he imagined he smelled chlorine wafting down the corridor behind him, as faint as a suppressed memory.

"Its most common form is a gas. But if it's stored at a very low temperature or under intense pressure, it becomes liquid. My husband had these canisters, each one not much bigger than a can of pinto beans, that did exactly that. Every few weeks he would loosen the top of one, just a little, just enough to make air, then drop it into the pool like a grenade. He got them specially, off the market. One was all it took to kill any germs in the water. A day or two later he'd fish out the empty canister with a net.

"He picked me up by the armpits and sat me down on the work bench. I watched him rummage around in a drawer. I didn't try to move. I don't think I remembered how to, without help. He pulled out a snorkel mask and put it on, then rummaged some more. Still he hadn't said a word to me. That *heat*. He was dripping so much he might have just climbed out of the pool, and I remember thinking he looked incredibly silly, puttering around in his birthday suit with goggles on and a tube pointing up above his head. I didn't see the canister in his hand when he walked up to me. He covered my mouth and nose with his palm, and my eyes went wide. They were still wide when he whacked the cap off the canister and brought it, hissing, up to my face. The last thing I saw before the garage melted, the last thing I've *ever* seen, was my husband staring at me through a fogged snorkel mask, his lips stretched around the mouthpiece."

Mark was gripping the table. He let go.

"My recollection of everything after that is muddled. I *know* I ended up at the hospital and was there for almost a month, that there were complications, infections, and the doctors were eventually forced to perform surgery. But what I *remember* is an eternity of sliding between consciousness and sleep, a never-ending nightmare where I slipped from dreams where I could see, dreams where I watched my children move by the blue light of their bedroom, into a pool of blackness and pain. I thought I was in hell. Now I know I only peeked at it." She took a long breath. "When I went home—"

"Weren't there questions?"

"My husband said it was an accident, said I opened the canister in the dark not realizing what it was, and when I could speak in words again, I said the same thing."

Mark bit down until the urge to scream passed. "Why?"

"Because I was lost. Because it was dark and I couldn't find my kids and his hand was there."

A memory rose up: crawling in darkness. The kitchen dimmed as a cloud passed below the sun. "Then what?"

"What more do you need to know?"

"All of it." Now it was Tommy Mark thought of, Tommy moaning behind a closed bathroom door. "I need to know everything."

"*Everything* would take more days than there's left in the year to tell. Everything would mean talking about the afternoon Alex scraped his knees in the backyard and rinsed off a little, not thinking, in the pool. Or the time Alice brought home the stray dog she found in the neighborhood. Everything would require describing their birthday parties. Long doting affairs, they were. They started the eve of, at dusk, and carried on until morning. Everything would mean discussing home-school lessons and extracurricular activities and how I laid awake each night, listening to the sounds down the hall. I could hear very clearly after my chlorine treatment, you understand. I could hear *everything*."

"The outline then," said Mark.

She turned her head to one side, pulling the skin smooth on her cheek, and for a moment he could make out the delicate curve of the jawbone beneath, a shadow of Alice. "My husband was not the type of man to want once. He wanted again and again and again. When it came to food he liked, he could eat the same thing every night, cooked the same way each time, and never get sick of it. The more he tasted something, the hungrier he became for it." She grimaced like someone swallowing a bad lump of meat. "I hoped it would become better for my children, that he would lose interest the older they got. But it grew worse. Sometimes I heard Alice laughing and laughing. Sometimes I heard Alex calling him—'*Dad! Dad!*'—the way you call a dog back to you when it gets excited and jumps all over your friend. Sometimes, when I washed their sheets in the morning, I smelled blood as well as urine."

Mark was gripping onto the table again.

"I was useful to him, you see. That's why he kept me around. I did the laundry, I made meals, I answered the door when neighbors came calling, which wasn't very often. I—"

Her throat gulped.

"How else were you useful to him?" Mark said.

"I—"

"How else were you useful to your husband?" His voice sounded cold. He felt cold.

"They were thirteen," she said quietly. "They were going to run away. I heard them whispering about it in their bedroom. My husband was leaving for a day, down to Boston, to see one of his pools finished, and Alex—Alex had bus tickets." She covered her face with both hands, muffling her words. "*I was scared. I was scared I'd lose them forever.*"

Mark relinquished his hold on the table and sat back in his chair.

"He never went anywhere without one of them after that. If he walked down the street to visit a neighbor, he took his son or daughter with him, and left the other at home. Then one day he and Alex went out for groceries and they took too long coming back. Alice ran when she heard the sirens. She got there in time to see."

"The bridge," said Mark.

Beverly spread her fingers, revealing black slivers of lens. "You never said how. You never said how you knew about the chlorine."

He tried to think of a lie, something that wouldn't sound insane, and decided he didn't much care what this woman thought either way. "Do you believe in ghosts, Mrs. Stokes?"

She lowered her hands. Again he had the distinct impression she was staring at him.

"I don't sleep anymore. I don't eat except when I'm so empty I feel I might float. I've been alone in this dark house—and it is always, always dark—for over a decade. I haven't looked at my children in twice that long. Once a year, they visit me. Sometimes they bring me flowers." Tears rolled down her cheeks. "You tell me, Mark, that you don't have any jokes."

Beverly took off her sunglasses. Two pits the color and texture of prunes leaked below her eyebrows.

"And you ask me if I believe in ghosts?"

• • •

Oil was a flexible medium—*fluid*. Wet, paint could be scraped off. Dried, it allowed for fresh layers, for new images to be born on top of, or recreate, the old. Alice's vision for the river that had been lost and found again was not overly complex. All it required was a removal of one winding shoreline, a modifying of the second, and an expansion of the star-blushed water. But once she'd constructed the body she spent hours more sharpening it, adding details as fine and chaotic as the blond hairs on the low of Mark's back. Vivid wasn't enough. Imperfect wasn't enough. She wanted the canvas to *live*.

At half past one, as her husband began his journey back from Vermont, Alice went into the office and placed the painting out of sight on the desk behind her ocean, before returning to the living room. The furious click of a keyboard carried through the house. She heard the sound but didn't process it. She was too thirsty.

Too hungry.

Fresh waxpaper, clean brush, pigments in a row. Alice clipped the bathroom to the easel and in one glance took it in: rounded floor tiles, lidded toilet, tiny sink and plain bathtub all shadowed in red steam. It *looked* finished, the same way the ocean looked finished, but it wasn't. The other day when she stopped, she'd been about to . . .

About to what?

She remembered sitting at the counter in a post-paint high, wondering why Alex hadn't come home yet. She'd propped her elbows, gone to set her chin in her hands, and almost drawn a smear on her cheek.

A *blue* smear.

Staring at the bathtub, Alice opened the jar of Ultramine. She wondered. She wondered. Then she stopped wondering and slipped into that thoughtless, selfless state of mind which all the best and most truthful things in life—art, lovemaking—share as foundation. When she set down the brush, a storm was raging beneath the bathtub's oversized and gushing faucet. Waves foamed over the walls, dark blue, and spilled down onto the floor. Alice picked her easel up by the base, carried it into the office, and returned for her palette. She walked slowly, her eyes wide open, like someone in a trance. Like someone who has just awakened.

Back in the office she restructured the clock, pushing the three paintings of the corridor back one hour apiece to make room for the bathroom. She placed this at eleven, gave one last look at the overflowing tub, then picked up her still-wet, still-blue brush from the palette and moved herself to midnight.

The ocean rolled.

She could see it now, the shape below the surface. It reached from the top of the canvas to the bottom, floating underneath the waves.

It was Tommy.

• • •

Mark arrived in Manxfield at dusk. The smell of his trip north clung to him, a stench of dust and secrets. He drove to the hotel for a change of clothes.

Also, one other thing.

He had to make sure no one was waiting for him there.

The sky hung a darkening shawl over Longreave. Inside, the dark felt colder—bigger—than it did out. He collected his backpack, switched on the lantern, and locked the door behind him before heading up the staircase. The sledgehammer was leaning against the wall in the basement, where he'd left it after hearing Alice call his name from the beach, and the absence of it made his hands feel heavier somehow.

In every blink he saw a pair of weeping sockets. With every step he heard an old voice creaking from the floorboards.

I was useful to him, you see.

In his mind, for the thousandth time, Mark held up a stick lighter and revealed the broken face hovering over him in the dark. And, for the thousandth time, his mind turned to the sledgehammer. The Pool Salesman had waited to visit until Mooney was gone, had even moved the lanterns into the hall out of Mark's reach. Why hadn't the Pool Salesman simply picked up the sledgehammer and caved in Mark's sleeping head?

How was *he*, Mark Currier, useful to *him*?

Mark stepped into 401 and as light touched the game on the nightstand, his father whispered, *You never could make any sense of the board around you.* Black had caught the white king in an unexpected fork. After the next move, no matter what, Mark would lose his queen. He wrung his tie, just as he had while leaving Alice's childhood home.

"Did your husband play chess?" he'd asked Beverly at the door.

"I couldn't say," she'd responded. "But there are many things about my husband that remain a mystery."

Mark had asked one more question before departing. Mark had asked Beverly her husband's name, and he hadn't been surprised by the answer. Like Alice once told him, the world was struggling toward synchronicity.

"I know who you are," he whispered to the board. "I know who you are, *Franklin* Stokes, and I won't let you have my son."

His son.

Mark walked slowly to the bathroom. The head of his shadow slid up the door and aligned itself with the hole gouged in the wood. As he stepped inside, his loafers squelched on the moist tile. "Tommy?"

The tub was empty.

Mark let out the breath he hadn't realized he'd been holding and then backtracked to the dresser for a fresh pair of clothes to wear home. At the thought of seeing Alice, his insides gave a happy—almost desperate—clench.

There was a sound, very close.

He turned.

From the dark under the bed came a low, twisted moan.

•••

Tommy's shadow darkened as it rose until pieces of him, jet black, breached the surface. A hand with fingers like snubs of charcoal reached from the belly of a wave; a kneecap and calf emerged along another wave's crest. Toes protruded in a spray of foam. Finally came the suggestion of a face. A smudge of chin, a sharp line of cheekbones, a blurred oval of mouth. His eyes were open underwater. His eyes were dark ocean blue.

Alice stepped back, one hand on her stomach. She felt as though she'd just pushed something terrible and wonderful out of her. And yet, as she stared at those wide, watching eyes . . .

"What do you *want*?"

Alice tightened her grip on the brush. The journey through the house had led her here, to him. It had taken back her to the bathroom and showed her what had been there since the beginning, waiting inside her, beneath the waves. At one in the morning, a raw dawn. At two, the front yard. At three, the living room. She moved from hour to hour. She moved like the hand on a clock. Four, a spoiled staircase. Five, a dripping bed and dead end. Back downstairs, skip six. Seven, the kitchen. Eight, nine, ten, the corridor. Eleven, the bathroom. Twelve, the ocean.

Alice paused, a hitch in her step. She started around a second time, faster. Sun, yard, sunken footprints. Stairs, bedroom, kitchen. Hall, hall, hall. Bathtub, storm. She paused again, started again, taking long strides. The canvases bled together. A wounded sun bloodied the front lawn of a house. Footprints led up the furred lumps of a staircase. A bloated bed sat before a sliding glass door, which stared out to a hallway that reached to a hazy bathroom, where a tub contained an ocean that contained Tommy . . . and now she was running. Running. All detail fled the canvases. The paintings became a rope connected only by color.

Red, red, red, red, red, red . . . blue.

There, at midnight, Alice stopped in front of her ocean. It wasn't like the rest, Geoff said. It didn't belong.

He was right. It didn't.

Because it wasn't finished.

She cleaned her brush, changed out the waxpaper, and mixed fresh paint using the powder from one of the jars Mark had tried to purchase. Careful not to touch Tommy, she drew a swath of red across the canvas. Her heart began to hammer. Lifting her arm, she colored in a bit more. For the next hour she kept her jaws tight and breathed thinly out of her nose. She applied long deep strokes to the bellies of the waves, shorter scratching strokes to the swells, and hard dabs to the crests. When her hand lowered once and for all, the only spots of blue left on the canvas were Tommy's eyes.

She stared.

The ocean was no longer an ocean. At least, not an ocean of water. The hungry anatomy that had swallowed her son had only been a skeleton. She'd given it skin. *Clothed* it. Where there'd been bellies, there were now fibrous twists and tangles, like yarn. The foaming mouth that had spit up Tommy's foot was transformed into a deep pocket, pebbled lips replaced by stitches. Her son reached up to her, a dark shadow drowning in red, his body woven into a frayed sea of cloth.

Alice dropped her brush. Turning to the door, she stepped on the handle and cracked it in half. She walked through the living room. She walked through the kitchen. As she passed the table, she saw it set for three people.

All the plates were bare.

Her brother looked up from his computer and smiled when she entered his room. "Hey there, you'll love this one. It's about—"

"Your hat."

He touched his head. "What?"

"You left it here when you left, but then it was gone."

"What are you talking about?" He pulled away as she reached the bed. "Alice, what's—"

She crawled onto his chest. The computer fell. "It was you."

"Alice." His pulse was visible in his neck.

She put her hands around it. "You."

"Lis, I—"

Squeezing, "You." She saw his eyes widen, saw the pupils constrict. "You." He squirmed beneath her, his bad leg kicking off the bed. "You." His hand pushed up at her face, and she bit it, sunk her teeth into his flesh. A whistling scream escaped his mouth. He twisted loose.

"Lis . . . I'm . . . *sorry.*"

Then she had his throat again, and he had hers. Tight. She squeezed, nails in his skin, squeezed. Gouts of blood welled beneath her fingertips, and she squeezed. The bed rippled like a pool. Alex began to sink. She followed him down, squeezing, squeezing. His winter hat darkened and became a shadow, became her son's face on the canvas, and she knew. She knew. She always knew. She knew, she knew, she new

she new she

new

• • •

Mark shone the lantern beneath the bed with a trembling hand. Far back, in the dust below the headboard, the light touched a naked, sobbing body.

"I knew," said Alice. "I *knew.*"

III. The Artist

Chapter Thirty-Seven
November 24th

Alex Stokes tucked his sister into bed. He laid her on her back, pulled the covers over her neck, and fluffed her pillow. Red droplets spattered her face. He wiped at the drops as they came, smearing her eyelids and cheeks and lips, but still they continued to fall. Was the ceiling leaking? He looked up to check and the room darkened and his head became heavy, a lump of marble on his shoulders.

There was a crash.

The lights woke up again, and he was on the floor. He blinked down at blood, *his* blood, his bright and pooling blood. With a cry, he began a backwards crawl across the wet boards. The bed bobbed away, and then he was staggering down the hall to the bathroom, leaving handprints on the walls. He stopped at the mirror. His hat was askew and his throat oozed on both sides, as though he'd been sucked on by vampires. Suked and suked and suked, and who was dressed for Halloween now? Who was the monster now you now you now?

His reflection started to laugh. The laughter caught on and soon he was laughing, too. Laughing, laughing, laughing, his hands gripping the sink, his mouth big and dark on his face. The hole under his left ear gave a juicy spritz. He leaned close to the mirror, quiet. There was something wedged in that hole, something off-white, buried in his skin.

A fingernail.

Blood gushed as he pulled it loose, and he felt the world turn soft and red and sticky. He managed to get the hand towel off the rack and against his throat. Then he tipped forward, his forehead to the mirror, and shut his eyes.

"What are you doing here, Uncle Alex?"

He twisted.

A hot bath had been drawn in the tub and inside it sat Tommy, propped up one elbow. He was staring the other way, toward . . .

"Shhhhhh."

Alex looked over and saw himself—but not himself—standing with his back to the closed bathroom door. This Alex was dressed for winter and wearing no hat. A finger was raised conspiratorially to his lips.

"Uncle—"

"Be quiet," said Hatless Him. His hair roamed about in trembly wisps. Frozen tears mapped his cheeks, touching the corners of his grin. "Mom will hear. She hears *everything*."

Alex remembered walking aimlessly through the cold, his limbs stiff and his bad leg throbbing like a rotten tooth, only to find himself back at the house where he'd started. He remembered standing inside the kitchen, shivering and lost, smelling the slow-cook of vegetables in the oven. And he remembered hearing a little splash down the hall, and going to the sound the way a moth goes to a feeble light in a dark room, his hand around the box in his pocket, a smile thawing the frosted grimace on his face.

"You're not supposed to be here," said Tommy.

"I brought your gift." Hatless Him sat down on the tub's edge. He pulled out a tiny box wrapped in blue. "When Alice and I were kids, we always gave each other our presents the day before our birthday. The presents we *wanted* to give, I mean. Not the presents we were made to give."

Tommy shifted, making waves inside the tub. "Mom said to wait."

"We had our own parties. Secret parties *he* wasn't invited to." Hatless Him held out the box. There was an eagerness in his eyes, and also an emptiness.

"I can't."

"It's yours."

"I can't."

"Go on, take it."

"Uncle Alex," Tommy said, "why don't you just go home?"

Hatless Him twitched. His face unraveled into wrinkles, as though some vital thread holding it together had been snipped. "You shut up." He gave Tommy a light shove. A schoolyard shove. Tommy slipped under the water. He came up sputtering, bangs pasted to his forehead, and recoiled from his uncle, who was now reaching out to help and blinking in shock, or terror, or both. "I'm sorry, I didn't mean, I'm sorry."

A scream chased the choking breath out of Tommy's throat, then the helping hand became a silencing hand as it clamped over his mouth. Hatless Him twisted toward the door, bracing for footsteps to come pounding down the hall. They didn't. The bath slopped. Kicking feet, clawing fingers. Four long seconds, four Mississippis, passed before Hatless Him turned back to the tub. When he did, he let go and muffled a scream of his own.

Tommy surfaced.

For a moment.

His jaws locked open as a slow, strange shuddering took hold of his body. He sank back down, smoothly, easily, almost calmly. His mouth filled. His moan garbled. His eyes, now underwater, rolled up to the whites.

At the sink Alex watched himself watch in horror, until he could watch no more. He limped out of the bathroom. He shut the door behind him. The sound of little, lapping waves followed him down the hall. "I only wanted to give him his present. I—I—"

He slipped in blood and caught himself on the guestroom doorway.

"You have to believe me, Alice. *Alice.*"

Alice didn't respond.

Warmth trickled from the hand towel. He stumbled across the room, too fast, and landed against the dresser. Something rattled inside the top drawer. He opened it and pulled out the steak knife. *Geoff's* steak knife.

The day melted outside the window.

Alex held up the knife, and a flicker of movement reflected off the meat-flecked blade. He turned. Alice was sitting upright. Her red mask had come off. Her face was young, very young, and except for a pair of bruises beneath her eyes, very pretty. She was herself as she'd been the day of the accident at the bridge.

Except it had been no accident.

"I don't know how much more," she said, and stopped there, just stopped, nothing left.

A teenage boy emerged. Hair hung down his neck in tawny, knotted ropes. Stick arms poked from the sleeves of his dirtied white t-shirt. He walked smoothly over to the bed, no limp, and sat down next to Alice. "Look up, Lis."

"What for?"

"I mean literally. Look *up*."

She lifted her head. "Okay. So?"

"Now look down."

As she did, the boy flicked her nose and made her jolt.

"See? Isn't looking up better?"

She gave him a light shove on the chest. A schoolyard shove. "Jerk."

"Why don't you get some rest?"

"I can't."

"Try."

"I can't."

Alex flinched.

"Sure you can," said Teenage Him.

"It's grocery day. It's my turn."

"I'll go."

"But—"

"I'll tell Dad your stomach's hurting." Teenage Him took her by the shoulders. "Lay thyself down now. Come on."

As her head hit the pillow, Alice began to blink slowly. Her voice slurred. "You'll stay awhile, won't you?"

"Sure I will."

"Tell me a story."

"Okay." Teenage Him hummed. "Once upon a rhyme, a lowly musical note named Baritone decided to climb the scales. He was armless and so, needless to say, any sort of ascension would prove difficult. Which is why he asked for help from—"

Alice's eyes had closed and her breathing had deepened.

Teenage Him pulled the covers to her chin and then sat there looking down at her, a solemn expression on his face.

Alex dragged the steak knife across his thighs. Its teeth chewed back and forth, eating through his swim trunks into his flesh. He was thinking of men. Men who pushed open doors late at night. Men who left bite marks. Men who made promises they couldn't keep, who said that people changed, who *lied*. They were all the same, all stabbers. All looking for a wound to plunge their pricks in. And if there was no wound, well, they had the tool to make one.

Red trickled down his right shin.

He told them. He warned them to leave Alice alone, and look what had happened. Look where Alice had ended up the moment a man walked back into her life. Things always came around to where they started. Things always came back around. After Geoff's bed, Alice spent two weeks in bed. How long would she spend in bed *now*?

Alex's legs streamed blood onto his bare feet.

"He's not going to hurt you anymore," Teenage Him whispered, and kissed his sister softly on her head. "Goodbye, Lis."

As Alex-the-boy left her side, Alex-the-man took his place. The knife was tight in his hand, fresh meat caught in the serration. "They're not going to hurt you anymore."

He gave her a kiss, marking his lips in the blood on her brow.

He said goodbye.

The boy was in the hallway. Alex walked past him into the kitchen, where he found his other former self limping ahead, hands wet with bathwater, feathery hair adrift. The table was set for three. A brand new, bright red winter hat sat on one of the plates. As yesterday's Alex paused to pick up the hat and put it on, today's Alex hobbled out through the sliding door alone, his hat in tatters and his fingers loose on the steak knife, a trail of broken and bloody footprints shining after him in the waning daylight.

• • •

For minutes nothing moved in 401, no sound but the trapped drag of a moan. Alice's sideways face swam in and out of darkness below the bed, eyes blue and empty, mouth black and silent. She was not the one moaning. Not anymore.

No, thought Mark, sitting with his back to the dresser and his hands between his legs. *No. No.* "No."

The spell of stillness broke.

He grabbed his lantern, tore it from his backpack, and lurched for the door. A wilted voice called out, *"Maaaaaaark,"* as 401 closed behind him. He ran down the stairwell, stumbling, tripping, falling through Longreave foot by foot, flight after flight. Alice was at home. She was wearing a pair of earrings, not a necklace of bruises. She was at their house, and it was *their* house because she was *there.*

He reached the lobby. He didn't notice that the air had a smell, or that his were not the only footsteps creaking on the floorboards. The front door appeared, and he slammed into it, throwing back a wild splash of light from the lantern that revealed for an instant the tall, bloated form advancing on him from behind.

The key *thunk*ed in the lock. Then his head hit the door, and a black flashbulb popped behind his eyes. His legs crumpled. He felt a large and soft hand over his face, felt himself being lifted, being turned. Through the cracks of fingers, he watched darkness run like water off the Pool Salesman's hanging jaws.

He had time for one thought: *Franklin Stokes found his flesh.*

The lights went out for good.

•••

A pretty little thing, she was. Slim in the waist, fat in the chest, with eyes that betrayed a hint of hopelessness. She had been sitting at the end of the bar, nursing a drink as tall as herself, and one look from those big sad gazers had told Geoff she was his type. He escorted her up the steps to his apartment, a hand on the low of her back, his pinky trespassing over her waistline.

"You live here?" she said in awe, and just a bit of fear. Just a taste.

"Here and New York, but mostly here." He reached into the pocket of his open leather jacket. That was when:

"Hiya, Jeff!"

Geoff spun around on a pale and smiling face. Something punched him low in the stomach. Bethany began to scream. He backed into the apartment door. The smiling face floated toward him above a loosely-tied burgundy scarf, and his first cold shock of surprise melted into a warm, almost sleepy calm.

"You."

"Me," agreed Alice.

"You came back."

"I sure did."

There was a strange, deep tug in his belly, as though someone had tied a rope behind his naval. Bethany's scream continued, and that reminded him. He had forgotten his manners. When an old friend comes to visit, you're supposed to introduce your new friend. "Alice, this is . . ."

What was the girl's name?

He tried to turn his head, but his neck had locked into place. The tugging sensation moved higher.

"Do you want to come in?" he asked Alice.

"I'm afraid not tonight," she said, still smiling. "I've got another date."

"Oh."

The girl doubled up on her scream, and Alice noticed her for the first time. "It's okay," said Alice. "You're safe now, Alice."

"But *you're* Alice," Geoff said. Then his neck unlocked and his head lolled forward, and he saw the hand climbing his body, moving in and out in gentle sawing motions. The hand was holding a large zipper, and his skin had opened around it like a second leather coat. The zipper stopped between his ribs, stuck, and his eyes widened in recognition.

"My knife."

The rest out of Geoff's mouth was blood.

• • •

Alex had been confused for a moment, but he realized now that the girl on Geoff's stoop wasn't Alice. Alice was at home sleeping. He tucked the knife into his swim trunks as he limped down to the car. Most days it was a devil to find parking in Boston, but not today. Today Alex might as well have been the devil himself for all his good luck. He paused as the headline for a Now You Now struck him—but no, that wouldn't work. Satan didn't have any silent letters.

Black ice crunched under his bare feet. He hopped behind the wheel, yelped, and pulled the knife out of his trunks. Silly Sally. He would have given his prick a nice little nick, if he had a prick to nick.

Prik?

Nik?

Two blocks later, his good luck said goodbye. He was sitting at a nasty red light, sentenced to an eternity of watching gay couples stroll across the street, when sirens drowned out the radio and emergency vehicles blew through the intersection, headed the way he'd come. He craned his neck after them. Had he driven past an accident without noticing? As their lights flashed off the brownstones, the light overhead turned green. He lifted his foot from a shallow pool of blood and pressed on the gas.

Eventually, a sign pointed him back onto the freeway.

The road looped around and arched onto a bridge lined by guardrails. Thirty feet below, traffic rushed like a bright river.

Suddenly there were three hands on the wheel.

He yanked to the left as the other hand yanked to the right. The car swerved across the opposite lane and kissed the guardrail. Then Alex had control again. He steered back over the yellow line, trembling, then looked into the passenger seat.

His fourteen year old self sat there, looking at him sadly.

"But I'm not Dad," said Alex.

The boy kept on staring as the bridge ended and Alex joined the southbound traffic out of Boston, toward Manxfield.

Toward Longreave.

•••

Alice Currier was afraid.

Mark had been here with her, but she didn't know where *here* was, had never been inside a room like this in her life. She'd been on top of a bed, on top of Alex, sinking, sinking, and now she was under a bed, and the floor down here was too soft for carpet. Too pink for carpet. Too warm. Through a reddish, swimming haze she could just make out the dresser. The shape of Mark's body was impressed in the wood, only she didn't think it was wood, just like she didn't think the handles sagging heavily off the drawers were steel.

This can't be.

She closed her eyes, and if it had been black behind her eyelids she might never have opened them again. But it wasn't black. It was pink. Rosy pink, like an eclipse. Fear put hands on her throat and squeezed. She tried to crawl, but the floor refused to let her go. She squirmed inside an Alice-shaped mold, trapped, the bed above threatening to press down and seal her away. There came a sound like moist, smacking lips as her right leg freed itself. She wormed out into the open and then got up off the ground. Relief turned to horror. She was naked. Completely naked, her body as slick as candy that had been sucked on and spit back out. And around her . . . around her . . .

The walls bellied in and the bed bulged, but it was still the room she'd lived in with Mark and Tommy. It was still 401.

"Longreave," she said. Her voice sounded hollow.

She turned for the window, but the curtains were covered in spidery little hairs that reminded her of the stuff that grows in the dark of a cast, and she decided she didn't want to look outside after all. Her eyes landed on Mark's chessboard. The pieces, placed on ovals rather than squares, were pink and red rather than white and black. The face of the red king was extra long, as though his mouth were hanging open.

Alice didn't want to look at him either.

She moved through slow-churning haze to a doorway that would have been at home inside a beating heart. The bathroom sweated. Fat red droplets clung to the toilet, the mirror, the sink. She couldn't tell if the tub, waiting sleek and low in the back, was empty or not. She wasn't about to check. As fast as her feet could carry her, Alice made for the exit.

She paused.

Turned toward the closet.

The panels on its doors were bent into smiles and frowns, and each smile, each frown, was exhaling the haze that swam within the room. As she watched, the air grew thicker, bloodier, until the closet was hidden from sight.

Alice gripped the doorknob and felt it give in her hand.

Outside 401 stretched a long pink corridor. She could see all the way to its distant end, which was twisted ever so slightly out of true.

"Hello?"

Longreave swallowed her voice.

A moist thud, like meat dropped onto a butcher's slab, startled Alice into a trot. The door to 401 had closed, and the ground where she'd walked was already refilling her footprints. She moved past other rooms, all of them shut, silent. Cobwebs dangled off drooping lamps, although no spider had ever spun anything so damp, or so red.

She stopped at the stairwell. Should she go down?

Did she have any choice?

The steps were rounded and not quite firm, and the railing was a vine-like thing held up by bowed posts. As she descended, the stillness grew around her, heavy on her skin and ears, a deep-water weight of silence. Emerging onto the second floor, she looked left to a dead end and then right to the far-off archway that led to the foyer, where she'd sat on occasion with Mark and Tommy, playing in the sunlight through the bay window. Past that was the annex. She'd never been in the annex. The word bothered her. It sounded like *ax* hiding behind an extra syllable.

The lobby staircase was longer than she remembered, and *snakier*, running side to side as well as down. She was standing over it when her neck prickled and her body stiffened and her head turned slowly, slowly, toward the dead end of the hall.

There was no one there.

She'd only imagined being watched.

Alice started down the steps and bit by bit, Longreave's main floor revealed itself. After the stairwell and corridors, the lobby yawned, a warm wide-open where folds wrinkled the ceiling and the ground rolled like waves in a frozen ocean. A shapeless mass—the front desk?—hunkered under heavy drapes of cobweb. She scanned the other way and as her gaze passed over the hotel's monolithic front door, movement caught her eye.

Colorful movement.

In the red and pink of the lobby, the blue leapt out at her. It was flowing, like spilled paint, only it was flowing both in *and* out, washing over the couches below the mantelpiece. At its limits the tide was the airy blue of cotton candy, or a freshly-chlorinated pool, but it deepened to navy at the center. There, sitting at the heart of the tide on a table whose legs leaned, overflowing like a bottomless bucket, was a lantern.

Alice floated toward the couches (if they could be called that, with their hunched and lumpy backs). On the closest lay her husband. His eyes were closed. His chest was moving shallowly. "Mark." She touched his shoulder. Shook him. Took his hand and held his knuckles to her trembling lips. "Mark, wake up." Past the flowing blue around her, past the staircase and front desk and bathrooms, separated by the vast unmoving sea of the lobby, stood the pink wall that marked the other end of the hotel, and she shouldn't be able to see that far with a single lantern, especially a lantern that didn't even shine. She pulled Mark's face to hers. "Please, please, wake up."

His breath stirred the air between them.

Then the air was still again.

Deathly still.

Alice backed away, a hand over her mouth. She couldn't feel her breath. She couldn't feel her breath because she wasn't breathing. The mantelpiece squished into her, and she twisted around to find herself staring at the painting above it. A building rippled on the canvas like a reflection on water, its architecture swimming madly, pinkly, against a blue ocean background. The building was Longreave. *Her* Longreave.

No.

Alice ran across the lobby to the hotel's heavy oak door. It was still heavy, but no longer oak. Its half-moon handles stretched as she pulled on them, and with a sound like skin unpeeling from hot leather, the door opened. On the other side stood darkness, utter darkness, all the colors in the spectrum mixed together, the world outside Longreave blotted out, black. From somewhere over the threshold came the crashing of waves, then the door slammed and she was running again. Running on bare feet, running naked, running nowhere. She climbed the snaking staircase and kept running, past doors of different sizes, beneath cobwebs hung like viscera, down a corridor whose floors and walls and ceiling curved into one another without beginning or end. She heard Geoff talking about beasts and the bellies of beasts and families as beasts. She saw her brother on the toilet, bleeding himself out slice by slice, and he was wrong. Their father wasn't in him, in either of them. They were in their father.

They were inside the Pool Salesman.

Alice stopped under the archway to the foyer. The air was as still as a strangled breath. She turned to face the dead end of the hall.

"Hello Daddy."

Down in the lobby, the front door opened a second time and a figure limped into the dark to discover one light had been left on inside Longreave.

Further down, in the cellar, a small body in the boiler stirred.

The birthday party had begun.

Chapter Thirty-Eight
November 24th

The Pool Salesman was a man made of curves.

At six foot two and two hundred fifty pounds, he was heavy but not fat, his frame packed in equal parts adipose and muscle. The bulge of his calves connected to the plumper bulge of his thighs to the plumper still bulge of his buttocks. He had an expectant mother's protruding belly and poking navel, and a child's hairless skin. His breasts were full pouches, the nipples ringed like large bull's-eyes. In life his cheeks had been round and rosy. In death his cheeks were torn into extensions of his lips, and red was a color reserved for the blood streaming from his mouth and for the erection curving up between his legs.

He stood at the far end of the corridor, a wall of pink tissue against a pink tissue wall.

He took a step toward Alice, and all of Longreave trembled.

•••

When Mark was twelve he'd gone to bed one night with what he thought was the flu but was in fact appendicitis. He'd woken an hour later, covered in sweat, pain cleaving his stomach down the middle and filling his bowels with lead.

This pain was worse.

It found him floating at the bottom of some deep, black place and dragged him screaming to the surface. A face hung overhead, bloody and bodiless, depending from the dark like a spider from its web. "Hello, brother by law."

"*Al*," Mark gasped, "*ex*."

"That's a nasty bruise on your noggin. Real nasty. Honestly I'm not surprised you took a spill, what without any lights to see by, but what I don't understand is why on *earth* you'd decide to nap afterward." Alex peered down at Mark, one eye opened wider than the other. "Did your concussion make you sleepy?"

The pain changed shapes. It was a hot coal buried in his guts, and now it was a corkscrew winding beneath his ribs, and now it was blunted, mashing teeth. Warmth ran up the back of his coat. He moaned.

"What did. You do?"

"You told me to let you know if I needed anything, and I needed you to wake up, so I let you know."

Mark squirmed, but only his upper body moved. "My legs. I can't feel my legs."

"I should think not!" Alex laughed a single high-pitched note that threw back his head, revealing the blood-soaked towel tied around his throat. "Where do you think I'm sitting?"

Mark let his cheek drop and saw his lantern sitting on the coffee table a foot away. The lobby. They were in the lobby. A memory came to him, hazy, dim. His feet off the ground and his body pinned to the front door as an enormous, soft hand squeezed his face. He'd been running to go home, running from . . .

Maaaarrrrk.

"You," he whispered.

"What—what did you say?" Alex reached up to pick at his frayed hat.

There was a scratching sound beneath Mark, a sound like someone scraping the cushions with a pointed fingernail. "My wife."

"Your wife is what I came to talk to you about." Alex's voice remained cheerful, but cords of tension popped from his face. "She hasn't been feeling so well since you returned—not so well at all—and she's going to need rest to get back to herself again. A *lot* of rest. I think it'd be better for her if you don't see her again."

I knew, said an echo of Alice, *I knew, I always knew.*

The cords pulled, stretching Alex's lips into an agonized grin. "I warned you, Mark. I warned you to stay away."

I knew, I knew . . .

And then, before falling silent:

. . . Tommy.

Mark's pain hardened into something else. Something terrible. It must have showed on his face, for Alex recoiled like a man who has opened a closet and found a monster waiting for him among the clothes.

"You killed my son."

Alex's hand moved quickly, desperately. Mark felt a tickle in his side, starting where his back touched the cushions and then running through him, *sliding* through him. He reached for the coffee table as the tickle gave way to a warm, gushing release. Alex's hand reappeared, lifting a wet knife into the air.

The knife plunged.

Mark swung the lantern.

It painted a bright, arching blur on the air. Then it shattered against Alex's temple, and glass rained down in sudden darkness. There was a howl, a shift of weight. Mark rolled off the couch and landed on his chest. A tiny flame awoke inside the broken lantern, which was lying on the rug beside him. Clutching his stomach, he dragged himself onto his knees, onto his feet, and into the dark. Blood seeped through his fingers.

"*Maaarrk.*"

By the dying light, he saw Alex staggering after him through the lobby, the steak knife swinging from his arm.

•••

Alice ran down squishing stairs and across a porous floor. She ran between a black length of window and an elevator whose dial pointed down to nothing, nowhere. She ran to a second staircase twisting up and around the elevator out of sight, and as her foot sank into the first step, husky breathing filled the foyer.

Towering in the archway, the same archway she'd stepped through moments before, was the Pool Salesman. Blood spilled from his mouth and hissed on his stomach and rose over his face in threads of pink steam.

A scream grew inside the stillness of Alice's chest. Stumbling, falling, she climbed to the annex. Doors slid by, room numbers melting off placards, and just when it seemed the corridor would keep on going forever, bend after bend after bend, she reached a stairwell with steps so steep and small they almost formed a slide. She scrambled up to another corridor, the same as the last, and there was her father's ragged breathing . . . and there were his heavy squelching footsteps . . . and *there*, coming around the bend behind her, his bouncing belly. Alice fell onto the next set of stairs. The scream expanded behind her ribs, crushing her from the inside. She opened her mouth to let it out and—

Silence.

The stairwell was empty. Nothing at the bottom. Nothing plodding up the steps, eager and wet. She continued to the fourth floor, picked herself off the ground, and froze. The door to 4A hung out on knuckled hinges. Gathering up her courage, she tiptoed closer. In the room hovered that strange reddish haze. With her body pressed to the opposite wall, she inched past the doorway. She could see the outline of the bed inside, swollen like something about to burst. She could see nothing else.

Alice rounded the bend. The door to 4B was also open, but the haze inside was so thick it made a door of its own. She wondered what it would smell like, if she could smell. Then she realized she already knew.

It would smell like chlorine.

As she crept past the doorway, flat to the wall, the haze shifted. A small line parted its surface, followed by a second and a third, joining the first two. The letter *A*. More lines stitched together, writing her name on red, like an invitation.

Like a Valentine.

The last of Alice's sanity took flight. She ran around the final bend in the corridor and with no more staircases to climb, nowhere else to go, she went the only place left to her. 4C. Shut inside the room, she pressed her back to the door. Before her glistened a bed, crimson sheets tucked under a pigskin-pink pillow. The scraps of a fuzzy chair lay piled beneath the window, which was curtained. No haze floated on the air, not in the bathroom, not in the closet.

There was a sound in the hall.

And another.

And another.

Alice tensed as the footsteps stopped outside 4C. From the corner of her eye she watched the doorknob, waiting for it to turn. Then came a whisper, like the palm of a large hand moving up a shaved leg.

The whisper was inside the room.

The Pool Salesman walked out of the closet, his chin hanging to his chest, his arms spread for an embrace.

Alice screamed at last.

•••

Alex had never thought himself scared of the dark, but Alex had never been inside a dark such as this in his life. It was like black cloth over the eyes. It was like having no eyes at all.

But that was all right. He still had his ears.

Mark had been within slicing distance, but then the lantern had died for good and Alex had lost him. Now Mr. Hotel Manager was playing stealthy, creeping about like a mouse. Well, Alex could play that game too.

Alex knew how to be plenty quiet.

He leaned against the wall to his right and picked broken glass from his cheek, tucking the shards into the netting of his swim trunks. He didn't want them tinkling on the floor and giving away his position. No sir. Blood rode the prickly curve of his smile. He swallowed it down bit by bit, sip by sip, listening.

There was a muffled rattle.

"I'm coming, Mark! I'm coming!" Alex lunged forward and grappled around a projecting wall. The rattling became louder. "Almost there!" His knife went *swish-swish* in the darkness. He heard a creak of hinges and then a stir of cold air hit him and he slammed through a door as it was swinging shut. Things got confusing after that. First his footsteps became hollow, as if he were running on sheet metal. Next the floor sloped down beneath him. He stumbled. Something clattered off to his left. The thinking part of him questioned going after the sound, but the chasing part of him had already committed. He turned . . .

. . . and walked into open air.

Alex landed before he knew he was falling. A cold, pale pain bloomed in his hips like the buds of a winter flower. His legs buckled and his head struck concrete.

For a while the darkness was both inside him and out. Groaning, he moved his hand and discovered his fingers were still closed around the knife. He was lying curled on one side. The temperature had fallen with him, and the stale, dusty air of Longreave had grown staler, dustier. The lobby had smelled like a tomb. This place smelled like the inside of the coffin inside that tomb. A basement, in other words.

"Clever, clever," he called. "What did you throw for me?"

"Padlock," replied a hoarse voice.

Alex laughed as he crawled to his feet. Good old Mark had rattle-rattled the padlock off the door above and tossed said padlock off the high dive. "I never took you for a quick thinker."

"I learned it from an old friend."

"Thinking quick?"

"No. Fetch."

From somewhere in the distance came a deep, purring sound. A draft like someone's last breath touched Alex's face, and a chill tickled down his spine. "What game are you playing now?"

"Hide and seek."

Alex limped after Mark's voice, the ball of his right foot scraping on the concrete, his knife pointed out on an invisible arm. A second heartbeat throbbed inside his hip. A third drummed inside his head.

"Why'd you do it, Alex?"

He altered his course to the left. "Do what?"

"Kill your sister."

An image of Alice superimposed itself on the darkness. Her eyes were half closed and her hair hung down from her face in coppery strands, tickling a pair of forearms that reached up to a pair of hands wrapped around her throat. He slashed at the picture. "No!"

"Why, Alex?"

"I didn't—"

"You didn't mean to?"

"I didn't do anything to her." He hobbled faster. "She's at home. She's sick, so she's sleeping. You wouldn't know because you've been here. You're always here. It's always been here over her for you."

Something splashed far off. Alex swiveled on his heels, his knife veering like the needle of a malfunctioning compass.

"But I wasn't at Longreave today," said Mark. "I was in Vermont. Talking to your mother."

"You're a liar."

"Beverly had a lot of nice things to say about you. Not so many nice things to say about your old man though."

"Found you!" Alex took a leaping, spearing step, but all he got in return was the sound of panting further ahead.

"You drove him off the bridge."

"My father was a bastard. He was—you have no idea what he was. He was killing her. He deserved it."

"I agree with you there." Mark gave a wet cough. "What I want to know is, do you think he'd be proud of you for finishing what he started?"

Alex grabbed his pounding skull. "Shut up, shut up, shut up . . ."

It was quiet.

His fingers trailed down, dragging the hat off his head. He rotated in a slow, complete circle. "Mark?" The draft was a salty whisper on the air. He became aware of the purring again, a rising-falling static deep inside his ears.

There was a drip behind him.

He turned. "Mark?"

Plop.

"Mark, where are you?" Alex heard or thought he heard a series of little, creeping squishes advancing toward him through the dark. He took a limping step back, and another drop landed where his feet had just been. His body stopped against brick. From above came a deep purr, followed by a disintegrating crash. Waves. The ocean. He inched sideways down the wall, his knife out in front of him.

Something soft, *fleshy*, snagged the blade.

Alex buried a scream. He pulled the knife in and ran a trembling finger along its edge. Perched on its tip was a cold bead of water. "Mark," he said, "Mark, I think there's someone else in here with us."

Then, close:

"I forgot to warn you."

Alex whirled. Light blazed on and threw a tall, twisting shadow over him.

"Longreave is haunted."

The sledgehammer struck Alex in the mouth, slamming his head back against the wall and shattering his teeth and gums in a brick-red spray of chips.

•••

The Pool Salesman's belly pressed into Alice. He leaned in, the splinters of his jaws on display beneath unfolded cheeks, blood reaching down from his lips in steamy ropes. His mouth grew larger, larger, swallowing the room.

She looked down at the floor.

He took her chin. His fingers were more than soft, more than familiar. As he lifted her face, his breath touched her skin like the warm, ragged wind before a summer storm. Then came the rain. Little drops against her collarbone and breasts. Little drops so cold they burned. The Pool Salesman's eyes hovered inches from her own. She saw herself reflected in them, drowning in blue, black pupils over her mouths.

He ran his nails down her neck slowly, reverently, and the bruises gathered around her windpipe woke with a collective throb. His breath stopped for a moment. Then it started again, sawing and coarse, and he picked her up by the armpits the way he used to when she was a child. The room swayed as he carried her. Her toes dragged across the floor.

He let go.

Alice soaked into crimson sheets. Her father crawled up the bed on all fours, jaws drooling, penis nodding. His hand engulfed her breast. His weight lowered onto her. *Somewhere paint is drying on a canvas, somewhere stars are looking down on a beach, somewhere postcards, somewhere Mark, somewhere, somewhere.* Teeth glistening in a ruined mouth. Blood spitting hot on her cheeks. *Somewhere, somewhere, somewhere—*

Franklin Stokes lifted his head. His eyes brightened. The blue shined out of them like light from a swimming pool. As he climbed off the bed, relief filled Alice like a deep breath. *Thank you, oh thank you, thank you* . . . Then he turned to her with his arms raised, and she saw it in his hands, two and a half feet long and tapered to a crude point.

A broken chair leg.

A splinter.

A stake.

Its tip punched into her chest and the shaft followed, softer than wood, harder than flesh. Alice watched the stake disappear into her, shrinking in size, magic, until only six fuzzy inches poked up from her sternum. Pain arrived. Grinding, chewing, *burning* pain. Pain that clamped her jaws and bent her body skyward.

The Pool Salesman pointed at Alice, pointed at the bed, and then left her alone in the room to suffer. She writhed on red, in red. Blood as thick as paint and as black as oil welled between her breasts. *This is Hell. I died and found Hell inside Longreave.*

Someone or something—perhaps the hotel itself—heard her.

And agreed.

Smoke began to rise, feeble and gray, feeling up from the raw floor and curling off the pink walls as though 4C were a lump of meat cooking over flames.

• • •

Alex stayed upright for half a minute before he slumped down the wall to his butt.

Mark didn't make it nearly so long.

Something ran out of him as he let go of hammer. It drained from his body like ice water and left him empty, cold. He stumbled back and sat down hard, his right leg soaked red, the lantern hanging from his wrist by the handle. He'd looped it there, so he could turn the switch and swing at the same time. *It's a bracelet, a pretty bracelet.* His hands, remembering the crunch of bone, began to shake. Someone sat down beside him. He turned his head and there was Alex, blue eyes aimed up slightly into the darkness. They were the eyes of someone watching a show in a crowded theater. Blood dripped off the sledgehammer lodged between his jaws.

Plop . . . Plop . . .

Mark saw Tommy standing on a wet patch of concrete, his face closed, expressionless, and spoke with as much voice as he could muster. "Don't look. Don't look at him."

But Tommy wasn't looking at his uncle. He was looking at his father.

"Is it true? Is Mommy dead?"

A lump swelled and burst inside Mark's throat. Tears ran quietly down his cheeks.

Tommy gave a strange nod, almost a twitch. "Is she here? Like me?"

"Yes."

"Where?"

But Mark had realized something. "You remember."

"I listened. Like you said." Tommy reached to his hip, as though feeling for a revolver. "I listened to every word."

"And you're here."

"You're here," Tommy said simply.

A falling musical note carried into the cellar. Mark stared at the stacks of brick on the floor around him. He hadn't finished. He'd worked so hard, come so close, but—"Oh, kiddo. What do I do? *What do I do?*"

"It's okay, Daddy."

"I didn't, I didn't, I—"

"It's okay."

Tommy held him, and together they rocked to the ghostly rhythm of the ocean outside Longreave, rocked and rocked like lost souls onboard a sinking ship. Behind them a shadow broke away from the dark and stepped into the light, the black curve of its belly filling out, becoming flesh.

From his seat on the floor, Alex watched the show go on.

•••

As the smoke thickened in the air, stitching together like loose gray threads, Alice closed her eyes. Better the pink inside her than the pink out. Better to lie still and play dead, if she was dead already anyway. At least like this she wouldn't have to see her father come for her. She would only have to feel him.

"It's time to get up," said a voice as soft as soot.

She opened her eyes. By the bathroom stood a tall silhouette, shimmering darkly inside a cocoon of smoke.

"You can rest later." The smoke parted down the middle, and from it stepped a man Alice had only ever seen in photographs and in the buried lines of Mark's face. He looked heavy, thick in the arms, large in the stomach, but he moved with the lightness of a wind-blown shopping bag in a parking lot. She recoiled when she spotted his penis, but there was nothing lecherous in his solemn gaze. His dark eyes found hers and didn't wander. "Get up, Alice."

"I can't."

"Yes, you can. And you will."

The stake quivered. Black blood pooled between her breasts. "It *hurts*."

"It doesn't hurt if you don't want it to," said Frank Currier. Smoke drifted from his mouth, measuring the length of each uttered syllable on the air. "Nothing can hurt if you don't want it to. You don't have to be *here* if you don't want to."

She wanted to gasp at the pain. She couldn't. "Where else is there?"

"You'll find that out in time," he said. "But right now you have to get up."

"I'm stuck."

"Not there, you aren't. Not by that." Frank pointed a smoking finger at the stake. Then he aimed the finger at her head. "That's where you're stuck."

A living, agonized heart pounded inside her chest. "I don't—"

"Turn it off."

"Turn *what* off?"

"All of it."

Alice was beginning to understand her husband's quiet resentment of this man. "How the *hell* am I supposed to—"

"Close your eyes."

She did, but the pain was still there, hiding behind pink curtains. "It doesn't help."

"Think of something else," came Frank Currier's soft, smoky voice. "Something brighter."

Brighter, brighter. The pink behind her eyelids darkened. She felt herself sinking into the pain, sinking *through* it. Pinpricks of light winked awake across spreading black velvet. Waves played music on the shore as sand that wasn't sand . . .

"Now get up."

The dream collapsed around her, darkness and starlight running like water down a thirsty drain. "I can't. I can't. You have to *help* me."

"I'm afraid I don't have the stuff." Frank tapped the hollow of his windpipe and the skin there crumbled like old parchment. Smoke breathed out of the hole. "Call it the symptom of living a coward's life."

Alice let her arms fall limply to the bed. "I can't."

"You have to."

"What do you care what happens to me?"

"What's happened to you has already happened." Frank waited for her eyes to lift before he finished. "But it hasn't happened to Mark. Not yet."

"Mark?" She jerked, and the chair leg tugged at her insides. "What about Mark? He isn't—is he okay?"

"He's far from okay. Your brother saw to that."

"Alex?" Her head reeled from her husband, asleep down in the lobby, to a red hat atop an empty plate. "But—"

"Are you going to keep asking questions?" There was nothing soft in Frank Currier's voice now. "Or are you going to get off that bed?"

Alice wrapped her hands around the stake, and pulled. Blood bubbled from the wound. Cartilage tore inside her. She pulled until the walls began to throb, until the room and the hotel melted away and all that remained was an endless plane of pink across which bruises exploded like purple fireworks, and then she collapsed back onto the mattress, two more inches of not-wood sticking from her chest.

"Go the other way," said Frank Currier, arms crossed over his crisping paunch.

"*What other way?*" she shrieked.

He pointed his gun-barrel finger at the ceiling. "Up and over."

Alice set her jaws, planted her feet, and worked her elbows up beneath her. The sheets clung to her skin, warm, moist, and she thought of all the sheets that had ever clung to her in her life, all the stinking urine-soaked sheets on all the beds she'd ever slept in, been fucked in, drowned in. She thought of Geoff, thought of her brother, of her father, and she *pushed.*

Her spine scraped against the stake.

Her body rose.

Six inches of chair leg shrank to five . . . four . . . three. She pressed her palms down flat, her back unpeeling from the bed, her chest arching toward the ceiling. "You could've told me to do this," she hissed, "*before* I made the fucking thing longer."

"Don't waste your breath."

"I. Don't. Have. Any. God. Damn. Breath." The knob of the stake disappeared into her, and she screamed as her insides crunched to make room. She screamed in triumph. With a hearty, wine-cork *ponk,* the chair leg popped from her backside and she rolled off the bed onto the floor.

Frank Currier smiled down at her. "Well done."

"Where is he?" she said as she rose, one ragged hole oozing between her breasts and a second between her shoulder blades. "Where's my husband?"

"You don't know?"

"How would I?"

Frank's smile curled into a smirk. "You and Mark really are meant for each other."

"What's that supposed to mean?"

"You're both utterly clueless." Frank waved a diminishing hand. "He's in the cellar."

"Thanks," she spat, before stumbling to the door and out into the hall.

"Alice."

4C was a churning gray. Within the smoke, the outline of Frank body's blurred and fanned outward, losing its shape.

But his voice was clear.

"Your son is with him."

•••

"Daddy, get up."

The cellar had shrunken to Tommy's cold embrace, and Mark didn't want to get up ever again. "No."

"Stand up."

"*No.*"

"He's here."

That raised Mark's head. Across Tommy's cheek lay a long crooked gash—a wound fit for a cowboy. His pupils were swollen by fear. In the shadows behind him a pair of blue eyes sparkled with lantern light.

Franklin Stokes emerged from the dark, moving with the prolonged strides of a man walking through water. His belly spat like a griddle beneath his dripping jaws. Pink steam chlorinated the air around him.

Mark shoved off the ground on wobbly legs. He pushed Tommy to the side.

The Pool Salesman stopped. There was a moment of almost-silence, the wind howling distantly over Longreave's rooftop, as he stared at the body propped against the wall. He pointed at his dead son, lifted his finger, and pointed at Mark.

A question.

"Yes," Mark answered, and yanked the sledgehammer loose. Blood splashed the concrete. Teeth scattered. Alex's jaws bounced on torn hinges, then his head slumped forward and tucked itself between his carved legs.

A molar skipped between the Pool Salesman's feet.

His meaty hands came together in applause.

He took a step closer.

•••

Alice spiraled down through the annex, a large black eye weeping between her breasts. Memories welled inside her, pieces of a jigsaw puzzle fitting together. The cowboy blanket lying soaked on the bed in 401. Mark's voice. Telling her you had to take care of what was yours, even if it scared you, even if you didn't know how. Telling her the story of a boy who played hide and seek at his father's hotel.

Her son was in Longreave.

Her son had been in Longreave all along.

Alice flew past 2C and was rounding the bend when she found herself diving through the air. She crashed onto her hands and knees and looked back at what had tripped her. There was a head on the floor. A dog's head. It twisted and snarled. Foam dripped off its snapping jaws.

Alice's skin tightened on her bones.

The dog was *sick*.

Beside it the floor bulged like a pink latex glove and then a huge paw clawed into sight. Alice scrambled to her feet. The dog's neck was emerging, and were its hind legs dangling into the corridor below? Or was it crawling up from somewhere else entirely? A second bulge gave birth to a second paw, and she spun the other way. She had to hurry. Before the dog surfaced. She had to get to her husband. Except . . .

Except the dog she'd found in the park as a child hadn't actually been sick. It had been this big friendly lump napping behind a bench, and it had licked her hand and followed her home, and then her father had broken a tree branch and peeled off all the bark so the wood was nice and smooth, and *sick*, she'd told herself as he pushed on the branch, as the dog whimpered, as its mouth foamed, *sick, it was sick, sick, sick*.

Except this creature, stuck in the floor, reminded her of herself not so long ago.

Alice turned back. There was mud in the dog's rolling white eyes, and on its jowls, and between its claws, as though it were crawling out of the earth. As though Longreave to it was one large grave. *Perhaps the hotel is a blank canvas and all of us who are dead, all of us but Mark, are simply painting ourselves on its walls. But if I, Alice Currier, am the artist of my own afterlife, who handed me the brush?*

"Don't you bite me," she said.

The dog gave off a lurid heat. She gripped it by the scruff of the neck and felt things throbbing there, under the fur. *Sick*, whispered a voice, *sick*. She told the voice to shut up, and pulled as hard as she could. The floor stretched around the body squirming inside and finally ripped. From the flaps burst the dog, who tore off and left her sitting beside a deep pink fissure that healed itself in seconds and left not even a scar. She wondered a moment where the dog was headed, and then she was running the other way.

To the cellar.

To her husband.

To her son.

• • •

The Pool Salesman approached, mouth dripping red, eyes shining blue.

His prick nodded *yes, yes, yes,* between his legs.

Mark pushed Tommy into the corner, making space, then lurched forward with the sledgehammer raised high. He swung over his right shoulder, swung over his left, swung and swung, raining blows down on bare flesh. Something twisted with a warm gush in his side. He ignored it and swung on. But the Pool Salesman was built of different stuff than Longreave. He took the beating the way a couch takes a child's temper tantrum, or a bed takes a hard fuck. Now there were two of him, three of him, more, his bodies together forming a wall, his joined mouths as vast as the cellar. Mark gasped for breath. The hammer slipped, the ground tilted, and for one extended moment he was weightless. Then his cheek was on the concrete and he was staring at bricks stacked higher than he could see.

A heavy foot set down in front of his face.

The foot lifted and moved on.

Mark dragged his head after it. He saw the Pool Salesman advancing on Tommy, the shadow of his penis swollen grotesquely on the wall. "No," he said.

There was a sound.

Building in the dark, amassing volume like a bullet train amasses speed. A roaring-engine sound, tearing at the air, feeding off its own echoes. A sound that sang through his bones like the joyous beat of steel on stone.

Mooney.

One hundred soaring pounds hit the turning Franklin Stokes square in the chest. It might have been one thousand. The impact lifted him off his feet, slammed him against the wall, and shook dust down from the ceiling. Tommy ran, or crawled, or a combination of the two, and as the Pool Salesman reeled about with Mooney swinging from his right breast, Mark's gaze went to the sledgehammer lying beside the sole burning lantern.

"Daddy."

Mark shoved Tommy away. "Keep running. Keep running, and don't stop."

Fingers buried themselves deep into Mooney's jowls. Skin stretched from his locked jaws.

"But—"

"*Go!*"

Tommy's face twisted like a wrung dishcloth. He stumbled back through the dead ring of lanterns into the dark.

A wet-newspaper *riiiiiiiiiiiip* turned Mark's head.

The Pool Salesman's breast opened in a steaming gush. Mooney landed on his paws and dropped a clump of nippled meat, then the dance was on again and Mark was dragging himself toward the sledgehammer, belly to the ground. He knew that if he looked back he would see a trail of blood smeared behind him. He didn't care. The hammer was what mattered.

The hammer.

Mark was reaching out for it when a hand—not his hand—closed around its splintered handle and lifted it off the concrete.

Growls.

Rasping breaths.

A crunch.

Mooney thumped to the ground. His eyes were shut and his tongue was lolling and his back . . . there was something wrong with his back. It was supposed to run one direction, not two. As Mark realized what had happened, the sledgehammer came down and struck the dog again, breaking his neck.

The Pool Salesman stepped between them.

"You bastard," said Mark. "You—"

Mooney's jaws snapped and his teeth peeled a yellow bowstring of tendon from the Pool Salesman's left ankle. There was a long and awful howl. The hammer fell. And that was the end of it. Mooney relaxed his bite and his body went stiff and the Pool Salesman, now walking with a limp, plodded off into the darkness of Longreave's underbelly.

It was quiet as Mark lay down next to his old friend. "I told you not to come back. I told you. But it wasn't for me this time, was it?"

A pink flicker.

A twitch of tongue.

Mooney's chest expanded around a shuddering breath. His spine grated and jerked. His claws scraped at the concrete. As he began to move, to pull himself after the Pool Salesman and Tommy, Mark stared. Then he nodded. Then he smiled. "That's right, buddy. That's right." With a slow hand, he reached for the sledgehammer. "Who needs to stand when you can crawl."

• • •

Tommy ran through the dripping cellar. Its pipes gurgled and leaked, and its gray-blue walls and ceiling streamed. Water gushed down the shiny body of the Boil Her. He wasn't three years old. He knew that now. He was dead. Daddy taught him, the same way Daddy taught him you couldn't finish a job you never started. He was dead, like the bird he found floating in the fountain when he was three—when he was alive. He was dead, and no matter how hard he worked or how many bricks he put down, he'd stay dead.

But there were worse things.

There was Him.

Tommy looked back as he ran. A doll-sized Drippy Man raised Daddy's hammer up high. The hammer dropped. Tommy's dog (horse) hit the ground. He cried out and turned his head straight in time to spot the puddle. But not in time to stop. His legs tangled. He saw his face on a ripply mirror, saw flowing arms reach out to catch him.

Cold.

The water was cold. The water was as cold as the bathroom tile on his cheek, as cold as the Drippy Man's finger running down his neck, as cold as a cowboy's eyes staring down a gun. Tommy back-crawled out of the puddle and pulled himself into a tight ball. It wasn't fair. It wasn't fair that anything could be so cold when you were dead.

Don't stop.

Tommy lifted his head. Daddy told him keep running, not, "Keep running unless it's scary," and besides, it was okay to be scared. Daddy told him that, too. Across the puddle was the staircase to the annix, but that was only thinking long-ways. *Deep-ways* . . . who knew how far the puddle reached deep-ways, or if it had a bottom.

It did, he remembered.

Daddy had carried him across it.

But there might be holes, like on the Boil Her. There were holes you came up from and holes that went down and down and down, and what if there was a hole like *that* hiding in the puddle? He could walk right into it and sink forever.

A howl ripped at the air.

That decided Tommy. He got up and walked into the gray-blue water, not looking back—he wouldn't look back no matter what. His teeth chattered. His tongue felt limp and funny in his mouth, like it used to before a spotty time. He inched toward the staircase, testing the ground before each step. *No hole,* said his left big toe. *No hole,* said his right. Something began to drag behind him, scraping along with a lurch and a pause, a lurch and a pause, and he wouldn't look back. Whatever happened, he wouldn't look back. He would run and run, like Daddy said, and he wouldn't look back.

Tommy looked back.

The Drippy Man waded into the puddle. His left foot went flop, flop, flop, and around its chewed ankle the water bubbled and hissed like a boiling plot of blood.

•••

Alice ran around the lobby for what felt like an eternity, searching for a door and a staircase down, darting in and out of empty rooms, her desperation growing. She was starting to think she should have asked Frank Currier for directions to the cellar (or better yet, a map) when at last she found the trail. Spilled on the red of the couch and rug below, the blood was almost invisible, but it stood out dark against the pink floor. She followed the drops and smears and occasional footprint, and then she realized not all the footprints were the same.

Some were shoeprints.

Loafer prints.

Alice found a door hiding inside a niche. She banged through it and stopped over a ramp as soft as a tongue, leading down into the scarlet immensity before her. Walls, striated like muscle, touched a ceiling thick with cobwebs. Straight ahead towered a cherry swollen beyond proportion, three tons of overripe fruit supported by tubes that brought to mind diagrams of the female reproductive system.

But it was the size of the cellar that held Alice in awe.

Here was the hotel with no bedrooms or bathrooms, no corridors or staircases, no foyer to set apart the annex and no annex to be set apart. Here was Longreave without division or distinction, Longreave unwalled, every inch long and wide of the nineteenth-century relic exposed in one underground stretch, one red hallway to join all.

And someone sat dead at the far back corner of it.

The body was bent over with its face between its legs, which were dressed in a shredded pair of shorts—or swim trunks. She watched the hair float on Alex's skull and felt a slow, strange flutter of bird wings where her heart once beat.

Then some part of her, not her eyes, sensed movement.

She turned her gaze to the middle of the cellar. The only thing there was the bloated cherry, and that was utterly still, and yet the longer she stared, the more her neck tingled. Movement. Movement *there*.

Blue, flowing blue, spilled out from behind the cherry. Alice started down the ramp. She knew that blue, where it came from. It was light, or the likeness of light in this hellish Longreave, and it belonged to her husband.

Mark came into view. He resembled a man rowing a boat on solid ground, without a boat. In his hands was a large hammer that he was using as a paddle, dragging himself forward inches at a time, on his knees more than his feet. Something furry emerged behind him, scrunching and extending along the floor like a caterpillar. It paused and lifted a snout in her direction, and she recognized it finally as the dog from the annex.

So, there was another way down to the cellar.

She ran.

Mark's head turned at the sound of her footsteps. He looked straight at her, and kept looking, and kept looking. *You're in the dark. He can't see you.* Then she slowed, seeing *him* clearly for the first time. A hole in his jacket peeked through to a deeper hole in his flesh. The blue of the lantern painted his blood purple as it seeped from his pantsleg.

"Mark," she said softly, stepping into the light (not light).

His face changed. The sledgehammer wobbled and he fell back against the wall. "*Oh God, Alice. Oh God.*"

She glanced down at the cartilage and bone on display inside her chest. Nothing she could say would change anything, so she said nothing. She sat down over him, took his hand, and placed it firmly on his wound. "We need to get you help. Do you have your phone?"

"No," Mark mumbled. "I don't know. Maybe."

"Where?"

"Slacks."

"Right pocket or left?"

"Light. Right."

She dug under his soggy wallet until she found his phone. It was damp but otherwise normal. Like the rest of his clothes, like Mark himself, it had not been infected by her afterlife. "You're going to be okay," she said. "We're going to get you out of Longreave."

That woke him up. "I can't—I can't leave yet."

She pushed him gently back. "You have to, Mark. You don't have a choice."

The dog, still worming along, began to inch past her. Slivers of white showed through the mud in its eyes. It was more than sick now. Its neck was broken and its back was cracked in two, nothing holding together the body but flesh and fur. Its middle stretched as the front paws pulled, and bunched as the back paws pushed.

Alex had not done this.

"Mark," she said in the hollow voice death had given her. "Where's Tommy?"

He answered in the same voice. "Your father."

It seemed there were no secrets anymore.

Alice turned her head the direction the dog was crawling and saw a staircase spilling down into the cellar like a waterfall of melted pink wax. She put the phone in Mark's hand. "Call 911. Tell them where you are."

"I'm coming with you."

"No. You're not." She grabbed the dog by both ends and dragged it onto Mark's legs. "You stay, boy. *Stay.*"

"His name is Mooney."

She took the phone back, dialed, and returned it. "Tell them."

There were no tears in Mark's eyes as he looked at her. There was nothing in his eyes at all.

"You're going to be okay," she said.

Alice headed for the staircase, and unlike her son before her, she did not look back.

•••

Darkness pressed in around the lantern light. On the phone, the operator was shouting, *"What is your emergency? Sir? Ma'am? Sir? Are you there? Hello?"*

"Well, buddy, what do you say?"

Mooney lifted his head, extended a paw, and began to crawl.

"Yeah." Mark hung up the phone. "That's what I thought."

•••

Tommy left a trail of footprints down the corridor.

He fled past a room where washers sloshed and dryers did too, past a room where streams ran on the unmoving belt of a treadmill, past rooms where faucets drained into overflowing sinks.

A staircase.

He glanced back from the top.

The Drippy Man climbed the steps, his fat hands on the leaking walls. Tommy cried out and continued to run. The hallway blurred. Behind every door he heard panting, rasping, squelching. Threads of pink steam curled around his ankles. He lunged through a break in the wall and landed against another wall, this one cracked all over. Through the cracks he saw into the elevator shaft, only there was no elevator, and how did he know that? He'd never been told that. Rivers poured inside, running their way down and down and down. Then he was running again, too.

But only for a moment.

Tommy braked at the top of a staircase, staring down at the room his daddy had carried him through during their hunt for Mooney. Foil Her, it was called, like Boil Her. He'd walked through it on his own once (he remembered doing so and at the same time he didn't . . . the memory was like a wet footprint on the floor of his mind, shimmery but not solid), but the room had been dry then except for a few trickles.

It wasn't dry now.

Below the Foil Her's barred window, just like outside it, there was water. Murky, gray-blue water. Not a puddle, or even a big puddle, like in the cellar.

A pool.

Cold fingertips tickled the back of his neck. He tottered forward. The world flipped over once, twice, a thousand times.

And stopped with a crunch.

The staircase had turned on its head, and the Drippy Man was hanging by his feet from its top step. Blood spilled up his upside-down body. His eyes glowed behind the steam falling off his skin. Tommy moaned. He was lying by the edge of the pool, nowhere to go but into the water, and he couldn't go into the water. He'd have a spotty time if he went in the water, and that would be it, no drowning, no dying, just gray-blue water all around for the rest of time.

The Drippy Man walked down the staircase, his thing red like Uncle Alex's knife.

Tommy got up and pressed back against the wall. The elbow of his right arm was poking out of his skin, and the bone was as clear and brittle as an icicle. He raised his other hand and pointed a shaking, water-beaded finger at the Drippy Man's head.

"Bang."

The Drippy Man lifted his dangling foot. Its toes caught on the carpet and the leftover bits of his ankle folded.

"Bang."

Two stairs left.

"Bang."

One.

"Bang."

The Drippy Man stepped down in front of Tommy. Bone gleamed inside the oozing flap of his breast. His stomach was a sunburned pink, and it was whispering beneath the steady flow of his blood, whispering, *shhhhhhhhhhhhhh.* As he leaned over, his jaws slid around Tommy's raised hand, swallowing it.

"Bang."

A red drop landed on Tommy's fingertip and steam rose from it like gun smoke, curling slowly into the mash of gums and teeth above him. Hot breath rattled against his face. One large palm enveloped his cheek. Then a voice filled the Foil Her.

"GET THE FUCK AWAY FROM MY SON."

The Drippy Man turned.

Tommy looked up. His mother stood at the top of the staircase. Her chest was black with blood and her face was pale and terrible, and her eyes, her eyes . . .

Tommy had never seen eyes so cold.

Not even on a cowboy.

•••

Alice Currier was afraid.

She did not look down at Tommy. Not for a second. She looked down at her father and her father alone. At the hole in his chest, almost in line with the hole in her own. At the foot hanging from his left ankle, flopping as he limped up the stairs. At his erection, red and curved and dripping with the blood from his wounds. And soon he was looking down at *her*, the way he had during the dark nights of her childhood, his bright blue eyes overflowing with excitement and violence and bottomless drowning desire.

She stood her ground.

"You let my son be," she said, her voice low, steady. "You leave him alone. He is not your family."

His belly pressed against her.

"*I'm* your family. I know what you want, what you've always wanted." She ran her fingers up the open lips of his cheek. "I won't run from you or hide from you or fight you." Raising her other hand, she cupped his head between her palms. "There are no windows in Longreave, no real windows. Only bedrooms." His breathing slowed. She moved her thumbs along his brow, tracing the veins beneath his skin. "We're home again, Daddy. We're home, and you can have me for as long as you want."

He lifted her by the armpits and then started for the annex in big limping strides. The elevator shaft glided past, its tender back wall ribboned as though carved by a knife. She smiled down at him. "Look at me, Daddy."

He looked at her.

"Do I look like Mom to you?" she said, and plunged her thumbs into his eyes. Steam exploded from his mouth like smoke from a volcano's pit. "*Do I, Daddy?*" she shouted as cold blood welled around her knuckles. "*Do I?*"

He swung her around, bellowing, and slammed her against the elevator shaft. Her body lodged into the soft pink of its wall and for a moment she hung off the ground without any help. Then he pulled her free and slammed her again, again, again, her head lashing on her neck, Longreave reeling like the world outside a falling car, and as the wall crumbled from the blows and the pieces dropped wetly to the floor, she sunk her thumbs into his eye sockets as deep as they would go, as deep as any daughter and her father could ever go.

She sunk them to the roots.

• • •

The pounding started as Mark reached the annex's second floor. It carried through the walls, filling the dark corridor with a heavy beat, as though some giant black heart had woken inside Longreave. He looked back, tottering, one hand on the rail. The staircase stretched down behind him, jiggling piano keys for steps. Mooney was a pair of glowing white eyes at the bottom, his body untouched by the lantern light.

"I have to go," Mark said. "I'll see you there, wherever there is."

He went on alone, using the sledgehammer like a cane. The pounding grew louder. It echoed deep within his skull.

Thud. Thud. Thud.

He leaned against the wall, and for a moment it was the floor and he was lying down. Then the corridor straightened itself, and he continued. 2B crept toward him. Once upon a time he'd crawled to that room on his hands and knees. His world had been dark for so long, and he'd cried when he'd seen the light under the door.

There wasn't any light under the door now.

Mark rounded the final corner, and the heartbeat began to resound from the floor and ceiling. It rattled the dead lamps above his head. It vibrated the carpet under his feet. Beneath each thud he heard cracking, splintering.

He was close.

The handle of the sledgehammer became slippery. Mark slid down it to his knees. The lantern on his wrist seemed dimmer. Perhaps it was running out of gas. As he pushed himself up, gravity played a funny trick and dropped him against the wall.

When had it gotten so quiet?

A doorway appeared. On the other side stood a broad naked body. Wood littered the carpet around its feet. Its arms were raised in darkness. Mark inched forward, bent over at the waist. His left eye was open a crack. His right eye was closed.

There was a hole in the back of the elevator shaft.

The Pool Salesman held Alice up by the throat. Her hands were wrapped around his skull. Her feet dangled over emptiness. She saw Mark leaning in the doorway, and a despair that had not been there before awakened inside her eyes. Her lips shaped a word.

No.

But she'd never understood. She'd never known what it meant to begin a job, the responsibility that came with it, the unspoken oath of the first swing. It was a hard, cruel world, and it would leave you behind if you let it. It would turn your dreams to ghosts. A man had to work to keep up. He had to put his head down and his shoulders up and work, even if it killed him. He had to finish what he started, or he might as well be dead already.

Mark lifted the sledgehammer.

He saw the wall as it had been on the day David took him down into the cellar. The bricks sat loose in their salt-rotten mold, waiting to topple. Waiting for time or someone to tear it all down and put the whole sick thing of its misery.

He swung.

The hammer fell, and the lantern sparked momentarily, *beautifully* bright on impact, illuminating the steel mallet as it caved in the Pool Salesman's skull and embedded itself deep in bone. Alice came whipping around, swung like a ragdoll in her father's enormous hands. Mark felt her slam into him.

Her body was soft.

So was the floor.

Soft.

•••

As the Drippy Man used Mommy like a sledgehammer on the wall, Tommy crawled up the stairs. He barely made it to the top when Daddy stumbled through the doorway, swinging the real thing in his hands. The hammer smashed down, *crrrrruuuuuunch*, and a mad shout of joy exploded from Tommy's throat.

But the Drippy Man didn't fall.

Daddy did.

First Mommy crashed into him. Then the leaking glass jar he carried everywhere crashed into the wall. Then they *all* fell, one on top of the other, Daddy on his back on the floor, Mommy on her back on top of him, and the Drippy Man on top of them both, howling, the sledgehammer stuck inside his head like Mommy's fingers were stuck inside his eyes. He let go of her throat and wrenched the hammer loose. The hole it left gushed and steamed. He shook his roaring, drooling skull back and forth as he pawed at Mommy, digging into her chest and stomach like a dog searching for a bone in a sandbox. Pieces of flesh stuck to the walls and plopped onto the carpet. Her arms loosened, and her thumbs slid out of the Drippy Man's eye holes, now gushing and steaming, too, his head one big smoking Jack O'Lantern.

Tommy crawled through wood and meat and bits of bone. He took his mother's hand. She turned her head and smiled. "Happy birthday, cowboy." She squeezed his fingers. "Don't look, okay? No matter what."

Tommy closed his eyes.

In the blue-gray twilight waiting there, he heard his father whisper and it was almost like it had been a little while ago—yesterday, perhaps—when night was a warm place between two bodies and a pair of soft voices in the dark.

"I'm sorry, Alice. I'm so sorry. I tried."

"I know you did."

"I wanted to build something. But it wasn't for Longreave. It was for you. It was always you."

"I *saw*. You showed me. And I'm there with you now, and it's beautiful, honey. It's bright out, brighter than it is dark, and it doesn't hurt anymore."

The Drippy Man's rasps grew hoarser, uglier, and beneath the saw-blade of his breath Tommy heard something else.

Footsteps.

He cracked his eyelids. Above him, where a pair of blood-lined legs joined together, wept a long and crooked gash.

The legs limped on.

•••

Alice smiled. "It doesn't hurt anymore."

The Pool Salesman's head spewed red out of every orifice, small and large. He'd run out of pieces to pull off her and was groping down her body instead of from it, his hands pawing blindly, hungrily.

"Can you hear me, you bastard?" she said. "You can't hurt me anymore."

She listened to the ocean behind her, to the melody of its waves on the shore, as her father forced her legs apart. There was no ceiling overhead, only stars, millions of stars, spilled like beads across the night. Alice let go of herself as a child lets go of a kite, and as the string ran through her fingers, a gentle wind bore her away over the Atlantic. Now the stars were below as well as above. They lit the dark water as far as the eye could see, so that it was impossible to tell what was true and what was reflection, and she knew then that there was no end to light, just as there was no beginning to darkness. Light goes where light goes, and touches what it touches along the way, and its course may be altered but its spark will never be extinguished. And so it was with life, and the mirror of death, shining forever bright.

The last of the string left Alice's fingers.

She caught it.

Back in Longreave, she felt her father's weight lift off her. Her chest and stomach had been torn out by the handful, leaving her nothing to sit up with but her spine. Her spine was enough. She propped herself up on one elbow.

The Pool Salesman staggered back, an arm around his neck. Over his shoulder hung a face much like his own, blue eyes and shattered jaws and mouth clogged by debris. A hand reached under his belly, gripped his testicles, and pulled off his prick as easily as ripe fruit from the stem. The new wound poured and hissed like the rest. Her father was screaming from everywhere now, his whole body nothing but a collection of howling mouths. He stopped at the edge of the elevator shaft, swaying in his captor's embrace.

Alex looked at her, his pale hair carried up on an invisible draft. Blood dripped from his lips and steamed on their father's shoulder. He worked his broken mouth, wanting to tell her, needing to tell her—

"I know," she said.

Alex closed his eyes and took a step back. He and the Pool Salesman plunged out of sight.

In the moments that followed, Alice and Tommy and Mark all crawled to the edge of the elevator shaft.

Alice saw a throat, rounded and pink and twisting as it descended.

Tommy saw water dripping down walls as smooth and gray as the pipes under a bathtub.

Mark saw darkness no different than the darkness anywhere inside Longreave.

None of them heard the Pool Salesman and his son hit bottom, or had any reason to believe there was one.

• • •

"Mooney!"

Mark lay with his head in Alice's lap. He watched the cowboy hug his horse and receive a sideways lick in return. It was nice to watch.

"I'm supposed to remember Mooney," he said.

"What about him?"

"I don't know. My father said if I remember Mooney, it'll be all right."

"I met him. Your father."

"You did?"

"Yeah. He's kind of an asshole."

Alice smiled down over the ruin of her body.

Shadows played around the elevator shaft. Mark's eyelids grew heavy. As they shut, he saw a mouth sliding open into darkness.

He twitched awake. "What if he comes back?"

"He won't."

"How can you be sure?"

Alice turned her gaze to the ceiling, the smile softer but still there on her lips. "Longreave has corners again."

Mark thought about that and decided it made sense. He reached up with a hand that felt strangely heavy and brushed back the hair from her cheek. "You forgot your earrings."

"I guess maybe I did."

"It's okay if you can't find them. There are more." His hand fell. "I'll give you a new pair tomorrow."

"Mark."

He started to ask why she sounded so sad, then he realized there were tears running down his cheeks. "I'm crying."

Alice nodded.

"Where are we?"

"We're in Longreave, honey."

But Longreave was cold, and it wasn't cold here. It was warm, like a bed. He turned his cheek into Alice's stomach, which must have been wrapped in a blanket, because it felt rumpled and loose and damp.

Damp?

Then he remembered. Tommy was with them, and Tommy always left things a little wet. They were all together, and Mooney too, somewhere close. Mark could smell his awful breath. "I don't want to fall asleep," he said. "Don't let me fall asleep, okay?"

"Okay."

"Tell me a story."

Alice began to speak softly, the light lowering over her face, and Mark rode her voice down on gentle waves, down into darkness, down.

Chapter Thirty-Nine
?

Mark Currier woke inside a brick coffin. He reached for his throat, choking, and found wires there. The wires twisted up around his chin, and when he yanked them off, things began to beep and screech behind him.

He threw off his single sweaty sheet.

White figures blew into the room.

"I have to finish," he said, pulling at the arms around his chest and neck. "There's one layer left. It's my responsibility. I have to *finish*."

Chapter Forty
December 2ⁿᵈ

A police officer stepped into the room. Mark saw her, and she saw him see her, so he couldn't pretend to be asleep this time. He stared at the ceiling as he answered her questions.

Yes, he'd been living at Longreave. Yes, even though the utilities were off and he owned a house. Yes, he'd been working on the wall in the cellar, and yes, he'd put the hole in the bathroom door in 401. He couldn't say why, to tell the truth. No, he hadn't let Alex in. Yes, Alex had stabbed him and chased him through the hotel. Yes, he'd hit Alex in the face with a sledgehammer. No, he didn't remember why he crawled through the annex or knocked down the back wall of the elevator shaft, but it seemed like something he would do. The wall had been broken, and he'd been rebuilding broken things in Longreave his whole life.

"Do you remember placing the call to the ambulance?"

"No."

"You have no recollection as to what you said on the phone?"

"No."

"The transcript from your end reads, 'Hello? Is anyone there? I'm in Longreave. I'm in Longreave.'"

Mark didn't hear a question, so he didn't give an answer.

"Mr. Currier, our responders were looking for a woman. They were told a woman had called from inside Longreave, and then they found you."

A vent rattled: *hick, hick.*

"Must have been the static," said the cop, "Let's move on."

On they moved. No, he had no idea what caused the disagreement between his wife and brother-in-law. No, he didn't know anyone by the name of Geoffrey Maws. Yes, he'd been told all his belongings were waiting at the police station. No, he had nobody to pick them up for him. Yes, he was sure.

The cop closed her notebook and got up to leave. She paused by the door. "Oh, you'd probably be interested to know Weirhill set a date."

"Weirhill?"

"The owner of the hotel. Mr. Weirhill. It seems this whole . . . *situation* . . . startled his lawyers into action. I'm not surprised, personally. If it were me, I'd want to sweep all this under the rug as soon as possible, too."

"A date for what?"

"The demolition. They're knocking Longreave down a week from today."

Mark blinked and then continued staring at the ceiling.

• • •

The battery had died on his phone, but one of the nurses let Mark borrow a charger. She even wiped the blood off the screen, which was nice. He thought about thanking her, but it didn't seem worth the energy.

He had a call to make.

It was true what Beverly had said. She really did hear everything. She heard the bad news before Mark got past hello.

"Which one of them?" she whispered. "Alex? Is Alex—"

"Both."

There was a long pause.

"How?"

"Car accident."

"I think," said the voice of a little girl, "I think I'm going to go now. It's such a pretty day. I might even take a swim."

The line dropped.

Mark was lightheaded. He'd lost a lot of blood, the doctors said. Enough to fill a large coke bottle and then some. He turned off his phone and waited for the spell to pass. It did. They always did, in time.

•••

Sometimes it's longer than that . . .

•••

Mark sat up in bed, a feeling on his skin, a tingling in his neck. Nicholas Lorey was in the visitor's chair, his perfect black cap of hair for once not so perfect. The loafers on his feet had been polished recently. Obsessively.

"I meant to come by sooner. I wanted to." Nicholas pulled at his bowtie. "They tell me you're recovering well. That you're numbers are getting better." He went silent, perhaps remembering the numbers that had been the subject of their last conversation, which had ended with Mark yanking on his tie and telling him to go away, go away. "They announced the auction finally. For Longreave's goods. I've been keeping an eye out, you know. Always did fancy those Chesterfields."

Mark didn't mention that one of the Chesterfields was soaked in blood.

"It's tomorrow, the auction. The Lovers are going, too. For nostalgia, I think. They're no longer lovers, according to them. They still live together, though. And go to the same classes. And share the same car. But *fini* they are, absolutely. One hundred percent." Nicholas gave a bark of a laugh, completely unlike himself, and Mark thought of Mooney. *What about him? What do I have to remember?* "They've been asking about you. They heard on the news. We all did." He pulled at his bowtie again, grunted, and tore it off. "Don't even remember putting on this stupid thing. It's like it knew I was coming before I did. I looked down at myself in the car, and there it was on me, saying, *Hello, Nicholas, old friend, today is a Longreave day.*"

But Mark was still stuck on the last thing Nicholas had said, about everyone hearing on the news. "David should be here. It should be him here."

"You don't know," Nicholas said quietly.

"Know what?"

"Mark." Nicholas swallowed. "David passed away late last month."

I was hoping we could talk before I left for California.

"It was lung cancer. He had it a long time, I guess, without knowing. It spread. It was one of those pack-your-bag things. His daughter called me from out west. She said she was calling everyone over here to let them know. I thought she would have, I thought *he* would have, I had no idea you didn't . . ."

There was a crack on the ceiling. A bad one. Somebody wasn't doing their job, letting a crack like that go unnoticed.

". . . Mark?"

"I have a favor to ask."

"Yeah. Yeah, of course. Anything."

"I'll need to write you a check."

•••

Now You Now

Let's tak about cow milk, that lovely liquid you imbibe your children with as soon as you stop giving them Momy milk. Foks at the dairy farm would have you believe it's al fun and games and uderly strong bones, but did you now

Mark closed the document, which had popped up as he turned on the computer. He felt a slight, lingering chill as he signed onto the internet and followed the instructions the Lovers had given Nicholas to give to him. Setting up the program (Skype, it was called) and typing in their username was easy enough. Pressing the big green Call button was harder.

Their faces appeared on the screen. "Hi," they said together, trading uncertain smiles for less certain frowns.

"Hi," he said back.

The speakers let out a screech of feedback, and a fuzzy voice in the background said, "The first item we have is a Lifestyle TR200, manufacturing date 2006. We'll begin the bidding at $50."

"It's starting," said Julie. She sounded relieved.

"Turn it around so he can see," said Matthew. He sounded relieved, too.

The screen jostled and bounced and then Mark was staring down miniature bleachers at a smaller basketball court and an even tinier stage. Two men wheeled something gray across the three-point line.

"Buy it," said Mark.

"Are you sure? You never even used—"

"Buy the treadmill."

Chapter Forty-One
December 8th

Mark was discharged from the hospital the day before the demolition. There was a throb under his bandages, and a throb under his ribs. One was his wound and one was his heart, but he couldn't tell the difference. He walked out of the hospital with a shopping bag of bloodied personal items, including a blue tie that was no longer very blue. A health ambassador hailed him a cab, which he took across town to his truck. The tarp over its bed was weighed down by snow. He lifted a corner of the tarp, scooped up a handful of chilled earrings, and held them to his lips. Then he pulled out his shovel and tossed it into the passenger seat for later.

The road to Longreave was already roped off.

A wall of snow had been raised in front of his house. He knocked a piece of it down as he climbed onto the curb. Icicles dangled off his father's wicker chair. The bird's nest above the door was pale with frost.

He let himself inside.

His suitcase sat in the entryway along with his backpack, a lantern, and the rollup bag containing his chess set. His copy of the Amateur's Mind was tucked through the handles. After all Nicholas and the Lovers had done for him, Mark supposed he should have told them he was getting out of the hospital. But then they would have wanted to bring him home, and some things a man had to do alone. He took another step, and shut the door to the office.

That would come later.

Or never.

The hotel's mantelpiece took up the entire back wall of the living room. Above the shale ledge was a pair of nails leftover from family photographs. Mark squeezed between the treadmill and coffee table. He picked up the painting lying on the Chesterfield, carried it to the mantelpiece, and hung it there.

Longreave stared down at him, windows rounded into glowing blue eyes.

Chapter Forty-Two
December 9th

Midnight.

Mark slid between two houses and hopped a fence. Stars burning in the black-ice sky lit the beach. He stole down the sand with his shovel and lantern, one side of the world solid, the other side wild and heaving darkness. In the middle, where the line blurred, stood Longreave.

Its four stories of salt-scabbed brick threw no shadow.

Its rooms held no light.

Waves crashed and wind howled as he pried off the boards he'd hammered up months ago. When the last was ripped loose, he turned his shovel on the window. The pane shattered in and a piece of the Atlantic exploded on the shore and everywhere around him everything was breaking, coming undone, finally undone. Then the tide pulled back, the tinkling stopped, and the night put itself together again.

It was quiet inside the office.

He stood there catching his breath, the ocean far away, a background sound of static. In the dark he could see plants hanging over a cluttered desk. "I'm here, David. I'm here and we can talk now. David, I'm sorry."

He switched on the lantern.

The office was empty.

Mark stumbled out under the staircase. The front desk was gone. So were the room keys and the hooks on which they'd hung. He pushed across the lobby, a hand on his side. His stitches chewed at his skin. His stomach pounded like a drum. He shouldered into the cellar and caught himself on the doorframe, swaying out over the drop where the ramp had been, the glow of his lantern swinging madly in the dark. "*Tommmmmmmy,*" he called. "*Moooooooney.*"

A voice called back to him.

His own.

He backpedalled into the lobby and began to jump from floorboard to squeaky floorboard, playing Longreave like a piano. "Can you hear me, David?" he shouted. "Can you hear me, Dad? I'm home! Everyone, I'm home!"

A chain rattled outside the front door.

The door groaned.

Mark choked on cold, watery panic and ran for the staircase. The beam of a flashlight flicked about the dark lobby as he climbed.

Up.

Up.

Up.

He reached the top floor and went the only way he knew to go, to the only place he had left. But 401 was locked. Everything was locked in Longreave. Bile in his mouth, he backed up to the opposite wall and then lunged at the door. Wood splintered and stitches tore and he stumbled into the room. His room.

Where he stopped.

A woman stood at the window, its curtain taken down and wrapped around her slender body.

"Alice."

She turned as he spoke, and the lantern light touched a face from his childhood.

"Hi, dear. I've been waiting for you." His mother pointed at the corner where the nightstand used to sit. "We never finished our game."

•••

"Come here," she said. "Let me look at you."

The carpet was soft beneath his feet, so soft it wasn't there. Mark felt himself sinking as he walked, losing height, becoming the boy he'd always been to her. He wrapped his arms around her and for a moment couldn't comprehend how small she was, how her body could fit so easily into his arms. "*Mom.*"

"Careful, dear, you'll crush me."

He let go. "I think I need to—"

His butt hit the floor. She sat down next to him, folding the curtain beneath her as though wearing a dress.

"You," he said. "You're the black king."

"Whose copy of The Amateur's Mind did you think you were carrying around all this time?"

"Dad told me he got it from a yard sale."

"Of course he did. Watching you take after me must have been so hard on your poor father. He always was a jealous man." She smiled without a trace of bitterness. "We drove each other crazy. It's part of why I married him, maybe even most of why. When you're young, like we were when we met, insanity often masquerades as love."

In life his mother's eyes had sometimes been green, sometimes blue, depending on the season. Now they were in between, like Longreave, on the middle of a spectrum whose breadth could only be glimpsed in the right light.

"So," she said, "have you been practicing?"

"No. I've been—I wanted to—but I couldn't. I can't." Something twisted and caught inside his chest, like the knob of a locked door. "They're going to knock down Longreave. They're going to take it away."

His mother leaned in close. Her breath smelled of the pomegranates that grew behind their house in the summer. "You know why you never beat me in any of our games? Why you'll never beat me?"

"Because you're better?"

She nodded. "And why am I better?"

"I don't know." He looked down at the lantern glowing between them. "Because you studied more? Because you worked harder than I did?"

"Because I'm dead." She lifted his chin. "And I get to see the *whole* board."

The pound of footsteps. Climbing. Running.

"No." Mark sat up against the wall. "No. Not yet. It's not enough time. There hasn't been enough time."

"There's nothing *but* time. Time is all there is."

"But we haven't even, but I haven't—Mooney." He twisted to her. "I need to remember Mooney, and it'll be all right."

"Your father told you that?"

"Yes. But I don't know *what*. I don't know what to remember."

The footsteps paused at the fourth floor. Then they started again, each one louder than the last.

His mother sighed. A pinprick of red appeared in her right eye. "Frank always was awful at giving advice."

Flickers played outside the broken door.

"Mark, you don't need to remember Mooney." Blood spread across the white of her eye, the blue-green of her iris, the black of her pupil. "You need to forget Mooney. Forget everything you ever knew about him." She turned the switch on the lantern, and the room went dark. "Tear it all down."

The beam of the flashlight swept into 401, where Mark sat alone.

• • •

Weirhill Security handed him over to the police, who put him in the back of a car, which pulled away so quickly that Longreave seemed to collapse through the back window, falling, falling, gone.

• • •

The clock outside the holding cell hit 1:48.

"Mr. Weirhill called," said the cop looking in through the bars. "He said he has no interest in pressing charges. In fact he asked us to do you a favor."

1:49.

"He asked us not to let you watch."

The second hand turned and turned, like a finger describing a circle, like the gears inside the world.

1:50.

1:51.

1:52 . . .

• • •

9:00.

Mark heard a deep, guttural *whomp*, a note of subliminal bass. He heard it inside his bones and heart and nowhere else. The cell was silent. He put his head in his hands and stayed that way until the cops made him leave.

• • •

The crowd had cleared from the caution tape.

A salt-white cloud hung over the coast. On the beach beneath the cloud lay an enormous pile of dust, chunks of wood and stone poking out here and there like bones after cremation. Excavators scooped yellow claws inside Longreave's remains. Ashy waves groped at the shore. Seagulls dove for fish.

Mark left.

•••

The house was unlocked.

Mark started up the stairs, paused, and walked back down to the closed room by the entryway. For several minutes he didn't move, just stood there in front of the door, like an artist in front of a canvas.

At last he went into the office.

He stopped over a broken brush, surrounded in red, seeing red, seeing the clock that Alice had built out of easels, a clock painted in her blood and Tommy's blood and the blood of all the dreams he'd ever had for them, for himself, all of it stolen and devoured and digested by a hungry world.

Tear it down.

Like a wall.

Tear it *down*.

He dug his fingers into one o'clock, opened the sun like the wound that it was, and pulled the whole easel to the ground.

Two o'clock.

There was the house, *their* house, the place that had been home and was now only a place. He saw the crack below the bending porch where he'd learned about death on a hot summer afternoon. Mooney, breath like garbage cans ripened by the sun, body a bundle of sick heat, round eyes as bright as—no. Remember none of it, not the warmth of the mud or the lumps in his neck or the prickly wires on his snout. Topple the house, tear it down.

Three o'clock.

The living room in which Mooney had waited every day to tackle Mark after school. Gone, swiped off the easel, forgotten.

Four o'clock.

Mark ran up the stairs, tripping and laughing as Mooney bounded up in pursuit. Now the stairs were falling, and the boy and dog were falling with them.

Five o'clock.

Bed. Slobber on the covers after a fierce wrestle. He ripped the mattress out of the canvas, leaving a hole in the room, in his memory.

No six o'clock existed.

He peeled seven into shreds, and Mooney had never chased him dizzy around the kitchen counter. He tipped eight, nine, and ten over in a row, and goodbye to those hours of fetch played in the corridor, goodbye. The game was over. The game had never begun.

Eleven.

Go away bathroom, and go away Mooney, stop lapping up all the water in the tub and stealing the bubbles, you couldn't have done that anyway. All that soap would have made you sick. All those gallons and gallons would have burst your stomach. Only a dead Mooney could have done that. Only a dead Mooney could have sucked down a bath like that.

Only a dead Mooney . . .

Mark slowed before twelve o'clock, where a blue-eyed shadow reached up from a blood-red ocean, and pushed the easel over almost gently. Behind it on the desk, in the same spot the divorce form once rested, lay one last painting next to an empty frame.

He stopped.

Everything stopped.

It was the beach at night, and it *was* brighter than it was dark. The shore sparkled with starlight, or perhaps the stars sparkled with shorelight. Jewels and the reflection of jewels lit the waves, each individual spec shining out its own drowned life, their combined radiance filling the ocean. Mark picked up the canvas and with careful fingers slid it into the frame. He carried the painting through the rubble and into the living room, where he hung it over the mantelpiece beside Longreave.

Rebuild it.

Brick by brick.

Rebuild it.

His mother brings a dog home from the pound, and Mark is so exultant he tackles them both. He is four, and it is fall. His father smokes on the wicker chair as Mark and his new friend roll around in the leaves. The moon shines in the dog's eyes, and Mark thinks of a name. Winter arrives. They retreat indoors to eat and grow as young boys and dogs do. And *boy* does Mooney grow. His paws become so large and awkward that he sounds like someone plodding about the house in snowshoes. By spring he has filled into them. He is one hundred pounds and twice the size of Mark, a bulldozer with a tongue. It slobbers over Mark's face every chance it gets and leaves his skin smelling like dog chow, an odor that is not entirely unpleasant. The days warm and Mooney's breath goes bad. Mark laughs at first. Then he worries for reasons he does not quite understand. There are things under the fur on Mooney's neck, loose and fatty things, and the dog is tired more than he used to be, more than Mark thinks is right. A heat wave heralds summer, and Mooney spends as much time asleep as he does awake. It's the temperature, Dad says. But Mark *knows*. He knows what he's too young to know. It is a feeling inside him, an open space in his chest, like the cupboard where he puts his action figures. But nothing goes there, nothing fits, and it only grows larger until one day Mooney disappears. Mark looks for him everywhere. He looks in the closet and under the bed. He even looks in the bathtub. When he finally stumbles outside calling Mooney's name, the hole is as big as he is. It wants to suck him down from the inside and swallow him. He hears a sound beneath the porch and crawls under the steps into the mud, where he finds what he has been waiting to find. There he stays long after his parents have gone down the street searching for him, long after Mooney has stopped breathing.

They dig a hole in the backyard by the pomegranate tree, which his mom says will now grow twice as good. She puts a rock on the grave. The rock gets rained on and sinks into the ground.

Mark is five.

He is quiet on his first day of school. He sits by himself while the other kids color and talk. At noon his mom takes him home. He climbs the porch ahead of her. He turns the doorknob. The door moves on its own and an inhuman face with moon-white eyes and a long drippy tongue comes lolling out of the house. He lands hard. His mother screams. His father rushes downstairs and screams, too. They can see the dog drool running down their son's cheeks and the paw prints digging into his shirt. They can see nothing else. But Mark is laughing. Mooney is back, Mooney is home, and Mark won't stop laughing. Soon he will have to crawl under the porch again to say goodbye, and eventually there will come a day when he lets go of his friend for good, when their grand reunions and bitter farewells are forgotten and their time together fades into a fond memory, but for now this moment is all that matters. Mooney came back. Mooney came *back*.

"It wasn't Longreave." Mark stared beyond the beach to the ocean, where a blurred line joined the waters of a past painting to the waves of the present. "It was me."

Lips brushed his ear.

And a soft voice whispered,

"Always."

July 2013 – May 19th, 2014.

You're here. You've finished, or you've skipped to the end looking for a photo of me with my hand stroking my beard. In which case you're out of luck, because like my beard, no such thing exists. Whatever brought you to this page, you took a gamble first. You opened Longreave and gave a little of your life to it.

Thank you.

If you'd be willing to sacrifice a few more moments by writing a brief, honest review on Amazon, I'd greatly appreciate it. Reviews help a book find its audience. Without them, the seats down there stay empty. So throw that tomato, clap those hands, shout, scream, flail, break dance in the aisles or set the building on fire, just make some noise. And get out before the cops come.

See you next time around, I hope.

Until then, love letters and death threats can be directed to dbhfiction@gmail.com.

Made in the USA
Columbia, SC
08 June 2021